WE ALL FALL DOWN

BOOK TWO IN THE
OF LOVE AND MADNESS SERIES

LONE SPARROW PRESS

KAREN CIMMS

WE ALL FALL DOWN

Cover Designer: Garrett Cimms
Cover Photographer: Lisa Hopstock, hopstockphoto.com
Interior Designer: The Write Assistants
Editing: Lisa Poisso, lisapoisso.com

ISBN: 978-0-9974867-2-8

FOREWORD

We All Fall Down is the second book in the *Of Love and Madness* series. It is not a standalone and it is strongly recommended that you read *At This Moment* before reading this book to fully understand and appreciate these characters.

It is not a typical romance, but it is a love story. It is dark, and it is gritty. I hope you'll trust me.

The third book, *All I Ever Wanted*, will complete the series.

To my favorite lead guitarist
I love you, Guman.
Thank you for filling my world with music.

Parting is all we know of heaven, and all we need of hell.
—Emily Dickinson

CHAPTER 1

JULY 19, 2012

The short-term parking lot shimmered like an urban mirage. Miami had been hot. At least there had been the occasional ocean breeze to punctuate the wet, heavy air. No such luck in Newark.

Billy fished an elastic band from his pocket, gathered his thick, blond mane into a double loop, and leaned against the windowed walls of the terminal. The cool glass felt good against his sweat-soaked back. As for the rest of him? It was like standing in front of an open oven door.

A steady line of cars and shuttles cozied up to the curb, spewing fumes into the still, dense air. If Eddie didn't show soon, Billy swore he'd leave the little shit's crap all over the sidewalk and hail a cab.

Mirrored aviator shades covered his bloodshot eyes, but nothing could disguise the pounding in his head. The dizzying waves rising from the pavement and the familiar rocking motion of his latest hangover made him want to find a dark corner and sleep until this rollercoaster came to a complete stop. And when it did, he'd like to get his hands around the neck of Stonestreet's tour manager and personally thank him for booking such an early flight.

The opportunity was unlikely to present itself, since he'd been fired hours earlier.

He folded his arms across his chest and closed his eyes, trying to make sense of the last twelve hours and ruminate on what he'd done to fuck up this time.

Mistake number one had been dropping acid. He hadn't done it in years, but when Eddie had shown up with a couple of hits, he figured what the hell. He was no choirboy, and this tour was kicking his ass. One more night and he would be home free, at least for a couple of weeks.

But what a night. He could still hear the roar of the crowd jammed into AmericanAirlines Arena. When the band started playing "Escaping to Perdition," he did what he always did, what he was paid to do: hang back and provide the rhythm and accents. But somewhere after the first verse, something snapped. Maybe it was the acid. Or maybe he was sick of playing second fiddle to a hack who couldn't even win at *Guitar Hero* without backup. Whatever the case, he lost himself in the music and before he knew it, he'd commandeered Mick's big solo.

And he was whaling on that motherfucker.

Even now, baking on the hot sidewalk a thousand miles from Miami, he still felt those notes pulsing through his fingertips. It was like being in a trance. Before he knew it, he'd crossed Mick's invisible line. His fingers had flown up and down the neck of his Les Paul custom. The frets had all but disappeared, and his fingers moved as if on glass. Each note reverberated through him, shooting out like sparks.

Mick let him have his moment. And it was the way he'd always dreamed it would be. He was front and center—Billy McDonald—and the crowd went crazy. When he opened his eyes and realized twenty thousand fans were screaming for him, he fell to his knees. And he didn't miss one fucking note.

2

The rest of the show had been a blur, but that feeling? No one could take that from him. It was the best night of his career—or at least it had been, for about three hours.

Stonestreet was a hard-partying band, and the end of a grueling nine weeks on the road was as good a reason to party as any. Limos deposited them at the hotel, where the booze flowed, weed was plentiful, and there was more than enough high-grade cocaine and half-naked women to go around.

It was tough, but he knew where to draw the line. The guilt he felt from cheating on Katie twenty years earlier had never left him. The risk of a few moments of pleasure wasn't worth losing the only other good thing in his life. He tried to stay away from the hard stuff too, but he was only human. If he needed a little something now and then, he wasn't hurting anybody.

But last night? Last night, the shit had finally hit the fan. Fueled by whiskey and coke and a few hours' resentment, Mick had launched into a tirade about Billy stealing his solo. Billy tried to shine him on, but he wasn't about to apologize to that horse's ass. Everyone knew that on his worst day, Billy was ten times better than Mick McAvoy could ever hope to be.

Things had gotten ugly. He'd been getting up to leave when Mick threw the first punch. He missed, but it didn't matter. Not since Billy was ten had anyone taken a swing at him and walked away in one piece.

His fist connected with Mick's jaw. Mick's feet flew out from under him, and he rolled ass-backward over the bass player, who was on his knees doing lines of coke off some groupie's tits.

It had been pretty comical until Mick fired him.

The rest of the night had been spent nursing his ego and a bottle of Jack. Things with the band had been rough, but last night's show had been amazing. And now it was over.

Billy glanced at his watch. A little past eleven. Plenty of time to get home, although the thought of facing Katie made his head throb.

Happy birthday, babe. I got fired! That was gonna go over real well.

The rumbling of his stomach reminded him he hadn't eaten, although the thought of food nauseated him—or maybe it was the heat. If he hadn't lost his driver's license, he'd be on the road by now. In the meantime, he longed for a little hair of the dog and a shower. He'd been so out of it last night he'd lost track of time. Not only had he not had time for a shower, he'd almost missed his plane.

He dug a toothpick from his pocket and clamped it between his teeth. Maybe that would get his mind off wanting a drink.

A horn blared.

"Finally," he muttered as Eddie pulled up to the curb.

He threw his duffle bag and guitar cases in the back and slipped into the front seat while Eddie loaded his suitcases into the cargo area.

"Sorry about last night, man," the drummer said as he navigated the rented SUV onto 78. "But you were amazing. Holy shit! You should've seen Mick's face. He was acting like the big man, giving you the spotlight, but I could see that little vein pulsing on the side of his head."

"It felt pretty good. Hope I get to feel that way again someday."

"It'll happen, brother. God doesn't give you that kinda talent to hide it under a bushel. Know what I'm sayin'?"

"I hope so." Billy lowered his seat and closed his eyes. The cool breeze from the air conditioner soothed his aching head. "Thanks for the lift. I was hoping my kid would pick me up, but I forgot he's working at some camp in Colorado."

"No problem. I enjoy the company." They drove in silence for a few minutes before Eddie spoke again. "Hey, I'm a bit parched. Okay if we stop along the way for a little libation?"

Billy cocked an eye open. He needed a drink a hell of a lot more than he needed a nap.

"I think I could be persuaded."

CHAPTER 2

Kate hadn't even opened her eyes, and she was already hot and sticky. She squinted at the neon-green numbers on the bedside clock, but they just blinked back. She had worked well past midnight, then driven home in a horrendous downpour. Too keyed up to sleep, she'd finished off a half bottle of wine and waited for Billy to call.

But 3:13 had come and gone. No call. No "Happy Birthday."

It was the first time he'd forgotten. After almost twenty-four years, she should be glad he remembered her birthday at all. But that didn't mean it didn't hurt.

Usually whenever Billy was away on her birthday, he would call at exactly

3:13, the moment she had been born, and sing to her. And when he was home, he'd kiss her awake, then sing "Happy Birthday" while making love to her in a way that still took her breath away.

She'd waited about twenty minutes, then given up and gone to sleep

Forty-two. Where had the time gone?

They were still married. Considering Billy's line of work and that he was often away more than he was home, they'd probably set some sort of record. They had two beautiful children, and she was already a grandmother. Although to be honest, having become a grandmother at such a young age usually made her shudder. Especially since most of her friends from high school had teens and tweens. Some even had toddlers.

She stared up at the ceiling. *Don't go there, Kate.* Some of the old resentment bubbled to the surface. She'd wanted more children. They'd agreed to have more children. Then after Devin was born, Billy had gone and had a vasectomy. Without even discussing it with her! Yes, she and Devin had both almost died, but the doctor had said she could have more children.

She'd been devastated when she found out, and even though she could almost understand his reasoning—he wouldn't risk losing her again, he'd said—she hadn't been sure she could forgive him. Every now and then, when that feeling of loss would overtake her, she had to wonder if maybe she hadn't forgiven him after all.

Enough wallowing. It was her birthday! She threw off the sheet and climbed out of bed to look out over the back yard and fields beyond their two-hundred-year-old home. A hazy sun hung high in the sky. She must have slept a lot later than she'd intended.

"Guess I needed it." She stretched her arms over her head, feeling tiny pops along her spine.

She slipped into a pair of running shorts and a tank top, pulled her hair into a high ponytail, then made her way down the narrow, U-shaped stairway. Charlie, her yellow Lab, trotted close behind.

The clock over the stove was blinking too, so she dug her cell phone from her purse. It was already after ten. If she was going to get in a run, she better get moving before it got any hotter.

Outside the air covered her like an uncomfortable second skin. This might be her shortest run ever. She leaned against the porch post and pulled her knee up to her chest, stretching her hamstrings. Then did the same on the other side. Dipping forward for another stretch, she reached for the newspaper lying on the porch, and nearly dropped it when she read the headline. Her story had made the front page. That was a first, although it was the last story she'd want receiving good play.

"Must be a slow news day."

She shivered in spite of the cloying heat and plopped down on the wicker settee, recalling her editor's summons just twenty-four hours earlier.

~

"Kate!"

Her heart clenched as Sully bellowed her name through his glass-walled office. John "Sully" Sullivan was a sonofabitch. He was a dyed-in-the-wool, old-school, no-nonsense journalist, and he made no bones about the fact that he wouldn't have chosen a fluff reporter like Kate for his newsroom team when The Belleville News got bought out by the Examiner. If it had been up to him, she probably wouldn't have even been offered a job in the mailroom.

It had never been her intention to be a reporter. It just happened. After a blowup with Billy over money a few years earlier, she'd taken a part-time job for a local printer, who also happened to own two weekly newspapers. After a while, he had her doing some proofreading and then typing social news items, such as weddings and births. When he found out she'd wanted to be a writer back in college, he let her do a few feature stories. Nothing serious. Just feel-good pieces about local people. At best, she worked twenty hours a week. Even then Billy hated it, but had come to grudgingly accept her new interest. Except of course when it interfered with their time together. He wasn't so understanding then.

But everything changed when the owner died. Thinking he was doing Kate a favor, Mr. Holmes's son included her continued employment as part of the deal when he sold the newspapers. Since there were no part-time positions, and nothing available in the features section of the newspaper, she was more or less dumped into the newsroom.

Young Mr. Holmes seemed so proud of what he'd done on her behalf, Kate didn't have the heart to tell him she didn't really want the job. Despite having only a semester at Rutgers and no journalism background, she toughed it out as best she could, certain Sully resented her. Why else would he give her such boring, crappy assignments? Not that she wanted to be an investigative reporter either. Truthfully? She didn't know what she wanted.

She summoned her best smile before stepping through the gates of hell. "Yes?"

Sully frowned at her over horn-rimmed bifocals. "Sedge Stevens. Why haven't you done a profile on him?"

"The junkman?"

"Is there another Sedge Stevens?"

"No, but—"

"'But' is not an answer."

Flooded with insecurity, she felt sixteen again, standing before her mother trying to explain something she'd said or done but too nervous to find the words.

"Yes sir." Her voice squeaked. She cleared her throat. "I guess I don't understand why you'd want a profile on Stevens."

He planted his elbows on his desk. "If you had one ounce of news judgment, you'd see for yourself that Stevens is a ticking time bomb."

She wasn't sure she agreed with him but nodded anyway.

"How many township meetings has he been to this year?"

"All of them."

"Why?"

She rocked from one foot to the other. "Because the township wants him to clean up his property, and he wants them to mind their own business."

"And?"

"And . . . they're threatening to condemn the land?"

"Are you asking me or telling me?"

"Telling?"

"So then what was your question?"

"Um . . ."

"Your question, Kate?" His complexion resembled that of a winter tomato.

"My question was why do you want a story on Sedge Stevens?"

"And do you know the answer?"

Nerves caused her voice to ratchet up at the end of every sentence, making each sound like a question.

"You want his side of the story?"

Sully removed his glasses and rubbed the bridge of his nose.

She shifted her weight again. If he yelled at her for that, she'd know for sure he had been possessed by her mother. Which would actually explain quite a lot.

"Yes, Kate." He sighed audibly. "I want his side of the story. Why doesn't he want to clean up the property? Why does he think he doesn't have to abide by the same law everybody else does? What does he plan to do if they keep pushing him? And I want pictures. Ace is on this afternoon. Let him know when you're ready."

"What's my deadline?" Damn squeaky voice.

He glared as if she'd completely lost her mind.

"It's j-just that I'm off tomorrow for my birthday, and I'd asked you about taking a couple weeks off?" Her hands fluttered about as if they had somewhere else to be. She should have brought a pen and a notepad in with her. At least that would have given her something to do with her hands. They traveled down her hips. *Why don't these pants have pockets?* "You said you'd think about it. My husband's coming—"

"Is today your birthday?" He clasped his hands over his stomach and actually smiled at her.

"No." She smiled back. "Tomorrow, but I have another story to fin—"

"So you're working today, correct?"

"Yes, but—"

"Then I suggest you get busy." He snapped his glasses back on and spun his chair around so that she was staring at its back.

"Yes sir."

She began backing out of his office, but before she could complete her escape, he angled toward her again. "What's the other story?"

"A personality profile on the old guy who makes furniture and decorates it with beer caps and resin."

He nodded, although she was sure such a story wouldn't even be on his radar.

"No rush. Have it filed by nine a.m. tomorrow. I want the piece on Stevens filed by nine tonight."

A short time later, she was downshifting her Saab convertible as they climbed the winding road up to Stevens's place.

"Where the hell are we going?" Ace asked.

"That's exactly where we're going. Hell."

She'd tried to find a phone number for Stevens, but no luck. Hermits didn't have phones. Or electricity or running water or working sewer systems, either.

Covering Washington Township committee meetings was one of her most boring assignments. The area consisted of several large farms and a handful of smaller tracts, most of them newly subdivided from old family farms that had been sold off to developers. The only story to come out of the meetings recently had been an ongoing dispute between the township and Stevens. Overgrown and cluttered, the only thing his land produced these days was junk.

Kate attempted to pull into the craggy dirt driveway but changed her mind when she saw the deep ruts. It would serve no purpose to leave her muffler as a calling card.

"Nice welcome," Ace said, aiming his Nikon at one of the many NO TRESPASSING and KEEP OUT signs skirting the perimeter of the property. "I think you're right. Sully hates you." He climbed out after Kate pulled as far off the narrow roadway as she dared. "I'm just trying to figure out what the hell I did that I had to come with you."

"Whatever it was, it must've been awful."

The grass was knee high in spots, and a tangle of thorny shrubs and scrub oak edged Stevens's driveway.

"So what's this guy's story?" Ace asked.

"I guess he grew up here and never left. From what I've learned, he rarely leaves the property except to come to township meetings." Kate swatted at a mosquito that landed on her arm, grateful to be wearing slacks and flats. "Over the years he's added to his collection—junk cars, trucks." She pointed to a rusted-out school bus. "That showed up about ten years ago. No one ever sees him bring anything up here, and nothing ever seems to leave, but he claims he's a junk dealer."

She kept her voice low, although the only other sound was the buzzing of gnats and the chirping of crickets in the high grass.

"He's pretty self-sufficient. Grows his own food, and judging by what the neighbors say about random bursts of gunfire, he shoots the rest. I guess it wasn't a big deal years ago, but now that they've been subdividing some of the larger farms and people are moving closer, the new neighbors want him gone."

"Hey, as far as I'm concerned, live and let live," Ace said. "If the old coot isn't bothering anybody, leave him alone."

"I agree, but now that you can see the junk from the road, they're making it a problem. Plus, he has a pack of dogs that he lets loose, and they've been known to terrorize his neighbors, even though some of them are over a half mile away."

Ace froze. "Are you fucking kidding me? He's got wild dogs running loose, and we're just strolling up to the front door? I hope you brought your gun."

"Hardly. Anyway, over the past few years, the township's been flooded with complaints about him, the junkyard, the dogs. They've issued citations and fines. When the sheriff attempted to serve him with another notice recently, he chased him off with a rifle."

Ace lowered his camera. "What the hell are we doing here?"

"I'm wondering that myself," she grumbled.

Stevens had begun to show up at meetings back in January, warning township officials to stay off his land. He'd stand in the back of the room near the door, glaring at committee members until they gave him the floor.

His presence made Kate's usual position in the back of the room more difficult to maintain over the past few months, as it was obvious it had been a long time since Stevens had made contact with soap and water. His overalls were stained with dirt, grease, and God knows what else, although the stench gave her a good idea. His flannel shirt was torn and frayed at the collar, and his jacket was as filthy as his overalls. While his hair was long and white, his beard was stained yellow, and his teeth (or what she could see of them) were brown nubs. He had a violent, hacking cough.

Kate had written about Stevens and the ongoing dispute faithfully each month, but only in the barest details. The man frightened her, and she didn't want to provoke him. If he wasn't hurting anyone, who cared what his property looked like?

As she and Ace rounded the curve in the driveway, the trailer came into view.

"My husband would kill me if he had any idea where I was or what I was doing."

"Give me his number. I'll call and tell him what you're up to, and then we can get the hell out of here." Ace's voice was low, but his sarcasm came through loud and clear.

Ignoring him, Kate led the way out into the open past the skeletons of rusted vehicles, old washing machines and refrigerators, and piles of rotting wood.

At the far side of the clearing, a row of ramshackle doghouses leaned against one another for support. Chained to them were some of the ugliest, meanest dogs she'd ever seen. They barked and pulled on their leads, causing the lean-to structures to quiver.

This might be one of the stupidest, most dangerous things she'd ever done.

"Mr. Stevens?" she called. "Hello! My name's Kate Donaldson. This is Ace Jackson. We're with the *Evening Examiner*. We'd like to talk to you about your situation with the township. I'd like to help you tell your side of the story."

The dogs grew more frantic.

"Mr. Stevens?"

Even if he couldn't hear her, he had to be curious about the barking by now.

Ace advanced closer to the trailer, which was leaning dangerously to one side as if the supports had given way. The glass was broken out of a window, and a tattered piece of cloth waved in the afternoon breeze. The wooden steps to the door had collapsed, and Kate wondered how anyone could safely enter or exit. A rat made its way along the sill plate into a gaping hole at the bottom of the rotting door. The hair on her arms stood at attention.

Maybe Stevens wasn't home. Odd, given he was a known hermit who rarely left his property. Ace zeroed in on the trailer and then stepped to the side, aiming his zoom at the dogs but not daring to go any closer.

After shooting for a few minutes, he turned to her.

"I'm good. As far as I'm concerned, I don't need anything else. Let's get the hell out of here. I feel like we've already pushed our luck."

Kate agreed. She had given it her best, and they'd more than worn out their welcome with the dogs. Watching her step in the tall grass, she picked her way along tires and assorted garbage. A snake slithered past, and she let out a screech and grabbed Ace's arm.

"Jesus fucking—" he cried.

"Shh!" The groan of gears echoed in the distance. They exchanged panicked glances. Although she had set out with the intention of making contact with Stevens, the idea had begun to terrify her.

Ace gripped her arm and tugged her away from the driveway. "I say neither of us admit we saw him and we get out of here now. This is one disturbed individual, and my gut says go."

Kate nodded, and they dove into a cluster of trees, hoping for enough cover to hide them when Stevens stopped at the entrance to his driveway.

They were still a good twenty or thirty yards from her car. Kate could see it; spots of bright red through the thick overgrowth. The truck rattled toward them, but then she heard the brakes grind. The only other sound came from the dogs. Their frenzied barking continued.

The engine roared, and the truck barreled down the driveway. In his haste, Stevens drove right past the spot where they crouched behind an old truck. His vehicle squealed and bounced over the ruts. When they were fairly certain he wouldn't be able to see them in his rearview mirror, they ran. It wouldn't take him long to figure out the intruder had left.

Kate ran to the driver's side of the Saab. Ace was still closing the passenger door when she began pulling away. She didn't even stop to fasten her seat belt and kept going as fast as she dared until they reached the main road.

Nerves pushed her another couple of miles before she finally pulled over. "Oh my God," she gasped.

Ace glared at her. "I need this job, but you're married to a goddamn rock star. What the hell is your problem?"

Willing her heart to slow down, she'd shrugged and tried to smile. "Just stubborn, I guess."

Kate unfolded the paper and scooted back in the settee. A copyeditor had made some changes, but it remained her story.

'KEEP OFF MY LAND!': TOWNSHIP THREATENS JUNKMAN WITH CONDEMNATION

BY EVENING EXAMINER STAFF

Sedge Stevens bothers no one and wants no one to bother him.

At least that's what he keeps telling Washington Township committee members at their monthly meetings.

Stevens, who lives on a 20-acre tract of land that has been in his family for generations, prefers to keep to himself but has made it a point to attend committee meetings since the beginning of the year. He claims items on his property are related to his business as a junk dealer and that the township is harassing him. According to township records, Stevens holds no license to operate a business from his property.

Stevens's ire peaked last month when the township issued a threat of condemnation. If he does not clean up the property, the committee has promised to proceed in court and condemn the land.

Stevens, who was unable to be reached for comment, has told the committee publicly in no uncertain terms, "Keep off my land."

"We've tried to work with Sedge for well over a year now," says Ainsworth Koch, committee chairman. "He just won't listen. I know of some old-timers who've even offered to go up there and help him clean up, but he refuses. He's tying our hands in this."

Stevens, 52, has lived on Indian Hill Road all his life. According to property tax records, a small wooden cabin was erected on the land around 1890 by Gordon Stevens. The cabin was destroyed by fire in 1972. Stevens remained, and it is assumed he resides in a large, dilapidated trailer on the property not visible from the main road.

A check of utility providers in the area indicates there is no running water or electricity.

"Mr. Stevens's property is an eyesore and he is a menace," says Roger Kiernan, a nearby property owner. "We live a good quarter mile away, yet his dogs have terrorized my wife and children, and I've even seen rats and other vermin in the woods between our two properties. No one should live like that, and I'll be damned if we'll suffer because he chooses to do so."

Kiernan has vociferously complained about Stevens's property and has threatened the township with a lawsuit if it does not follow through with the condemnation.

According to Committeewoman Ellen Day, there have been "generous offers" to purchase the land from Stevens, including a recent offer of close to $1 million from the McMillon Group of Bernardsville, developers of luxury housing.

"Mr. Stevens could live very comfortably somewhere else if he would accept any one of several offers made to him," says Day. "It would be a shame for him to lose the land when he could just sell it."

As for Stevens, he's vowed not to sell and, it seems, not to remediate any issues on his property, declaring it his land to do with as he sees fit.

The township, however, disagrees and has threatened to proceed with condemnation if Stevens does not clean up the property within the next 60 days.

Kate folded the paper and set it on the wicker table, relieved that not only did her story sit below the fold, it had been attributed to "Evening Examiner staff" instead of her byline—perhaps the only concession Sully would ever give her. Good call. She hadn't wanted to do the story in the first place, and certainly didn't want Stevens hassling her at the next meeting.

She tightened her ponytail and stood. How had she gone from typing wedding announcements and taking stationery orders to risking her life to stick her nose into other people's business?

Maybe Billy was right. She was just stubborn.

Not the most disciplined of runners, Kate had gone about two miles before the heat and humidity got the better of her. She jogged up her long, gravel driveway, into the back yard, and headed straight for her garden. Last night's rain had brought no relief in the way of cooler temperatures, but at least she wouldn't have to water.

She twisted a ripe, red beefsteak tomato from the vine, careful not to tug too hard lest it explode in her hand. She plucked a second one. She cradled the pair, warm and heavy, in the hem of her tank top, relishing the bitter scent of the vine on her fingers. Jersey tomatoes. There was nothing better. At the herb garden near the back door, she pinched off a handful of basil leaves. A tomato salad would be good. And there was leftover ham. She'd throw together a quiche, too. She had to be a little crazy to turn on the oven with the temperature inching close to a hundred, but she wasn't about to let the last of the ham go to waste. Besides, once Billy got home, she wouldn't be spending a lot of time in the kitchen, especially since he'd been gone for almost nine weeks.

After putting together her quiche, Kate set the timer for forty-five minutes, then dashed upstairs for a quick shower. She was pawing through the dresses in her closet, trying to decide what she would wear to dinner, when the phone rang. A lovely harmony of male voices behind one very loud, tone-deaf lead answered her greeting.

"I see you hired the Gay Men's Chorus of New York," she joked when the birthday song ended.

"I'm crushed! Didn't you like that?" Joey asked.

"Loved it."

"How's the birthday girl?"

"Great. I'm enjoying a quiet afternoon, and Billy is taking me out to dinner tonight."

"'Great,' she lied," he answered, his tone mocking.

"I'm not lying."

"Do you want me to come out?"

"No. I said I'm great. I went for a run, and I have a quiche in the oven. Devin is still in the wilds of Colorado, but he sent me a beautiful card and promised to take me to dinner when he gets home next month. Rhiannon will probably be here later with the boys, and Billy should be home sometime this afternoon. It's all good."

"Do you want me to come out?" he asked again, acting as if she'd just told him her plans included reading Sylvia Plath and sticking her head in the oven.

"Did you hear anything I said?"

"Yes. You said Rhiannon will *probably* be there, which means she won't. And you said Billy *should* be home this afternoon, which means don't count on it. You also said you went for a run, which begs me to ask where is my Kate and what have you done with her?"

He was as exasperating as ever.

"Rhiannon will come by at some point, if not to see me then to see her father."

"True."

"The first leg of Billy's tour ended last night, so he has to come home eventually. And I started running a while ago. I told you that, remember? If I want my husband to keep chasing me, I need to stay in shape."

"There goes my breakfast."

Kate recognized the sarcasm in Joey's voice, but that was about all she heard. She wandered back into the bathroom and took a good look at herself in the mirror. Not too bad. Her hair was still long and dark, although she'd been known to yank out a gray straggler on occasion. She was still slim but put out extra effort to stay fit. And thanks to the constant supply of exorbitantly expensive beauty products Joey provided her with, plus some pretty good genes, she looked years younger than her chronological age. She brought her face closer to the mirror. At least she hoped so.

Joey was still talking.

"Sorry. What did you say?"

"I said I would've been there if it weren't for this interview. Remember? Pizzazz! has been named one of the top boutiques in Soho. They're coming today for a story, photos, the whole thing. We should wrap up by six or seven. You sure you don't want me to come out when we're done?"

"Don't be silly."

Gravel crunched in the driveway. Expecting Billy, she peeked outside and saw the delivery truck from Flora Dora's.

"Gotta go. Flower delivery heading my way! Love you!"

Kate dropped the worn SpongeBob SquarePants beach towel she'd wrapped around herself, slipped into her robe, and raced downstairs.

She yanked open the door to find a sullen young man with heavy-framed glasses and a smattering of leopard spots tattooed on his neck, holding a large gift basket filled with fruit and an assortment of snacks. Her hand drifted to her own neck as she took in the painful-looking artwork.

"I guess these are for you." He thrust the basket toward her. The card attached to the cellophane read: WITH SYMPATHY.

"Ha-ha. Someone's a real comedian."

He looked confused.

"'With sympathy?'" She frowned. "Today's my birthday. Someone thinks they're funny."

He shook his head. "I don't think so. Aren't you Beulah Howard?"

"Do I look like a Beulah?" She scanned the card again. "Wait! Beulah Howard? Did something happen to Shorty?"

The young man shrugged. "I dunno. All I know is this goes to Beulah Howard." Given his tone, you would have thought she was the one wasting his time.

"The Howards live at 200 Park Street. This is 200 River Street. That's the back of their house right there." She pointed to a small, neat yard that backed up to her driveway, and started to explain that their house had been built in the early 1800s, and then as property had been sold off, other houses had been built, leaving them facing the backs of the newer homes. Given the look on his face he clearly wasn't interested in any fun facts about early Belleville.

"Sorry." He tugged the gift basket from her hands and headed for his van.

"You sure you don't have anything for me?" she called after him.

He gave her a suspicious look. "Who are you?"

"Kate Donaldson. Or maybe Kate McDonald?"

"Which is it?" he asked sarcastically.

"Either, actually. My name is Donaldson, but my husband also goes by Billy McDonald. So . . ." The look he was giving her was sour, and her smile began to slip. Why was she letting this hipster wannabe make her feel uncomfortable in her own home?

She cleared her throat. "Do you have anything in your truck for me?"

"Um, no. Pretty sure I don't." More sarcasm. He plodded back toward the van.

"Nope, nope, nope," Kate said as she closed the door. "I'm not gonna let this ruin my day."

CHAPTER 3

The Hilltop Tavern was dark and cool. It also hadn't changed in twenty years. Hard to believe they'd squeezed a four-piece up on a stage barely big enough for a duo. Compared to last night in Miami, it was damn depressing. Billy had come a long way, and it sucked balls to think he might be heading back to places like this.

He settled onto the rickety stool. Elbows on the bar, he massaged his temples and tried to dissolve the gnawing melancholy weaving its way into his gut. If he could just shake this hangover.

The barmaid dropped napkins in front of him and Eddie. Tanned like a leather saddle, she was probably in her mid-sixties. Bleached blond hair was piled high atop her head, and her neon pink lips matched her shirt. Good thing he was wearing shades.

"What can I get ya, sugar?" Her voice rasped like a rusty hinge.

Here was his salvation, even if she wasn't easy on the eyes. Or the ears.

"What've you got on tap?"

"Miller and Bud."

He made a face. "Nah. Jack Daniels, rocks."

She looked at Eddie.

"Budweiser."

The old broad pulled a frosted mug from a freezer beneath the bar and slid it under the tap.

"I used to play here, back in the day," Billy told Eddie as he watched the golden liquid rise in the mug, wishing she'd hurry the fuck up.

"No shit? Think they'd remember you?"

"Doubtful. That was over twenty years ago."

The barmaid set Eddie's beer in front of him, then picked up the bottle of Jack. Amber liquid splashed over the ice, and his mouth watered.

"Thanks, hon." He tossed a twenty on the bar and raised the glass to his lips. The alcohol hadn't had time to chill, but it felt good going down.

"You said you played here?" Her voice was like nails on a chalkboard.

He chewed on an ice cube. "Long time ago."

"Take off the glasses." It was more of an order than a request.

He slid the shades partway down his nose.

"All the way."

Eddie snorted. "That's what she said."

Billy slipped off his glasses.

"No way!" She slapped her palm down on the surface of the bar so hard it had to have stung. "Earl! Earl! Get the hell out here!"

Billy's hangover roared back to life. "Shit," he muttered.

The door to the kitchen swung open, and a monster of a man emerged— Earl, Billy assumed. Thick around the middle, he wore an apron so stained and dirty it looked as if he'd been butchering hogs instead of flipping burgers.

"Chrissakes, Doris, what the hell you hollerin' about?"

"Look." She pointed at Billy.

"Look at what?"

"Look!" She wagged a gnarled finger in Billy's face.

"What am I looking at?"

"Who! Who are you looking at!"

"I dunno," Earl yelled back, clearly annoyed at the interruption. "*Who* am I looking at?"

"Look!"

Earl zeroed in for a closer look, frowning, while Billy leaned away from the scrutiny. Earl turned to Doris, about to speak, but then turned back for another look.

"No fuckin' way!" His mouth unhinged, and he gaped at Billy.

"I told you!"

"You didn't tell me nothin'." Earl's attention snapped back to Doris. "You asked me. You didn't tell me. I woulda figured it out myself."

Eddie leaned over. "What the hell are they talking about?"

"Who the hell knows?" Actually, that was a lie. Billy knew there was a damn good chance she recognized him. The sick feeling seeping into his stomach echoed the one already in his head. All he'd wanted was a quiet drink, something to dull the sharp edges of his hangover.

Doris waved her hand in Earl's face, dismissing his ignorance.

"I can't believe it." Earl gaped at Billy like he was witnessing the second coming, or at the very least, a member of the advance team.

"I'll bite," Billy said after a fortifying sip. "You don't believe what?" These two were irritating the piss out of him.

"Billy McDonald, right?" Doris asked.

He nodded.

"I'll be damned," Earl said.

Eddie brayed like a donkey. "Maybe they were at the concert last night."

"Call him on the cellular phone," Doris demanded. "Get him down here." She turned and gave Billy a look that was probably meant to be seductive but instead caused the hair on the back of his neck to stand up. "You boys ain't in a hurry, are ya?"

"Well . . ." He didn't know what she wanted, but he was pretty sure he wanted no part of it.

"C'mon, you can wait. Drinks are on the house. Make yourselves comfortable. We gotta get our boy here."

"Hey, if drinks are on the house . . ." Eddie drained his mug, then pushed it forward. With a wink, Doris snatched it up and hurried to refill it.

Billy lifted his glass in a toast. He didn't know to what, but a free drink was a free drink. Besides, it was exactly what he needed.

"He's on his way," Earl said, bustling back in from the kitchen.

"Did ya tell him?" Doris asked.

"No! I don't wanna ruin the surprise."

"What surprise?" Eddie whispered.

This time Billy was clueless. "Your guess is as good as mine." He drained his glass and pushed it forward. It was refilled immediately.

The comfortable numbness that accompanied the free drinks was doubly appreciated once Billy realized that he was the surprise.

He was polishing off his second Jack when a doughy ginger came in through a back door and joined the woman behind the bar.

"Well?" she said.

Billy glanced from the newcomer to Doris.

"You remember our son Chris, don't you? Of course he was only in high school the last time you saw him, but we never forgot how you used to let him sit in with the band." She beamed up at her son.

"Of course." *Not a clue.* "Bass player, right?"

"Keyboard."

"Right." Billy clicked his tongue and triggered an index finger.

No fucking clue.

"Chris is a musician, too," Doris added. Billy eyed the ham hocks at the end of the guy's wrists. "Teaches down at the elementary center."

Teaching music to fourth-graders?

"That's terrific, man. Keeping the dream alive. Love it."

Kill me now.

Doris had been ignoring Billy's empty glass since her progeny arrived. He pushed it closer. A firm but gentle reminder: *Free booze, remember?*

Chris stepped behind the bar and filled Billy's glass with ice.

"Jack Daniels, right?" He grinned. "See? I remembered."

Wow—and that wasn't creepy at all. Billy responded with the cool-guy chin tip.

Chris refilled Eddie's mug, then grabbed another frosted mug from the freezer and filled it half-full with root beer.

Doris cackled, sending a chill down Billy's spine. "Can you believe it? Practically grew up in a barroom and he doesn't even drink."

"Hard to believe," Billy answered, eyeing up Chris. He certainly looked as if he liked to eat.

Doris stepped away to wait on some other customers but returned in a flash, carrying a picture she'd snatched off the wall back from when he'd "made it big," as she put it.

"Would you mind?" she asked.

"Certainly, darlin'." He manufactured a grin, mostly because she'd finally lowered her voice. Other than the epic hangover, he sure as hell didn't feel like a star, but he obliged her. As long as she kept pouring, he'd sign her droopy left tit if she wanted.

Mother and son kept the drinks flowing for the next hour. By the time Chris invited them back to his house to jam, Billy's headache had retreated somewhat. That, or he was too numb to care. He glanced at his watch. Two o'clock. They could jam for an hour or two, and he would still get home before Kate. Besides, Eddie, who couldn't sit still for very long anyway, already had one foot out the door. The kid needed Ritalin or something.

Chris lived less than a mile from the bar, and since he wasn't drinking, he drove. He pulled up in front of a small ranch-style house just off the highway. It was dark and musty inside. Judging by the early dorm room décor and the fine layer of dust, he wasn't married. Probably didn't even have a girlfriend.

Billy took in the depressing surroundings. What the hell was he doing? He had someone waiting for him at home. Someone he hadn't seen in over two months.

He hung back. "Maybe we should get going," he said to Eddie. "Katie's going to be home in a couple hours—"

"C'mon, man, you said yourself she doesn't get home until six." Eddie picked up an old Ovation leaning against the sofa and handed it to him. "Let's just jam for a few, then we'll head out." He leaned closer. "You polished off a half bottle of Jack back there. It's payback time, bro."

Truthfully? He didn't give a fuck. The only strings attached to those drinks were the ones that had kept him tied to his barstool until he'd met Doris's son. Mission accomplished.

"Half hour, then we'll go. Promise."

Eddie had the wheels, so Billy had no choice. He plucked a chord on the Ovation and cringed. He tightened the strings. After one song, they'd slipped again. There was no snap, no crispness. They probably hadn't been changed this decade; rubber bands would have made a better sound. This was frustrating. He wanted a shower and to lie down in his own bed, with a naked Katie beside him.

He leaned the guitar against the edge of the couch and stood.

"Dude." He gave Eddie a pointed look. "Now. Okay?"

Eddie's eyes flickered to their host, who was rolling a joint. Chris lit up, took a hit, and handed it to the drummer.

"You don't drink, but you smoke weed?" Eddie asked in a tight voice, holding his breath and passing the joint to Billy.

"Nah. Don't like the way it makes me feel." Chris winked. "But that's not all I got." He pulled a metal tin from a shelf over the sofa and dumped out several rocks of cocaine and a razor. He cut them into six neat, thin lines on the glass-topped coffee table.

Billy's brain was saying no. The rest of him was still in rock-star party mode.

"What the fuck," he grumbled, giving in way too easily. "Won't be getting much of this once I get home."

He'd promised to quit the hard stuff a few years ago when Katie had caught wind of his dabbling with some serious shit and had all but packed her bags. He had quit, more or less, other than a little pot now and then. And that shit was practically legal. This last tour? Yeah, that was such a clusterfuck, it shouldn't count at all. He would hit rewind. Just as soon as he got home.

He snorted a couple of lines, but the rush was temporary. His lack of sleep conspired with the weed and JD, and he could barely keep his eyes open. Figured. Two months on the road, half of it sleeping on a cushy tour bus and the other half in five-star hotels, and he couldn't sleep worth a damn. Now he was nodding off on some stranger's disgusting couch. Such a bad idea.

It couldn't have been more than a few minutes. Eddie was shaking him awake. "C'mon, man. It's almost five. We gotta get the car and hit the road."

"Shit," Billy groaned. He couldn't focus, let alone stand and walk.

Chris was bent over the table, snorting another line.

"We gotta split," Eddie said. "You gotta take us back to my car. Now."

Chris dropped onto his ample ass and laughed. "I can't drive, dude. If my parents saw me right now, they'd kill me."

"What are you? Forty? Who gives a fuck what they think? C'mon man, we gotta get back to my car. His old lady's gonna kill him if I don't get him home."

As enamored as he'd originally been of seeing Billy, Chris no longer seemed to care.

Eddie helped Billy to his feet. "Fucking little shit!" he yelled over his shoulder as he guided Billy to the door.

By the time they reached Eddie's car, Billy had sobered up enough to realize he'd better call Kate. He dug into the pockets of his jeans but came up empty.

"Shit."

"What?" Eddie asked, unlocking the SUV.

"I think I left my phone on the bar." The parking lot was full now. Happy hour. "I'll be right back." He needed to get in and out without Doris and Earl telling everyone who he was.

No such luck.

"There he is," Doris called out as soon as he stepped into the packed barroom.

Billy gave her a tense smile. He ducked his head and stepped toward the bar. "Did I leave my phone here?"

"You sure did, honey. Got it right here." She scanned the shelves behind her, looking puzzled. "It was here a minute ago."

Earl stood at the end of the bar, surrounded by several patrons.

"Earl!" she yelled. "You seen Billy's phone?"

The big man turned, looking like he was about to shoot off his mouth to his wife, but when his eyes fell on Billy, he froze. Probably because Billy's cell phone was in his hands. And if Billy wasn't mistaken, he was currently scrolling through his contact list.

"What the fuck you doing?"

"We was just looking to see if you got any famous phone numbers in here," Earl confessed.

"Give me the damn phone."

Before Earl could respond, a blonde in her mid-twenties snatched it from his hands and tucked it down the front of her blouse.

"Come and get it," she teased, taking a step toward him and squeezing her shoulders together.

Unsmiling, Billy held out his hand. He wasn't in the mood for games. "May I please have my phone?"

"I said come get it." She leaned forward, giving her breasts a little shake while the crowd gathered around her egged her on.

He continued holding out his hand. "My phone. Now."

Eddie burst through the front door. "What the hell are you doin'? We gotta get goin' if you're gonna get home in time."

"Give me my phone," Billy repeated. If this chick couldn't tell he wasn't fooling around, there was something seriously wrong with her. He knew how this could go. He could just smile, play along. Then he could reach in, cop a feel, and probably sign her tits or something. It wouldn't be the first time. He just wasn't in the mood.

Apparently, she wasn't very good at reading people, because she just laughed.

"Come and get it. You know you wanna." She was inches from him now, taunting him.

"She have your phone?" Eddie asked, getting up to speed.

If Billy had turned to answer, he might have been able to stop him. But he hadn't; he'd continued glaring down at the blonde. Eddie's hand sliced through the air, yanking the front of the chick's blouse and tearing it nearly in half. The glass face of the phone shattered as it crashed to the floor.

"What the fuck?" The girl screeched and clutched at the two halves of her shredded shirt.

It wasn't clear who threw the first punch—not that it mattered. Some tank with a shaved head and a sick amount of ink tackled Eddie from behind.

Someone else jumped into the fray, knocking Billy into the bar. Not cool. Billy spun, grabbed him around the neck, then kneed the bastard in the groin when he wouldn't go down.

From the corner of his eye, he saw someone about to pounce from atop the bar. Billy reached around and used the dude's own momentum to swing him forward. Then he pulled back, landing his fist just under the Neanderthal's jaw and sending him backward through a large plate glass window. The man lay motionless and bleeding, his legs still in the bar and his torso outside, cradled by the boxwood hedge. It didn't look like he was breathing.

Eddie groaned as he tried to stand. "Let's get the fuck outta here." His eye was swelling shut and a trickle of blood ran from the corner of his mouth.

"Not so fast." Earl stepped between them and the door, pointing a baseball bat in Billy's direction. "Ain't nobody going nowhere until the cops get here."

The jukebox, blasting something by Lynyrd Skynyrd only moments before, had gone silent. Distant sirens filled the gap, and before long, red and blue lights reflected off the jagged shards of glass clinging to what was left of the window.

Billy slumped against the bar. He could have been home hours ago, showered, shaved, and if he was lucky, enjoying a quickie with his wife before celebrating her birthday.

But no, he had to have a fucking drink.

CHAPTER 4

The call went straight to voicemail—again. Kate tossed her phone on the counter and yanked open the refrigerator. At least she'd made the quiche earlier. She should stick a candle in it and take a picture, post it on Facebook. *Happy birthday to me.*

It was almost eight. She should have allowed Joey to come and take her to dinner like he'd offered. Let Billy come home and wonder where she was. See how he liked it.

The microwave beeped.

"Ow! Damn it!" Kate yanked her hand away from the hot plate, almost dropping it. She stood at the kitchen sink and held her fingers under the faucet. The cold water soothed the burn but did nothing for the sting of being stood up on her birthday. Tears filled her eyes and she blinked rapidly. Should she be angry? Worried? Actually, she was both. Sixty-forty; anger was definitely in the lead.

She poured a glass of wine, slipped a dish towel over her reddened fingers, picked up her dinner, and carried it into the living room, where she curled up on the couch.

"Happy birthday, Kate." She raised her glass to Anderson Cooper while keeping her eyes on the crawl at the bottom of the screen. Had there been some disaster she didn't know about or an accident on Route 78? She was an expert at finding excuses for Billy's behavior, even if she was the only one buying them.

She closed her eyes. Maybe he'd missed his flight or lost his phone. Or maybe he'd forgotten to recharge it. That was probably it. He'd forgotten to recharge the phone. Of course that was more like something she'd do, but it was possible. Right?

⁓

The ringing of her cell phone startled her awake.

"Mrs. McDonald?"

"Yes?" She squinted at the cable box below the TV: 11:38.

"Listen." The caller lowered his voice to a whisper. "Your husband's been arrested. The Andrewsville Police Department has him in custody."

"What?" Her body jerked forward. "Who is this?"

"Let's just say I'm a fan. I thought someone should let you know."

"What happened?"

"Bar fight. He's been arrested for public drunkenness, destruction of private property, assault, and aggravated assault."

Pretty informed for a fan. "How do you know all this?"

"Can't say. I'm gonna give you a number. Call and identify yourself. Just say you understand he was arrested. This way you'll know I'm telling you the truth."

"Who are you?"

His voice dropped so low, it was almost impossible to hear him.

"Look, I wanted to give you a heads-up. After you confirm that he's there, you should call your attorney. He'll be arraigned this evening."

Before she could ask how the caller had gotten her number, the line went dead. Billy took great pains to keep his private life separate. No random fan would have been able to get their home phone number.

Hands shaking, she called information and asked for the number of the Andrewsville Police Department. It was the same number the caller had given her. After calling and confirming what she'd been told, she grabbed the little black clutch she'd left near the back door and hurried to her car. She plugged the address for the jail into her GPS. She knew where she was going. Sort of. She'd been to Andrewsville before. Billy had even played there years ago with Viper at some little hole in the wall. Although why he'd been there today instead of coming home, she had no idea.

Belleville was asleep. The homes Kate passed were dark, their inhabitants tucked away for the night. Even the main street was empty and deserted. Streetlights flickered across her dashboard as she headed out of town. It was late, certainly too late to be making phone calls, but she dialed anyway.

It rang several times before a sleepy voice answered.

"I'm sorry to wake you, Tommy." She steadied her voice. "It's Kate. Billy's been arrested."

"Jesus," he whispered. "What happened?"

That's what she'd like to know. Sounding a lot calmer than she felt, Kate repeated what the caller had told her, none of which answered the real question: Why?

It was quiet for so long she wondered if Tom had fallen back to sleep.

"Hang on a sec."

She heard movement on the other end, then the quiet snap of a door. "So some stranger calls, gives you a number, and you call it, then jump in the car in the middle of the night?"

Her fingers tightened over the steering wheel. "Give me a little credit, Tommy. I looked up the number for the Andrewsville PD first. It's the same number he gave me."

He sighed loudly. Or maybe he yawned.

"Billy was supposed to land at Newark this morning, and he was hitching a ride with Eddie Anderson, Stonestreet's drummer. He should've been home this afternoon. I tried calling him earlier, but the calls just go to voicemail.

31

We were supposed to go out for . . ." This was humiliating, and she hated that she sounded whiney and pathetic. "I ended up falling asleep on the couch."

She definitely heard a yawn that time. "Let me call ahead and see what's what."

"Thanks, Tommy. I'm sorry to wake you."

"I'm sorry you had to wake me, too."

The dashboard clock ticked off the final two minutes of her birthday.

"Yeah, well. That's the glamorous life of being married to a rock star, right?" Her attempt to lighten the mood fell flat.

"I guess," Tom said, commiserating. "I'll give you a call when I know something."

She hung up and angrily pushed buttons on her radio until she found a station playing smooth jazz, hoping the mellow music would keep her relaxed. It didn't.

This wouldn't be the first time she'd had to pick Billy up from jail. He'd had a couple of DUI arrests and convictions and was due to get his license back next year. Of course, that might change now.

What the hell had happened between getting off the plane and that phone call? Aggravated assault? *Jesus.* He had a temper—she'd seen it more times than she cared to admit—but other than the fight with his old partner not long after they'd met, she'd never known him to get physical with anyone. Threaten? Yes, but faced with a glowering giant just over six foot four, people thought twice before pissing him off.

How could a simple ride home have landed him in so much trouble?

CHAPTER 5

It had to be at least ten degrees warmer in Andrewsville. Thick, sticky air wrapped itself around Kate like a woolen sweater, which was exactly what she wished she had once she stepped through the glass doors of the county jail and was hit with an icy, arctic blast. She'd left in such a hurry, she hadn't thought to grab a sweater or shawl and now, catching sight of her reflection as she registered with the officer behind the thick glass, she was sorry she hadn't taken time to change.

The strapless black leather mini dress, chunky gold necklace, and strappy platform sandals were better suited for a trendy restaurant, not the waiting area of a county jail. It was the kind of outfit she only wore when she was with Billy, and not having seen him for two months, she'd been hoping to knock his socks off.

If the image in the glass was a true reflection, she wasn't living up to anyone's idea of a trophy wife. Her makeup was smudged and her messy bun was more sloppy than messy. She looked like a high-priced call girl down on her luck.

The officer behind the desk gave her a hard look, and she hoped they wouldn't make her pee into a cup before she could take Billy home.

"I'm here for my husband. William Donaldson." No one ever called Billy that, but it was his legal name, and what was on his state ID card.

"Have a seat."

"Do you have any idea how long—"

"Take a seat, ma'am."

Kate mumbled a thank-you, although for what, she had no idea.

There was a seat available on the far side of the room. It was the middle of the night, for God's sake. Why were there so many people here? Was Andrewsville such a hotbed of overnight crime? Several pairs of eyes followed her as she crossed the waiting room, making her feel even more uncomfortable. Cold, hard plastic bit into the backs of her bare legs as she sat. The short leather skirt rode up her thighs. She struggled to wiggle it down, but it wouldn't give. Not only did she look like a hooker, she was displaying leg as if she were open for business.

She offered an embarrassed smile at the older couple sitting across from her. The man's grin was met with the back of the woman's hand across his chest and a barely disguised "*Puta!*" hurled in her direction. Kate didn't speak Spanish, but the meaning was clear. An angry flurry of words followed and the couple moved so that they no longer faced her.

She uncrossed her legs and sat straight in the narrow chair, her ankles pressed together. Eyes down, she fidgeted in her purse. Cell phone, driver's license, debit card, lip gloss. She twirled the square tube of lip gloss between her fingers—Nars Super Orgasm. *Seems appropriate.* She dropped the lip gloss back into her purse and rubbed her fingers above the bridge of her nose, trying to smooth some of the tension gathered there.

Billy had been gone nine weeks. Every day had been hard. The nights, even harder. He'd left the Tuesday after Mother's Day, and typical of a night before he headed out on tour, they hadn't gotten much sleep.

She had woken to find his side of the bed empty. Afraid he might leave before she got up, she raced downstairs and found him leaning against the counter in the kitchen, half awake, waiting for the coffee to brew.

"Were you going to leave without saying goodbye?"

The edges of his lips curled. "We said goodbye several times last night, didn't we?"

She couldn't return his smile. The dread she'd felt since he'd gotten this gig filled her to the brim. Stonestreet was a hard-partying band, and Billy had been hired to replace the rhythm guitarist, who'd died of a drug overdose six months earlier. Billy had accused her of overreacting, but it scared her. He'd promised her no more hard drugs, and she wanted to believe him, but he'd made lots of promises over the years—and more than once, she'd been disappointed.

"Katie." He frowned, but his eyes were soft. "We talked about this. This is a great opportunity. I'm getting to do what I love with a band that's already paid its dues. This is a good thing."

She twisted a long strand of hair between her fingers. "It's a long time."

"I've been gone this long before. I'll fly you out whenever I have a day off. Promise."

"You know I have to work."

"No. You don't." Gone was the cajoling tone he'd used moments earlier. "That's all you."

"Yes, I do. I have a job."

Irritation clouded his face. "Let's not start this before I have to leave, okay?" The set of his jaw spoke volumes about how he felt about her working.

Kate slipped her arms around his waist and nodded. She squeezed her eyes shut and pressed her face into his chest. He smelled of soap and lemongrass—distinctly Billy. A calloused finger lifted her chin, and his tongue captured a lone tear that had slipped from her eye and raced down her cheek.

His mouth covered hers. Warm and salty. His hands reached lower. Cradling her bottom, he lifted her and set her on the kitchen island. Then he untied her light silk robe and ran his hands over her breasts, cupping them before trailing his long fingers down to her waist. Sliding his way down her legs, he hooked his hands around her knees and pulled her closer to the edge, then knelt before her.

"What are you doing?" she asked as his lips brushed the inside of her knee.

There was a devilish gleam in his blue-gray eyes. "If you don't know, I guess I'm not doing it very well."

His tongue traveled the length of her thigh.

"Your car's going to be here . . ." Her words faded to a low hum. She wove her fingers through his hair, pulling him closer. Soft moans filled the quiet kitchen until she finally tumbled over some invisible cliff. He kissed her thigh, then stood and began unbuckling his belt.

"Your car—"

"Can wait," he answered, his eyes fixed on hers.

It was quick and gritty and very much unlike the lazy lovemaking that had kept them awake most of the night. He was tucking himself in when she heard the crunch of gravel. All of his guitars and equipment had been picked up earlier and loaded for the tour, except for his favorite Strat and the duffle bag holding a few changes of clothes and his personal things. He slung the bag over his shoulder and picked up the hard travel case, then leaned in for a final kiss.

"Wash your face," she reminded him, her arms clinging to his neck.

"No way." He grinned, running his tongue over his bottom lip. "I want to taste you for as long as possible."

He had done everything in his power that morning to distract her. And while he still made her weak in the knees, right about now, sitting under the harsh fluorescent lighting in the jailhouse waiting room, freezing her ass off, she wanted to kill him.

She grabbed a magazine off the table beside her. It was an old copy of *People*—in Spanish. No matter. It was all about the pictures anyway. She flipped through the pages until she shivered so violently she almost knocked her bag from her lap. Her teeth chattering, she tossed the magazine back on the table and rubbed her arms with her hands to try to generate some heat and silently cursed the county for spending its tax dollars so foolishly. Hopefully the arraignment would be over before she came down with pneumonia.

When she could no longer stand it, she got up and told the clerk she'd be out front. The woman shrugged, clearly not caring where the hooker waited for her criminal husband.

The difference between the inside and the outside had to be at least twenty degrees. Kate leaned against the building, the bricks still warm from baking in the sun all day, and tried to visualize what was in her trunk. A spare tire, a beach chair, and a large, sand-covered blanket from the trip down the shore in May. Until Devin had left for college, she could have counted on finding a sweatshirt or raincoat, a lesson learned from years of standing cold and wet on the sidelines at his sporting events.

The door to the building opened. Chilled air followed a man in a suit out into the balmy night. "Mrs. Donaldson?"

Finally.

"I heard you speaking to the clerk. I'm Sgt. Sterling." Holding out his hand, he stepped closer. "I'm the anonymous caller. I normally wouldn't have done that, but it seemed at first your husband wasn't going to call anyone."

He tipped his head toward the building, and she presumed, in the direction of wherever it was Billy was being held. "I'm kind of a fan."

He winced. Maybe because he realized he sounded more like a fourteen-year-old girl than a police sergeant. "I just thought I'd give you a heads-up. I'm sure once he's arraigned, he'll be wanting out of here real quick."

He slipped out of his jacket and held it out. "Besides, I saw you on the closed-circuit. You seemed, um, cold."

It was a nice gesture, although the gun holstered against his chest set her teeth on edge.

She held up a hand. "I can't," she said, although what she really wanted was to tear it from his hands. "Will he be arraigned soon?"

"Hard to tell. Turns out now that he's sobered up some, he opted to call his attorney. Once he gets here, it'll depend on the judge. Guess I shouldn't have bothered you after all."

His eyes dropped to her leather-covered breasts, then snapped back up to her face. At least he had the decency to look embarrassed. "Looks like you must have been in the middle of something."

The dress was going in the trash the minute she got home. "It's my birthday. Or it was my birthday. I was waiting for my husband to get home and take me to dinner." She forced a smile. "I fell asleep on the couch. All dressed up and no place to go, ya know." Once she started rambling, it was hard to stop. "Then you called, and I left so quickly I didn't think about what I was wearing." She looked down at her short skirt and her bare legs. "I must look pretty ridiculous." Her thumb hooked in the direction of the sign on the building. "Here, of all places. I think some of those people in there think I'm a working girl."

The look he gave her was slow and lingering and maybe a little too long for a man who had to be at least ten years her junior. "I don't know if ridiculous would be the word I'd use."

Her face felt warmer than the eighty-plus-degree air temperature dictated. At least it was too dark for him to notice.

"Well, whether or not you're looking for business, I don't recommend standing out here this time of night. Hopefully, your attorney will be here soon. He can deal with the magistrate, and you can be on your way. In the meantime, I suggest you stay in the waiting room."

She scanned the rough-looking block. "But it's so cold in there."

He thrust the jacket into her hands. "Please. I insist. Just leave it at the front desk when you go. Besides, I feel guilty for dragging you out in the middle of the night."

"Don't." Grateful, she slipped her arms into the sleeves. "If you hadn't called, I still wouldn't know where he was, so thank you."

He escorted her back to the waiting room. "Good luck. I hope it won't be much longer."

The room had cleared somewhat since she'd first entered, and there was a seat available in the far corner. Shaking with exhaustion, Kate tucked her clutch up under her arm and pulled the jacket tightly around her. Leaning her head against the wall, she closed her eyes. By the time she felt someone tapping her shoulder, she'd lost all track of time.

"Hey," Tom slipped into the chair beside her. "How're you doing?"

She squinted against the harsh fluorescent light. "I've been better. What time is it?"

He glanced at his watch. "Almost three."

"Oh, Tommy. I'm sorry."

"Nothing for you to be sorry about. He'll be released soon. They're processing him now." His lips formed a thin, straight line. "Listen, Kate . . ."

Judging by the look on his face and the way he was holding back, things were far worse than what she'd been told. "Just tell me. At least no one died, right?"

"Well, no." Deep lines creased his forehead. "He's still in surgery."

Oh, shit. She hadn't been serious.

"It's just that when they towed Billy's friend's vehicle to the impound lot, an inspection was done of their belongings. Billy had cocaine, marijuana, and a wooden pipe stashed in his guitar case."

She clenched her fist so tightly her nails bit into her palm. So much for promising he'd stop using hard drugs. Of course, he probably didn't consider cocaine a hard drug—not compared to, say, heroin. *C'mon, Kate. Perspective.*

"In addition to the initial charges, he's also facing possession and possession of drug paraphernalia. Because of his prior arrest record—and I don't think his attitude in there helped, either—the magistrate originally set bail at a hundred thousand dollars."

She could feel herself deflate.

Tom reached out as if to pat her knee but blanched at the bare leg below his hand. With no safe surface, he drew his hand closed and pulled back. "Just so you know, I had to drop a couple of names in there. The magistrate lowered bail to fifty grand, and he's allowing you to post ten percent."

"You didn't!" That was the last thing she wanted.

"The quicker we get him out of here, the better. There'll likely be a court reporter stopping by to check on the overnight arrests soon, and once they learn he's here, it'll just be a matter of time before it's in the news anyway. It's not going to be a secret, Kate. Might as well use Doug's connections to get him out of here without photos."

Doug, her son-in-law. Although Rhiannon was far too young to marry, despite being older than Kate was when she married Billy, her daughter had married into a well-connected, moneyed family. Her husband was an attorney. His father, Douglas Sr., was a county judge with political ambitions. Kate couldn't help but wonder how the conversation unfolded on the ninth hole when it came to his honor's questionable in-laws.

"I've yet to sort it all out," Tom said, "but you may want to hire Doug's firm for this anyway. If Billy's convicted, there's a chance he could see jail time, not to mention fines of at least fifty thousand dollars or more. Don't panic yet, but let's not rule that out, okay?"

"Too late. I started panicking when I got the phone call, and I moved right into apoplexy when you said 'possession.'" She shook her head as if that could make it go away. Maybe she was still asleep. Maybe Tom wasn't even here yet. Maybe, please God, she was still at home, asleep on the couch, and Billy had missed his plane and lost his cell phone—

"You okay?"

No. Definitely not okay.

She gave him a tremulous smile. "Maybe he should stay behind bars. It might be safer, given the way I'm feeling about now."

Tom looked uncomfortable, but got down to business and explained what the charges were. Although it sounded grim, the man Billy assaulted most likely didn't have any life-threatening injuries. That was the most serious charge. If they could prove Billy was defending himself or his friend, it might help.

"We'll do whatever we can to limit the damage, but keep an open mind about Doug's firm."

Kate let out a long, deep breath she hadn't even realized she'd been holding and leaned back. When she shivered, Tommy slipped an arm around her.

They hadn't known each other well growing up; Tommy had been a few years ahead of her in school and more Joey's friend. Once he'd joined his father's practice, he became their attorney, which included dealing with Billy's previous arrests for possession and DWI.

Tommy was so solid, so sensible. Probably a good husband, too—responsible and trustworthy, a man who came to the rescue, not someone who needed rescuing. He made a good living, had a beautiful home. Would she have been happy with someone so sweet and safe? With her thumb, she spun her engagement ring around her finger.

If she were a betting person, she'd wager that Tommy and Stephanie had sex every Saturday night from eleven to eleven fifteen. Then it was church the next morning, brunch at the club, and dinner with his parents Sunday evening. The thought of Tommy taking Stephanie up against the wall in the shower didn't quite ring true.

Safe. Secure. Boring.

Was there something wrong with her that she'd choose hot, steamy shower sex over a husband who was home every night and hadn't once lost his license? She sighed, loudly.

"You sure you're okay?"

"Yeah," she lied.

A door clanged open. Tom stood and walked toward the hallway, then nodded in her direction. She tucked her clutch under her arm and followed.

Billy's back was to her as she came around the corner. Snug black jeans hugged his long legs. A long-sleeved black shirt with the tails out and the cuffs turned up showed off the tattoos covering his forearms. His hair was messy and loose, hanging well past his shoulders. He and Tommy were speaking, and when Tommy glanced in her direction, Billy turned slowly, then snapped back to Tommy when he realized who was standing behind him.

"What the fuck is she doing here?" he practically growled. "I didn't tell you to call her."

"He didn't call me," she answered, hurt as well as angry. "And is that all you have to say?"

The man standing before her was a far cry from the one she'd kissed goodbye over two months ago. His neatly trimmed goatee had grown out into a scraggly beard. He needed a shower badly, and although it was the middle of the night, he wore sunglasses. A long, thin cut above his eyebrow was held together with several Steri-Strips. Another near the bridge of his nose had begun to swell. An angry red mark blossomed on his cheek, and there were hints that his eye would soon be black and blue.

"If I wanted you here, I would've called you. You shouldn't be here." He scowled at Tommy as if he were the reason behind all of them being there.

Kate slipped off the sergeant's jacket. "Neither should you." She tapped on the thick glass to get the desk officer's attention, then waited by the inner door until she came around to retrieve the jacket.

Billy watched as she walked back, his mouth curling into that trademark smile, the one that still caused her to melt like a teenager.

Not this time. This time, she was pissed.

"Well, I see you came dressed to impress." His grin grew, and the cut on his bottom lip split open, blood welling in the spot. A memory flashed before her of a night long ago when she hadn't been nearly as angry as she was now, yet she had punched him in the stomach. Tempting.

"Let's go." She started toward the exit.

Billy shoved his wallet, keys, and a handful of loose change and guitar picks into his pocket. He jammed his cell phone, which had a broken screen, into the other pocket.

"Where's the rest of my stuff?" he demanded.

"Everything that was in the van has been secured," Tommy explained. "You can wait until they bring it down, or you can come back and get it tomorrow."

"Do you have any idea how much that Gibson is worth? Not to mention the stuff in my bag."

The woman behind the glass eyed him warily.

"If something happens to any of it. If one fucking pick is missing—"

Tommy stepped close, the muscles in his jaw clenched. "I'm going to strongly suggest you not stand here and threaten the Andrewsville Police Department, especially within hearing range of witnesses and under surveillance of a closed-circuit television."

Billy glanced up at the camera and flipped it off with both hands. "This sucks balls." With one last glare at Tommy, he jammed his hands in his pockets and leaned against the wall, ignoring both of them.

It was like she'd been dropped from the sky after being caught up in a tornado. After all these years, she thought she'd seen every possible side of her husband, but this was one Billy she hadn't met before. Sure, he could be a bit of a jerk the first day or two coming off a long tour. She attributed that to the sharp dichotomy between life on the road and life as a husband and father. He kept the two separate, but there had to be some blurring of lines as he made the transition from the guy who had roadies do his dirty work while on tour to the guy who had to take out the trash and clean up after the dog at home.

And of course she'd seen him angry and nasty. His temper was legendary: Billy McDonald, bad boy of rock 'n' roll. Personally, she thought much of it had been grossly exaggerated. At least she had thought so.

An officer appeared with Billy's guitars and duffle bag. After signing off, Billy grabbed his things and headed for the exit without waiting for Kate, letting the door swing closed behind him. Part of her wanted to drop to the floor and remain there in protest. She was that tired and that angry. Besides, she had the keys. He wasn't going anywhere.

"Are you sure you're going to be okay?" Tommy asked.

"Honestly?" Her heels clicked across the tile floor. "I have no idea. I'll get through tonight. No promises about tomorrow. You may have to bail me out of jail."

"If you don't want to drive back with him, I'll take him."

Throwing a frown in Tommy's direction, she shook her head. "We'll be fine. Go home. Tell Stephanie I'm sorry. I'll call you tomorrow so we can figure out where we go from here."

Billy was waiting at the end of the sidewalk. She ignored him as she passed.

When they reached his car, Tommy leaned in and kissed her cheek.

"Hey!" Billy called from several yards away. "Go kiss your own wife!"

He'd been in jail for hours, yet the way he staggered, Kate couldn't help wondering if he was still drunk or stoned. Or maybe he'd just been knocked senseless in the fight.

She looked up at Tommy. "There've been lots of women over the years who've wanted to take Billy McDonald home, but that's my job. I'm the lucky one."

CHAPTER 6

Billy lowered himself into the front of Kate's Saab, then dropped the seat and closed his eyes. She slid in beside him and waited.

No explanations. No apology. No nothing.

Her anger building, she plugged in her iPhone, logged onto Pandora, and queued up a heavy metal station, hoping the loud, pounding music would add to the headache he was probably nursing. To be honest, what she really wanted to do was pound him with her fists. She'd never been this furious, and it was only the beginning.

Because of this boneheaded stunt, they could lose everything. He promised her he'd quit using hard drugs years ago, especially after she found out he'd been messing with heroin. This was exactly why she hadn't wanted him to take the gig with Stonestreet. Each time he had called, she could tell something wasn't quite right. He'd denied anything was wrong, but she could feel the tension radiating off him even though they were hundreds, sometimes thousands of miles apart. He never said anything outright. Of course he didn't want her to worry. He also didn't want her to think she'd been right.

Unfortunately, being right gave her little satisfaction.

When the urge to throttle him had faded and she was calm enough to drive, she pulled out of the parking lot.

Despite the abrasive rhythm and screeching vocals of AC/DC and Metallica, bands he'd cut his teeth on, Billy was asleep before she'd gone more than a couple of blocks. James Hetfield screamed out the lyrics to "Battery"; Billy snored; and Kate's head threatened to explode.

She pulled over and keyed in Justin Bieber. After an endless string of "baby, baby, baby," Billy lifted his head and glared at her.

"What the fuck is this?" he grumbled.

She focused on the empty highway.

"Turn it off!" he bellowed. "Jesus Christ, Kate, it's giving me a headache!" He unfastened his seatbelt and rolled toward the window.

She raised the volume. If she'd known the words, she would've sung along.

Billy jerked himself up and smacked the off button with his open palm. He pushed the seat back as far as it would go and lay back down.

She waited a minute, then turned it back on.

"Turn it off!"

When she did nothing, he reached over and slammed the dashboard, then grabbed her phone from the cup holder.

"Turn it on again and I'll throw this out the fucking window! Jesus, Kate. Gimme a fucking break."

He slept, and she seethed in silence the rest of the way home. The voices in her head imagined the fight they would have. Imagining it was usually as far as she got, though. Billy would misbehave, and after stewing for a few hours, she would hand him a Get Out of Jail Free card.

She cringed; that analogy hit a little too close to home this time.

It was after four by the time she nosed the Saab up the driveway. She reached over to wake Billy, who was snoring loudly, but stopped herself. He could sleep in the damn car for all she cared.

She got out and slammed the door. Hard.

She let Charlie out, put the plate and fork from her birthday dinner into the dishwasher, and grabbed the bottle of white zinfandel from the refrigerator. She filled her wine glass and was heading upstairs when Billy came crashing through the screen door. The strap from his duffle bag caught the handle, and he tugged so hard she thought he would tear it off.

"Were you gonna let me sleep in the car all night?"

She glared at him over the top of her glass.

"Whatever." He shook his head dismissively, as if he were the one who deserved to be angry.

He emptied his pockets on the kitchen counter, slipped off his sunglasses, and tucked them into the neck of his shirt.

"I'm starving." He yanked open the refrigerator and peered inside. "What've we got to eat?"

He helped himself to a bottle of Molson and turned expectantly toward her, curious as to what she was going to feed him. Kate's blood pressure ticked up a few points. His eye was already turning black and blue. In addition to the cuts on his nose and forehead, there was a small cut above his cheekbone she hadn't seen earlier, near a faded scar from a long-ago fight. Even so, he seemed more obnoxious than hurt.

Her fingers tightened on the bowl of her wine glass until she thought it might shatter. "Are you serious?"

"What? I haven't eaten since . . ." He scrubbed a hand over his scraggly beard. "I don't know. Maybe before the show or something. I'm hungry." He poked around in the refrigerator and pulled out the quiche, made a face, and asked if there was something else.

"You're unbelievable," she muttered.

As she tried to move past him, Billy grabbed her wrist, and she recognized a different kind of hunger.

"I didn't tell you how beautiful you look." His finger traced the line of her jaw, a slow smile curled his lips.

She knew all too well that if she spoke, she would likely regret it. They needed to put a night between them and sort things out in the morning. Morning, hah! She glanced at the clock above the stove, still blinking from the storm. What was she thinking? He wouldn't be functional until midafternoon at the earliest.

He dragged her toward him and buried his face in her neck. Ugh. Sweat and whiskey seeped through his pores.

"It's been too long, Katie. I need you." And just like that, he went from arrogant to contrite, maybe even pleading. "I get crazy when we're apart." His breath, warm in her ear, triggered the tiny hairs along her arm. "How 'bout we head upstairs? I need a shower first." His teeth scraped the nape of her neck to just behind her ear. "Of course, you could join me."

She pushed against his chest, but his hold tightened.

"Ouch." The sweetness evaporated as quickly as it had come. "For such a hot-looking piece of ass, you're pretty damn cold."

That was it. "You're a jerk." She yanked her wrist from his grip, grabbed her wine glass, and stomped up the steps.

"Aw, c'mon. Don't be mad." His laughter following her until she slammed the bedroom door.

She struggled to remove the strappy sandals, then kicked them into the closet. She grabbed an old, comfortable nightgown, cursing the couple of hundred bucks she'd dropped at Victoria's Secret to welcome Billy home, and then locked the bathroom door behind her.

Most of her makeup was now under her eyes, giving her the look of a tired Goth. Lovely. She grabbed a washcloth and scrubbed. After patting her face dry, she peeled off the leather dress and slipped into her nightgown. The habit of brushing her hair one hundred strokes each night before bed, something Joey had ingrained in her, was so strong she didn't think she'd be able to sleep if she didn't do it. The routine soothed her, and if ever she needed soothing, tonight was the night.

Perched on the edge of the tub, she dragged the brush through her hair and replayed the day in her head. What a birthday. A flower delivery that wasn't for her. No phone call from either of her children.

And now?

She wouldn't even acknowledge her birthday from now on. Totally not worth it.

She snapped off the light and came out to find Billy sprawled sideways across the handmade quilt, naked and snoring loudly. His clothes lay in a pile on the floor next to his duffle bag.

"Oh, for crying out loud!" She shook him. The snoring stuttered, but his eyelids didn't even flicker. "Billy!" She shook him again. Nothing.

She yanked her pillow from under his arm and stormed downstairs to spend the night curled up on the living room sofa as all the reasons she didn't deserve to be in this position played over and over in her head.

CHAPTER 7

Night loosened its grip, and early morning gray gave way to dusky pink. Kate shuffled to the kitchen. She filled the coffee pot with water, then dumped half out. Billy wouldn't be getting up for a long time, and when he did, he could make his own damn coffee. She mixed up a batch of oatmeal and topped it with a handful of early blackberries to make it palatable.

After breakfast, she dressed and headed to the garden. It was too hot and she was too tired for a run. Besides, the tomatoes were ripening quickly, and this was as good a time as any to make marinara. Staying busy might also keep her mind off wanting to march upstairs and strangle the snoring, naked elephant asleep in her bed.

She was about to dump a bowl of diced plum tomatoes into the sautéed garlic when she heard a knock on the front door. Her eyes darted to the clock over the stove. It had still been blinking last night but now declared it was a little past nine. Billy must have fixed it while she was getting ready for bed. Typical. There were far more important things in his life that needed fixing, but he was worried about the damn clock.

From where Kate stood, she could see straight through the dining room—originally the main living area—to the front door, where a neatly dressed young man stood on the porch, holding a clipboard.

She wiped her hands on a dish towel and headed for the door.

"Good morning. My name is Mr. Johannson. I'm here to see William Donaldson."

Kate tried not to smile at the formality of his greeting, especially from someone so young. "I'm sorry, Mr. Donaldson is still asleep. I don't anticipate he'll be up for several hours. Can I help you with something?"

"Are you Mrs. Donaldson?"

"Yes."

"I have a repossession notice for a 2010 Saab convertible belonging to Mr. Donaldson."

Her heart sank. "I don't understand." She opened the door and motioned for him to enter.

"Mr. Donaldson is two payments behind. As of tomorrow, it'll be three. He needs to make those payments now, or the car goes."

Kate could feel her blood pressure ratcheting back up. She pointed at the dining room table. "Have a seat. I'll see if I can wake him."

Judging by the snoring she heard from the top of the stairs, it wouldn't be easy.

She gave him a rough shake. "Billy. Wake up."

Nothing. She tried again, harder, but it was no use.

She dropped onto the edge of the bed. There was a little money in her savings account, but other than that, she had nothing. She didn't even know where Billy kept the checkbook. His refusal to relinquish the financial reins had been a sore spot in their marriage for years, but no matter how much she had argued, he wouldn't budge. He was doing her a favor, he'd said—one less thing for her to worry about. Unfortunately, that wasn't always the case, and even though he gave her an allowance like some 1960s housewife, she'd been caught short more times than she cared to remember. It was insulting and embarrassing, and it was the exact reason she'd taken a job. Another marital bone of contention.

Sad and desperate flew out the open window. Hello, furious.

She grabbed her own checkbook. There wasn't much in her account, but maybe Mr. Johannson would take a check for one payment and Billy could send the rest later. She'd make him walk his ass all the way to the post office, too.

Turned out that wouldn't be sufficient.

"It has to be a certified check, or you can call this number and make a payment with a debit card." He handed her a business card.

She had less than $1,500 in her savings account and only a few hundred in checking. "How much?"

"At $437.58 per month, that would be $1,312.74 total."

It would practically wipe her out.

"I have to transfer money first." The words on the card were all a jumble. She wasn't even sure if she was holding it right side up. "Let me get my laptop."

The sticky air seemed thick as well, and she moved in slow motion.

"Are you sure I can't get you something to drink?" she asked as she plugged in the laptop and waited for it to boot up. This was humiliating, true, but it didn't mean she shouldn't still be gracious. "Maybe something cold?"

"No, thank you." He looked uncomfortable. "I'm really sorry to do this."

She felt a need to fill the silence. "It must be a pretty horrible job."

"Not exactly my dream job, but with the economy the way it's been, there are lots of available jobs in collections . . ."

"They say it's getting better." Was it? She had no idea. For someone who worked in news, she didn't follow it as closely as she should. She tapped an impatient finger on the table.

"Let's hope. By the way, my name is Jason."

"Kate."

When the computer finally booted up, she logged in and transferred most of her savings into her checking account, then dialed the number he had given her to make the payment. While she waited on hold, she made small talk, trying to ease the discomfort they both felt.

"I kinda hate my job, too."

"Really?"

Actually, no. She didn't hate it. She was more or less ambivalent. "I'm a reporter."

"You don't enjoy that?"

She shrugged. "When I started, I worked for the local weekly. I handled all the fluff—weddings, engagements, birth announcements. I wrote some features, too. At least it was something I enjoyed. And the family who owned the paper, they were wonderful. Old Mr. Holmes was a sweetheart."

"So what happened?"

"When he died, his son sold the paper to the *Evening Examiner*. Everything changed. He thought he was doing me a favor and included my job as part of the deal when he sold the paper." She shrugged. "I felt obligated to tough it out." She wrinkled her nose. "My boss pretty much hates me. I'm either too stupid or too stubborn to leave."

Jason nodded. "I know how you feel. Trust me, there's no joy in knowing each job you complete successfully is going to upset the people you come in contact with."

"I don't know what's worse, being miserable or making others miserable."

"I think I'd rather be miserable."

She gave him a sad smile. "Guess you have the worst job."

"Yeah, and people like you make it even harder."

"That's a nice thing to say."

After she had confirmed her payment, Jason rose to leave.

Kate held out her hand. "Thank you."

He chuckled as he took it. "For what? Trying to repossess your car?"

"No. That wasn't cool. But you could be a real jerk with a job like this, and you're not." She walked him to the door. "Believe it or not, this last half hour with you has been the best part of the past twenty-four hours."

He looked shocked. "Wow. I hope your luck changes."

She sighed. "Me, too."

CHAPTER 8

This was not cooking weather. A smart person would have just cut up a few tomatoes for salad or bruschetta, but two people could only eat so many. Kate couldn't stand seeing her hard work rotting on the vine.

She stood at the Viking range, one of Billy's few household splurges, and tried to visualize her anger dissolving into the thick, rich sauce. No such luck. She was getting hotter by the minute, and not from the temperature, which was on track to hit a hundred by late afternoon.

Cooking usually cleared her head, but not today. Her thoughts were melting like the sweat trickling down her back. She stretched, trying to work a kink from her neck. This was almost unbearable. Maybe the heat made everything seem worse than it really was.

"Right," she grumbled. "It will all be a bad dream once this heat wave breaks." She wound her ponytail into a messy knot on top of her head, the sudden coolness against her damp neck a brief respite.

The sound of feet thumped overhead. Charlie, who was stretched out on the cool brick of the dining room hearth, lifted his head and let out a lazy woof.

The floor creaked. Then the inevitable bump into the antique demilune table, followed by mumbled cursing and the sound of running water.

When the shower stopped a short time later, the ominous riff from *Jaws* cued up on a loop inside Kate's head. "Here we go," she muttered.

She was rinsing the last batch of plum tomatoes when Billy's arms wound around her. The scent of fresh lemongrass from his shampoo enveloped her. His shirt was unbuttoned, his skin warm and damp from the shower. He pressed his mouth against her neck. The beard was gone. His hair dragged against her bare shoulders leaving cool, wet tracks as he kissed the spot behind her ear.

"Dance with me," he purred. "I've missed you."

The crack in her heart grew a little wider.

It would be so easy to turn around, bury her face in his chest. She'd done it hundreds of times. Made excuses. Looked the other way. But this time, hurt and disappointment weighed her down. Her feet were rooted to the floor. She couldn't dance. She could barely move.

Billy tugged gently, trying to turn her toward him, but anger won out over instinct. She twisted far enough that his lips landed on her temple.

"What's your problem?" He seemed surprised, even a little irritated.

She turned the heat on under the congealed blob of oatmeal that had been sitting on the back burner all morning and jabbed at it angrily with a wooden spoon, attempting to mash it back into something edible.

Billy shrugged at the snub and pulled a stool up to the counter. "What're you making?"

He was doing his best to sound casual, but she wasn't in the mood. She punctuated her silence with another stir of the oatmeal, which had begun to stick to the bottom of the Calphalon pot.

"I could go for some eggs Benedict. I'm starving. I don't think I ate at all yesterday. At least that I can remember." He laughed as if this was funny.

She pulled a paper plate from a cupboard over the microwave and slapped a spoonful of oatmeal on it. With a dark look, she shoved it across the counter.

"Oatmeal?" He seemed truly offended. "I hate oatmeal. C'mon, babe. Eggs Benedict, and I promise I'll take you to your favorite restaurant tonight to make up for yesterday." He tried to charm her with his smile. "Or how about I call a car and we head to the city. We'll go for the whole weekend, whatever you want."

She stirred her marinara and tried to steady herself.

"What the hell's your problem?" His patience was vanishing quickly. "I know you're pissed, okay? I fucked up. I've had a couple of bad days myself. I don't need shit from you too."

She shot him an evil look, then began scraping the burned oatmeal into the garbage disposal. The pot was probably ruined.

"Aww, babe," he sighed, pulling a Jekyll and Hyde. "Did you think I forgot your birthday?"

Her head snapped up. "Please stop. Eat your oatmeal and stop talking."

He eased himself off the stool, fixing her with the smile that had reduced her to putty a million times. A few hours of sleep and a shower had done him some good, but she could see now that he'd lost weight. The marks on his face were also more noticeable. A large bruise, the color of an eggplant, was partially visible near his ribcage.

His ragged appearance was worrisome—but she refused to let him off the hook this time. She reminded herself of the near repossession of her car and his lack of apology. She turned back to her scorched pot and her own simmering anger.

Over the sound of running water, she heard the familiar click of the latches on his guitar case and the sound of strings being tuned.

"I know what'll make you feel better."

She recognized the first few notes of one of her favorites, a Journey song he played for her now and then, especially on the rare occasions she would come to a gig. His voice was warm and soft when he wanted it to be. She had to give him credit; he was really trying to nail this performance.

She leaned against the sink, her arms folded, her lips pursed.

When he was done, he settled the guitar in the case and snapped one latch shut. It was a habit he'd had ever since the day Devin had tried to play roadie and picked up the unfastened guitar case. Billy's prized Martin, the guitar his grandfather had given him when he was ten, had crashed to the ground, the body cracking. Hungover and suffering from a lack of sleep, Billy's visceral response had frightened even her. More importantly, the incident had left five-year-old Devin trembling. She'd almost hated him that day. When Billy had calmed down, he apologized to both of them, but it was something she'd never forgotten. And to his credit, it was something Billy made sure he'd never forget, either. Instead of having the guitar repaired, he left it the way it was. The crack didn't affect the sound, but it did rub the inside of his arm when he played, scratching it raw if he played a long time. It was a small price to pay, he said, to help him remember never to lose his temper with either of his children again.

With the guitar safely stored away, he cocked his head and gave her a tentative smile. When she remained silent, he moved toward her, arms open, but before he could speak, she cut him off.

"Get out."

He stopped short. "What?"

"Get. Out."

Confusion flooded his face. "I don't—what?"

"Get out of my house."

"Your house?" He shook his head and chuckled. "I hate to tell—"

She pointed at the door. "Get out!"

"What the hell's wrong with you?"

The warm tone he'd used moments earlier had disappeared, and Kate's reason along with it. She picked up the pot she'd been scrubbing and flung it as hard as she could.

For someone so obviously hungover, he demonstrated impressive reflexes, ducking as the pot sailed over his head and crashed into the wall behind him. But the near miss flipped some switch in his head, and she wasn't sure what he would do as he moved toward her, his eyes on fire.

For that matter, she wasn't sure what she would do, especially after she grabbed the large kitchen knife she'd been using to chop garlic.

"Get out," she demanded. Bile rose in the back of her throat, and sweat trickled down her back. Faint or throw up? Maybe she'd do both.

"You've lost your fucking mind." He started up the stairs.

"No!" she cried, coming around the island and advancing on him. "Out. Now!"

"I have no shoes, *Kate*." His voice hung on the *T*, sharp and final. "You want me to leave barefoot?"

"Get out!" She thrust the knife in front of her like a sword. Maybe she had lost her mind. Or maybe he just made her crazy.

He watched her from the bottom step, a slow smile blossoming.

"C'mon, babe. Put that down and come here." His throaty little laugh infuriated her. "You know you're sexy when you get all fired up."

Maybe they were both crazy.

"We've been away from each other too long. I know what you need. You need me. Put that down and come here."

He licked his lower lip, catching it in his teeth. One eyebrow arched suggestively. Her heart thumped as she lowered her arm. What the hell was she doing?

The phone rang. The sound was like a bucket of ice water. She let it go to voicemail.

"I mean it, Billy. Go." She motioned toward the door with the knife. Was this what it felt like to lose your mind?

"I give up." He threw his hands up and continued to climb the stairs. Kate spied his boots near the door.

"No! Just get out. I'll get your damn boots."

The look on his face was one of extreme disappointment, as if she'd been the one to let him down. Slowly—deliberately infuriating her—he descended the stairs. When he neared the door, he turned back.

She sent a vase filled with pink knockout roses sailing past his head. It crashed into the wall, sending flowers, water, and glass spewing in every direction.

"I'm going, you psycho bitch," he snarled. The screen banged open against the side of the house, then slammed shut.

When he reached the sidewalk, Billy turned and ran his hand through his hair. She advanced to the doorway, still brandishing the knife.

"C'mon, babe," he pleaded. "Let's talk about this."

If he didn't start to walk away right now, she was convinced she would turn into some type of maniac. Flashes of white dotted her vision. She closed her eyes. Dear God, was she having a stroke?

He mistook her hesitation for an opportunity. "Katie, please, let me explain."

"Stop!" she screamed, but he continued toward the front door.

She grabbed the guitar case off the table, and as his foot touched the first step, she opened the door and flung it as hard as she could. It glanced off his left shoulder and skidded across the sidewalk.

"What the fuck?" he bellowed.

"Leave now, or I'll call the police!"

She threw first one boot and then the other in the direction of his head. The first landed in the grass. The second rolled into the driveway.

A curtain moved at the Howard house in front of them. On top of everything else, they apparently now had an audience.

"For what?" he shouted. "I didn't lay a hand on you. Call the fucking cops. I'll have you arrested for threatening to kill me and destroying my property."

"If you don't go now, I'll destroy more than one guitar. I'll go after that whole room upstairs, piece by piece. And I will call the cops. I bet you have something illegal stashed around here. A little pot? Some coke? You must take me for the biggest idiot that ever walked this earth. It's over, Billy. I'm done. I can't do this anymore!"

Something was about to burst in her brain. Sharp pain stabbed behind her eyes. Flashes of light made it all but impossible to see. Billy stood there looking at her like he had no idea who she was. Their eyes locked, and she saw their life together flashing before her. This must be what dying felt like.

The crunch of gravel brought her back to the present.

Rhiannon. Kate dropped her forehead against the doorjamb. Daddy's little girl.

Well, wasn't this just perfect?

CHAPTER 9

Kate watched the silver Volvo make its way up the driveway and over Billy's boot.

Rhiannon neared the bend that would take her behind the house. She lowered the window and waved. "Hi, Daddy! The boys can't wait to see you!"

Identical blond heads bobbed in the back seat, craning to catch a glimpse of their Poppy.

Kate headed to the kitchen. This was the last thing she needed. She set the knife on the cutting board. The usual commotion could be heard from the driveway. One boy was screaming, and the other was yelling something unintelligible.

Rhiannon had had her father wrapped around her little finger since the day she was born. Blond and petite, with Billy's blue eyes and charming smile, she'd been head cheerleader and homecoming queen in high school and president of her sorority at Rutgers. She'd met Doug during the short time she actually held a job, working in an off-campus pub. The relationship blossomed, although the job didn't last. Rhiannon claimed the late hours and required weekends cut into her study time. Barely carrying a 2.5 GPA, she couldn't have been studying all that hard.

Doug had been in his first year of law school when they met, and although Rhiannon was only a junior, they married as soon as he graduated. They enjoyed a delayed honeymoon to Turks and Caicos after his sitting for the bar exam, then settled into a five-thousand-square-foot McMansion in an upscale Pittstown neighborhood.

The screaming grew louder as Rhiannon came through the kitchen door carrying the source of the noise in one arm and dragging the second twin, who looked suspiciously guilty, by the hand.

"Can you help me? Please?" She spoke as if this was somehow her mother's fault.

Kate took the crying child and carried him to the sink, where she wet a paper towel with cool water and started to gently dab his face.

"What's the matter, buddy?" she cooed.

Dalton stiffened like a board and screamed. Kate cringed, certain her eardrum had just been pierced.

"He wants a cookie," explained Rhiannon. "I stopped at Starbucks, and he demanded a cookie. I said 'No cookies.' I gave him a cracker, but he didn't want it, so he's been screaming for the last twenty minutes. My head is about to explode."

Kate set Dalton on the floor, where he continued his tantrum, kicking her in the process.

"I have homemade oatmeal cookies." Kate stepped over the child and reached for a large glass apothecary jar on the counter.

"I said no cookies!" Rhiannon snapped. "You listen as well as they do." Then, as if someone had flipped a switch, her mood changed, her face brightening as if lit from within. "Where's Daddy? Is he still out front?"

All smiles, she rushed to the front door.

Billy sat on the steps. He had one boot on and was trying to work his foot into the one crushed by the Volvo.

Rhiannon flew through the door and threw her arms around his waist when he stood. "I'm so happy to see you. Did you and Mom have fun last night? I'm sorry I didn't get here yesterday, but the boys were so cranky. They wouldn't nap. You know how it is. What're you doing out here?"

She stopped squeezing him long enough to look up and froze. "What happened to your face?" She turned to her mother, her mouth open in horror.

"Why are you looking at me?" Kate asked. "I didn't do it."

Billy glanced at Kate. "Somebody took my phone and—"

"You were mugged?" Rhiannon threw her arms around him as if he were Lazarus returned from the dead.

Kate rolled her eyes and watched from inside the screen door, holding Dayton while Dalton's screams from the kitchen unwound from air-gulping sobs to low whimpers.

Billy returned his daughter's hug, giving Kate a pleading look over the top of her head. She frowned and held open the door.

"How's the tour going?" Rhiannon took her father by the hand and led him into the house. "How long are you home? I asked Mom, but she never knows what's going on."

Kate stood to the side as they walked past into the dining room.

"Where's Dalton?" Rhiannon asked, her smile fading.

"On the floor in the kitchen."

"Mom!" she cried. "You left him lying on a dirty kitchen floor?"

Kate handed Dayton to Billy, who proceeded to cover the boy with kisses and tickles while she went to retrieve the tearstained, sweaty Dalton. Despite a whimper now and then, he had fallen asleep on the cool tile floor. She thought about joining him.

Instead, she picked him up and carried him into the dining room.

"You two catch up," she whispered as she headed upstairs with the sleeping child. "I'll put him down in the music room."

Once she'd settled Dalton into the portable crib, Kate sank down onto the futon, exhausted from lack of sleep. On the wall above the crib hung several guitars: a Fender Telecaster and a Jazzmaster, a couple of basses, and an Epiphone acoustic. A mandolin with rosewood and turquoise inlays Kate had bought Billy the first Christmas after they were married hung in the center.

Directly across from her hung a large family portrait Joey had taken not long after Devin was born. As outrageous as it was, it had been her idea, and Billy loved it. He'd used it on the back of one of his early albums, and it had been used in several articles about him years ago. It was Kate's version of American Gothic: Billy on the right, holding Rhiannon instead of a pitchfork, and Kate on the left, holding a newborn Devin. The unconventional part was that they were all naked, or at least they appeared to be. Kate's long hair covered her breasts, and the picture stopped above her belly button—no long, vertical scar from her emergency C-section—and a critically private point on the much taller Billy.

The portrait had been a silent dig at her controlling, disapproving mother. It had hung over the fireplace for years until the day Devin demanded it be removed. His friends seemed to gravitate to it, and truthfully, having preteen boys leering at her was just plain creepy. The photo was moved to Billy's music room, which was off limits to even the most precocious prepubescents.

So many memories, Kate thought, looking at the portrait and the collection of instruments, some hanging in their assigned places, others on stands waiting for Billy to bring them to life. Her eyes stopped on an empty stand, and she felt the nausea return. His favorite, the Martin, belonged there. She hoped it hadn't been damaged when she'd thrown it.

Feeling the room and the memories closing in on her, she made a hasty retreat just as Rhiannon was coming up the steps.

"He's fine," she whispered. "He's sleeping."

"You need to come downstairs." Rhiannon looked somber. *Damn it.* Billy must have told her what happened?

"Look, sweetheart, I really don't want to get into this with you."

"There's a police officer here, Mom. You need to come downstairs."

Kate's heart nearly stopped. "Oh my God. Devin?"

Rhiannon shook her head fiercely. "Devin's fine. He's here to see you."

Digger Johnson waited in the doorway. Billy remained seated at the dining room table, holding Dayton and trying to make small talk, but Digger just stood there looking uncomfortable.

"Rhiannon, could you excuse us?" The officer asked after Kate appeared.

"Daddy?" She turned to Billy.

Of course Rhiannon would believe her father trumped the chief of police.

"I'm sure everything's okay," Billy said. "Just do as he asks."

Rhiannon took Dayton, then looked from Billy to Kate, back to Digger.

"Why don't you and Dayton go pick me a nice bouquet for the table?" Kate asked.

"Flowers! I forgot. I have flowers for you." Rhiannon squinched her face. "Happy belated birthday."

Although her stomach was churning, Kate gave her daughter a reassuring smile, then motioned with her head toward the backyard.

Digger waited until Rhiannon left, then walked into the kitchen to make sure she was out of hearing range. Billy and Kate exchanged angry glances.

"I'm responding to a complaint of a domestic in progress," Digger said, sounding very official. "Since it doesn't look like anything's going on, other than that," he pointed at the shattered vase, "one of you better start talking."

Shards of broken glass and wilted flowers littered a puddle of water between the door and an antique cupboard.

Billy cocked an eyebrow at her. "Really?"

"I didn't call anyone!" She turned to face the officer. "Digger, I did not call anyone. I don't know what—"

"No, Kate," he interrupted. "The call was about you."

She gasped. "What?"

"We got a report of a domestic in progress—with a weapon."

Digger walked back into the kitchen and returned with the knife she'd been waving in the air not too long ago.

"I . . . I just . . ."

Billy rose and moved toward Kate.

"Freeze!" Digger ordered. "I mean it. Sit down!" He motioned to the seat Billy had vacated.

Billy hung back, but he didn't sit.

"What's going on, Kate?" Digger spoke calmly, but she continued to trip over her words.

Billy held up his hands. "C'mon, Digger. Is this a joke? Katie wouldn't hurt a fly, and you know it."

"Billy," Digger snarled. "Sit down and shut the fuck up. I don't wanna hear a word out of you unless I ask for it. I'm not falling for your bullshit now, just like I never fell for it in the past."

Billy glared at Digger, the muscle in his jaw flickering.

Kate blinked rapidly. Exhaustion, anger, and now fear had taken control of her brain. A low hum buzzed in her ears as if a swarm of bees had somehow gotten into the house. She began to rock.

"Look what you're doin' to her!" Ignoring the officer, Billy crossed the room. He slipped his arm around her shoulders, and her body naturally gravitated toward his.

Digger moved his hand to his service revolver and warned Billy again to back away.

"No. You don't come into my house and terrorize my wife. Who the hell called you? There's nothing going on here."

Digger pulled a small notebook from his shirt pocket. "We got a call that there was screaming and yelling coming from your residence. A man exited the front door. Following that, Mrs. Donaldson stood in the doorway, waving a large knife in a threatening manner. She then threw a large object out the door, hitting said man"—he pointed at Billy—"in the shoulder, followed by a pair of shoes."

"Boots," Kate corrected softly.

Billy squeezed her shoulder, probably warning her to stay quiet. Her anger from earlier resurfaced as she remembered the twitching curtain.

"Who called you? Mrs. Howard?"

"Katie." Billy's voice carried a warning note.

"You be quiet," Digger commanded.

"No. Katie, please. Let me." Billy sounded almost desperate. "Yeah, we had a fight. Okay? Yesterday was Kate's birthday and I forgot. Can you blame her? I mean, I'm a jackass, right?"

"Shut up, Billy. I've known you were a jackass for years, and I also know what happened yesterday and the night before. You made the national news, rock star, so don't feed me any of your bullshit, 'cause I'm not buying it."

National news? Kate glanced up at Billy, but he was focused on Digger.

"Digger, c'mon. We've known each other a long time. Kate was pissed, but she didn't threaten me, and she didn't throw anything either. I don't know what that old bat saw."

Billy pulled Kate in front of him and wrapped his arms around her. "I love this woman with all my heart, and she loves me. I'd never hurt her. Same goes for her. Let's just say it was a case of mistaken identity and call it a day. Okay?"

Digger didn't seem like he was buying it.

Kate forced a smile. "Yep," she said, choking on her words. "Forgot my birthday."

Even all these years—long after his high school crush on her should have faded—Digger still looked at her a little too long and made her a little too uncomfortable. She leaned back into Billy's embrace, then lifted her hands to rest on his arms.

"Just a lover's quarrel," she continued. "This man makes me crazy sometimes."

She tilted her head and smiled up at Billy.

He squeezed tighter, then bent to whisper so only she could hear. "You know how much I love you, right?"

"Uh-huh." She nodded, still smiling at Digger.

Looking defeated, Digger put the knife on the dining room table. "If I get another call, I'm running you both in. And you—" He pointed at Billy. "Don't even cross against the light, or I swear to God I'll make it my business to see you serve time."

"Absolutely, officer."

She couldn't see him, but she knew he was giving Digger a cocky grin.

Even after the door to the cruiser slammed shut and the engine started, they didn't move. Billy's arms remained wrapped tightly around her. He dragged his nose through her hair, then rested his cheek on top of her head.

"You can let me go now," she said softly.

"No."

"Billy, please." She tugged on his arms, but he held on tighter.

"I can't." His voice was a frightened whisper. "I'm afraid if I let go, I might never hold you again."

A chill skittered up her spine.

She closed her eyes and breathed in his achingly familiar scent—lemongrass, Jack Daniels, and something very much his own. She leaned back and let him hold her. Maybe it would be the last time. She swiveled in his arms, put her hands on either side of his face, and kissed him. He pressed a hand against her waist, pulling her to him as her knees turned to jelly.

"What the hell is going on?" Rhiannon demanded.

Kate broke free. She wiped her mouth and noticed the iron taste of blood. She didn't know if it was hers or if the cut on Billy's lip had opened again. "Nothing, sweetheart." She called on every ounce of strength she had. "Everything's fine."

"Well," Rhiannon continued, indignant, "I was scared out of my—"

"Honey, could you please help your dad out?" Kate wrapped her arms around her own torso. "He needs a place to stay."

"Katie!"

"And we'd really appreciate if you could help him until he can find a place of his own. You've got that big house, and the boys really haven't had much time with their poppy."

"Mom!"

"Thanks, sweetheart."

The look on Billy's face was one she hadn't seen before. He seemed destroyed, and it almost made her change her mind.

"I love you. I do. I just can't do this anymore. I'm sorry." She spoke with no emotion. "Could you lock up on your way out? And Rhiannon, would you please turn off the stove? I'm sure my sauce burned a while ago."

Kate started up the stairs, reminding herself to keep moving, since it seemed her body had forgotten how: right leg, left leg, repeat. "Good night." Her voice was hollow.

"Mom!"

She kept walking.

"Mom?" Rhiannon spoke softly, a hint of fear in her voice. "It's only three o'clock."

When she reached her room, Kate locked the door behind her, then sat stiffly on the edge of the bed. There was a soft tap on the door.

"Mom?"

A moment or two later—or maybe an hour, she had no idea—Billy knocked.

"Baby, please open the door. We can fix this." He jiggled the handle. "Katie, please talk to me."

She didn't move.

He cursed and demanded to know when she'd had a lock installed. The lock had always been there; he'd just never been on the other side of it. There was a soft thud and by the muffled sound of his voice, Kate pictured his battered face against the door. He begged. He pleaded. He finally apologized. His voice grew hoarse, but he never stopped talking, reminding her of the good times, of how much he loved her, of everything that was at stake. After a long while, she heard the full length of him slide down the door and onto the floor.

Her body had gone numb. She no longer felt the intense heat. Her skin was dry, and the jabbing pain behind her eyes was gone. She had checked out. Blessed nothingness. The fact that her spine was still holding her in an upright position as she sat on the bed seemed nothing short of a miracle.

She stared out the window. Tall stalks of corn swayed in neat rows behind the house. Beyond the field, she could see the top of the bleachers at the far end of the high school stadium. Every now and then, the crack of a bat or the distant roar of a small crowd floated toward her. A child cried. Dayton. Or Dalton. Maybe both.

The shadows lengthened. Rhiannon's car started up. Then it was gone.

Dusk arrived. The shouts from the stadium faded. The sun made its descent on the opposite side of the house.

It was quiet, yet Billy was still there. Once Rhiannon left, he must have started drinking. It wasn't long before he was pounding on the door, demanding she open it. Then he threatened to kick it in. When that didn't work, he pleaded again and cried her name out loud.

Kate lay down. She had never experienced this level of exhaustion. She didn't want to think. She didn't want to feel. She just wanted to go to sleep for a good, long time, but she couldn't. She continued to stare, numb and dry-eyed, at the wall.

Other than the occasional mumble, Billy had grown quiet.

Gravel crunched in the driveway. Maybe Rhiannon had returned, or

Digger, given Billy's shouts and threats. The back door opened and closed, followed by heavy footsteps on the stairs.

"C'mon, Billy. Time to go." Kate recognized Doug's voice. "You need to let her be."

Kate's lip quivered. Her breathing quickened, and tears pricked her eyes.

"Leave me alone," Billy cried. "I'm not leaving." He pounded the door again. "Katie!"

The rest was mumbled—drunken slurs and angry sobs.

"Billy, don't make this harder than it is."

"Get the fuck away from me! Don't make me hurt you!"

The windows were open, yet Kate struggled to breathe.

"She wants you to leave." Doug's voice was calm but firm. "You need to respect her. You owe her this—"

"No!"

The force of the single word reverberated inside her, drawing her up from the bed. Her fist pressed to her mouth, she moved toward the door. She reached for the knob. There was a loud thud, and the door shuddered in its frame.

"Come on, Billy. Let's go."

Billy's drunken rambling continued. Her head rested against the door, her hand on the knob. One more second.

Her heart said open the door. Her brain said: *Enough.*

There was movement on the other side, followed by muffled grunts and footsteps.

"That's it. Just lean on me."

Billy's words were unintelligible as they moved down the hall.

"I'm sure she does, but you have to give her some space. Give her a little time."

The back door slammed shut.

Kate stood at the window overlooking the driveway, watching Doug help Billy across the pavement. He loaded him into the passenger seat of the Lexus, then buckled him in like a child. When he lifted his face toward their bedroom window, and she could see his anguished expression, her heart split the rest of the way.

The car disappeared around the bend. Exhausted and numb, she lay down and stared at the ceiling overhead. Anything more would be impossible.

CHAPTER 10

Kate woke with a start, her heart pounding. Other than the neon light of the clock, the room was dark. Her body felt stiff, her eyes burning. Her mouth was dry and her stomach lurched with nausea. She rolled onto her back and blinked up at the ceiling, trying to let her eyes adjust to the darkness.

The pounding continued. It wasn't her heart.

She fumbled for the lamp. Soft light filled the room. Her eyes fell on Billy's pile of discarded clothes. The fog of confusion faded, and heartache roared back to life.

Still the pounding. Someone called her name.

She stumbled downstairs, flicking on lights along the way, until she was met with a frantic face peering in her back door.

She flipped the lock and pulled it open. "What are you doing here?"

"Oh my God! I've been calling you for three hours!" Joey screeched in her face. "I finally got in the car and started driving. Why didn't you answer the phone? I was worried sick! What the hell's going on?"

"It's over." Even the words hurt.

"Oh, honey," he frowned, leading her into the kitchen. "You've said that before."

She stared back at him. "No, I haven't."

He dismissed her with a flick of his wrist. "It was only a matter of time."

"Please don't start."

From the day they'd met, Billy and Joey had held a mutual dislike for each other that had even bordered on ugly. In more recent years they had at least been civil, although Joey couldn't resist making a snarky comment if the opportunity presented itself.

"I'm sorry you're hurting," he said. "C'mere."

Kate buried her face against his designer T-shirt. In the arms of her dearest, closest friend, she let go.

Joey held her for a while, then pulled away. "God, you're an ugly crier. Are you ready to tell me what's going on?"

She nodded, and he guided her to a chair in the dining room.

"I'll make some tea, and you can tell me what happened."

She pulled her legs up, then rested her chin on her knees. Holding up her head felt like too much of an effort.

"Or maybe something stronger?" He gave a lift of his brows.

"No. Tea. My throat hurts. But you go ahead," she added between heaving breaths.

Joey pulled a bottle of shiraz from his messenger bag, found a glass with a large bowl, and filled it three-quarters of the way. He sniffed, sipped, swallowed. Satisfied, he retreated to the kitchen to put the kettle on.

"What the hell is this?" He stood in the doorway holding her large sauce pot. Inside was a thick, reddish brown mess.

"Marinara."

"Remind me not to come for your next Italian night," he muttered.

"What time is it?" Kate asked.

The battery was dead in the hand-painted Vaillancourt clock that hung over the fireplace in the dining room. In all the drama of the past day, Billy must have missed it.

"It's a little after three," Joey called from the kitchen.

Cabinet doors banged open and closed as he searched for tea bags and a mug. It hurt too much to call across the room, so she got up and walked into the kitchen.

"In the morning?" She had been asleep for hours.

"No, in the afternoon. We're having an eclipse." There was that trademark sarcasm.

She pulled a stool up to the counter, where she noticed a large bouquet of stargazer lilies and gardenias in an antique agateware coffeepot—the flowers from Rhiannon and the boys. In the sink sat the pot of dark brown marinara, and on the counter lay the dented saucepan she had hurled at Billy's head. She leaned over to look into the dining room. The shattered glass had been cleaned up.

"Lemon and honey?"

She nodded. "So how'd you know?"

"Rhiannon called, hysterical. She said she came to surprise you for your birthday—I know, a day late." Joey rolled his eyes. "She said you threw her father out. A police officer came to arrest you. You've completely lost your mind. And there's just no talking to you." He recited all of this in a sing-song voice. "Yada, yada, yada. I asked if she'd been drinking, and then she really lost it. She said she had all she could deal with trying to take care of her father, who I assume is doing the actual drinking, and that somebody had better straighten you out. She called Devin, but he's not answering his phone."

Kate groaned and covered her face with her hands.

Joey poured the boiling water into Kate's mug and pulled up a stool. Rubbing his hand on her back, he asked for the non-hysterical version. She began with the arrival of the sympathy fruit basket and ended with Doug's removal of Billy. Reliving it didn't make it easier, but Joey listened quietly, holding her when she cried.

By the time she had finished, the line of trees that edged her property was becoming visible through the kitchen window.

"I don't know what I'm going to do. I'm tired of being hurt and disappointed. I didn't want him to take this gig, but he wouldn't listen. I could tell when he called me that he was stressed and miserable. Not that he would ever admit it. And it's obvious he's been lying. If he lied about the drugs, what else is he lying about? What if he ends up in jail? Or we lose the house? I don't know if I can handle this."

Joey threaded his fingers between hers. "Come to New York. Stay as long as you want. Let me take care of you for a while."

"What good would that do? That won't fix anything. Plus I have a job, remember? Sully would love nothing more than an excuse to fire me. I asked him for some time off because Billy was coming home. He gave me two days. He's not going to change his mind."

"They can't do without you for a little while? Just tell them Romeo is at it again."

Kate shook her head. "Sully doesn't care. He just expects to see a newspaper every day. Besides, I need the money."

She choked up again thinking of the humiliation when the sweet young man came to repossess her car.

When she told Joey, his jaw tightened.

"Why didn't you tell me it was this bad?"

"I don't know how bad it is or even *if* it's bad. I have no idea." She shook her head. "I can't take your money. I need to figure this out myself, on my own."

"You'll never be on your own, Kate. I'm always here for you. Always." He squeezed her hand, then leaned forward and rubbed his nose against hers.

She tried to smile.

As night surrendered into a pink dawn, promising another hot day, Joey put Kate's cup in the sink, topped off his glass, then turned out the light.

"Let's go. I'm putting you to bed, and I'm gonna head for that futon myself. If I can't sleep, I'll snip all the strings on that collection up there." He winked.

Upstairs, after she came back out of the bathroom dressed in one of Billy's old T-shirts, he sat her on the edge of the bed and began brushing her hair.

"One hundred strokes a night. Right?"

"Um-hmmm." It was all she could do to remain upright.

When he finished, she lay down.

"Do you need anything?" he asked, pulling the covers up to her chin.

She shook her head, and her eyes filled with tears. "No. I'm just so tired."

"Then it's a good thing you're in bed." He walked to each window and pulled the drapes closed. "It's Saturday. Sleep all day if you want." He pointed to the phone, sitting off the hook on the nightstand, and frowned. "Should I hang this up?"

"I guess."

He kissed her forehead. "I'm right down the hall if you need me."

Charlie nosed at the edge of the covers, already intent on settling onto Billy's side of the bed.

"C'mon, Charlie. You're sleeping with me, you lucky fellow. Mommy needs sleep, and you aren't waking her up at the crack of noon. Let's go."

A rooster crowed in the distance.

"That settles it," said Joey. "Now it really is bedtime. If you get used to these hours, you'll fit right in in New York." He blew her a kiss. "Right down the hall. Okay?"

She closed her eyes. When she heard the door to the music room close, she rolled over to Billy's side, buried her face in his pillow, and cried herself to sleep.

CHAPTER 11

Joey stared into a bowl of fresh eggs. Knowing Kate, she'd probably plucked them out from under the chicken's ass herself. He should probably do something with them, like crack them into a hot pan. But then what? Cooking wasn't his thing; in fact, living in Manhattan, it wasn't even on his radar. But here, in no man's land—

There was a knock at the back door, three soft taps.

"Hey," he said when he saw Tom on the other side of the screen. He opened the door and let him in.

"When did you get here?" Tom was wearing running shorts and a Fighting Irish T-shirt. Sweat trickled down his temples, and his shirt was damp. His short, sandy hair stood up in spikes around his head.

Joey held his finger to his lips. "Kate's sleeping. I got here around three. Rhiannon called me."

"Where's Billy?"

Joey shook his head and huffed. "Gone. She threw him out."

"Shit. When?"

"Yesterday, right after Chief Asshat came to arrest her."

He didn't give Tom much time to react before he relayed everything Kate had told him, including the kid who had come to repossess her car and the visit from Digger.

"That's too bad."

"No, it's not!" Joey shook his head furiously. "It's about time is what it is. Actually, it's about twenty-four years too late."

"She loves him, Joey."

"She'll get over it."

Still irritated, he motioned for Tom to follow him into the kitchen, where he held out the bowl of eggs. "What do you do with these?"

"Eggs?"

"I know they're eggs. I want to make Kate breakfast."

"You?" Tom laughed.

Joey gave him the stink eye and folded his arms over his chest.

"Allow me." Tom washed his hands, then ran a dishtowel under some cool water and draped it around his neck. "Omelet?"

Joey snuggled into a stool at the kitchen island. "Yes, please." He let out an exaggerated sigh. "I'm starving. And don't forget the coffee."

"You haven't had coffee yet?" Tom glanced at his watch. "It's almost noon.

Joey leaned back on the stool and dropped a hand to his hip. "Is there a Starbucks around here I don't know about?" He waggled a half cup of cold tea. "Then no. I can't figure out how to work that thing." The newfangled coffeemaker on the counter mocked him. "I'm treading water here."

With a smirk, Tom filled the reservoir with water, scooped some ground coffee into the basket, and set it to brew. He cracked several eggs into a bowl and whipped them into a froth with a utensil that might have been left over from the Middle Ages, moving efficiently around the kitchen.

Satisfied that his caffeine fix was close at hand, Joey hopped off the stool and made his way to the other side, where Tom had just dropped a large pat of butter into a skillet. He took Tom's hand and paused, listening to the silence. Convinced that Kate was still asleep, he pulled Tom into the laundry room off the kitchen.

"I hate this." He wrapped his arms around Tom's waist and rested his head on his shoulder.

"I know." Tom pressed his lips to Joey's head. "I hate sneaking around as much as you do. I'm just not ready."

"Not ready for what?" Joey pulled back. "Not ready to be who you are? For fuck's sake. Anyone who can't accept that, then the hell with them. That's not someone you need in your life, is it?"

"I know. I hate hurting you, but my parents . . . They won't understand."

Joey plucked Tom's shirt away from his damp skin and ran his fingers along the base of his spine. "Being gay is nothing new, Tommy. It isn't something we came up with just to shock people, you know."

He felt rather than heard Tom sigh.

"I know, but what about Stephanie? She'll take Lian, and then I'll have nothing."

Joey pulled away. "You won't have nothing. You'll have me!"

"I didn't mean it like that. I'm just not as strong as you." Tom lifted Joey's chin and kissed him. "You know I love you, don't you? And I promise, next month we'll get away. I've already told Stephanie that you're looking to open a boutique in Boston and you need me to review the paperwork. We'll head up to Maine. For a whole week this time."

The prospect of having Tom to himself for an entire week was exciting, but he was tired of living his life in pieces, never able to step out into public with the man he loved.

But it was more than that. "It's bad enough this sneaking around for years—*years*—and only seeing each other when you can get away, but I hate lying to Kate."

"I know, but you can't tell her," Tom whispered frantically. "You can't!"

"I won't. I just don't like it."

"I'm trying. I am. Someday I'll be strong enough, I promise. Then we won't hide from anybody."

"I'll be old and gray by then."

"I'll love you even when you're old and gray," Tom promised, running his fingers through Joey's halo of dark curls, "and maybe even if you're bald."

"God forbid."

The aroma of fresh-brewed coffee filled the air. Other than the hum of the coffeemaker and the steady tick of the clock in the dining room, the house was still.

He pushed Tom against the washing machine and closed the door.

Breakfast—even his precious coffee—would have to wait a little longer.

CHAPTER 12

The buzzing was back, only this time it wasn't in Kate's head. Her cell phone shimmied on the bedside table. It was probably Billy, but Kate wasn't ready to talk to him. She was about to send it to voicemail, when Sully's name popped up.

She should have ignored him as well.

In a tone just short of barking, he informed her that not only had the Associated Press released an entertainment brief about an altercation Billy had in Miami with Mick McAvoy, leading to his subsequent termination from Stonestreet—which was news to her—but the story of his arrest in Andrewsville was also moving on the entertainment and state wires. That was bad enough, but what was currently making Sully's head threaten to explode was that another major daily in the same market as the *Evening Examiner* had picked up both pieces. Although Kate used her legal name of Donaldson, the competition had identified her as Billy's wife—and given the name of her employer.

Reporters should write the news, not make the news, Sully reminded her loudly. As if she'd played any part in this mess. He put her on a two-week administrative leave—with pay, he grudgingly added—to "let things die down." In an attempt to soften the punishment, he told her Sedge Stevens had called the newspaper several times, "huffing and puffing" about the article she'd written. Because of that, Sully thought it best to send a more seasoned reporter to the next meeting in case things came to a head between Stevens and the committee, as if it would be difficult for her to report on something more contentious than squabbling neighbors.

Kate hung up and stared at the ceiling. She wanted to pull the covers over her head. Instead, she let the promise of fresh coffee and the aroma of sautéed onions lure her downstairs.

Bright sunlight hit her face, and she squinted as she stepped outside. "Morning."

Tommy and Joey sat at the table on the patio, shaded by a large, colorful umbrella. Kate ran her hand lightly across Tommy's shoulder and bent to kiss Joey on the head.

"Morning, Mary Sunshine," Joey sang. "How'd you sleep?"

She shrugged. "I slept."

"How're you doing?" Tommy poured her a cup of coffee from a carafe on the table and handed it to her.

She wrapped her hands around the mug and took a sip. "Hmm." Surprised, she looked at Joey, who pointed at Tommy.

"Cinnamon," Tommy said.

"Nice." Actually, it was perfect. "How am I doing? I don't know. Kinda numb, worn out. I slept, yet I feel so tired."

She took another bracing sip, then zeroed in on Tommy. "Do I want to know how bad it is?"

He toyed with the mug in front of him. "I don't really know yet. I've read the affidavit, and I've got some questions. I haven't spoken to Billy, of course, but there are a few things that don't make sense."

She listened and nodded.

"Just keep in mind what I said about getting Doug's firm involved."

She started to protest.

"I know you don't want him in the middle, but his firm has more experience with this stuff. And to be honest, it might get expensive. You know I'd do my best, but my dad owns our firm as well, and Billy isn't my father-in-law."

"I say put him in jail and throw away the key." Joey's response to Kate's glare was all wide-eyed innocence. "What?"

With a frown and a subtle shake of his head, Tom rose.

"I made an omelet, Kate. Let me get it, and then I have to head home and shower. We have a family picnic this afternoon. Stephanie will be wondering what happened to me."

"Yeah," Joey muttered, "the family's coming."

The screen door slammed shut, and Kate poked him. "What's wrong with you?"

"Nothing." He flashed a toothy smile. "It's the heat. Makes me cranky."

"I'll say."

Joey played with the remnants of his breakfast, making a face with scraps of egg, adding eyes and a mouth with a couple of drops of ketchup. When he fashioned a hat for his creation out of what was left of his toast, she knew he was avoiding something.

"Joey?"

"Hmm?"

"Why are you sitting on the newspaper?"

He gave his ear a scratch. "What?"

"You're sitting on the newspaper."

"I am?"

He was a terrible actor and a worse liar.

"Yes. Why are you sitting on the newspaper?"

"Um, I didn't want to get my khakis dirty?"

"Let me see."

He shook his head and wrinkled his nose. "It's just full of bad news. Nothing you'd want to see."

She held out her hand and wiggled her fingers.

"Don't say I didn't warn you." He lifted a cheek so she could tug the newspaper out from under him.

She stared at the headline and gasped: SUSPECT HELD IN MOVIE MASSACRE

"Oh my God. When did this happen?"

Looking confused, Joey followed her gaze.

"Oh, crap. You didn't know about that, did you?"

She'd been so wrapped up in her own nightmare, she'd had no idea.

"Some nutcase burst into a movie theater and started shooting," he explained. "Killed about a dozen people and wounded a lot more. This shit is getting ridiculous. As far as I'm concerned, they can take all the guns and pitch them into the ocean."

"Do they know why?" Kate stared at the print, seeing nothing beyond the headline and the picture on the front page.

"Who knows?"

The carnage made her sick to her stomach. "The world's a pretty scary place sometimes."

The screen door swung open and Tom reappeared, carrying a tray with Kate's omelet, a cloth napkin, silverware, a small bowl of ketchup, and a glass of orange juice.

"Wow. If this is the kind of service your firm delivers, you can bail my husband out of jail any time."

"That's not even funny," Joey said.

"I know." Kate set the paper down and forced a smile. "But hey, I just got two weeks off for bad behavior—not mine, but still."

She caught the pointed look Tom gave Joey.

"I thought you weren't going to let her see the paper."

"I didn't," Joey said, his teeth clenched. "She took it."

"I knew it." Kate dropped her fork and snatched up the paper. She'd been so distracted by the front page she hadn't looked inside.

Joey tried to grab it, but she was too quick.

"Page three?" she moaned. "I'd hoped it would have been buried in the back."

At the top of the page was a three-column color picture of Billy in handcuffs, being led to an awaiting squad car. She slumped forward and pushed her plate away.

"What I don't understand is how they got a picture," Joey said.

"Cell phones," Kate and Tom answered at the same time. She nodded while Tom continued.

"Everybody has a cell phone. If they see anything they think is newsworthy, they take a picture. Somebody at the bar recognized him."

"I guess that settles it." Kate folded the paper and set it beside her plate. "If I can figure out what to do with Charlie, I just might take you up on your offer."

"Good," Joey stood. "The faster I get out of this town, the better. Eat!"

"I'll take Charlie," Tom offered.

Joey let out a sharp laugh. "I don't think Stephanie's going to be too happy about that."

Kate reached under the table to pat Charlie, who was panting near her feet. "Aww, he's just a puppy."

"He's not a puppy," Joey said. "He's nuts."

"Maybe a little nuts. He's mellow now because of the heat. He's a good boy, but he can be bit of a handful."

"It'll be fine," Tom assured her. "It's about time I took a stand for something in my house."

CHAPTER 13

"Can you fucking believe this?" Rhiannon threw the *New York Post* on the breakfast table.

Doug shot her a warning look over his copy of *The New York Times.* The twins sat in high chairs on either side of her.

"Like they know what that means," she snapped.

Doug folded his paper and set it down in front of him. "Believe what?"

"Page Six." She tapped her finger on the article. Before he could see what she was pointing at, she yanked the newspaper back and read it aloud.

"Under the Sightings column," she explained. "'Stylist Joey Buccacino squires a mysterious, dark-haired beauty to a quiet table at RSVP in the Village. Word on the street? It's best gal pal Kate McDonald, wife of bad-boy rocker Billy McDonald, late of Stonestreet and the Andrewsville City Jail.'"

She flashed the paper at him. "There's even a picture. My father's here, eating his heart out, and she's partying all over New York with Uncle Joey."

Doug leaned over to look at the blurb and photo. "That's your mother all right—dressed head to toe in black and wearing dark glasses that cover half her face. She looks like she's going to a funeral. The article says 'a quiet table at RSVP.' Sounds like they went to dinner, Rhiannon, not a rave."

She hated when he was so condescending.

"And your father may be eating his heart out, but it's the 'drowning his sorrow' part that concerns me. You promised you'd speak to him about that."

Rhiannon stared back in stony silence.

"If I know your mother, she's not partying," he continued. "Joey's probably dragging her out, trying to get her mind off what happened. She needs a break, Rhiannon. I'm sure once she and your father each get some perspective, they'll be able to work things out."

He shoveled a bite of egg white and spinach omelet into his mouth, then pushed the plate away. "Besides, I've never seen two people more in love than your parents, in spite of their issues."

"What the hell does that mean?" She slammed her blueberry, avocado, and spirulina detox smoothie onto the table. Black liquid splattered onto her mother's picture. "You don't think we're in love?"

"I didn't say that. And now I'm leaving." He rose from the table and kissed the tops of the two little blond heads, avoiding the sticky fingers that reached for him. Then because he was a very smart man who knew how to push her buttons, he pulled her to her feet and grabbed her around the waist, bent her over backward, and kissed her until she went limp in his arms.

"Better," she said, staggering when he let go.

"Good." He slapped her on the ass with his folded newspaper and called over his shoulder on his way out. "Talk to your father."

⌒〜

"This is just great." Kate tossed the *Post* on the table between the two deck chairs in Joey's rooftop garden. "I was supposed to stay out of the news."

"Oh, relax." Joey tilted his head toward the sun. "If they fire you, you can come live with me."

Ten blocks away, the Freedom Tower loomed over his Tribeca loft and lower Manhattan. As impressive as all this was, it wasn't home.

"I can't. Even if they fire me."

Joey lowered his Prada sunglasses. "Why not?"

"Because I have a life, Joey, and it's not in New York."

"You're taking him back, aren't you?"

Yes?

"I don't know. Shouldn't I at least try to make it work?"

"What the hell have you been doing all these years?" he demanded. "You've been trying too hard for too long, and you have the footprints all over you to prove it."

"It's not like that."

"No?" he snorted. "You could've fooled me."

"Joey, you can't understand. You've never really been in love. If you had, you'd understand that sometimes there are sacrifices you need to make or things you must do even if you don't want to because you love this other person. Billy is . . . complicated."

It was hard to defend Billy, even to her best friend, when she was unable to explain his past without betraying him. She knew so little of it herself, but what she did know was not her story to tell.

"You don't know what his life was like—"

"I call bullshit, Kate." Gripping the sides of his chair, Joey leaned forward. "You keep giving him a free pass because of his past. Well, you know what? Who didn't have a shitty past? And when is enough enough? He's been with you longer than he lived that mysterious past. Shouldn't he have gotten over it by now?" He threw himself back and turned away, chewing on the pad of his thumb.

"Why do you hate him so much?"

Joey seemed to be composing himself. He cocked his head toward her. "I don't hate him."

"I know you say that, but there are times—like now—I don't think I believe you."

He lifted his wineglass and stared into its depths. "I don't hate him," he repeated, his tone softer this time. "It's just . . . You deserve so much more, Kate. You deserve someone who loves you and who would never—"

A horn blared from seven floors below them.

"Never what?"

Joey shook his head. "Nothing. Someone who would never be an ass, that's what."

"Well, that's a pretty rare quality in a human being, isn't it?" She chuckled. "I mean, let he amongst us who has never been an ass cast the first stone."

"You know what I mean."

"I do. And I also know that Billy, regardless of his faults—and I am fully aware of them, all of them—loves me. I'd bet anything his substance abuse issues are triggered by his past. It doesn't help that he works in an industry that dispenses pills and cocaine like breath mints. Trust me, Joey, I'm not okay with what he did, but he usually has it under control. I don't know what happened this time, but I do know I didn't even give him a chance to explain."

She ignored the face he made.

"And you need to remember I've never had a strong sense of self, yet he's loved me with all my flaws. My childhood left a lot to be desired, but he had it much harder. Maybe that's why I've always let him slide. I admit I'm an enabler, and that hasn't done either of us any good. I need to go home and talk to him, put my foot down. Tell him if he gets help and gets sober, then we can work on it."

She wanted him to agree with her.

"How much do you love him?" Joey tugged his glasses down to reveal his eyes. "Honestly. How much?"

She answered without hesitation. "I love him so much, I believe I would die without him."

Her shoulders lifted in surrender, and she steeled herself for his recriminations.

Instead, he surprised her with a smile. "So what you're telling me is that if you really love someone, there may be times when you'll have to do something you don't want in order to make that person happy, because in the long run, it will be the best for both of you?"

She couldn't leave Billy. She was angry and hurt, but it would be easier to cut her heart out and try to live without it than to live without him.

"I think so."

The edges of Joey's lips curled. "Maybe I do understand."

"Finally! It's only taken you . . ."

The smile on his face expanded, as the realization of what he was saying seeped in. "Joey. Do you mean there's someone—"

"Let's just leave it at that, okay?"

"But—"

He shook his head and waved his arms dramatically, as if magically erasing what he just said.

"So, Saturday," he said, clumsily changing the subject. "I think Saturday morning, you might want to pack your stuff and get the hell out of here." He took her hand and squeezed. "You have a lot of work to do."

Yeah. She did.

He stood. "That's settled, then. How about we order in, since you're intent not to make Page Six two days in a row and I'm the most interesting thing in the city this summer since everyone else is in the Hamptons."

She laughed and nodded.

"How about sushi?"

"How about not?"

"Good thing you don't live here. You'd never survive."

"True," she agreed. "I'd cook, but your cabinets are empty. You don't even have salt and pepper."

"That's because this is New York, I don't cook, and I want sushi," he said. "Go online and see what Takahachi has that you'll eat, then order what you want and get me the sushi and sashimi platter. I'm gonna take a quick shower, and then I'll take a walk and pick it up. And if you want to make a phone call while I'm gone, feel free."

Kate opened his laptop. "When did you become so understanding, or are you really and truly finally in love?"

"Don't worry about it." The little grin he tried to hide gave him away. "And don't forget, you're my date for that restaurant opening Friday night. Some Texas thing. Huge slabs of meat—right up your alley. I'll get you a blond wig, and we'll dress you up to look like Marilyn Monroe so no one will know it's you."

He gave her a wink, and she gave him the finger.

"You're a grandmother, you know," he pointed out.

She flipped him off with the other hand too.

After Joey left to pick up dinner, Kate retrieved her cell phone. The battery was low, only about ten percent. That meant no long phone call, which could be good. She really didn't want to get into anything with Billy over the phone. For someone who'd somehow forgotten to call her on her birthday, he'd left her a couple of dozen texts and nearly twenty voicemails. No way could this be a quick phone call. And if he sounded drunk or stoned, she'd change her mind altogether.

Better to just go home Saturday and call him then. She still had a week off from work. That should give them some time to work on things. In the past, she'd tried talking to him about AA, but he'd always blown it off, swearing he didn't have a problem. But after losing his gig with the band and the possibility of facing serious jail time, not to mention losing her, he might finally be ready to admit he had a problem.

CHAPTER 14

Billy stood in his kitchen and keyed Kate's number into his phone again, and again it went straight to voicemail. He'd lost track of how many times he'd called over the past five days. She didn't want to talk to him. She'd been pissed before, but never like this, and never for this long.

Pissed he could deal with. But the disappointment on her face that night? That was the killer. When he'd turned and seen Katie standing there behind him—in the fucking county jail—he'd about lost it. It had been bad enough knowing he would have to tell her what he'd done, but to have her there? To have her see him being released from jail and collect his things like a fucking criminal?

Of course he'd been angry.

So what had he done? Slammed down his walls and made it worse. He'd taken it out on her because he'd been too ashamed to admit he was wrong and say he was sorry. He hadn't started that damn bar fight. What was he supposed to have done? Walk away? Leave Eddie to fight off three goons by himself? It would've served the little fucker right for causing the fight in the first place—but still.

He unscrewed the cap on a bottle of twenty-one-year-old Scotch. It nearly killed him, but he poured it down the drain. A dozen bottles lined the kitchen counter. Condemned prisoners all, and he was the executioner. He dumped them one by one, even Kate's wine. If he was going to do this, there could be no survivors.

Despair seeped in. With nothing to numb it, he had no choice but to feel it.

He'd been sober for two days, almost. It wasn't easy. When he'd gone to help himself to Doug's Irish whiskey, Rhiannon had stopped him. She'd hemmed and hawed and never did get to the point, but he eventually figured out that Doug wasn't cool with his drinking in the house, especially around the kids. He couldn't blame him. If someone had been acting like a jackass in front of his kids, he wouldn't have been as diplomatic.

So after Rhiannon had taken him to town for an appointment with Tom, who'd mentioned he was dog-sitting Charlie, Billy talked her into leaving him at the house. She'd seemed more than a little relieved. Kate wasn't home, so what difference did it make? When she came home and threw him out again, he'd deal with it then. Or not.

In the meantime, he'd at least show her he was trying. He unscrewed the cap on a bottle of Tanqueray and began to pour. Even the fumes were intoxicating.

His eyes dampened, but as much as he hated doing this, he knew he wasn't getting misty over his disappearing liquor supply. He'd run so far and so fast from his roots, it surprised him to realize he hadn't escaped them at all. He was no better than either of his parents: a lying, manipulative mother and a violent drunk of a father. His only saving grace was that he'd never laid a hand on his wife or kids.

But he'd left it up to Katie to create his idea of the perfect family, with little to no effort on his part. There was more to being a good husband and father than not knocking his wife's teeth loose or putting his kid in the hospital. But beyond that, he hadn't done much better. In trying to follow his dream, he'd become unreliable and selfish. There were times when he'd made good money and others when he had to scramble to find work. His career had been filled with so many spectacular highs and lows.

And there was only one way he knew how to ride that roller coaster. When things were good, he had an excuse to party and celebrate. When they were bad, he needed to dull the frustration.

Either way, he'd been checking out on what was important for years. But this time, he'd really fucked up, and he wasn't sure he could fix it. After the highest high and lowest low of his career in the span of less than twenty-four hours, he may have destroyed what was most important to him.

To top it all off, Katie really thought he'd forgotten her birthday. He hadn't. He'd spent almost a thousand bucks on a bracelet that he'd never had a chance to give her. It was still in the bottom of his duffle bag.

Two bottles of Grey Goose were next. Why the hell had he bought the expensive stuff?

As he poured, he pictured Kate dressed for her birthday dinner. Even sleepy, her hair mussed and her makeup smudged, she was the best thing he'd seen since he'd walked out of their kitchen nine weeks earlier. Thinking about her in that filthy jail waiting room made it a little easier to pour the next bottle down the drain.

He set aside a couple of bottles of Kate's expensive liqueurs—surely he could keep his hands off those—and continued carrying out his self-imposed sentence. When he got to the forty-dollar bottle of Jack Daniels Single Barrel that Devin had given him for his birthday, his heart nearly broke. There was a reason he'd left this one for last. He opened the bottle and breathed deeply. His mouth watered. He tipped it but stopped as soon as the first drop hit the sink.

He tilted the bottle again. The whiskey rolled toward the neck. Just a little more. His arm hovered, his hand shook.

He lowered the bottle. He couldn't do it. He listed in his head all the reasons not to dump it: It was a gift. It was wasteful. If he only had a little now and then, it wouldn't be a big deal. He didn't have a drinking problem. It was drugs that had gotten him in the most trouble, and he could stop that shit any time; he just used them to party or take the edge off before a gig. He didn't need them.

He was in control.

To prove it, he pulled a glass from the cabinet and filled it with ice. He poured. Not too much. Two inches. That was enough, and really, the ice made it look like a lot more. He swirled the amber liquid a few times, chilling it, and took a sip. It trickled down his throat, the icy burn slipping through the center of his chest and fading into the recesses of his stomach.

He could do this. It was just a matter of knowing when to stop.

CHAPTER 15

A cab ride anywhere in Manhattan during rush hour was a fool's adventure. The trip from Joey's loft to Mercy West was only about ten blocks, but Kate had hailed a cab, praying it would get her there faster. Just a couple of blocks from the hospital at a standstill on Broadway, she opted to run the rest of the way. She paid the driver and jumped out, nearly getting hit by another cab trying to make a new path through the gridlock.

She kicked off her heels, snatched them up and ran barefoot through the streets of lower Manhattan. At the emergency room, she slipped them back on and waited for a clerk.

"I got a call that my friend was brought in." She struggled to catch her breath. "Joey Buccacino."

The woman keyed some information into the computer. "I'm sorry. We can only give information to family."

"We're family. I'm his only family. Look." Kate's voice was rising. "Obviously you have my name because someone called me. I'm his emergency contact. Please tell me where he is!"

"Have a seat. I'll see what I can do."

"Can you at least tell me what happened?"

"Ma'am. Have a seat. I'll see what I can do."

Kate slipped into a seat near the front desk to ensure she wouldn't be easily forgotten, and pulled out her cell phone. Before she could reconsider, her fingers were flying over the keyboard: "Joey at Mercy West. No one telling me anything."

A few minutes later, her phone vibrated.

"On my way."

She palmed the phone and pressed it to her chest. Billy had disappointed her over and over. Yet despite the fact that she'd ordered him out of their home and not spoken to him for over a week, he hadn't even asked what she wanted of him. He was on his way.

Of course, knowing Joey, he could have fainted because he cut himself. She stifled a nervous giggle. It's not like it hadn't happened before. Maybe she should tell Billy to wait, in case it turned out to be something silly. Then again, if Joey were able, he'd have called her himself.

Fear gnawed at her belly, and she couldn't shake the feeling that something was very wrong.

She sent Billy another message. "How?"

A few seconds later: "Giving Thompson kid $100 to drive me."

The Thompson kid? That meant Billy was at home. She started to send him the heart emoji but decided against it. Instead, she just typed "Thanks," then added one more word: "Scared."

The wait was nerve-wracking, especially not knowing anything. Anxiety had her wanting to pace the waiting room, but she was too afraid to leave her seat, afraid they'd come looking for her and she would miss them. Instead, she remained seated, swinging her leg frantically.

She was about to text the location of the hospital to Billy when a man walked up and held out his hand. A. PATEL, MD was embroidered on the left side of his white coat.

"Can you come with me, Mrs. Donaldson?"

Kate followed him into a small office near the waiting room. He closed the door and invited her to sit down.

"This is highly irregular, but looking at Mr. Buccacino's cell phone, we see he has indicated you as the first contact in case of emergency. Given there are no other contacts or family members highlighted, I assume you would be the proper person—the only person—we have available to discuss his condition."

He continued speaking, but her mind stumbled over the next thing he said. "I'm sorry. What?"

"I said Mr. Buccacino suffered several bullet wounds."

"I don't understand. Bullet wounds. How? Where?" Her fingers gripped and twisted the soft chiffon fabric of her dress. The dress Joey had bought her to wear to the restaurant opening. The one he was supposed to be taking her to. Right now. She wanted to tell the doctor to cut the crap and let Joey know they were going to be late.

Trying to stay in the moment, she focused on the doctor's eyes. Pale green, set under thick white brows, startling compared to the caramel color of his skin. A random smattering of dark, raised freckles dotted his nose and cheeks.

He caught on that she was having trouble following him and began to speak as if she had some type of mental impairment. "I don't have all the details, but it appears to have been a robbery. Mr. Buccacino was found in an alley behind a boutique in Soho. He was shot three times, twice in the chest and once in his left leg."

It felt as if he had reached inside her chest and was squeezing her heart and lungs.

"Are you all right?"

Of course she wasn't all right. She nodded anyway.

"Mr. Buccacino lost a lot of blood before they found him. The bullets were fired at close range, and they did a lot of damage."

She began to rock.

"He's still in surgery, but it is very serious. I can take you up to the ICU trauma unit where they'll bring him after surgery. I'm sure you'll be more comfortable there."

Dazed, Kate followed him down the hall and into an elevator. When the doors opened, he led her past a large waiting room to a much smaller room. Unlike the harsh lighting and plastic chairs in the first room, it was comfortably furnished. There was a small sofa and upholstered chairs, end tables. Lamps bathed the room in warm light.

She stumbled as she backed away.

"This is where you take people to tell them someone died, isn't it?"

He didn't deny what she'd asked. "Please. I think you'll be more comfortable here. There's an officer in the hospital, and I'm sure he'll want to speak with you. There will be fewer distractions here."

He motioned for her to sit and asked if he could get her something to drink. She shook her head and chose a chair nearest the door.

After he left, she fired off another text.

"Where are you?"

"On my way. Any news?"

"Bad."

A few minutes ticked by.

"How bad?"

How could she write in a text message that the best friend she's ever had, would ever have, could be dying? If she wrote it, it would be real. She couldn't simply push delete to make it go away.

She searched the emoji on her phone. When she found the one resembling a broken heart, she pushed send.

A few seconds later: "I'm sorry."

She wanted to text him back and demand he not say that—not yet— but she couldn't. She didn't have the strength to be confrontational. Instead, she wrapped her arms around her waist and rocked. It was a habit of self-soothing she'd developed as a child, one she was frequently scolded for, which only made the desire stronger. There was no one to tell her to stop, and she needed the comfort it gave her.

She had no idea how long she sat there—twenty minutes, a half hour, maybe longer. It seemed like an eternity.

"Mrs. Donaldson?"

Two men stood in the doorway. Sport coats, ties. Definitely not doctors.

"I'm Lieutenant Burke, this is Detective Gullickson. We're with the sixth precinct. We have some questions you may be able to help us with. We'll try to answer any questions you might have, if we can."

The lieutenant pulled a notebook from his pocket and began to read. "At 15:37 hours, we got a call for a man with multiple gunshot wounds in an alley near Broome and Watts streets."

"He has a shop there." Kate's voice was barely audible. "It's new." She counted on her fingers. Noon was twelve. Then thirteen, fourteen. Fifteen would be three o'clock. So at 3:37. What had she been doing at 3:37? Why didn't he just *say* 3:37?

"He had no identification on him, but the people in the shop, the person who found him, told us who he was."

A loophole! She became animated. "Maybe they were wrong. Maybe it's not him. You don't know for sure, right?"

The officers exchanged glances.

"One of his employees"—Lt. Burke flipped back a few pages in his notebook—"a Ginger Lane, identified the victim as Joey Buccacino."

The loophole vanished. Ginger had worked for Joey for several years. Kate's eyes fell to a stain in the carpet near the detective's foot.

"Ms. Lane wasn't sure how long he'd been gone or why he stepped into the alley. His cell phone was on his desk. He had no wallet, and it wasn't inside the shop. We believe it was a robbery."

Kate couldn't speak. Nodding was also difficult.

Lt. Burke continued. "He had nothing of value on him. Did he normally wear jewelry? A ring? Cuff links?"

None of this was important. All that mattered was that they fix him. "I don't know. I can't think." She started rocking again.

Detective Gullickson pulled up a chair and sat directly in front of her. "Mrs. Donaldson? If you can identify any jewelry or anything else that might have been stolen, when the perp tries to fence it, it'll be a lot easier for us to track down the sonofabitch who did this. Do you understand?"

Kate met the detective's eyes and winced; they were the same soft gray as Joey's.

She pictured Joey leaving the loft that morning. He'd been wearing a purple houndstooth blazer, a charcoal gray vest, and a pink patterned tie. There was a matching handkerchief in his breast pocket.

"He has a ring he wears on his right hand, ring finger. I think it's platinum. Looks like a wedding ring. I could probably draw it. He never took that off. If he's not wearing it, it was stolen."

The lieutenant made notes as she spoke.

"Anything else?" Detective Gullickson asked.

She nodded. "Cuff links. Silver cylinders with purple enamel stripes."

Lt. Burke nodded. "This is good."

Trying to picture Joey made her want to cry.

"A TAG Heuer watch. Polished steel. I know he had that on this morning. I remember him looking at it when he was leaving, to remind me what time to be ready. We're supposed to be . . ."

She took a few deep breaths.

"Is there anything else?" the detective asked.

Meeting the detective's eyes, she shook her head. "It's bad, isn't it?"

CHAPTER 16

It was quiet in the ICU waiting room. People sat alone, separated by a chair or two, or gathered in small groups of two and three. Billy scanned the room. No Katie. Frustrated, he ran his hand through his hair. The nurse had said she was in the waiting room. He continued down the hall. Maybe there was another waiting room somewhere.

He was about to ask when he saw her. Her head was lowered, her hair loose, a shiny, chestnut curtain making it difficult to see her face, but he'd know her anywhere. A man sat in front of her, head bent to her level.

"Excuse me." Billy tried to shoulder past the man standing in the doorway, but the gorilla held out his arm, blocking him from entering the room.

"Not now. There's a waiting room down the hall." His voice carried a warning note, one Billy had no intention of heeding.

"Katie."

Her head jerked up, and the look on her face just about tore his heart in two. The dude in the doorway stepped aside to let Billy pass, while his buddy stood and pulled the chair away. Billy dropped to his knees in its place and tucked a strand of hair behind her ear.

"Are you okay?"

She shook her head.

"Come here." He guided her from the chair to a nearby sofa, then sat beside her, pulling her close against him.

With Kate's body settled against his, Billy directed his attention to the two men. Short hair, shiny shoes, jaded expressions. Cops, most likely.

"I'm her husband. What the hell's goin' on?"

Turned out they were cops. NYPD. The one who'd been talking to Kate, a lieutenant, introduced himself and his partner, then for Billy's benefit, he ran down what they'd already told her. Once he'd finished, he held out a card. Kate stared as if she hadn't a clue what to do with it. Billy took it and tucked it into his pocket.

"Just give us a call if you have any questions or remember anything of significance."

As they were leaving, the officer by the door spoke. "We'll do our best, Mrs. Donaldson, but if this was just a case of your friend being in the wrong place at the wrong time and we don't come up with any witnesses, it's going to be difficult to find whoever did this."

Kate continued staring after the officers left, while Billy tried to process what had happened.

Joey? Shot? It made no sense. There was no way in hell he would've tussled with someone trying to take his wallet. Joey was a lot of things, but stupid wasn't one of them.

Kate took a deep, shaky breath.

"Babe, are you okay?"

"I don't know," she said. "I think I'm in shock."

Billy tightened his hold and pressed his lips to the top of her head. "I've got you."

The tension in her body unspooled, as if she'd been waiting for assurance that he was truly there for her.

They sat in silence, insulated from the world while the trauma unit hummed with activity just outside the door.

"What's this?" Kate ran a finger over the raised, blistered edges of the Celtic symbol he'd recently had tattooed where his wedding ring should be. "You stopped wearing your ring?"

"Just till it heals." He spread his fingers wider, tilting his hand so she could see her name written in script on the inside of his finger. He turned his hand again so she could see the words ALWAYS AND FOREVER tattooed on the other side nearest his pinkie.

He maneuvered his body until his eyes met hers. "Because it is forever."

She traced the words with the tip of her pinky. "Every time we fight, you get another tattoo. You're a walking testament to marital discord."

"It was more than a fight this time, Katie."

Her eyes fell to the three Japanese symbols tattooed on the inside of his wrist: Harmony, tranquility, family. A reminder of another time when he'd lost his temper, only that time he'd walked out on Kate. His body was inked with a roadmap of emotions, reminders to keep himself in check.

Her fingers traveled to another tattoo, script that started at the first joint of his right thumb and ran along the edge of his hand and around his wrist.

"You got this right after Devin was born. I don't remember any fight."

As part of his wedding vows, he had quoted from the poet Pedro Calderón de la Barca: "When love is not madness, it is not love." On his hand was inked what he'd said after reciting that quote and the date of their wedding: YOU ARE MY MADNESS AND MY LOVE—MAY 20, 1989.

The words were a double-edged sword, a brand to remind him of the best and worst things he'd ever done: marrying Katie and being unfaithful to her the night Devin was born. The purpose of the tattoo was not penance for having fought with her. It was there because he wanted to never unzip his pants again without knowing what he could lose.

"We didn't fight." Strong as ever, the guilt caused his throat to tighten. He threaded their fingers together. "I just wanted a reminder of what you mean to me."

There was a quiet sadness on her face. "I never needed any reminders,

Billy. Your name was tattooed on my heart before I was born."

"Oh, Katie." He slipped his hand against the base of her neck and pressed his forehead to hers. "I know this isn't the right time, but I'm so afraid of losing you. Everything is so fucked. Things with the band . . . You were right. I don't even think it's about the music with those guys. It was bad from the beginning. I got more respect doing studio work than I ever got out on that stage with Mick McAvoy. It all went to shit pretty fast. That last night . . ."

He pulled in a deep breath, remembering the feeling of standing on that stage, the vibrations moving through him, both from the music and the crowd. It was a feeling like none he'd ever had throughout his career.

"That last night was what I know it should've been all along, and then afterward . . ." His sigh was so deep he felt smaller, diminished. "I let it get out of control. Shit went down with Mick, and I got fired."

He wished he could see her face, see if she understood he wasn't just being a total fuck-up, but she kept her head down, her finger tracing an endless pattern over those words as if she might decode them and discover their true meaning.

His lips touched her hair. He wanted her mouth, wanted her to look up and let him know they were okay, but she didn't move. She didn't pull away, either. At least there was that.

"Do you know how humiliating it was for me to turn around and see you standing there in the jail that night? To know you were there because of me?" He ran his thumb along her neck just below her ear. "It was just another reminder of what a fuck-up I am. And then instead of apologizing, I turned into a giant dick and made it worse."

"Yeah." Kate wrapped her fingers around his wrist. "You did."

"And speaking of giant dicks."

A small chuckle escaped. "Yeah."

"When going through the mail, I saw a couple of past due notices for your car. I took care of all the other bills before heading out on tour, but somehow I missed that one."

"Yep."

"When I saw it was about to be repossessed, I called the bank."

"Too late."

"Yeah, they told me. I'm sorry, babe."

She shrugged.

"I paid it off. You won't have to worry again. And, I transferred money into your bank account.

Kate let go of his wrist. "Thank you, but still, we really need to talk—"

"Mrs. Donaldson?" A slight man in hospital green surgical scrubs stood in the doorway. "I'm Dr. Evans."

The tension that had been in Kate's body when Billy first arrived seemed to return all at once. The doctor stepped into the room and held out his hand. It was small, but his fingers were long and narrow. Good hands for a piano player, or even bass.

"I'm one of the surgeons who was working on Mr. Buccacino."

Of course, a surgeon made more sense.

"I assume you spoke with the police?"

Kate cleared her throat. "Yes."

The chair the detective had vacated stuttered across the carpet as the doctor pulled it directly in front of Kate. He sat resting his elbows on his knees, bringing his face level with hers.

"As I'm sure you've been told, Mr. Buccacino was shot three times. The wound to his leg was superficial, but the other two bullets caused massive trauma to his chest and lungs. One of the bullets punctured his lung. As a result, his lung collapsed, which resulted in a significant decrease in oxygen delivery to his vital organs as well as bleeding into his chest cavity." He looked from Kate to Billy, as if gauging their level of comprehension. "We've transfused several units of blood, and we were able to repair the damage. He's out of surgery, and once he's stable and awake, we'll be moving him to a room in the ICU."

Kate's fingers closed around the soft peach fabric draping her thighs, twisting it until much of her leg was exposed. Billy dropped his hand over hers and squeezed, stilling it.

"He's going to be okay, right?"

"It's really too early to say. He's ill. Very ill. The next twelve to twenty-four hours will be critical." The doctor stood. "It could be another hour or so before they bring him up from recovery. Once he's settled in, you can see him."

After he'd gone, Kate remained rigid, staring at the empty chair in front of her.

"Babe? Can I do anything for you? Are you hungry?"

She shook her head. "No, but coffee might be good. We'll probably be here for a while."

It was late and the cafeteria was closed, but there was a small café off the lobby that had coffee, two kinds of soup, and an assortment of sandwiches and salads. Billy wasn't hungry either, but he bought a ham and cheese panini and a cup of minestrone. It was a small miracle that he got Kate to take a few bites of the sandwich and eat almost half of the soup.

She crumpled up a paper napkin and pushed it inside the empty cup. "Tell me he's going to make it."

It didn't take much to realize she wasn't looking for facts. She wanted assurances. Promises he couldn't make.

"I'm sure they're doing everything they can. You heard Dr. Evans. We just have to wait and see."

She pressed her palms against the table to help her stand, as if she were suddenly decades older. "We should head back upstairs. I want to be there when he gets to his room."

Back in the ICU, the floor was quieter than it had been earlier, but there were still more people about than one might expect to see at that hour. Fear and grief were etched on the faces of the people moving through the hall. Kate wore a similar expression as the nurse led them to Joey's room. She hung back at the threshold.

"You okay?" Billy asked.

She took a deep breath and blew it out slowly, visibly steeling herself. He wrapped his hand around hers and waited. When she nodded, he led her into the room.

Other than a ghostly pallor, and lips that were more blue than pink, Joey looked much like himself. Bandages wound around his chest. Two tubes ran from the right side of his chest to a canister on the floor next to the bed. Wires connected him to various machines and monitors, tracking his blood pressure, his oxygen levels, his heart rate.

Billy guided Kate to a chair beside the bed, though she refused to sit.

"He'll drift in and out," the nurse explained. "Mostly out. Plus he needs to rest, so if he wakes, try not to tire him out. Just let him know you're here.

That's enough for now."

An hour passed. Kate hadn't taken her eyes off Joey since they'd walked into the room. Billy had stood alongside her at first, but as the caffeine wore off and exhaustion wrapped itself around his bones, he uncoiled into a chair near the door.

"Shouldn't he have woken by now?" Kate's voice was raspy. "Joey? I'm here. Billy, too. Can you hear me?"

Billy half expected Joey to grimace at the mention of his name. The two of them had come to an uncomfortable truce over the years, but he was certain Joey still hated him. After that horrible night—the night he'd won his one and only Grammy, the night his son had been born without him knowing, the night he'd been too drunk and dusted to realize his former agent had her mouth wrapped around his cock until it was too late—he'd been forced to turn to Joey. He'd had to beg Joey to keep Christa from ratting him out to Kate, especially after Billy had fired her and immediately cut all ties.

Even though Joey hated Billy for what he'd done, he'd somehow managed to convince Christa to back off. And she had—at least as far as Kate was concerned. Billy, on the other hand, had remained fair game. Over the years, Christa, who was one of the most powerful agents in the business if not *the* most powerful player, had done everything she could to see that his career never took off. Sure, he'd made a living doing what he loved—a good one most of the time, playing in someone else's band—but whenever he'd tried to break out on his own, she'd crushed him. The only record companies that would work with him were small independents. He'd recorded a few albums, but without the big money for tours and promotions and the clout to get him airplay, he had been doomed before he'd even gotten started.

It was frustrating and depressing, but at least Kate had never found out. It was one of the main reasons he'd kept her as far away from his business as possible. She'd never traveled with him and rarely met the musicians he played with. He lived in two different worlds. It was the only way he could deal with it.

Clearly, he was doing a shit job of balancing the two.

Billy shifted uncomfortably in the wooden chair. Kate had grown up with a mother who hadn't wanted her and who never missed an opportunity to let her know it. Her father had been unable to stand up to the cruel, uncaring woman he'd married. But she'd always had Joey. Unlike Billy, whose one stupid act more than twenty years ago could have destroyed her, Joey had remained Kate's one true constant. The only person who'd never hurt her. Never let her down. And now there was a chance she could lose him.

Billy sat up with a jerk, forcing himself to remain alert. If this went on much longer, he was going to need something a hell of a lot stronger than caffeine. He rested his head against the wall and watched through drooping eyelids as Kate stroked Joey's hand. She prattled on, reminding Joey of things they'd done as children, continuing unrelentingly as if trying to lure him into opening his eyes.

A nervous chuckle slipped out, and Kate's head snapped up.

He rubbed his hands over his eyes. "Sorry, I just thought of something funny. I was just thinking, the way you've been talking kind of nonstop, if he were to wake up right now, he'd probably tell you to shut up."

Her lips twitched, and she lightly traced the line of Joey's brow with the tip of her finger. "You would too, wouldn't you?"

Billy stifled a yawn and checked his watch. It was a little after two. "How long have you been here?"

"I don't know. I think it was around five. I texted you as soon as I got here."

His heart thumped. She'd reached out to him right away. A small victory, but it filled him with hope.

Kate stood suddenly.

"What's wrong?"

"He squeezed my hand. Joey? It's Kate, honey. Can you hear me?" She turned to Billy. "It's weak, but I felt it."

Over the next few moments, Joey's fingers twitched. His eyelids fluttered.

"Are you in any pain?" Kate asked when his eyes had remained open for more than a few seconds.

It was slight, but he definitely moved his head: *No.*

She leaned closer and spoke louder. "Joey. You had an accident, but you're going to be okay."

He blinked several times and tried to focus on Kate's face. "What happened?" he asked eventually. His voice was strange, thin, as if he were speaking into a rubber balloon.

Kate brushed a strand of hair away from his face. "You were mugged. Behind the new shop. Do you remember?"

He shook his head, and his eyes closed for a few moments. When he opened them again, they landed on Billy.

"Kate."

"What, sweetie?"

A few seconds passed. "I need to talk to you. Alone." He tipped his chin toward Billy. "Please."

"Um . . .okay." She turned. "Would you give us a few minutes?"

Billy pushed himself from the chair. Of course Joey wanted him gone. Two bullets to the chest, and the first thing he wants to do was remind her why she'd left him. He supposed he should feel more generous toward someone who'd almost died, but old habits die hard.

CHAPTER 17

Joey gripped her hand tightly. "Kate, listen to me."

There was desperation in his voice.

"Joey. What is it?"

"Tom. You need to call Tom."

Tom? Oh dear God. Had he been doing something illegal when he'd been shot?

"Now? It's the middle of the night? Why would you need a lawyer in the middle of the night?"

"Kate, please. Just listen." He coughed, then grimaced in pain. "You can't tell anyone what I'm going to tell you. No one. Promise me."

"Okay."

"Not even Billy."

She nodded. "I promise."

He closed his eyes and took several quick, short breaths before opening them again.

"Tom and me. We're together."

"I don't understand what you mean. Together how?"

"In love, Kate." The numbers on the monitor keeping track of his heart rate crept upward.

"I don't . . . How can you and Tommy . . . Seriously? Is that what you were hinting at yesterday?"

He nodded.

"But . . . Stephanie. He's married."

"No one knows. And you can't tell anyone. But I need you to call him. Tell him what happened, where I am. Now."

She couldn't wrap her head around this. Tommy? And Joey? She was too tired for it to sink in.

"And Kate?" He gripped her hand before she could leave. "If anything happens . . . promise me . . . you'll be there for him."

His breathing was short and choppy.

"Stop. Nothing's going to happen. You're going to be fine, okay? I'm going to find Billy and have him stay with you, and I'll go call Tommy. You're going to be fine. And when you're all better, Mr. Buccacino, you're gonna have some 'splaining to do."

The corner of his mouth quirked up. It was a weak attempt at a smile, but it was something.

No longer struggling to speak, his heart rate began to tick back down. Kate breathed a sigh of relief and dropped a kiss on his forehead.

He was going to be fine.

⁓

Now that she needed to make this call, Kate couldn't get enough bars on her phone for even a text. Which is how she found herself outside, alone on a nearly deserted New York City street in the middle of the night. It was foolish, but personal safety was the least of her worries.

The night air hung on her like a loose, damp sweater. She shuffled to the end of the block alongside brick walls still giving off warmth from the previous day's heat. A *Daily News* truck rumbled past, leaving a cloud of diesel fumes in its wake. She filled her lungs with the pervasive stink of the city and dialed Tommy's number.

An irritated female voice answered.

Damn it.

"Hi, Stephanie. It's Kate Donaldson. I'm sorry to call so late—er, early—but I need to talk to Tommy."

"Tom," Stephanie corrected. "Dear God, Kate, it's the middle of the night. Did your husband get arrested *again?*"

Bitch. Kate had always tried to give Stephanie the benefit of the doubt, even though she never understood what Tom saw in her. He was sweet and down to earth. But Stephanie? She lorded it over people in a town where there was no need for lording of any kind. What Joey had told her a few minutes earlier began to make bit more sense.

"I know it's late, and I apologize, but I need to talk to Tomm—" She caught herself just in time.

"He's not here. He's at a conference in Pittsburgh. You can try his cell, but I'm not sure he'll answer it. He usually turns it off at night—for obvious reasons."

Kate didn't miss the dig. "Do you know where he's staying, in case I can't reach him on his cell?"

"Do you really need to do this in the middle of the night? Can't you just let Billy sleep it off wherever he is and just pick him up in the morning?"

Kate's fingers tightened around the phone. "Look, I'm sorry to wake you. I am. But I need to get hold of Tom tonight."

Stephanie let out an audible huff. "Hold on."

At least a minute went by, and if Kate hadn't heard the sound of someone moving about on the other end of the call, she'd have thought they'd been disconnected.

"I hope he's charging you plenty for all these late-night emergencies," Stephanie grumbled when she came back on. "He's staying at the Fairmont. I don't have the number. You'll have to look it up."

"That's fine, thank you." Although it galled her, she forced herself to make one more attempt at being polite. "I'm really sorry, Stephanie. I hope I won't have to call you again."

Ever.

Tommy's cell phone went straight to voicemail, so she searched for the Fairmont instead. Once the call was transferred to his room, he answered on the second ring.

"Kate? What's wrong? Is it Billy?"

"No, not Billy." How would she do this? She should have thought this through, figured out what she should say. "It's Joey."

Silence. "What's going on?"

"He asked me to call you. He's at Mercy West in Lower Manhattan. We're not sure exactly what happened, but he was probably mugged."

"Oh shit. Is he all right?"

"He's out of surgery—"

"Surgery!"

"He's stable. He was shot, Tommy—but he's stable. He's awake and talking, and he told me . . . He told me to call you."

"He's going to be okay, though, right?"

"I don't know. The surgeon says the next twelve to twenty-four hours are critical. But he's awake, so that's good. I think he wants you to come."

"I'm in Pittsburgh. Shit. Let me think." She heard rustling in the background. "Can I talk to him?"

"I'm on the street in front of the hospital. I couldn't get a signal inside. I didn't even notice if there was a phone in his room. Look, when I get back upstairs, if there's a phone, we'll call you, okay? On your cell. You're coming, right?"

"Yeah, I just need to pack, and I'll catch the next flight out. Oh God. I don't know how quickly I can get there." More silence, then, "Kate?"

"Yeah?"

"So he told you?"

"Yeah."

He was silent for another moment. "Tell him I love him."

Her throat felt as if it would close on her, but she forced the words out anyway.

"I will."

CHAPTER 18

Billy stood awkwardly in the doorway to Joey's room. Kate had ushered him back in before disappearing to use the ladies room. She'd been gone so long, he wondered if he should go after her.

Joey's eyes had been closed when Billy first returned, but now he was awake and staring up at the ceiling. The two of them alone; it was as awkward as fuck.

Billy broke the uncomfortable silence. "How're you feeling?"

"Like someone shot me in the chest."

Always the smartass.

"Can I get you anything? Do anything for you?"

"Well, I'm dying of thirst."

"Probably shouldn't use that word around Kate. She's freaked out enough."

Billy hesitantly picked up a Styrofoam cup filled with ice chips. Like this wasn't weird, spoon-feeding a forty-some-year-old man. "It's the best I can do, man."

Joey opened his mouth. Billy touched the spoon to his bottom lip and tipped it. He hadn't done this since Devin had begun shoveling Cheerios (and anything else he could get his hands on) into his mouth.

"More?"

Joey nodded. His eyes locked with Billy's as the spoon rose again. "It's bad, isn't it?"

Billy looked away. He didn't want to be in this position. Joey was flighty. He might not take the fact that he could die very well, and Billy wasn't about to be the one to tell him and find out.

"You'll be fine."

"Don't shit me. I have three holes in me I didn't have this morning."

Damn, this was uncomfortable. "I don't know. They said the next twenty-four hours are critical. I guess after that, you should be good." That might have been the stupidest thing he'd ever said.

"I want a priest. Tell Kate when she gets back." He crooked a finger for Billy to come closer. "Listen."

Joey was gasping after every few words. The nasal cannula feeding him additional oxygen didn't seem to be doing much good. "Kate's fragile. You really . . . hurt her this time. You can't keep . . . fucking around."

Before Billy could answer, Joey raised a hand.

"Save it. Just love her." He took a ragged breath. "That's all I'm asking. Just love her more."

"How can you say that? Does she honestly think I don't love her?"

Joey's face contorted, and Billy felt a twinge of guilt. This wasn't an appropriate conversation right now.

There was a low, sharp whistle as Joey grappled for another breath. "Just do it."

Billy's response caught in his throat. Blood gushed through the tubes in Joey's chest. The canister on the floor collecting the blood and other fluids in his lungs was nearly full. Why hadn't he noticed that earlier?

Joey's eyes rolled back as one of the monitors began beeping. A loud, steady alarm sounded.

"Shit!" Where the hell was that call button?

Two nurses rushed into the room. One headed straight for Joey while the other began yanking the curtain closed around him.

"You'll need to step outside."

Shit, shit, shit. Where the hell was Katie?

"Now, please."

The curtain snapped between them.

Billy dashed into the hallway. Where the hell was she? Maybe she'd gone down to the café. He stepped toward the elevator but stopped. What if she came back and he wasn't there?

Dr. Evans came charging around the nurses station and disappeared into Joey's room, followed by two more staff members. The monitor finally stopped screaming.

Billy was standing at the door to the ladies room, about to knock, when the medical team burst into the hall, wheeling Joey in the opposite direction.

"Hey!" He jogged toward the commotion. "What's happening?"

One nurse slowed down. "They're taking him back into surgery. He's bleeding out."

Bleeding out?

"Is he going to be okay?"

The nurse called over her shoulder as she hurried to catch up. "Someone will be out to see you as soon as they have some answers. If you'll go back to the waiting room, I'll let them know where to find you."

The disappeared around the corner just seconds before Kate stepped off the elevator at the opposite end of the hall, holding two cups of coffee.

This wasn't good.

She handed him a tall paper cup as he reached her side. "I figured we could stand more coffee, since the chances of either of us getting any sleep tonight is about zilch." She took a sip while he just stared at the cup in his hands, still not sure what to say. "What're you doing out here? Is Dr. Evans in with him?"

Billy shook his head. "C'mon. Let's have a seat in the waiting room."

"No. Let's wait until they're finished. I don't want him to be alone."

"He's not. C'mon." He gripped her elbow firmly and steered her toward the waiting room.

Once there, she returned to the exact spot where she'd sat several hours earlier. "How long do you think they'll be?"

"Who?"

"Whoever's in there with him."

Billy lowered himself onto the sofa beside her. He placed his coffee on a side table.

"They had to rush him back into surgery."

He grabbed her cup before she could drop it.

"What . . ."

What happened? He had no fucking clue. Probably best not to tell her about all that blood. "I don't know. The monitors went off and some nurses came in, then Dr. Evans. They made me leave, and then they were rushing him down the hall. They said someone would come see us as soon as they had something to report."

"Was he awake?"

He didn't want to upset her, but he couldn't bring himself to give her false hope either. "I don't know. I don't think so. He was talking, but he seemed to be having a hard time breathing. It happened really fast. I'm not sure."

He slipped an arm around her shoulder and pulled her in. "He's in good hands. Why don't you try and rest? Close your eyes. It might be a while before we know anything."

He expected her to argue, but she didn't—and probably not because she agreed but because she was either in shock or just too damn tired.

Predicting the future wasn't one of his talents, but he had a sick feeling that this time, he might be able to call it with dead-on accuracy.

Kate's head snapped up. She blinked several times before recalling where she was and why. Billy's arm still held her, but his head was tilted back and his mouth open. A drop of saliva pooled in the corner. She gently brushed it away with her thumb.

"Mrs. Donaldson?"

Dr. Evans stood in the doorway looking tired and grim. He crossed the small room and lowered himself into the chair across from them as Billy stirred.

"Shortly after four o'clock, Mr. Buccacino began bleeding heavily. We thought we had the injuries from the gunshot wounds repaired, but there was more vascular damage than we initially realized. We've tried to repair it, but he continues to bleed at a dangerous rate. We've given him multiple transfusions."

He tugged the green scrub cap off his head and crushed it in his hands. "We're not making any progress, and we aren't able to repair all the injuries while he continues to bleed. He's in what we call DIC, disseminated intravascular coagulation. He's experiencing massive bleeding and clotting at the same time. DIC is very difficult to treat. What we've done for now is to pack the injured area in an attempt to apply pressure to the bleeding and allow him to stabilize so we can catch up on fluids and blood transfusions and give his body a chance to rest. We're moving him back to the ICU. Once we feel he's strong enough—say, sometime in the next twelve to twenty-four hours—we'll go back into the OR and see if we can repair the rest of the damage."

She stared at the green of Dr. Evans's scrub top. His words floated above her head like angry gnats.

Billy cleared his throat and sat forward. "So you missed something the first time."

"No, we didn't miss anything, but the repair didn't hold as well as we would have hoped. Vascular repairs, especially venous repairs as opposed to arterial, can be very tenuous. They can break open if a patient's blood pressure goes too high. Sometimes the extent of damaged tissue is greater than expected due to the shear forces and heat generated by the passing bullet. This can create a secondary injury, not initially identified, that causes the repair to break down or give out, which is what happened with Mr. Buccacino."

"But you can fix this, right?" Kate's voice was froggy. "You give him some time to rest, and then you go back in and fix it."

"That's the plan. But you need to understand his condition is grave. The best we can do right now is hope and pray we can control the bleeding and get him stable enough to try again."

Whatever confidence Dr. Evans had inspired in her earlier faded.

"Is he going to die?" The question slipped out before she could stop it.

The look in his eyes told her all she needed to know. "We'll do whatever we can to see that doesn't happen."

She put her hand on Billy's thigh and pushed herself up, willing her knees not to buckle. If she gave in to the fear raging inside of her, she'd be lost.

"I want to see him. Now."

~

Joey's chest rose and fell. A machine was breathing for him, hissing as it did. Bags of blood and fluids hung on poles, running into his body to replace what he'd lost.

Kate stood at the foot of his bed. "Can I touch him?"

"Of course. If you'd like to hold his hand or kiss him, yes, that's fine," Dr. Evans said.

Billy guided her toward a chair, which was good, since her body wasn't quite sure what to do next. She perched on the edge of the seat and lifted Joey's hand. It was cold and limp. She covered it with her own and wished she could somehow reach his other hand as well, hold them both at the same time.

"Oh shit," Billy said.

She looked up.

"I forgot. Everything happened so quickly. Joey wants a priest."

"He said that?"

Billy nodded. "I'm sorry. I forgot with everything going on. Is there someone you need me to call?"

Dr. Evans stepped in. "I'll have the unit clerk take care of it. We have a list of priests on call."

Why couldn't he say that it wouldn't be necessary, that they were jumping to conclusions and that Joey would be fine? She blinked to relieve the burning behind her eyes. Unable to use her words, she answered with a quick bob of her head.

It turned out there was a priest already in the hospital, there to administer the Sacrament of Last Rites to another patient. Two for one, Kate thought bitterly. Wouldn't want to impose, have him make two trips.

She leaned on Billy, her mind see-sawing between grief and anger as the priest read the prayers. It's just a precaution, she reminded herself. A just-in-case. It didn't mean he was going to die. The priest anointed Joey with holy oil, leaving behind a greasy cross on his forehead. A precaution. A blessing. He was going to be fine.

When the priest left, Kate reclaimed Joey's hand. She sat very still, hoping to feel even the slightest movement, but there was nothing. She tried to pray, but it was like fighting a riptide forcing her further away from where she wanted to be.

They had been friends for so long. At almost every important moment, practically as far back as she could remember, Joey had been there. He'd walked her down the aisle when she married Billy, and he'd rushed her to the hospital and stayed with her the night Devin was born. He was godfather to both her children. Hardly a day went by that they didn't speak.

The monitor beeped steadily. The ventilator hissed. Joey's blood pressure was dropping as his heart rate inched upward.

While the prayers she'd said all her life escaped her, the lyrics to "Amazing Grace," one of their favorite hymns, filled her until the words bubbled up, spilling over her lips and she began to sing. But her voice betrayed her and was no competition for the tears streaming down her face.

From behind her, Billy's voice rose up, echoing through the trauma unit and carrying into the rooms. Voices muted, and visitors who had kept vigil through the night on death watches of their own stepped into the hall. Nurses, doctors, and technicians paused what they were doing. The sick and the dying turned their heads. Surely some of them must have thought it was the voice of an angel they were hearing.

When he'd finished, Billy rested his hands on Kate's shoulders while she stared at the faint pulse flickering beneath Joey's jaw. More than the machines, which threatened to betray them both, this told her he was still with her.

She tried to ignore the beeping and hissing, but she couldn't ignore the vibration of her phone. *Tommy.* How could she have forgotten?

She swiped her finger across the screen: "Leaving LaGuardia. Be there 35–40 min."

"Who's that?" Billy asked.

"Tommy. He's on his way."

"Tommy? Tommy Reilly? What the hell for?"

Kate stared at the screen. She never lied to Billy, but Joey had been adamant. So she told the truth—sort of. "He's Joey's lawyer."

"So?" Billy waved his hand at the bed. "Obviously he isn't in any shape to talk business."

"No, but they're friends too."

He looked at her as if she'd grown two heads. "Since when? I've known Joey for twenty-five years, and not once have I ever heard him mention Tom."

Kate's fingers twitched over the screen on her phone. Should she give Tommy an update? No. Probably best to wait. He'd be there soon enough. She dropped the phone back in her bag and looked up to see that Billy was waiting for an answer.

"Why do you care? This has nothing to do with you." It came out much more defensive than she'd intended.

"I just don't want this turning into some sort of circus. You're stressed enough." He scrubbed a hand over his face. "Never mind. I'm just tired and cranky."

An alarm pierced the soft sounds around them.

Kate sprang to her feet. "What's wrong?"

Medical personnel began bursting into the room. Billy moved almost as quickly, pulling her out of the way.

A nurse stepped between them and Joey's bed.

"What's happening? What's wrong?" Kate repeated.

"Please. You'll have to step outside." The nurse raised her arms as if it were possible to shield them from what was going on behind her and herded them into the corridor.

Time passed slowly. Minutes seemed like hours. Kate paced the small waiting room, waving Billy off whenever he tried to get her to sit.

"I can't. I feel like I've been sitting for days." A picture of Jesus watched her from the wall behind the small sofa where Billy sat. Why hadn't she noticed it before? She tried again to pray. This time the words didn't fail her. She was halfway through the Lord's Prayer when she sensed someone had entered the room.

"Katie," Billy said, his voice gentle.

She stared at the painting.

Thy kingdom come, thy will be d—

"Katie." His arm curled around her shoulder, warm and strong. Her body ached to lean into him, but her mind pulled away. "Dr. Evans is here."

She shook her head. "No."

"Babe . . ."

"No!"

Billy stepped between her and Jesus. She closed her eyes, refusing to look at him. He gripped the tops of her arms and pulled her nearer, then he pressed his lips against her forehead.

"Katie. Dr. Evans is here to talk to us, and we need to listen to him."

She opened her eyes slowly and lifted her chin. Her worse fears were written all over Billy's face. Either she was leaning on him, or he was holding her up—it was difficult to tell which. She straightened and turned.

Dr. Evans was leaning against the door frame. Twin half-moons of sweat darkened his scrubs beneath his arms. Exhaustion lined his face. "I'm sorry. His heart couldn't keep up with the stress to his body. He went into ventricular tachycardia. We did everything we could. I'm very sorry."

She should say something. Anything. The best she could do was a barely perceptible nod of her head.

"A nurse will be in to get you soon if you'd like to go in, say goodbye."

Nothing.

"Babe?"

She nodded at Billy, then at the doctor. "Thank you."

Billy guided her to the sofa. A raw, gaping hole opened up inside her. Joey's heart couldn't take it? Well neither could hers. A world without Joey? It didn't seem possible. Her body began to shiver. Billy drew her closer, wrapped his arms around her, but it didn't help.

Outside, the sun was rising, but inside, everything had turned dark and cold.

Billy wanted to leave. Take Kate home. Now. Standing over Joey's body wasn't going to bring him back, and it wasn't going to do her any good either. But she wouldn't hear of it.

"Besides," she said, pressing a tissue under her red-rimmed eyes as they stood outside the door to Joey's room. "I told you, Tommy's coming."

What the hell for? It made no sense, but he wasn't about to argue. There was no point in Tom coming to the hospital, just to turn around and drive home again.

"You ready?" he asked, girding himself for what would happen when he walked her through that door.

Before she could answer, the elevator at the end of the corridor chimed. The doors slid open and Tom stepped off. Kate pulled away and flew straight at him. She threw her arms around him and whispered in his ear. Tom leaned against her, his arms circling her waist and his head close to hers.

What the hell? An unsettling jealousy washed over him as he watched his wife and his lawyer hugging it out in front of him. It went on so long he wanted to stalk over and tear Kate out of Tom's arms, but he didn't. His caveman behavior had landed him in enough trouble recently. And maybe Tom and Joey had been friends. Hell, he didn't know all Joey's friends, that's for sure. He watched and waited, maybe not patiently, but he kept his mouth shut.

When they finally broke apart and walked toward Joey's room, Billy reached for Kate's hand.

She waved him off. "It's okay. Just wait for me in the other room. We're just going to say our goodbyes." She nodded at him, as if he would understand what the hell she meant and pulled the door closed behind her, leaving him alone in the empty hallway.

What the ever-loving fuck? Billy stood gaping at the door, his mouth open.

"Just love her, that's all I'm asking."

Billy dragged his hands through his hair, staring at the closed door as Joey's words played over again in his head.

"Just love her more."

More? How was that even possible?

CHAPTER 19

Dark, noiseless, suffocating. Joey's loft wore death like a shroud. The surrounding buildings blocked out the sun's last rays, and other than the dim light from a table lamp, the apartment was gloomy. Even the sound of traffic seven floors below was muted.

Although he was alone, Billy spoke in low tones as he arranged for a car to pick Devin up at the airport. He'd spent much of the past two days making arrangements for the few things that had to be done. Joey, the ultimate control freak, had already planned almost every last detail of his funeral. The only thing he hadn't been able to control was when or how he would die.

Billy scanned the list Tom had faxed a day earlier. He'd called the musicians' union and finalized details for a string quartet, organist, choir, and—even Kate was surprised by the last item—a bagpiper. Hopefully his own Celtic roots would behave themselves. The damn things always made him tear up.

After calling Rhiannon to check on the program and remind her what she needed to bring, Billy stretched, working out a kink in his neck. It was almost eight, and he was starving. Kate needed to eat as well. He removed a half-empty bottle of white zinfandel from the refrigerator and uncorked it. Just one quick swallow? *Dig in, man.* He pulled out a bottle of water for himself, then carried both up the spiral staircase to the rooftop garden.

The sky had turned deep shades of inky-blue and pink. The setting sun reflected off the glass-faced buildings of lower Manhattan. Curled on a chaise lounge, Kate stared off into nothingness, unaware that he had returned. Her empty wine glass sat on a nearby table. Billy refilled it, then reached down and kneaded the tight muscles in her shoulders, working his thumbs into the knots at the base of her neck. Her head dropped forward and she let out a deep sigh. He lifted her hair and draped it over her shoulder, longing to press his lips against the top of her spine.

"How're you doing?" he asked after working on her neck and shoulders for a few minutes. He pulled a chair alongside her.

She gave him a weak smile. "Numb."

He was well-acquainted with the feeling. "Devin's all set. He's flying into Newark tomorrow afternoon. There'll be a car waiting to pick him up."

"Thank you."

You're welcome seemed so formal. He nodded instead.

"I asked if he wanted to stay with Rhiannon and Doug at the hotel, but he said he'd rather be here with you."

"My baby."

He chuckled softly. "That's one big baby."

Lights in nearby buildings were beginning to flicker on.

"It seems so quiet, doesn't it?" she asked.

"Yeah, I was thinking that myself." He stretched his legs out in front of him and leaned back. An airplane passed overhead, the last rays of sunlight glittering on its silver skin. "Why didn't we ever move to the city?"

Kate raised her eyebrows. "I don't ever remember discussing that."

"Really? I thought it was something we both wanted. I'm sure we talked about it."

She studied the wine in her glass as if it held some mystical answers. "Life didn't turn out the way either of us planned, did it?"

"I don't know," he said, suddenly feeling defensive. "There are some things I'd change, but overall—"

Her cell phone interrupted him.

"It's Tom. I have to take this." She rose and walked to the other side of the roof, almost out of earshot.

"Hey, sweetie," she said, her voice soft. "How're you doing?"

Billy's jaw tightened. He leaned into his chair, threw his head back, and emptied the bottle of water. Too bad it wasn't Jack Daniels. His fingers dug into the edge of the chair when she asked Tom if he wanted to stay at the loft.

"It would be uncomfortable," she whispered. "I understand."

She hung up and came back to sit on the chaise. He searched her face for a sign of what was going on with Tom, but all he saw was the same quiet grief she'd worn for the past two days. He wanted to ask why it would be "uncomfortable," but held his tongue once she reached across the glass-topped table between them to trace the black swirls of the tattoo on his forearm.

"Thank you." Her chin quivered. "You've really stepped up. You have no idea how much it means to me."

He took her hand, and she made no effort to pull it back.

"I was just telling Tommy how wonderful you've been through all this."

Funny. That part, he hadn't heard.

After dinner—sushi for him and the old standby sweet and sour chicken for Kate—Billy offered to do the dishes, but she insisted. When the kitchen was spotless the way Joey liked it, she joined him on the ultramodern leather sofa.

"What're you watching?"

"*Pawn Stars.*"

When she made a face, he held out the remote, but she shook her head.

"I don't care. It's not like I'm paying attention anyway." She shifted her weight, and tucked her legs beneath her. A few minutes later, she leaned forward and turned in the other direction. "This couch isn't very comfortable, is it?"

"Not really, why? You wanna sleep on it?"

"Not really." She wrapped her arms around the ikat pillow in her lap, bringing it to her chest. "I feel bad. You're doing so much, and you look so tired."

The loft had two bedrooms. Kate had declared Joey's room off limits, and she had been using the tiny guest room. After Billy had put her to bed the previous night, he settled in on the couch, not wanting to make any assumptions as far as their relationship was concerned, but he hadn't been able to sleep a wink. He'd ended up on the roof, stretched out on the chaise lounge until the sun came up just before six and nearly blinded him.

"If you'd be more comfortable, you can sleep with me."

The corners of his mouth quirked up.

"I said *sleep*."

He lifted his hands to proclaim his innocence.

"It's just that the next couple of days are going to be hard, and you need sleep too. This sofa probably cost a fortune, but it's not comfortable. I'm not sure it's even meant for sitting on, let alone sleeping."

"I hear you." He stifled a yawn. "If that's a firm offer, I'd love to take you up on a good night's sleep because I'm fried."

~

Billy had left his briefs on—an unusual concession to their unusual situation—and was well over on the right side of the bed facing the window when Kate came in later. She took her time washing her face and brushing her hair in hopes that he'd be asleep by the time she climbed in beside him.

She turned off the bedside lamp, but the room was still flooded with light from the street. It didn't bother her, but Billy was obviously still awake.

"Do you want me to pull the shade?" she asked.

He rolled toward her and lifted himself up onto his elbow, his face just inches from hers, his hair caressing her cheek. "I'm so tired, I don't think it'll matter."

His breath was warm on her face. Maybe this wasn't a good idea, or maybe she should've slept on the couch. She wanted to touch his face, wrap her arms around him. She missed him so much, but everything was such a mess.

Sex wouldn't fix anything. It would be another way of shoving everything under the rug until next time. A week ago, she'd been certain it was over, but her heart had convinced her otherwise. Next time, they might not be so lucky.

"Good night, Katie."

"Night." She tried to swallow the lump in her throat.

He leaned forward. Her mind went blank as he dragged his nose along the edge of her jaw. He pressed his lips against the corner of her mouth, and her heart slammed into her rib cage. She wanted to kiss him back, to run her fingers through his hair and hold onto him for dear life, but she didn't dare. She knew exactly what would happen if she moved.

When he was finished with her mouth, he kissed the tip of her nose and then her forehead. "I love you," he whispered before rolling away, his back to her.

She kept her body still, although her heart was ricocheting in her chest. Could he feel it? Surely he knew what he did to her. Before long, she could tell by his breathing that he had fallen asleep.

Only then did she allow herself to take a full breath.

CHAPTER 20

Nothing had changed. Friends laughed at an outdoor café. People stood in line to see the latest flick at a Soho cinema. A man pushed a baby stroller, holding hands with a woman who carried a fluffy white dog with a blue bow on its head strapped into a harness on her chest.

Life went on in spite of death.

Crammed into the back of Doug's Lexus with Kate and Devin, Billy couldn't help but marvel at the contrast. The silence in the car was deafening. Other than the muted hum of voices and traffic outside, the only sound came from the mindless thrumming of Kate's finger over the silver cuff bracelet he had given her before they left for the wake.

She'd been standing in the rooftop garden, looking out over Tribeca toward the Freedom Tower, when he came up behind her and put his hands on her shoulders. Surprisingly, she leaned into him. Other than the times she'd allowed him to hold her when she cried or kiss her good night, they'd hardly touched. Emboldened, he wrapped his arms around her. He felt rather than heard her sigh. They stood there watching the sun reflect off the glass of the lone tower as it lowered in the late afternoon sky. He would have stood there as long as she wanted—until the sun fell all the way into the Pacific Ocean, if need be.

"You okay?" he asked.

"No, but I will be."

"I have something for you." Taking her hand, he led her to a chair. He sat across from her and pulled the iconic blue box from his pocket.

"What's this?"

"I'm ashamed to say it's your birthday present, but that's what it is. I'm sorry I didn't give it to you before. I had it. I even have the receipt, if you don't believe me. I bought it in Atlanta. I was too busy screwing up to give it to you."

She rested the box in her lap as carefully as if he'd told her it was a vial of nitroglycerin.

"Open it."

She tugged off the white satin ribbon, letting it drift to the floor, and lifted the bracelet from the box.

"They're olive leaves," he said. "Of course I didn't know I'd be needing an olive branch when I bought it. Kind of appropriate, don't you think?"

"It's beautiful." She slipped it over her delicate wrist, admiring it, and then leaned forward and kissed him—a kiss that started out chaste, but she took it further. Much further.

At that moment, he'd believed he was forgiven, that no matter what happened, they'd be okay.

But now he wasn't so sure.

They'd arrived at the wake early to allow time to see Joey alone. Billy assumed he would take Kate in first so she could have a private farewell, but she wanted to wait, so he sat on a chair in the hall. Maybe she was trying to come to grips with saying her last goodbye. He fidgeted nervously and was about to stand up and try to gently hurry her along when Tom arrived.

As soon as she saw him, Kate flew to his side.

Every muscle in Billy's body tensed as she slipped her arm around Tom's waist and kissed his cheek. And the whispering—what the fuck was that about? When he didn't think he could stand it a moment longer, he walked over and shook Tom's hand—even though he would have preferred ripping his head off—then slipped a proprietary arm around Kate's shoulders.

"We need to go in now if you want any time alone with Joey. There are a lot of people expected and—"

She patted his hand and gave him a tight smile. "I know. Thank you."

Then, incredibly, she turned away from him and slipped her hand into the crook of Tom's arm. "Tom? Would you mind?"

Tom opened his mouth but said nothing. At least the fucker had the decency to behave like whatever was going on was wrong. Regardless, Billy still wanted to pound him into the carpet.

"Katie!" His voice was louder than he intended. "What're you doing? I'll take you."

She patted Billy's arm dismissively. "I know, but Tom would like a moment, too." Then she fucking winked at him. As if that would make him understand.

Well, it didn't.

Tom shifted nervously. "Yeah." The bastard cleared his throat. "If you don't mind."

Billy gritted his teeth so hard he thought his jaw would crack. He nodded and forced his fists to unclench as he watched his wife do one of the hardest things she'd ever had to do—on the arm of another man.

"What the hell was that about?"

Rhiannon stood at his side. Billy shook his head as the door to the viewing parlor closed, leaving him on one side and Kate and Tom on the other.

"I have no idea."

He was still pissed when Doug dropped them off at the loft after the wake. Kate remained standing by the curb, looking lost.

"You coming?"

If Kate caught the irritation in his voice, she didn't react. "Can we walk?"

Yeah, because a casual stroll through Tribeca was what he felt like doing about now. What he really wanted was to wait for her to go to sleep so he could find where Joey had stashed his liquor. Instead, he jammed the keys back into his pocket.

"Sure. Where do you want to go?"

"The waterfront."

He pressed his hand against the small of her back as they crossed Hudson Street, then jammed it back into his pocket. He studied her face in the lights from the shops and street lamps as they navigated the cobblestone street.

"Katie?"

She brushed away a lone tear and glanced up. "What?"

She was grieving. It was killing him to have things so strained between them, but now wasn't the right time to discuss his failings as a life partner.

He shook his head. "Nothing. You okay?"

She shrugged.

Fuck it. Maybe he was overreacting about this shit with Tom. It was probably nothing. She'd said Joey and Tom were friends. He was just in a bad place right now, letting things get the better of him. A drink would help clear his head, but he couldn't go there. Not if he had a prayer of fixing things with Kate. He slipped his arm around her shoulder and tucked her into his side. When they got to the end of the street, they found a bench and sat. Across the river, the lights of Jersey City twinkled on the water.

"Remember when we lived in Bayonne, and we'd sit in the little park and watch the water?"

"I think I can remember back that far." He gave her a sidelong glance and smiled.

"Maybe we should've stayed there."

"Maybe. I think they're considered waterfront condos now."

She looked up, incredulous. "No way."

"Yep. We probably couldn't afford it anymore."

"I'll be damned."

"Besides, we needed a bigger place."

She nodded. "We did. But something happened to us. It's like as soon as we bought that house, life became serious or something. Something changed."

His stomach turned over. He shook his head. "Nothing changed."

She gave a low but derisive snort. "You didn't want to move there, and just like our wedding, you offered and I jumped at it without thinking what was best for you."

"You were thinking about what was best for us. I was just thinking about myself. You were right."

"I don't know." She traced a crack in the sidewalk with the toe of her black funeral heels. "I'm sorry."

"For what?"

"For standing in your way, holding you back."

"Never." He vehemently shook his head. "I'll never be sorry. Neither should you."

But her phone was ringing, and he had no idea if she'd heard him. Without so much as an apology for the interruption, she jumped up and walked to the railing that lined the sidewalk as she answered. "Hi, Tommy."

Billy slouched lower on the bench. He wanted to throw her goddamn phone into the Hudson. Instead, he reached into the pocket of his suit jacket and pulled out the bottle of tranquilizers he had insisted her doctor prescribe for her in case she needed them to get through the funeral. He popped one into his mouth and swallowed it dry. He needed it more than she did. After all, she had Tommy.

CHAPTER 21

It should have been raining. Slow. Steady. An unrelenting drizzle. The kind of rain that chills you to the bone and makes you wonder if you'll ever be warm again.

At least that would have made sense.

Kate stepped from the limo, squinting in spite of her dark glasses. Outlined against a clear cerulean sky, the historic stone building with its massive ionic columns looked more like a Greek temple than a Catholic church. It was Joey's church, and the pastor knew him. She took comfort in that. She wouldn't have been able to bear it if the priest had begun his sermon with "I didn't really know Joseph . . ."

A steady stream of somberly clad mourners made their way up the steps like ants to a picnic. She smoothed the peplum of her black silk dress, remembering the old Italian women who sat on the benches outside their Bayonne apartment building when she and Billy were first married. Black crows, he had called them, each in some perpetual state of mourning. She finally understood how grief could make itself at home and never leave.

Billy had offered her a tranquilizer before they'd left the loft, and she'd practically bitten his head off, insisting not everyone needed to mask their feelings. She had instantly regretted the attack, and was regretting it again now as she balanced on wobbly knees.

"Ready?" Billy asked, closing his hand over hers.

"Not really, but I guess it doesn't matter, does it?"

He squeezed her hand as they walked up the steps and into St. Peter's. Devin stood at the entrance and together, he and Billy escorted her to the front pew, where Rhiannon and Doug were already seated.

Tom was sitting directly behind them. She'd begged him to sit up front with her, but he refused, saying it wouldn't look right. Her heart was breaking for him. The pain she felt at losing Joey was unbearable, but Tom's had to be worse. No matter how much she loved Joey, the truth was she loved her husband more. Flesh and blood and with more than enough faults to go around, he sat beside her, loving her, holding her up. Tom had nothing but a sham of a marriage, and the love of his life was dead—gone, and he couldn't even grieve openly.

It wasn't the time or the place, but she felt a sudden need to apologize to Billy—for throwing him out, for the pain she knew she'd caused him.

She grabbed his arm. "Billy," she whispered, "I'm sorry. I should've told you sooner—"

The swell of the organ and the rumble of hundreds of mourners rising to their feet cut her off.

He looked down questioningly as he helped her stand.

"Later," she whispered, squeezing his arm, unable to say anything more.

It would be a long, hard day, but they would talk tonight. There were things that had to be said, things that couldn't wait.

Life was too short.

⁓

Billy was torn. He wanted to do this for Kate, and for Joey, but he would have preferred to remain seated beside her. He picked up his guitar and took a seat on the stool alongside the altar, almost directly in front of Kate. Balancing on one foot, he hooked the other through the bottom rung.

No sooner had he began playing "Songbird" when Tom, who had somehow situated himself behind Kate, leaned forward and began whispering in her ear. And damn if she didn't turn around, take his hand, and hold it throughout the entire song.

He wanted to stand up and tear the two of them apart. Playing in church wasn't his thing, but he knew glaring at someone while he did probably wasn't acceptable protocol. He needed to focus, but all he could think about were Kate's last few words. What had she been about to apologize for?

When he finished, Kate turned around, the expression on her face unreadable. She was sad. Yeah, he got that. But there was more. She'd said she was sorry. For what? Something she'd done? That made no sense. He was the one who needed to do the apologizing.

Or was her apology for something she was about to do?

He tried to swallow the rock lodged in his throat and made his way to the piano.

Sorry for what?

If he didn't get his shit together, he would never pull this off. He needed a drink. The bottle of tranquilizers rattled in his pocket, taunting him. If he could turn away for a second—

The sound of strings filled the church with the opening bars of "You Raise Me Up."

He was a professional. Hell, he'd played under just about every circumstance. Except for one—fear of the unknown.

His eyes found Kate. At least she was paying attention now. Tom sat behind her, wearing shades like he was a motherfucking rock star and not some dweeb lawyer who was dangerously close to having his face bashed in.

Sorry. For. What?

Someone had the foresight to put the sheet music on the piano, and although he hadn't thought he would need it, he was grateful. It gave him focus. He concentrated on his hands and his voice, not what was or wasn't going on right under his fucking nose.

When the song was finally over, he slipped into the pew beside Kate, who looked as if she were about to lose it. He nudged Rhiannon, who pulled a bottle of water from her oversized handbag. He reached into his pocket, took out the lorazepam, and handed a pill to Kate. She'd refused to take anything earlier. Now, with shaking hands, she put it on her tongue and took a sip from the bottle he held out to her.

"Is one enough?" Her face was wet with tears, and her breathing had become ragged.

He took out another and split it in half, then handed one of the halves to her. After she swallowed it, he took the water from her and popped the other half into his mouth. For no other reason than to keep him from knocking Tom into next week.

It shouldn't take long for her to feel the effects of the drug. Even if it didn't numb her, it might soften some of the sharp edges of her grief. He pulled her close and rocked her back and forth until finally, under the drone of the prayers and mumbo jumbo around them, he felt her begin to relax.

CHAPTER 22

Billy slid his empty glass across the polished mahogany surface.

"Another Jack Daniels?"

Like he needed to ask. He fixed the bartender in an angry glare and watched the man's bright smile slide off his face. Other than the short time he'd spent pushing overpriced salmon around his plate, he'd occupied a stool at the end of the bar, far enough from the loud, swarming crowd to discourage anyone from engaging him in conversation. Combined with the tranquilizer he'd taken earlier, he should be a zombie by now.

Just recalling Kate's invitation for Tom to join them in the limo after the funeral made him want to snatch the goddamn bottle from the bartender's hand and skip the glass altogether. He didn't know what the fuck was going on between the two of them, but he was damn sure going to find out.

He motioned to the glass. "Just keep 'em comin'."

He tore at the noose around his neck until the knot came loose, yanked his tie through the stiff collar, and jammed it into the pocket of his suit jacket.

A dull ache wound itself into a knot at the base of his skull. How long did these things drag on for anyway? If it wasn't for the open bar, he might have voluntarily switched places with Joey.

Shitty thing to think—but still.

He was lifting the freshly refilled glass to his lips when a petite blonde sidled up next to him. She leaned against the bar with her elbows against the edge, thrusting out her chest in the process. Bile burned the back of his throat at a whiff of her expensive perfume.

Could this day get any worse?

"Howdy, stranger."

Just the sound of her voice set his teeth on edge. His grunt should have warned her to stay the fuck away. He stared into his half-full glass, wanting the woman beside him to disappear.

"You don't sound very happy to see me."

He swirled the glass slowly. "I have no feelings about you one way or the other." He tossed back another mouthful.

She let out a low chuckle. "Oh, I doubt that."

Actually, she was right. He still hated her more than he'd hated just about anyone. Christa Dunphy had been the biggest mistake of his life. He'd paid twenty-some years of guilt for ten minutes with her in a back room, and if wrapping his hands around her throat and choking the life out of her would have made it all go away, he'd have done it in a heartbeat.

He glanced at his former agent. Fashionably styled hair. Artfully applied makeup. Tight, low-cut black suit.

"You trolling funerals for hookups now?"

"Ouch." She chuckled. "Who pissed in your Cheerios?"

He tossed back his drink and set the glass down clumsily. The bartender skipped the formality and simply reached for the JD. About time.

"Seems there was a time you weren't all that averse to hooking up." Christa leaned in close, her voice barely a whisper.

Billy crunched into an ice cube. "I'm a lot smarter than I was then."

"Really?" She tapped his elbow with her Chanel clutch. "Correct me if I'm wrong, but weren't you in not one but two fights recently, not to mention getting fired from one of the best gigs you've had in years?" She bared her teeth in a wicked smile, then hissed at him under her breath. "Sounds like you aren't any smarter than when we first met."

The bartender set down her Scotch, neat.

She narrowed her eyes at Billy. "You know, poor little Kate has been through so much. She certainly didn't deserve this. Maybe it's time she and I finally have that little talk. You know, I promised Joey I wouldn't say anything to her, but now that he's gone . . ." She shrugged. "I'm sure she'll thank me for letting her in on our little secret after all these years."

A red haze clouded his vision, and it was all he could do not to wrap his fingers around her throat and snap her neck. Instead, he took a long pull on his glass. He slammed it on the bar and wiped his mouth on the back of his hand. The bartender silently refilled the glass, then edged away to the other end of the bar.

Billy was drunk. Stinking drunk. But the edges that should have been dulled by pills and the half bottle of whiskey had been honed to a sharp, deadly point.

He rose, staggered a step toward Christa, and smiled, his bottom lip catching in his teeth. It was clearly not the response she'd expected, and he almost grinned when he saw how much he'd unnerved her.

Lowering his head, he brought his mouth so close to her ear she would feel the words as much as hear them. "You still want me?"

He pressed his arm against hers, his smile growing at her sharp intake of air.

Christa's eyes grew round and dark, her fingers dancing across her thick gold necklace. He could read her body language as if the words had been embroidered onto the lapels of her designer suit. Her chin rose.

Billy leaned so close the hairs of his mustache brushed against her ear.

"You still wanna fuck me?"

She swallowed. Her chest rose and fell, and the skin along her forearms prickled with gooseflesh.

Lids lowered, his eyes locked on hers. He lifted his glass and opened his mouth, tipping it until a slow trickle of whiskey rolled past his lips. He ran his tongue over the rim of his glass, then sucked on an ice cube, turning it over in his mouth.

Christa looked as if she were about to combust. Her eyes settled on his mouth, and she licked her lips as if she could taste the whiskey there.

He cocked an eyebrow, waiting for her answer.

She chewed on her lower lip. Her eyes darted back and forth.

"You know I do," she said finally, her voice low and husky.

"Yeah?"

His smile widened to a grin for the briefest second. Then he pulled up to his full height.

"Fuck you, you fucking cunt," he snarled. "You get within fifteen feet of my wife, I'll break your fucking neck."

He drained his glass and slammed it down, leaving Christa speechless as he pushed off the bar.

He needed Kate. But even as he turned away from Christa, all he could see was Tom's arm on the back of her chair, their heads bent close together, deep in conversation.

"Fuck this shit."

He headed for the door. If he didn't get out of there, he just might kill somebody.

CHAPTER 23

Kate woke to the sound of muffled voices, one angry and one irritated. Billy had returned, and he was probably drunk. She punched the pillow and pulled it over her head in an attempt to drown out whatever was going on outside her door.

She'd gone to bed hours earlier. Anger had kept her awake, but exhaustion had finally won out. Before saying good night to Devin, she'd covered Joey's expensive sofa with sheets and left a pillow and a blanket. Billy was not welcome in her bed. Not tonight. And to make sure he got the message, she'd locked the bedroom door.

When it grew quiet again, she slipped out from under the pillow and rolled onto her side, away from the window and the empty half of the bed, hoping Billy would have passed out by now.

Unfortunately, she was now wide awake, her brain slipping into overdrive. They should head home tomorrow. Being in Joey's apartment was a constant reminder that he wasn't there. Not that going home would make accepting his death any easier, but at least she could sleep in her own bed, work in her garden, occupy her mind along with her hands. Could it be that easy? Doubtful.

And of course there was this situation with Billy. They needed to talk, and after today, even more so. He couldn't keep this up; this path of self-destruction would ruin them both.

Footsteps echoed outside the door, followed by the rattle of the doorknob. Did he seriously expect her to let him in after what he'd done? He shook it again, harder this time, causing the door to shiver in its frame. She slammed her open palms against the mattress and prayed he'd wise up and head for the couch. Better yet, back to New Jersey.

"Katie! Open the damn door!"

When she didn't respond, he kicked it.

God damn it. She threw off the covers and climbed out of bed. If he woke Devin or damaged that door . . .

Kate unlocked the door and yanked it open, narrowly missing a fist in her face.

Billy staggered past her, reeking of alcohol, sweat, and cigarettes. "I wanna go to bed."

She grabbed his arm. "Sleep on the couch. I don't want you in here."

"Tough shit." He shook her off like a bug.

One of his cuff links was missing and his sleeve flapped open. He fumbled with the buttons of his shirt. When they refused to cooperate, he tore it open. Buttons pinged against the wall and rolled across the floor.

Years of experience had taught Kate that Billy didn't respond well to anger, although this behavior? This was totally out of character for him, at least when it came to her. In the past, if he was angry with her, he'd leave. Stay away until he calmed down. Not that he had any right to be angry. What made it worse, she'd never seen him this drunk.

It wasn't easy, but she forced herself to speak calmly.

"Don't do this, Billy. Please. Not tonight."

He glared down at her, and the look on his face caused her to take a step back. Even in the dim light, his eyes were wild, his pupils nearly eclipsing all of the blue. A chill skittered up her spine. Drinking wasn't all he'd been doing.

He shrugged out of his shirt and dropped it onto the floor, then tore at the buckle on his belt. "I'm not sleepin' on any fuckin' couch!"

A siren sliced through the night, its echo mimicking the beating of her heart.

"Lower your voice. Please." She spoke softly, a contradiction to the rage practically screaming inside of her.

"I'll yell if I want." He yanked his briefs off and kicked them across the room, stumbling before catching himself on the edge of the dresser. Given his level of intoxication, he should have fallen flat on his face. It would have served him right, too. Instead, he turned and tried to stare her down—a silent challenge, although for what she had no idea.

She couldn't deal with this, not right now. Whatever the hell he'd gone and done, she wasn't having it. The past few days had been awful, and this? This was too much. She collapsed onto the bed and dropped her head into her hands.

"Do you have to do this tonight?"

She didn't hear him move, but she could feel him standing before her. Of course. Now he wanted to apologize. After abandoning and humiliating her, when it was time to climb into bed, now he was sorry.

Only he wasn't.

Sharp pain bit into her upper arm as he yanked her to her feet.

"Ow! You're hurting me." She tried to wrench away, but his grip was too strong. "Let go!"

Billy's grip tightened and he forced her onto her toes, bringing her face close to his. The muscles corded in his neck and shoulders. Beads of sweat trickled from his temples. The shiver of fear she'd felt earlier spread across her chest. Something was very, very wrong.

She sucked in a deep breath and spoke slowly through her clenched teeth. "Let me go."

His eyes were dark holes, his pupils so dilated they were almost black. He stared without blinking. With a cold, ugly laugh, he shoved her onto the bed.

She tried to roll, but he caught her leg with his knee, pinning her into place and lowering his body over hers.

"What're you gonna do, Katie? Huh?"

His weight was crushing her, his body slick with sweat. She struggled to breathe.

"Get off!" Flattening her palms against his chest, she pushed, but he didn't budge.

"Go ahead, push me away." He pressed against her, forcing out whatever air remained in her lungs. When his mouth sought hers, she turned away, his lips brushing her cheek.

"You wanna play games?" He snarled into her ear. "Not a good idea, babe, 'cause I'm sick of your fucking games."

Billy twisted his hand in her hair, holding her still as his mouth met hers. Pain tore through her scalp. She struggled, but it was no use. Keeping her hair wound taut in his fist, he dragged his tongue over the shell of her ear, then lightly bit her neck. He moved on to the fleshy part of her shoulder and bit her again; this time hard enough to make her cry out.

"Why are you doing this to me?"

In the dull, gray light, his eyes met hers. "I'm taking what's mine. Just so you know, it's not yours to give away." His teeth crashed into hers, splitting her lip, the coppery taste of blood filling her mouth.

He relaxed his grip and shifted his focus to her breasts. She yanked her arm out from under him and swung, hitting him squarely on the side of his head. He reared up, and with a roar, slapped her hard across her face.

Stunned, she sucked in a lungful of air. Billy had never raised a hand to her, let alone struck her. The shock hurt more than the blow itself.

Adrenaline pumped through her veins, and she struggled harder. "You have lost your fucking mind!"

Billy raised his hand again. Time stopped. His fingers curled into a fist. The noise from the street fell away, leaving behind only the sound of her blood rushing through her veins, and the rhythmic thump of her own heart. His arm cocked back slowly, as if the air had grown thick.

He was going to hit her. Again. Given his size and strength, he would hurt more than her pride this time.

In that second, their eyes locked. In his she saw a flash of recognition, one single moment of clarity, as if he understood what he'd just done and what he was about to do. Time sped up again, his fist dropped, and the density that had swallowed them disappeared.

"Don't you hit me," he growled. "Don't you ever fucking hit me."

Panting as if he'd run a long distance, he stared down at her, his chest heaving. Gently, he threaded his fingers through her hair, then lowered his face over hers. His kiss was softer. Tender, even. As if he himself didn't know what the hell he was doing.

"It's been too long, baby," he murmured, his lips brushing her ear.

When her nightgown got in his way, he tore it in two. His mouth found her breasts, sucking and kneading them. At one point he bit her, hard enough, she was sure, to have broken the skin. A scream rose in her throat, but he covered her mouth with his own. He kissed her face and her throat, all the while mumbling words that made no sense.

She wanted to strike out against him, to kick and scream. But she didn't. She wasn't strong enough to fight him, so she stopped trying. And screaming would bring Devin. Then what? No. She couldn't do that. She would endure whatever happened. But tomorrow? Tomorrow he would put his ass in rehab or else.

"Hold me!" he demanded. "Put your fuckin' arms around me, and hold me like you mean it."

His grip on her hair tightened and he pulled until she thought he would wrench it from its roots.

"Stop it! You're hurting me."

He eased up, but only a little. Kate wound her arms around him. Taut, hard muscles rippled beneath her fingers. She could feel each vertebra, every rib. His skin was slick, wet. Sweat dripped onto her.

His rambling became more incoherent, and although it would have been wise to just give in and let him do what he wanted, knowing he wasn't in his right mind, her instinct and outrage won out when he dropped to the ground between her thighs. Without thinking, she pulled her leg up and kicked her foot hard against his shoulder. With barely a grunt at her assault, he flipped her over effortlessly and slapped her ass. Then he began to massage it, as if this were all some kind of normal sex play. He ran his tongue over the burn, then bit her again.

She balled up the sheets and blankets and screamed into the mattress. As frightened as she was for herself, she was more afraid to wake Devin. No longer able to control the tears, she sobbed into the bedding. It was as if he didn't even hear her.

When he had done all the surface damage he could manage, and more emotional damage than she could gauge, he dragged her onto the floor, pushed her knees apart, and forced himself inside her. His body was hot where it touched hers, and he was sweating so much that she was as wet as he was.

It couldn't have been worse if a stranger had dragged her into a dark alley. Though that meant she could have been lying in the street or even dead by now, either alternative might have been preferable to being attacked by the man she loved.

But it was what happened next that cut her to her very core.

Billy's face was outlined by the ghostly blue-gray light coming from outside the window. He grabbed her by her hair and tilted her face until their eyes locked.

"There're plenty of woman I wouldn't have to force to do what you're doing right now. There's a regular parade of pussy at my fingertips." He pulled her so close she could feel his words on her face. "Fuck. I could've had Christa on her knees again today if I wanted." He glared down at her. "All these years I felt guilty, while you're carrying on under my nose like I'm some kinda fucking moron."

A knife through her heart would have been kinder. The pain and humiliation of what he'd done to her was nothing. All that mattered were his words: *on her knees again.*

Nausea gripped her.

On her knees. Again.

The words that destroyed her seemed to have strengthened him. With renewed vigor, he took her roughly, pounding hard against her hips until he eventually cried out and collapsed in a massive, wet, panting heap, pinning her to the floor. After a few minutes, he lifted his head. His eyes, dark and wild, found hers.

"You're mine, Katie," he growled. "Don't you ever forget it."

Hours may have passed. It was hard to tell. Kate lay still, her heart shredded, torn from her chest. She'd been ready to make excuses for him, convinced he'd taken some drug he wasn't used to. But his confession? That hurt worse than anything he could have done. There were no excuses to make for that. Tears trailed from her eyes into her ears. She couldn't even raise her arms to wipe them away.

Billy groaned. His body shifted, and when she was certain he had passed out, she shimmied out from under him. A web of pain spread over her lower back and her hips. Her groin ached, and her legs seemed unable to support her. If she could just get to Joey's room . . . And if Billy came looking for her, she would call the police.

After separating her robe from the tangled sheets, Kate gingerly stepped out into the apartment. Except for the light from nearby buildings, it was dark, and thankfully, the door to the roof was closed. Devin wouldn't have heard anything. She crossed the apartment as quietly as she could, each step an agonizing reminder of what Billy had done to her.

By the time she reached Joey's room, her body was shaking. She locked the door. She wanted nothing more than to collapse on the floor, but if she did, she might never get up again. She gripped the doorknob for support as her eyes swept the immaculate, tastefully decorated space. More than anywhere else in the apartment, this was where she felt Joey's presence the most. She'd avoided it since he'd died, other than to pick out the clothes to bury him in, but she let it wrap around her now. A safe haven. It was as if he were there, protecting her.

She choked back a sob. That she would need protecting from Billy crushed her. Yet here she was.

Gathering what little strength she had left, she made a mental blueprint of the marks he might have left on her, to minimize the shock when she turned on the light. She pushed off the door as if she needed the momentum to move, slipped into Joey's bathroom, and with an attempt at a deep, calming breath, she flipped on the light.

What she saw stole that breath away.

Her cheeks, neck, and shoulders were scarlet and raw-looking from the stubble on his face, and her lower lip was split and bleeding. When she ran a shaky hand through her hair, long pieces came out between her fingers.

Facing the full-length mirrors, she dropped her robe. Ugly red and purple bruises covered her body. Marks were already forming on the underside of her arm where Billy's fingers had dug into her flesh. Teeth marks marred her left breast, shoulder, and inner thighs. A handprint was still visible across her backside.

Who was this woman staring back at her, and who had done this to her? She knew the truth, but she couldn't grasp the reality of it. How was this even possible?

Kate stared at her reflection and cried. She cried so hard, and with such great, racking sobs, she had to bury her face in a towel so she wouldn't wake Devin—or, God forbid, Billy. When she felt she could bear it, she stepped into the shower, allowing the water to nearly scald her as she scrubbed at the marks Billy had left upon her flesh, marks that would fade eventually.

But the way he'd shredded her heart?

That would be permanent.

Billy woke sometime before dawn. The carpet was rough on his face. His body was hot, sweaty. Groaning, he pushed himself to his feet. Where the hell was he, and why was he on the floor? He was burning up. Fragments of memory flashed like a broken strobe, but nothing he could grab hold of. His muscles ached. His heart was beating too fast. His head pounded. His mouth felt like it was filled with cotton.

Gray light from the street swirled around him, turning his stomach, making him dizzy. He lifted himself onto the bed, trying not to wake Kate and praying the room would stop spinning. It felt like he was spiraling through space. He needed grounding. His hand snaked toward her, fingers reaching, but they came up empty.

His head jerked up and his stomach pitched. Why wasn't she in bed? It had to be late. His hand swept the nightstand. Where the hell was his watch?

He flicked on the bedside lamp, squinting against the brightness. His clothes were strewn about the room. He spotted his briefs, stood clumsily, and slipped them on. Then he checked his pants pockets. No watch. He'd taken it off. But where?

When the walls stopped trying to fall and crush him, he staggered to the door, unsure if he was even standing straight. The apartment was dark and silent. The couch was made up for sleeping, but it lay empty. Maybe she'd gone up to the roof.

He climbed the stairs, holding onto the railing with both hands to keep from falling. Devin was asleep on the chaise, despite the city sounds drifting up from below. No Kate. He made his way back downstairs with careful steps and tried Joey's door. Locked.

An ugly thought raced through his head: Tom. He stared hard at the door, as if he might be able to see through to the other side and find Kate in bed with—

His throat tightened.

What the hell was he thinking? Kate would never . . . Would she?

He grabbed his chest, thinking his heart might explode. If he didn't lie down, he was going to be sick. His head was as full of cotton as his mouth. He stumbled back into the kitchen and snatched a bottle of water from the refrigerator, but the cabinets and bathroom medicine chest mocked him in his search for aspirin. There was never any fucking aspirin when he needed it.

He returned to the bedroom, dragging his hand along the walls to keep himself upright, and climbed into bed, where he prayed for sleep or death.

Either would do.

CHAPTER 24

Soft scratching noises rose from deep in the recesses of his brain, but Billy chose to ignore them. When they didn't stop, he rolled over to find Kate poking around in the closet.

The sunlight was downright painful. "Babe?" he mumbled. "What time is it?"

"Early." Her voice was low but sharp. "Go back to sleep."

He rolled onto his side. "Did Devin leave?"

"Yes."

Kate yanked at something in the closet, and a hanger clattered to the floor. He squeezed his eyes shut and groaned, then rubbed his temples with the tips of his fingers.

"Could you find me some aspirin? Please? I have a killer headache." He forced his eyes open a little wider. "Then come lie down with me."

Kate seemed determined to reach something in the bottom of the closet. "I have to get dressed."

Through eyes open no wider than slits, he watched her grip the edge of the wall and lower herself to pick up what she'd dropped, groaning as she did.

"You okay?"

"Fine."

"You don't sound fine."

She steadied herself against the wall. "I'm fine," she repeated, her voice like ice.

Might as well get it over with. He forced himself to sit up.

"I'm sorry about yesterday. I know you must be disappointed. There's no excuse. I let you down. Again."

"Disappointed?" She looked at him like he'd grown two heads. "You think I'm disappointed?"

He couldn't come to grips with the venom in her tone. "Yeah, well, I'm kinda disappointed in you, too, you know. And hurt."

Her mouth fell open. "You're disappointed in me?"

"Yeah. And hurt."

Her face was a total blank. "I can't even begin to formulate a response to that."

She moved toward the door.

He needed to make this right, to get to the bottom of whatever was going on with Tom. It was probably nothing—but whatever it was, it was going to stop. In spite of his desperate need for more sleep and a handful of aspirin, he rose from the bed. The room spun like a Tilt-a-Whirl. He wished he could remember whatever the fuck he'd taken last night, because whatever it was, he wanted to make sure he'd never do it again.

"Katie." He grimaced at the sound of his own voice echoing inside his head. "Don't walk away from me." He reached for her but she ducked, crying out as she did.

"Don't touch me!"

Her voice was a dagger between his eyes. He pulled back and rubbed his hand over his face, then reached for her again.

"Don't!" She held her free hand up as if to stop him.

It did, but after the shock of her response wore off, he took another step. "Katie?" The room spun and his stomach threatened to empty its contents on the bedroom floor.

"No!" She moved backward through the door and into the bright light of the living room.

"What's wrong with you?" Marks were visible on her face, throat, and chest. "What the hell is all over your neck?"

"Stay away from me."

He grabbed her arm gently, wanting to see what she was hiding, but let go when she let out an anguished, painful cry.

Blood pounded in his ears. His jaw clenched, and his fists curled. "What happened to you?" If somebody had hurt her . . .

Her eyes were filled with fear and something else, something he'd never seen before. Something feral.

Icy fingers gripped the base of his spine, creeping upward. "Katie. What's wrong?" Images spun through his head so quickly they made him dizzy, and he found himself holding onto the door frame to keep from falling.

Moving as if every step was painful, she tossed the clothing in her arms onto the sofa. Then she faced him and untied her robe, letting it drop in a heap around her ankles.

His reaction was visceral, as red as the blood smeared on her chin from the split in her lip. Anger roared in his ears. Her body was covered with bruises and bites.

Words escaped him. Black-and-white memories tumbled in his brain along with a pain that was almost debilitating. His heart pounded dangerously.

"I'll kill whoever did this." The sound of his voice, only a whisper, made him sick.

He squeezed his eyes shut, jammed his palms into his eye sockets, and pressed. When he opened his eyes, it was all still there—every welt, every bruise.

The images in his head clicked into place like a Rubik's Cube, from an abstract puzzle to the beginning of a memory.

He began to shake.

"No," he whispered as more memories dropped into place. "It's not possible." He swallowed the bile inching up this throat.

Kate turned so he could see her back as well. An ugly welt across her bottom. Purple fingerprints dotting her upper arms.

It made no sense. "I don't . . . I could never . . ." He shook his head, trying to clear it, searching for an explanation, a piece of memory he could pull out and examine.

"I was drinking." He toggled between a memory and an explanation. "A lot. I remember that. I went to a bar in the Village, and someone had a joint, and we went out back. I did a few lines of coke . . ." He rubbed his wrist. "My watch."

Kate looked even angrier.

"No, listen. I gave someone my watch." He stared at the floor as more images clicked into place. "Meth." He said it so softly she might not have heard. He cleared his throat. "Crystal meth. I was snorting crystal meth. That has to be it."

Meth? What the hell was wrong with him? He wanted to drop to his knees, beg her to listen, to understand. "I'm not sure, Katie. Please. Let me think." He took another step toward her, holding out his hands. "I can't believe I did that." His voice broke and he swallowed a sob. "I love you. I would never hurt you."

A lone tear rolled down her cheek.

"Being raped by a stranger in an alley would have been easier to live through than what you did to me." Each word was a dagger, plunged into his heart. "And it would have been over quicker. And maybe I would have been dead instead of just wishing I were."

Another painful cry escaped as she bent to pick up her robe. She slipped it on, cinching the belt tightly around her waist.

He wanted to go to her, comfort her. Jesus. He needed her to comfort him. This was some fucked-up nightmare. But he couldn't move.

"And if that wasn't bad enough"—her voice broke—"you cheated."

His heart slammed against his ribs. "No! Never. That's not true."

"You're a liar!" She took a step toward him as if she would strike him. "You told me yourself. You said you could've had her again yesterday if you wanted. You were actually bragging."

His eyes dropped to the floor, unable to face her, but it was too late. The shock on his face must have been all she needed to confirm it.

"How stupid am I?" She wrapped her arms around her waist. "We had our problems, but I always thought we were better than that. All these people over the years telling me I should expect you to cheat. It was the nature of the business, they said, but I swore that would never be us. How they must have laughed at me. I thought we were special. I thought as long as we had love and respect, we could deal with all the rest. I was an idiot!"

He reached for her. "No, Katie, it wasn't like that. It was a long time ago. It meant nothing."

"Stop!" She covered her ears with her hands, her mouth contorting with grief. "Nothing you say can change what you've done."

He needed to explain, to hold her. "Katie, please."

"You are not the boy I married." The words cut through him, jagged shards of glass spilling out between pitiful sobs. "You're a monster. You have finally become your father. Get your stuff and get out. If you're not gone in fifteen minutes, I'm calling the police—and I will press charges."

Every step she took away was as painful to watch as it must have been for her to take. Before she closed and locked the bedroom door, she faced him one last time.

"I never want to see you again. Ever."

CHAPTER 25

Devin stood on the corner of Leonard and Hudson streets feeling guilty. He'd never really lied to his mother before, at least that he could remember. This was a pretty shitty time to start, too, but he couldn't help it. After the bullshit his father had pulled after the funeral, he didn't want to be anywhere near him. At least he'd been able to get out of Uncle Joey's apartment before he'd woken up.

The city was surprisingly refreshing that morning. That, or getting out from under all the sadness made it seem that way.

A little red car waited at the light. Devin stepped up to the curb and waved. When it pulled alongside him, he climbed in, leaned over, and kissed the driver.

"Want me to drive?"

"I've made it this far without getting run off the road by some maniac—might as well go the rest of the way." She flashed a big smile.

He couldn't resist, so he kissed her again.

The cabbie behind them laid on the horn.

"I'm going! I'm going!" she shouted, nosing the car out onto Leonard Street. "Good grief. This is a hundred times worse than Pittsburgh traffic any day."

Danielle Kelly was the prettiest girl he'd ever seen: expressive eyes the color of melted chocolate and a thick mane of chestnut curls framing her heart-shaped face. At just a tad over five feet tall, compared to his six foot five, they made an odd couple, but they'd hit it off immediately. She was not only pretty, she was brilliant, well-informed, and socially conscious, which as far as he was concerned made her even more beautiful.

Watching her white-knuckle the steering wheel of her ridiculously small car, he couldn't stop grinning.

"What?" She took her eyes off the road for only a second, even though they weren't even moving.

"Nothing. I'm just glad to see you. I missed you."

She chanced a quick smile, then returned her focus to the Manhattan traffic.

It had been ten long weeks since they had seen each other, but Devin loved what he was doing. A summer working with kids whose fathers had skipped out long before they were born or were serving time for any number of offenses had shown him he'd found his calling. He couldn't compare himself to any of those kids even on the tiniest of margins, but he did feel a connection. He knew his own father would eventually come home, but he also knew what it was like to wish for a dad to be sitting in the stands at his baseball games or coaching his soccer team. He also knew what it was to have a father who didn't know when to say when.

Which reminded him of the bullshit his father had pulled after the funeral.

His guilt over escaping the city early dissolved. He was supposed to be heading for the airport to catch a plane back to Colorado for the last two weeks of his summer break. Danielle's summer internship with a newspaper in Pennsylvania had just ended. They had originally made plans for her to join him in Colorado, but with him having to return early for the funeral, they instead decided to escape to her family's weekend place in the Poconos. With her parents in Europe and his in New York, no one would be the wiser.

"I hate saying it," he said as she edged up Canal Street toward the Holland Tunnel, "but I'm glad to be out of there. I feel bad leaving my mom, but my father's being a jackass, and I can only take so much."

It felt good to share his feelings with someone for a change. He never spoke to anyone about his family. Most of his friends were in awe of his father, and whenever they came over, his dad played the humble rock star. Devin had thought he would die the time his father had pulled out a joint and offered to share it with them. That day, he envied each of his friends their dull accountant, truck-driving, factory-working fathers.

Danielle understood him. Talking to her was easy. She didn't judge.

She gave his hand a quick squeeze before regaining her death grip on the steering wheel. "Was it that bad?"

He shrugged, staring out the window. "Yesterday started out okay, all things considered, but at the luncheon afterward, he started drinking." He tugged on the shoulder strap. "He actually left the restaurant before it was over. I didn't see him go, or I'd have gone after him. I don't know what happened or why he did it. Left my mother there by herself. Even Rhiannon couldn't come up with an excuse this time—not that she didn't try."

"What did your mother do?"

"Nothing. She said he had to see someone, but I know damn well she was just covering for him." The cramped compartment made it difficult to stretch his legs. He shifted his weight, trying to get comfortable. "Sometimes I feel like I'm living in the *Valley of the Dolls*."

Danielle groaned. "Did you actually read that?"

He chuckled under his breath. "No, but you know what I mean. Did you?"

"Hardly."

Maybe he could stick his legs out the window.

He tugged gently on one of her curls, watching as it sprang back when he let go. "You know, if we're going to keep seeing each other, you're gonna have to get a bigger car."

"Yeah, I'll get right on that."

Her mouth quirked up into a smile, and if it wouldn't have freaked her out, he'd have stolen a quick kiss right then. Screw the traffic.

"In the meantime," she continued, "we can stop, and you can buy me breakfast and stretch those stilts of yours."

"That'll work. For now."

They stopped at the last diner before the interstate.

Devin carefully unfolded himself from the front seat. "I'm not kidding. I hope we have what it takes to survive a Volkswagen, because I feel like an accordion."

"It's not my fault you're a giant."

"You can blame my father for that, too."

"I will." She gave him a brilliant smile over the roof of her car. "If you ever let me meet him."

CHAPTER 26

Billy stood in the shadows a few hundred feet from the end of his driveway, hands jammed in his back pockets, careful to avoid the pool of light cast by the streetlight. It was unlikely anyone would drive by, especially at this hour, but there was the possibility that one of his neighbors might get up to take a piss. He didn't want anyone to see him lurking about.

Although if he were being honest, he had no fucks left to give. All he cared about was numbing the soul-sucking, gut-wrenching pain Kate had left him with. Whiskey wasn't doing it; it just made him sadder and sick. He didn't want to feel anything.

Not one damn thing.

If he didn't do something about it soon, he would lose his fucking mind.

Maybe he'd already lost it. He remembered almost nothing of the night of Joey's funeral. If it wasn't for the random flashbacks and nightmares, he'd swear it had never happened.

It made no sense. The idea that he was capable of physically hurting Kate was beyond him. It was impossible. Yet he'd done exactly that. And then, as if that weren't bad enough, he'd opened his big mouth and slit his own throat.

For twenty years, he'd successfully kept Kate from learning what had happened with Christa. He never allowed her to travel with any of the bands he played with, even when other wives and kids came along. On the rare occasions he flew her out to meet him on the road, it was always when he had a couple of days between shows, and they always stayed in a hotel away from the others. He told her he wanted to keep his two lives separate—and that was true, but mostly because he knew not only had Christa blabbed about what had happened to anyone who would listen, she'd made it sound like a lot more than giving him head in a back room while he was so blitzed he could barely remember his own name.

And in the end, he had gotten so wasted he'd told Kate himself. It made no fucking sense.

An engine growled from a few blocks away. Moments later, a sleek red Mustang turned the corner onto River Street. The driver killed the headlights as the muscle car rumbled to a stop. Billy emerged from the darkness and waited, pretty sure the passenger was sizing him up from inside the car.

After what seemed like too long, the dark-tinted window slid halfway open. The man looking up at him was right out of central casting—so much the movie version of a drug dealer that Billy wondered if he was being set up.

"Chooch?" he asked.

"Maybe."

Dick. Chooch, or whatever his name was, looked to be in his mid-twenties. His hair was long and black, and despite it being the middle of the night, he wore dark sunglasses. Thick gold chains dangled around his neck. On his right arm were several poorly executed tattoos. Billy could see nothing of the driver.

"Yes or no, I ain't got all night."

"Simmer down." Chooch flashed him an artificially white smile. "What you got for me?"

"What have you got for me?"

"Exactly what you asked for, man. Two 8-balls. Five caps. I even threw in a couple spikes. Gratis."

Spikes? He hadn't planned on shooting up, just snorting. Just something to get him over the hump. He'd done some messing around with needles years ago, but when Kate found out—

Fuck it. What difference did it make now?

"Let me see."

Chooch held up a magazine. Tucked between the pages were five small bags, each containing a tan powder the consistency of brown sugar, two syringes, plus another small bag with a couple of 8-balls of coke. Satisfied, Billy pulled four hundred-dollar bills from his pocket and handed them to Chooch.

The man motioned to the money and laughed. "I don't think so, rock star. Six bills."

Billy stared, stony-faced. He was going to kill Eddie. This guy wasn't supposed to know anything about him, not his name or what he did, which was part of the reason he was taking the risk of meeting him out on the street.

"You said four."

"That was before. You're forgetting travel time for me and my girl. One bill each, plus four bills for the smack and the blow."

He should have expected this. He tugged his wallet from his back pocket and peeled off another two hundred.

"Pleasure doing business with you, rock star."

Before he could answer, the car peeled away. Billy flipped over the magazine. Even in the dark of the night, he could see it was a copy of *Rolling Stone* from earlier in the year, the issue that announced he'd been hired to replace Alec Grant in Stonestreet.

So much for keeping a low profile. He rolled the magazine into a tube and slipped it into his back pocket and headed for his empty house.

CHAPTER 27

Since his parents would be in New York till Friday, Devin wasn't too concerned about driving back to Belleville to hook up with some friends. They decided to meet for dinner at La Cucina in Spring Lake. He just needed to make a quick stop at the house and pick up a jacket and tie, since he'd left his suit in New York with his mother.

And Danielle didn't know it yet, but he also planned to take his father's pickup rather than keep squeezing into her tin can of a car any longer than necessary.

"This is a cute little house," she said as they pulled around back. "I'm kind of surprised it's so small."

Devin snorted. "What did you expect? A gated entry with a pool and tennis court?"

Color rose in her cheeks.

"Just kidding," he said. "To be honest, I wouldn't like to live that way. I like this house. It's small, but it's home. My parents put an addition on about ten years ago, so it's a lot bigger than it used to be. It's nice, but my dad . . . He thinks it's too far from everything and too old. Every time something breaks or the roof leaks, he threatens to sell it. My mom grew up around here and she loves it, so after a while he quits grumbling. He's gone most of the time anyway. I don't know why he even cares."

Devin unfolded himself from Danielle's car and stretched. "I think you'll like the inside. My mom's decorated it in that primitive style like an old farmhouse."

"Sounds nice," she said as he unlocked the back door.

Loud music was coming from upstairs.

"Shit," he grumbled. "I didn't think they'd be home until Friday."

Dishes were piled in the sink. Empty liquor bottles lined the counter. It was obvious his father was home, if not his mother.

"Too late now. They probably heard us drive up."

But he wasn't ready for this, for introducing his parents to Danielle. It had nothing to do with her. He just wasn't ready to share her with his family. At least not yet.

"Dad! I'm home."

Nothing.

Alice in Chains was pumping through the speakers upstairs.

"Dad?" Devin took the steps two at a time.

He pushed open the door to the music room and found his father slumped on the futon, a belt loosely twisted around his arm and a syringe on the cushion beside him.

"Oh fuck!" He started toward his father, then turned back and yelled down the hall. "Dani! Danielle!"

He was rounding the top of the stairs when her face appeared below.

"Call 911! It's my dad. I think he OD'd!"

By the time Danielle made the call and raced upstairs, Devin had his father stretched out on the floor. He knelt beside him, trying to resuscitate him, while Layne Staley's vocals screamed in his ears.

"Could you please turn that off?" he asked between breaths.

"Yeah, of course." She picked her way over his father's bare feet.

A Bose stereo system sat on the upper shelf of a large wall unit that lined one side of the room. Danielle struggled to reach it. When she finally flicked the button and the music stopped, the room still hummed.

"The amp," he said between breaths. "It's the amp."

An electric guitar leaned precariously against the futon, plugged into an amplifier in the corner. A tiny red light glowed next to a power button. She pressed the button, and the hum died away. Silence filled the room.

Devin held his ear above his father's mouth. "I'm not sure, damn it." He exhaled sharply. "He might be breathing. I'm not sure."

"You're doing great."

He wanted to believe her, but the panic on her face told him she had no clue how he was doing.

He sat back on his heels and tried to fill his lungs. "Where the hell is that ambulance?"

She checked her watch, then tapped the face as if trying to make sure it was still ticking. It wasn't just him, then. She must have noticed how long the ambulance was taking.

As he crouched over his father again, his eyes passed over the carnage on the end table. Empty glasses and a half-full bottle of whiskey littered the top, along with some glassine bags and a spoon. Considering the belt he'd yanked off his father's arm and the hypodermic needle lying nearby, it didn't take a genius to figure out what had happened. The only question Devin had was why.

He pressed his fingertips into the space below his father's jaw. His neck bristled with several days of unshaved whiskers. At least he was still warm. Now if only he could find a pulse.

"It's weak, but I think I can feel a—I don't know. Damn it. I'm not sure." He yanked his hands through his hair and leaned back, linking his fingers together at the back of his neck.

Danielle knelt beside him and placed her fingers in roughly the same spot, then nodded. "I feel it."

A siren wailed in the distance.

She pushed up off the floor. "I'll go let them in."

Devin took a cleansing breath. "C'mon, Dad. Don't do this to us. Please."

He pressed the heel of his hands onto the center of his father's chest, laced his fingers together, and threw his weight into more chest compressions. Voices floated up the stairs, followed by heavy footsteps. A police officer dropped to his knees beside him, opened the small plastic box he was carrying, and snapped on a pair of latex gloves.

"You're a piece of work, you know that?"

Devin leaned back onto his heels, surprised. Then he realized it was his father the officer was grumbling at. The policeman tilted his father's head, checked his airway, then pulled a bag valve mask from the box.

"What happened?" he asked Devin.

Why: That's the question Devin wanted answered. It was obvious what had happened.

"I don't know. I came home and found him unconscious on the couch."

The officer's eyes scanned the room, landing on the items on the table. If Devin had to venture a guess, he'd say it was heroin.

Why?

The officer tipped his father's head back, raised his chin, and fitted a clear mask over his nose and mouth. He held the mask in place with one hand and began to pump the bag with the other. Devin held his breath as if it might help.

After a couple of minutes, the officer paused, took his father's pulse, and listened. He shook his head. Everything about his father seemed gray—his skin, the hair on his face, his lips.

Was he already gone? How the hell would he tell his mother? Jesus.

The officer replaced the mask and resumed squeezing the bag. "Breathe, you sonofabitch!"

A second set of sirens filled the air. Danielle disappeared again. Knowing he would only be in the way, Devin moved toward the door as a paramedic came racing up the stairs carrying a large orange box and a portable defibrillator. An oxygen tank was hoisted over her shoulder. Danielle was right behind her.

"Hey, Digger," the woman said, dropping to her knees. "What've we got here?"

The officer glanced up in acknowledgment but kept working the bag. "He was barely breathing when I arrived. His son was doing mouth-to-mouth and chest compressions, but his lips were still blue. His pulse was very weak. He's got needle marks in his left arm, and judging by the bags on the table"—he angled his head—"it's heroin."

She glanced at the table and squinted slightly, then nodded. She spoke to Devin calmly as she attached a cardiac monitor to his father's chest. "Was he breathing when you found him?"

Devin tucked his hands under his armpits. "I don't know. It didn't seem like it. His lips were blue, so I started mouth-to-mouth. If he was, it was weak. I couldn't feel a pulse, but maybe I was pressing too hard."

"You did good," she said. "Better safe than sorry."

Another EMT entered the room carrying a bright orange stretcher made of heavy plastic and unrolled it next to his father. The addition of three more adults to the tiny room made it feel claustrophobic.

Devin pressed himself against the wall and watched as they rolled his father onto the stretcher. The paramedic began an IV and did a blood stick, explaining as she worked that she was checking his blood sugar. She lifted his eyelid and flashed a tiny light in his pupil.

"Let's push point four milligrams of Narcan," she said to her partner.

The officer continued working the bag.

"You okay there, Digger?"

He nodded.

"Good. Just slow it down a bit. We don't want to hyperventilate him."

Digger grunted but did as she instructed. After she injected the Narcan into the IV, Digger pulled back the mask. She checked his pulse, then shook her head.

Devin felt Danielle's hand brush against his. A lifeline. He wrapped his large hand around her much smaller one and squeezed.

The officer replaced the mask and resumed bagging, counting quietly.

After strapping his father into the stretcher, they navigated down the hallway and the steep, narrow staircase, where they had to lower him almost upright in order to make the sharp turn. Once down, they placed him onto a litter set up in the dining room. The paramedic assessed him again and prepared for a second push of Narcan. Digger continued to breathe for him as she injected the opioid antagonist into his IV.

Seconds later, his father moaned, then he gagged. His head rolled as the EMT tilted the stretcher to the side. Digger reached for the mask, but his father got it first. He tore it off, then vomited forcefully onto the officer's leg and over his shoes. There hadn't been much in his stomach, but whatever it was, it was now all over the cop.

"Jesus Christ!" Digger yelled, jumping back.

Devin felt Danielle begin to titter beside him. She covered her mouth with her hand. If he weren't so frightened, he might have laughed with her.

"Oh, you mother—" Digger cut off when he saw Devin standing beside him.

His father's eyes, glazed at first, stared past the officer right at him.

"Oh, fuck," he mumbled. Then he closed his eyes and sank back against the litter.

The officer stood motionless in the small puddle.

Danielle quickly got herself under control. "I'll get something," she said, rushing from the room.

The paramedics were reassessing his father when she returned with a roll of paper towels and a wet dishrag for the officer. He sponged the wet vomit off his pant legs and shoes, then blotted them with the paper towels.

Danielle motioned to the small, wet pile on the floor. "I'll clean this up."

"You didn't expect me to do it, did you?" he snapped.

Devin looked up. What a jerk.

"No sir." She blinked several times, her big brown eyes tearing up.

There was no need to talk to her like that, and Devin was about to say so, when the paramedics began wheeling his father out of the house. He followed, needing to find out where they were taking him.

When the officer came outside a few minutes later, walking stiffly in his wet pants, he was carrying a plastic evidence bag that contained the syringe, spoon, and the glassine bags, as well as his father's belt. Devin knew the chances of him forgetting the evidence were pretty slim, but he'd hoped that was exactly what would have happened.

His father was mumbling and cursing as they loaded him into the rig. He seemed dazed and incoherent, not quite aware of what was going on around him.

Devin watched as the ambulance backed down the driveway, followed by the squad car. By the time it pulled out onto River Street, the high-pitched, repetitive beep was replaced by the wail of sirens.

"Let's go," Danielle said, coming up beside him. "We'll meet them there."

With no warning, Devin bent over and threw up onto the grass.

"Shit." He wiped his mouth with the back of his hand and waited to see if his stomach would betray him again. He pressed his thumb and fingers against the sting of tears in his eyes, praying he wouldn't humiliate himself even more by crying, too.

"Are you okay?" Danielle rubbed her hand over his back.

"I guess. Sorry."

"Don't be ridiculous. Go wash up. I'll take care of this." She motioned to the small puddle next to the brick walk.

"Don't worry about it."

"Go!" She pointed to the house.

He wasn't about to argue. By the time he'd rinsed out his mouth and locked up, Danielle had buried the contents of his stomach with some dirt she'd scooped out of the pachysandra bed with an empty flower pot.

The ride to the hospital was quiet. Their relationship had moved past the point where they felt it necessary to fill the silence. And really, what could he say? *I hope my dad's still alive when we get there.* Of course he felt that way. She knew that.

When they arrived at the hospital, he checked in at the desk and then settled into a hard plastic chair in the waiting room next to Danielle. "No news is good news, I guess."

"He'll be fine."

"I'm sorry about all this."

She swiveled in her chair so she was facing him. "Please stop saying that. None of this is your fault. Besides, I care about you, Devin—a lot. I'm glad I was here with you. Okay? So please stop telling me you're sorry."

He frowned as he watched a woman argue on a cell phone while her toddler ate spilled corn chips off the stained carpet.

"You know," he said, "I think I've expected this day since I was old enough to understand. You'd think I'd have been better prepared."

"You were prepared. You probably saved his life."

"Mr. Donaldson?" A man in a white coat approached them. "I'm Dr. Bergman."

Devin stood and nodded.

"How about we step in here for a minute?" He motioned to an office off the main waiting area.

Dr. Bergman closed the door and instructed Devin and Danielle to have a seat. He perched on the edge of the desk in front of them.

"The labs confirmed the paramedics' suspicion that it was a drug overdose. The paramedics followed protocol and gave him a couple of doses of Narcan, which counters the effects of the heroin. They were able to revive him before transport, and he remained awake, although he's not alert. Since he's been here, his blood pressure, breathing, and heart rhythms are returning to normal. However, the lab report also showed there were large amounts of cocaine and alcohol in his system."

"Jesus Christ," Devin muttered.

"Is this the first time something like this has happened?"

"I don't know. I guess. I know he smokes pot once in a while. But this?" He threw his arm up. "I don't know what the hell all this is about, if that's what you're asking."

"Not really. People don't usually inject heroin as their first foray into drug use. I meant has he overdosed before."

Devin shrugged. "Don't know. Sorry."

"We can speak to him about that later, when he's sober." Dr. Bergman jotted some notes on a clipboard, then set it down, crossed his arms, and zeroed in on Devin.

"I'm sorry, but I have to ask. Do you think this was an attempted suicide?"

"What? No!" Devin shook his head vehemently. "He and my mom were having some problems, but no way. I don't believe he'd do that. No. He's just an idiot."

The doctor's brows lifted. He jotted a few notes onto his clipboard.

"Since there was such an unusually high amount of drugs and alcohol in his system, and because we can't be certain that it wasn't a deliberate attempt to take his own life, I'm going to insist we keep him overnight and order that he speak with a psychiatrist in the morning. We'll let that doctor make the determination as to whether or not we need to keep him longer."

Devin took a deep breath and nodded.

"We're giving him IV fluids and oxygen, and we'll continue to monitor his vitals. Apparently he became aggressive and threatening in the ambulance, so we have him restrained until we're certain he's calmed down."

Devin winced. That sounded about right.

"Okay, then. We'll need you to fill out the necessary paperwork so we can check him in and—"

"You need to check him in under an assumed name," Danielle interrupted.

What?

"If word gets out he's here, the hospital is going to be swamped with fans. You have to keep this hush-hush."

Dr. Bergman turned to Devin.

"I mean it," she continued, inserting herself between Devin and the doctor. This was a side of Danielle Devin hadn't seen before. "Check him in as Devin Kelly or John Doe or even Eugene Fitzherbert. He'll sign whatever papers you need when he's able, but in the meantime, you have to keep his admission under wraps."

Devin mumbled something in agreement, not quite sure what to say.

"Who is he, if I might ask?"

"His legal name is William Donaldson," she said. "I'd rather not give you his stage name, but rest assured, it would be akin to letting the public know Jon Bon Jovi was here. Do you have the kind of security you'd need to keep people out and protect him at the same time?"

Devin's eyes grew rounder. It was getting harder to maintain a straight face.

"No." Dr. Bergman shook his head. "We really don't."

"Well then. I suggest you keep this as quiet as possible. You especially need to keep the news media out of here. Once they learn he's here . . ." She clicked her tongue. "I hate to think—"

"Absolutely." Dr. Bergman nodded efficiently. "We do have a protocol in place for this. I'll see what I can do. And you are?"

She thrust out her hand. "Danielle Kelly." She gave him a smile and a wink. "Let's just say I work for his manager. You make this happen, and I'll make sure the next time he performs in this area, you'll have front row seats."

"Oh, that's not necessary," Dr. Bergman said, although he looked like he was buying whatever she was selling.

"I insist." She gave him a professional nod. "When can we get him moved into a private room?"

"I'll get on that right away." He stood. "You can wait with him until we can move him. This way, you can make sure no one bothers him in the meantime."

"On behalf of the family and Mr. Fitzherbert, I'd like to thank you for your discretion."

Dr. Bergman led them through the emergency room to his father's bedside, then promised to return shortly and pulled the curtain tight.

Devin stepped closer to the bed. His father was either asleep or passed out. His skin had a grayish cast under his tan, his hair was stringy and tangled, and there were dark smudges beneath his eyes. He was connected to a variety of machines, including oxygen and some type of IV.

The image was jarring. Devin began to feel a wave of nausea just as Danielle's hand closed around his wrist.

It was hard to speak over the lump in his throat. "How long do you think they'll keep him strapped down?" he whispered, not expecting an answer.

"I think it's pretty common in these cases. When they push the opioid antagonist, sometimes patients react violently. I think they get pretty pissed that someone just killed their high."

"Who are you, Ms. Kelly?" He couldn't help smiling.

She slipped her sunglasses off from atop her head and tucked them into her purse. "I read. Plus working a police beat most of the summer, I learned a lot."

"So when did you become an agent, and who the hell is Eugene Fitzherbert?"

"Seriously? Eugene Fitzherbert is the love interest of Rapunzel in *Tangled*."

He had no idea what she was talking about. She rolled her eyes and frowned.

"From Disney? *Tangled?*"

He shook his head again.

"Man, you've led a sheltered life," she teased. "As for the other, I just figured your mother didn't need anything else to worry about right now. I asked the police officer if he could keep it quiet. It turns out he's a friend of your mom's. He said for her, he'd try, but not for your father. He wanted me to make sure I understood that."

That was an odd thing to say. Danielle just shrugged.

"With the drug packets and the needle right out in the open like that, I don't know that they won't charge him, but for now, I just wanted to keep it out of the news. That's why I told the doctor the same thing. I know your dad made some headlines a couple of weeks ago, and I didn't think any of you would want a repeat of that."

"I didn't even think of that. Thanks."

"Don't mention it." She smiled. "I did it for you. And your mom. I hope it works."

So did he. Danielle was right. This was absolutely the last thing his mother needed.

CHAPTER 28

Rhiannon stood over her father. She ran her fingers over his hair and whenever he let her, she held his hand. She had rushed to the hospital as soon as Devin called. He'd sounded scared on the phone, but now he was acting all pissy and pacing back and forth. You'd think it was Dad's fault, the way he was carrying on. Drug overdose? *Gimme a break.* Somebody had probably given him some bad stuff, and as distraught as he'd been over her mother's latest theatrics, he might have been a little careless. That's all.

She had no idea what had happened between the two of them this time, only that her mother had called and left a message the day before insisting that Rhiannon remind her father to have his things moved out before she returned home on Friday. She'd been ankle-deep in bubbles when her phone rang, and seriously, all this drama lately was just getting to be a bit much. She'd let the call go to voicemail and enjoyed the rest of her pedicure. She'd meant to check in with Dad, but the boys had playgroup and by the time they got home, they needed a nap. Then Dena had called, and to be honest, she just needed a break. So here she was, standing over her father in a hospital bed while her mother—well, who the hell knew?

"Daddy," she crooned, leaning closer. Ugh. He smelled, and not in a good way.

She pressed the tip of her finger under her nose. "Do you need anything? Something to drink, maybe?"

Devin snorted. "Yeah, I'll bet he needs a drink."

She shot her brother a dangerous look. He might be over a foot taller, but she could be a whole lot meaner.

"Water. Please." His voice cracked.

Rhiannon reached for the cup on the tray table, bent the straw, and held it to her father's lips. The water seemed to revive him. He sank back against the pillow as his eyes darted from her to Devin to Doug, who sat silently in the corner looking as if he'd rather be anywhere but there.

Then his watery blue-gray eyes settled on hers. "Where's your mother?"

Not this again. He'd woken several times over the past hour, and each time, he did little more than mumble and ask for Kate.

"We haven't called her." She glared at her brother. "Devin thinks we should wait."

"I need your mother." He pushed against the mattress and tried to sit up.

Rhiannon reached for the button and adjusted his position. "We're here, Daddy. Devin and I, and Doug."

"Where's Katie?"

Devin didn't give her a chance to answer. "She's still in New York. We're not calling her, and we're not telling her, so forget it."

"I need your mother."

"What the hell's wrong with you?" Devin demanded, throwing his hands up in the air.

"Daddy, you don't need Mom right now," she said, trying to soothe him while shooting daggers at her brother. "We're here. We'll take care of you."

She tucked the sheet over his chest and sniffed. "Frankly, I don't think she should be here. If she'd been home, this wouldn't have happened. I don't know what's going on with you two, but she can't keep throwing you out every time she gets a bug up her ass."

"Rhiannon," Doug said firmly. "That's enough."

Oh, no he didn't. "Excuse me? That is not enough. My father almost died. She needs to think about someone other than herself. I know she's grieving. We all are. But don't you dare tell me that's enough!"

She took a deep, cleansing breath. Thank God for yoga classes. She turned back to her father and smiled. "You don't need her. You have us."

Devin kicked the foot of the bed. "I'm done," he said, shaking his head. "I don't care anymore. You may be my father, but you don't deserve the title. You're a self-centered sonofabitch who thinks of no one but himself. You want Mom? Fuck you, Dad. I'm not calling her, and no one else better either." He gripped the edge of the bed. "I told them you weren't trying to kill yourself, and I don't believe you were. But I have to ask you this, *Dad*." He pronounced the word as if it left a bad taste in his mouth. "Were you trying to kill Mom?"

The look his father gave him would have frightened anyone else, and if Devin had been a bit younger, he might have hightailed it out of there.

"That isn't even worthy of an answer," her father replied.

In a feeble attempt to break the tension, Rhiannon grabbed the cup of water, sloshing drops of it onto the sheets, and held it to her father's lips. He angrily waved it away.

"Then what's this all about?" Devin asked. "You thought if you OD'd, she'd come running back?"

"It was an accident."

"Don't talk, Daddy," she pleaded. "You're straining your voice. Now, don't get upset. No one's blaming you."

"I am," Devin snapped. "I am most definitely blaming you."

The cup went flying as her father nearly shot out of the bed. "Who the fuck do you think you're talking to? I'm your father. You don't talk to me like that."

"Father?" Devin snorted. "What a joke."

A nurse flung the door open. "What's going on in here?" She folded her arms, looking ready to take on any one of them. "I can hear you all the way down the hall. You've got to keep your voices down, or I'll have security escort each and every one of you out of here."

"I'm sorry," Devin apologized.

Rhiannon echoed her brother's apology. The nurse gave them each a warning look, unimpressed with the unidentified rock star and his family. When her eyes reached Doug, he raised his hands, proclaiming his innocence. Rhiannon glared at him. Traitor.

With one last warning look, the nurse left, closing the door behind her.

"I'm going," Devin said. "I'm sorry you almost died, Dad. I'm sorry your life is so bad you can't handle it without resorting to drugs and alcohol. And I'm sorry I blew up at you, but I can't deal with you anymore. I'm done. You wanna drag yourself down? Go ahead, but you're not dragging me down with you. And for God's sake, stop dragging Mom down too. And if you can't get your shit together, let her go. She doesn't deserve this, and you sure as hell don't deserve her."

He dragged his hand through his hair and let out a loud whoosh of air, as if trying to expel the last of his anger. "You're my father, and I'll always love you, but I don't respect you. I don't think I want you in my life."

Without another word, he turned and walked out.

"Devin!" Rhiannon called after him. When he didn't respond, she turned to Doug. "Go get him! Make him come back and apologize!"

Doug stood but made no move for the door. "I'm sorry, Billy. I know you've been through a lot, but what you're doing is hurting the people who love you. If you don't stop now, it's going to get worse. I hope this serves as a wake-up call."

"Douglas!" she scolded. "You apologize right now!"

He picked up the jacket he'd neatly folded over the chair when he'd arrived earlier and draped it over his arm.

Then his warm brown eyes met hers. "With all due respect, sweetheart, get your head out of your ass."

She sputtered. Okay, maybe she was speechless. Who wouldn't be? Doug had never spoken to her like that, and she wasn't about to start tolerating it now.

While she floundered for a scathing comeback, Doug turned back toward his father-in-law.

"I really hope you'll leave Kate out of this."

She snapped her mouth shut as the door closed behind him. Fine. He could go home and put the twins to bed himself. See how he liked it. Another cleansing breath. She might need two yoga classes tomorrow. Maybe even a massage.

She summoned her brightest smile and turned back to her father, reaching to refluff the already fluffed pillow. She recognized the angry twitch along his jaw.

"Don't you listen to them, Daddy." She brushed an imaginary piece of fuzz from the corner of his pillow. "You didn't do anything wrong. You're dealing with a lot of—"

"Rhiannon, honey." His voice creaked as he spoke. "Please, sweetheart, just shut up."

~

The world outside Billy's room was shrouded in inky blackness. It was late. Or was it early? Not knowing made him antsy. He rubbed his hand over the space where his watch should have been and recalled the feeling of restraints strapped to his wrists. His stomach threatened to let loose whatever might be in there.

The last few days were a blur. He felt like Ray Milland in *The Lost Weekend*, only with better music.

He shivered. Either the air conditioning was turned up too high, or his body was still rebelling. He tugged the waffle-weave blanket up over his shoulder. The sheets were rough, and the pillow crinkled under his head when he moved. He wanted his own bed with the zillion-thread-count sheets and pillows with lumps in just the right places.

More than anything, he wanted Katie.

Through the large window of the private room, he watched the red lights of an airplane slice through the darkness. He pictured Kate standing in Joey's rooftop garden, her face tilted up at the night sky, dark hair tumbling down her back, her arms crossed, holding herself together. His heart tore the rest of the way, and he realized what he'd been doing since everything fell apart: hiding. Numbing himself from the fear of facing life without her.

But trying to kill himself? Subconsciously, maybe. He'd chosen the sweet relief of escape over reality, until that reality had finally reared up and hit him harder than his father ever had. As long as he lived, he would never forget the look on Devin's face when he came to. The mix of fear and disappointment. Disgust.

He'd spent the last twenty years trying to protect his family from his parents. Yet the demons he'd been fighting all this time had sunk their claws into him. As much as he hated him, his father's blood ran through his veins. He couldn't change that. He'd foolishly thought he'd succeeded in keeping his father away, grudgingly writing a check every month, paying his mother's blackmail. But his old man had been with him all along, inside him, waiting to get out. He had become his father—a violent, selfish man, destroying everything in his path.

That Katie loved him had been enough to prove he wasn't the monster his father was. So what had he done? He'd beaten and raped his own wife. He'd become the monster he'd always feared and hurt the person he loved the most.

Maybe he did want to die.

The memory of Joey's funeral flickered in his head, a slide show of black-and-white images. The rest of the day was still a blur. Either he couldn't remember, or he'd blocked it out. But the image of Katie the next morning—hurt, angry, damaged . . . That was burned into his brain.

More sober than he'd been in days, Billy felt the darkness rise up, threatening to swallow him. He was empty. Cold and lost. He wanted Katie. Needed her more than he'd ever needed her before.

It was all too much, and he had no one to blame but himself. Choking on a sob, he buried his face in the cheap, noisy pillow. And when it came, washing over him in great waves of darkness with nothing to stop it, he had no choice but to feel the pain he'd been running from all of his life.

CHAPTER 29

"Let me get this straight," Danielle said, climbing into the front of Devin's mother's Saab. "You're mad at your father and you refuse to speak to him or go visit him, but you're shopping for him so when he comes home tomorrow, he won't need anything."

Devin continued shoveling bags into the back seat of the car. "Something like that."

She smirked. "Just wondering."

He returned the cart and climbed in next to her. "Besides, he can't drive because his license was suspended, so at least this way he'll have some basic necessities. Plus, my mom should be home by the end of the week. I don't want her to have to worry about going to the store or anything."

He'd tried to keep up the impression that he was angry, but he was more hurt and disappointed than anything else. As far as he was concerned, there was no excuse for what his father had done. None.

"You're a good son. Speaking of which, have you told your mother you're not in Colorado?"

His thumbs tapped out a nervous rhythm atop the steering wheel. "I haven't spoken to her other than to text her that I landed. Besides, she thinks I'm out of cell phone range, so she won't even try to call me. One lie is enough. After I drop all this stuff at the house, we can head to the cabin. No one has to know anything. My father won't tell her. He's got his own mess to worry about."

He turned the key and waited for the rag top to open, then slipped the gearshift into reverse. They'd moved only a couple of feet when a truck appeared out of nowhere in his rearview mirror.

"Jesus Christ!" he said, slamming on the brakes.

An old pickup, perhaps once red but now faded to a rusty brown, had stopped directly behind them. The driver, who looked a bit like a deranged Santa, stared down at the car.

"Excuse me!" Devin called over his shoulder, trying to keep the annoyance he was feeling from his voice. "I'm trying to back up."

The man ignored him, as if he had every right to park in a lane of the SuperFresh parking lot.

Devin went to open his door, and Danielle grabbed his arm. "Please don't confront him." She stole another look at the stranger behind them. "He looks dangerous."

"I'm not going to confront him. I'm just going to point out nicely that he's in my way."

Devin's height was usually enough to make people think twice about challenging him, but apparently not this time. The man threw open the door of his pickup and jumped out rather quickly for someone with such a shaggy white beard and hair. A filthy T-shirt covered his thick barrel chest.

"Is there a problem?" Devin asked.

"Yeah, there's a problem." The stranger jabbed a finger at him. "You're the problem. I know who you are, and I'm warning you. Stay the hell off my land."

A crowd was forming a short distance away, but no one seemed willing to get involved. A clerk who'd been gathering carts dashed inside the supermarket.

Devin shook his head. "I'm sorry. I don't know you or what land you're talking about. I haven't been here all summer. You must have me confused with someone else."

The man began to speak but choked out a cough instead. "You're a fucking liar." He gasped several times, wheezing and jabbing wildly at the air. "I saw you. I'm gonna warn you once. Come on my property again, it'll be the last thing you do."

Devin raised his chin, trying not to lose his temper. "Listen to me—"

"Consider yourself warned!" The man coughed up a great gob of phlegm and spit it at Devin's feet. Then he climbed into his truck and sped off, gears grinding as hapless bystanders scurried out of his path.

Devin slid back into the driver's seat and heard Danielle reporting the incident over her cell phone.

"The police are on their way," she said, disconnecting the call.

"You didn't need to do that." He gripped the steering wheel, feeling more unnerved than he wanted to admit. He leaned back and stared up at the blue sky overhead.

As far as he was concerned, he was more than ready for this summer to be over.

CHAPTER 30

Billy wasn't even sure why he was knocking on Eileen Ryan's back door. He'd walked up the driveway to grab the mail, and the next thing he knew, he was knocking on her screen door. He could hear the television blaring in the living room. He knocked again, harder this time.

"Coming," she called.

Her voice sounded far off. This was a bad idea. She was probably in the middle of something. Maybe she was in the bathroom. Jesus. He didn't mean to drag her out of the bathroom.

He was about to call out "Never mind" when the volume on the television dropped.

"I'm coming."

Eileen had been their neighbor since they moved to Belleville. She'd also been Kate's seventh-grade English teacher. Over the years, she'd become like a second mother to Kate—more of a mother and grandmother than Evelyn Daniels had ever been. A widow, she'd retired years ago. Billy guessed she must be in her upper seventies by now.

What the hell was he doing here?

A gray cat meowed at him from the top of the stairs. A few seconds later, Eileen's feet shuffled into view. She swept the cat aside with a slippered foot. "Shoo! Henry, move!" Ignoring her, the cat hopped down the stairs ahead of her.

"Billy!" She unlocked the screen. "This is a surprise."

He hesitated in the doorway. "I don't want to trouble you."

She waved him in. "Nonsense."

He saw her eyes flick across the bruises lining the insides of his arm. They had faded from purple to a sickly yellowish green, but they were still prominent enough to be seen. He pushed his sunglasses up atop his head to hold back his hair, forgetting about the dark smudges beneath his bloodshot eyes until it was too late.

"It's no trouble." She followed him up the steps.

He couldn't remember being in this house more than a couple of times over the past twenty years. Both times, Kate had dragged him there for a holiday drink on Christmas Eve. He wanted to apologize, but really, what was the point after all this time?

"Are you hungry?" Before giving him a chance to answer, she darted into the living room to scoot her cat off the arm of her recliner just as he was about to take a bite of her sandwich.

"I'm sorry." He shuffled his feet. "You were eating lunch. I should go."

"Sit," she demanded. He obeyed. "How about a meat loaf sandwich?"

The thought of food still nauseated him. "No. Thanks." He swallowed the lump in his throat instead. "Have you talked to Katie?"

"Not since the funeral. I imagine she'll be home soon though."

He nodded, still unsure of why he was there. His eyes scanned the kitchen, as if the words he needed might be found in her cupboards or stacked on the drain board.

"Are you okay?" she asked.

It was a reasonable question, although the answer was pretty obvious. It was also more than likely that even if she hadn't heard the ambulance come screaming up the driveway a few nights ago, it wouldn't have taken long for gossip to make its way around town.

"No. Um, Kate doesn't know about the other night."

"That's probably for the best."

"Yeah." He stared at his hands. "I'm moving out. She wants me gone before she gets back."

Eileen lifted a gnarled old hand. It looked as if she were about to touch him, but at the last moment she pulled away. "I'm sorry, Billy. I didn't know that."

"I really fucked up big time." He looked up. "Shit. I'm sorry."

This time she didn't hold back. She reached out and patted his hand. "I agree," she said sternly. "You did fuck up."

Her language caught him off guard, and he couldn't help the smile that tugged at the corner of his mouth.

"What are you going to do about it?"

He played with the fringed edge of a woven placemat. "I think it's too late."

"You're not dead yet, are you? Although it's not from lack of trying."

Billy froze. "I wasn't trying . . ." He began again with more conviction. "I just wanted to dull the pain. It wasn't intentional. I just don't think I can live without her." His elbows crashed to the kitchen table, and he covered his eyes with the heels of his hands.

Eileen slid the wicker basket of paper napkins on the table in his direction. Then she got up and poured him a glass of iced tea.

He crumbled a handful of napkins and hastily wiped his face as she set the glass down before him.

"I'm sorry," he mumbled. For someone who never cried, he was making up for lost time.

"Tell me what happened."

He nodded, but he couldn't seem to begin. He took a sip of the tea and made a face—something bitter and herbal. He set the glass down and ran his thumb over the condensation running down the side.

Then he began to tell her about Miami and getting arrested.

"I already know that," she said, cutting him off. "I also know Kate had been planning on coming home before Joey was killed. She told me she wanted to try and work things out. Something must have changed her mind."

He wrapped his hands around the glass. "I think there's someone else."

It was difficult enough to think it, saying it out loud hurt like hell.

"What?" she said sharply. "You found someone else?"

His head snapped up. Was she fucking serious? "No. I think Katie has someone else."

"Now you're being an ass. What else?"

He frowned. "I'm serious."

"So am I. What else?"

He picked up a napkin and blew his nose. "Like I said . . ." He glared, daring her to contradict him. "I thought there was someone else, and it was eating at me. I had too much to drink at the luncheon after the funeral, and I was getting pissed, so I left."

"I remember," Eileen reminded him. "I was there."

It was one thing to tell someone about your bad behavior. It was another thing to realize they'd witnessed it firsthand.

"I went to some bar in the Village and I ran into some old friends, sort of. One thing led to another. We were partying, you know?"

She nodded.

"I was drinking. A lot. We were doing some coke. I know I did a few lines, more than a few. Then somebody pulled out some crystal meth. I usually don't touch that stuff, but I just didn't give a shit. Everything seemed so fucked up. I snorted that, too. I don't know if that's what pushed me over the edge, but I was just all kinds of fucked up."

He balled up a napkin and threw it onto the table.

"Sorry." He sunk lower into his chair. "I'm turning into a real lowlife."

When she didn't argue, he continued. "I don't remember making my way back to Joey's apartment, and I can't really remember what happened with Katie, but . . . I did something to her. I hurt her."

Eileen's fingers gripped the dish towel in her hands. "What do you mean 'hurt her'?"

"I hurt her." He dragged a hand through his hair and struggled to control his voice. "Physically. I might have hit her, I don't remember." He gulped for air. "And I guess I forced her . . ."

He couldn't even finish the sentence.

Eileen's mouth nearly unhinged. For a second, he thought she was about to launch herself across the table at him.

"How badly did you hurt her?"

He shrugged and shook his head. "Bad enough, I guess."

She twisted the dishrag into a thin rope. "Where is she now?"

"Still in New York. She left a message with Rhiannon to be gone before she comes home."

"Did you put her in the hospital?"

"My God, no. If I'd done that—I couldn't. I can't even imagine." He pressed his fingertips into his eyes, wishing he could erase the image of Kate the morning after. "I would have filled my veins so full of poison there would've been no bringing me back."

Eileen loosened her grip on the dishrag. She set it down on the table, laid it flat, and smoothed her hands over it.

"Why are you telling me all this?"

"I don't know. Because you care about her? Maybe because I want you to know how much I love her and how sorry I am." He shrugged. "Maybe I hope you'll tell her that. I'm not really sure."

She leaned forward until their eyes met. "I'm going to ask you again, Billy: What are you going to do about it?"

His head suddenly seemed too heavy to hold up on his own, so he dropped it into his hands. Tears streamed down his cheeks.

"I dunno."

She reached across the table and wrapped her fingers around his hand. "You know you need help, right?"

He nodded.

"It's hard. You know that too, right?"

Hell, yeah, he did.

"The way I see it, you have two choices. You can get help and get sober—

quit drinking, the drugs, everything. Or you can keep doing what you're doing and destroy everything you've worked for—your career, your family—and in the process, kill yourself and very likely Kate as well. Losing you will kill her."

He shook his head. "Doubtful. She's already finished with me. I told you, she's found someone else."

"And I said you're an ass."

He snorted, and despite everything, he couldn't help but smile.

"Listen." Eileen scooted her chair closer, then took both his hands in hers. "You work on getting your act together. Go to AA. Go to rehab. Do whatever it is you need to get better, and then worry about fixing things with Kate. Show her you're trying. Promise me you'll do that, and I promise to speak with her on your behalf. But I have to see you're trying."

A distant hope bloomed deep within him. "You think she'll listen?"

"I don't know. Since you don't even know what you did, I can't answer that. But I know she loves you. You don't stop loving someone overnight, no matter how stupid they are or how badly they behave."

The sound of gravel crunching floated in through the open screen door.

He stood slowly. "That's probably Rhiannon. I have to finish packing."

Eileen stood as well, even more slowly. He was about to head toward the door but stopped. He bent down and hugged her. "Thank you. I know you love my Katie. Maybe that's why I came to you."

She gave him a quick pat. "I do. Now you go take care of yourself, and I'll see what I can do."

Billy walked up the driveway, his hands jammed in his pockets. He was a pathetic excuse of a husband, and God knows he didn't deserve a second chance. But for the first time in days, he felt a tiny glimmer of hope.

CHAPTER 31

The drive from the train station in Dover was quiet at first. Kate thanked Eileen for picking her up, and they exchanged a few pleasantries. But while she didn't want to appear rude, she was too exhausted, physically and mentally, for conversation. She was content to stare out the window.

But Eileen seemed unusually chatty.

"You know what they say. God only gives us what we can handle."

Kate snorted. "You really believe that?"

"No, but I thought you'd appreciate it." She stole a quick glance at Kate and gave her a wry smile.

"I think I've reached my limit for this lifetime."

"I felt that way when Michael died."

Kate had only been a teenager then, but she knew Eileen's son had died from a drug overdose. "But you survived. I guess I will, too." She let out a long sigh, not sure she actually believed that at the moment.

"You will. I have faith in you. You have strength and grace. You'll come through this—all of it."

Eileen turned onto Kate's long, narrow driveway and pulled up close to the back door.

Now that she was home, the thought of facing an empty house made Kate's stomach turn. When she didn't open the door to get out, Eileen cut the engine.

"You want me to come in with you?"

Kate shook her head. "I don't know. I'm not sure if I want to go in."

"Baby steps," Eileen said, opening her door and climbing out. "Let's go."

The grass had grown several inches while she was gone, and tomatoes had gone bad on the vine. On the plus side, a riot of colorful zinnias greeted her in the flower bed along the driveway and the side of the garage.

Kate loaded her arms with the suitcases and clothing bags from the back seat, then forced herself to enter the home she'd lived in most of her life—the home she would now live in alone. Maybe she should have stayed in New York after all.

The house was quiet and stuffy. Charlie was still at the kennel, and no matter how tired she was, she would need to go get him.

The clock was blinking over the stove. And while there was always the possibility that he hadn't left, had waited to see her, thinking he could somehow change her mind, the blinking clock assured her that Billy was gone.

"He really left?" Kate asked.

"Yesterday afternoon."

She drew in a ragged breath and tamped down her emotions. "Good."

Eileen frowned. "Is that really what you want?"

Kate dropped her purse on the island. "What I want doesn't really matter." She pulled open the refrigerator and was surprised to see it had been freshly stocked. How could that be?

"Maybe you should give him a chance. Listen to what he has to say?"

Kate turned slowly. "You spoke to him?"

Eileen's shoulders lifted into a guilty shrug.

"When?"

"He came to see me yesterday."

Kate snorted. "Only took him twenty years."

"Be that as it may, he still came to see me."

"Why?"

"He's hurting."

"It's his own fault if he's hurting. He did this to himself."

"He knows that."

Kate's mouth dropped open. "Are you defending him?"

"I'm just telling you what I observed. He's hurting and he's sorry. Look, sweetie, I didn't mean to bring this up now."

"But you did mean to bring it up some time?"

Eileen shrugged and nodded.

Unbelievable. "Did he tell you what he did?"

"Not really. It seems he doesn't know the extent of it himself."

"No!" Kate said, her voice rising. "No, he doesn't, because he was so drugged out on something he turned into an animal!"

"Are you okay?"

From the look Eileen gave her, Kate might as well have just told her Billy had accidentally knocked her over in the schoolyard. Memories from that night closed in on her. Fear, anger, feeling helpless and betrayed. Eileen didn't have a clue.

"No, I'm not okay!" she snapped. "I don't know if I'll ever be okay."

"Of course you will. You're angry and hurt."

"I'm a lot more than angry and hurt."

The past two weeks had left her feeling like she'd been run over by a freight train, and she was trying hard not to give in to it again. She reached into the cabinet and pulled down a wine glass. Eileen didn't drink. And even if she did, Kate wasn't in the mood to invite her to stay.

"Did he tell you everything?"

"I told you he doesn't remember much."

"How convenient for him." She yanked open the refrigerator again. Of course there were no open bottles of wine. Billy would have polished those off his first night home. The champagne she'd bought to open the night of her birthday was still buried in the vegetable bin, where it could stay. Nothing to celebrate here.

She slammed the door so hard two magnets fell to the floor. "But what about the rest of it?"

Eileen shrugged. "I don't know what you mean."

Kate checked the wine rack in the dining room. Empty. What the hell? Had he thrown a party?

"I figured as much." She folded her arms across her chest and steadied herself. "Did he tell you he cheated?" Saying it out loud was like getting punched in the stomach all over again.

"Er, no. He didn't mention that."

Kate squeezed her eyes shut and pressed her fingertips to her temples. "I can't do this now." She took a breath deep enough to dislodge the weight that had settled on her chest. "I love you, and I thank you for picking me up, but I can't do this right now. I can't think about him. I have to unpack and go get Charlie."

And if I'd like a glass of wine to help me sleep, I'll have to stop at the goddamn liquor store as well.

Eileen pulled her in for a hug. "I didn't mean to upset you. You know I'm here for you, right?"

"I know." She already felt guilty for her little tirade. "I didn't mean to get short with you."

"Not at all. Do you want to come for dinner tonight?"

"Thanks, but no. I'm just going to get Charlie and go to bed early. I want to sleep in my own bed. I have a lot to catch up on tomorrow, and then I have to get ready to go back to work on Monday."

"Already?"

"Afraid so. I got two weeks off because of getting my name in the paper when Billy was arrested. And then I took a week's vacation after"—she swallowed—"you know. I have to go back to work, or I don't get paid. I'm really not in a position to lose my job." This time her voice did break. "I've already lost everything else."

Eileen squeezed her arm. "This too shall pass. You'll see."

Kate's eyes burned, but she refused to give in. She'd cried enough for two lifetimes.

"Yeah. We'll see."

CHAPTER 32

Tom held a bottle of shiraz in one hand and chardonnay in the other. He gave her a pathetic little smile.

"I didn't know what you were making, so I brought red and white."

Kate led the way into the kitchen, then put the white wine in the refrigerator. "I say we have the chardonnay with the salad and the shiraz with the steak."

While she searched for a corkscrew, Tom set his briefcase on the dining room table.

She eyed the expensive leather satchel. "If you were planning on a working dinner, Billy's not here. And I don't want to talk about him anyway."

Tom ran his hand over the back of his neck. "This has nothing to do with

Billy. Besides, he fired me."

"What?" Her mouth dropped. "Why?"

"I didn't talk to him. Doug called me yesterday. He apologized but said Billy was terminating my services and that his firm would be taking over his defense. Personally, I think that's the right move, but I still don't like getting fired."

"I'm sorry. I had no idea. We . . . we haven't spoken." She lifted her white canvas apron off a hook, slipped the strap over her head, and fastened it around her waist. "Actually, since you no longer represent Billy, maybe you can represent me."

He chuckled softly. "Why? Were you arrested, too?"

Chin up, just say it. "No. You can handle my divorce."

He dropped onto a stool next to the island. "You can't possibly be serious."

She reached into the basket on the counter and plucked out two ripe tomatoes.

"I am," she said, picking up the knife that had almost landed her in jail for domestic assault and running it through one of the tomatoes "I want a divorce."

Saying it out loud was a lot harder than she'd expected. It felt as if an elephant had backed into her and sat on her chest.

"It's kind of sudden, don't you think?"

Her mouth twisted into a strained smile. "I don't think Joey would've said that."

"I think he would."

"Hardly. He'd be popping the champagne by now."

"I don't know, Kate." He plucked a green olive from a tray on the counter and popped it into his mouth. "Joey may not have been Billy's biggest fan, but he understood how much you two loved each other. The sacrifices you made to stay together."

"If he were here now, he'd change his mind. Besides, I'm the only one who was making sacrifices, it seems."

"Maybe not."

"Trust me. The only sacrifices Billy ever made were the ones that benefited him."

Tom opened his mouth to speak, but she waved the knife, cutting him off before he had the chance to disagree.

"Let's not talk about it, okay?" She wiped her hands on a dish towel and forced a smile. "I want to talk about you and Joey. I know it's hard, but I want to know what he never told me." She struggled to keep her voice steady. "I need to know he was loved."

Tom's face softened. "He was. Very much. And you're right, I do need to talk about him. It's killing me, having to act like I only lost a casual acquaintance and a client, nothing more."

Some of the leftover pieces of her heart splintered. She set down the clove of garlic she'd been about to smash with the flat of her knife. She wanted to hear stories about Joey and Tom; needed to become familiar with another part of Joey that she could keep tucked inside her, next to their shared memories. But to do so, she was going to need a little help.

"How about something stronger while the wine chills?"

Tom nodded enthusiastically. "Martini?"

"All that was left in the liquor cabinet when I got back were some liqueurs and a bottle of vermouth, so while I was out today, I picked up a bottle of Ketel One." She pulled it from the freezer, as well as a large jar of olives from the refrigerator.

Tom mixed up a pitcher of dirty martinis and carried it out to the patio. Kate followed behind with the steaks and a platter of grilled shrimp with a sweet and spicy remoulade. Some people ate when they were stressed; Kate cooked. And with everything going on in her life, she wouldn't have been surprised to find out she was on the fast track for her own cooking show on Food Network.

While the steaks sizzled on the grill, Tom told her he and Joey had been together for years. The revelation hurt, more than just a little.

She speared two olives and slid them into her mouth.

"It was my fault he never told you," Tom said apologetically. "He begged me to let him. All the time."

"I never knew he could actually keep a secret." She remembered how close he'd come to telling her this very thing the day before the shooting.

Tom twisted the stem of his glass as he spoke. "I met Stephanie at Notre Dame. We dated for a while. Of course nothing came of it. Then after graduation, we drifted apart. I went to law school, and she went home to Chicago."

"But later when my parents learned my college girlfriend was single and living nearby, they pushed me to resume the relationship. I couldn't tell them I was gay, so I went along with it, again thinking nothing would come of it. Then her parents started pushing too, and it just got easier to do what they all wanted and get everybody off my back."

He drained what was left in his glass and poured himself another.

"Sounds like an episode of *Downton Abbey*."

"Indeed it does, Lady Grantham," Tom replied in his best aristocratic English. "I tried to make it work, but I just couldn't be close to her that way. I think she was actually relieved. We agreed to be discreet with our relationships outside the marriage. In fact, she took it so well I suspected there was someone else—or many someone elses. But to be honest, I didn't care. The only thing she was upset about was not being able to have a child. So we decided to adopt."

He skewered another shrimp, dipped it in the remoulade, and took a bite. "As for me and Joey, we reconnected about six years ago."

She nearly dropped her glass. "Reconnected? What do you mean, *re-connected?*"

Even in the waning light, the flush creeping up Tom's neck was visible.

"We had a little thing in high school."

"Shut up!" Kate's mouth dropped. "High school? How did I not know any of this?" Had there been any hints she'd missed somehow? High school? That was a million years ago. She wasn't sure if she was more shocked or hurt at being kept in the dark about something that had been so important to Joey.

"Did anyone know?"

"Not on purpose, but Joey's father caught us." Tom's complexion continued to deepen. "Together. That's why he threw him out. I took a summer job in South Bend right after that, mostly because I was afraid of running into his father or his brothers. I was also terrified the old bastard would go to my parents."

Joey had shown up under her window around midnight the night he'd graduated. She snuck him upstairs, where he told her he'd had a fight with his father and was leaving for New York in the morning. He vowed he would never set foot in Belleville again. He had come back, for her at least—and maybe Tom, who knows?—but he'd never gone to see his family again. At least not that she knew of.

Of course, it was painfully clear now that in some aspects of Joey's life, she knew very little.

"He told me he'd confessed to his father that he was gay and his father had thrown him out," she said. "He never said anything about being discovered."

Tom twirled his glass so hard several drops landed on his hand. He didn't seem to notice, staring across the yard as if watching the scenes from that night play over again. "He'd planned to tell him and expected the same reaction. After that, and his father chasing me out of the house, I never had the guts to tell my parents. It's not that I think my father would come after me with a baseball bat, but I'm fairly certain if he didn't drop dead initially, he'd disown me."

Kate didn't believe that for one second.

"What?" he asked. "You're looking at me the same way Joey did."

That made her smile. "Your parents might be a little shocked, but drop dead? Your father is an intelligent, thinking man. He's known a lot of people in his career, and I bet quite a few have been gay. I'm sure he knows they're no different than anyone else. So no, I don't believe he'd drop dead or disown you."

Tom's face shifted as he struggled with his emotions. "Don't you see? Even if you're right, I can't tell them now."

"Why?"

"Because if I couldn't do it while Joey was alive, what right do I have to do it now? I have no right to live openly. I forfeited that when Joey died."

She took his hand and held it across the glass-topped table. "That's ridiculous. I think he'd be proud of you for finding the courage."

"No. Besides, you're forgetting something."

Her gums had begun to feel pleasantly numb, thanks to two quickly downed martinis, so if she was having a hard time following his reasoning at this point, it wasn't her fault.

"Stephanie. If I humiliate Stephanie by coming out, she'll use that against me to take Lian. If that happens, then I would truly have nothing to live for anymore."

Kate rested her chin in the palm of her hand. "Oh, we're a fine pair. Both of us with so little to live for."

Tom nodded.

"Well," she gave him a weak smile, "until we get our shit together, how about we just live for each other and worry about the rest when we feel like it?"

He saluted her with an olive-skewered toothpick. "Sounds like a plan."

After dinner, which included both bottles of wine, Tom built a fire and they sat around the fire pit gazing up at the stars. It was very possible she might even have dozed off once or twice. Her brain was so foggy—something she was definitely okay with.

"We do have other business to talk about," Tom said, interrupting the murkiness, his face glowing orange in the firelight.

He had to be kidding. "What business?" She wasn't capable of discussing any business of any kind.

"The will. We have to set up a reading of the will."

"The will?" She squirmed deeper into her lawn chair. "I'm drunk. I don't want to talk about that right now."

"I understand, but you may not realize the extent of Joey's property and business dealings. It's substantial, Kate."

She shrugged impatiently. "He seriously didn't expect me to deal with any of that, did he?"

"Maybe not, but he also didn't expect to die at forty-three."

How could he possibly be lawyering right now? She wasn't even sure she'd be able to stand and walk back to the house.

"Can't we please put it off for a while?"

"Yes, but there are decisions to be made that affect other people, remember? There are employees with families and bills to pay."

"Can't you just do the reading or whatever and just let me deal with my part when I can manage it?"

"No—because everything goes to you."

She sat bolt upright, a lot more sober than she'd felt a minute earlier. "That's crazy. What about you?"

He laughed. "Now how would I explain that? It's all yours, Kate. But for the time being, as executor, I can manage things for you."

She hadn't even wrapped her head around Joey's death yet, and then there was the implosion of her marriage. And now she was supposed to run a multi-million dollar business? What the hell had Joey been thinking?

"Can you?"

"Do you mean am I capable?" Even in the firelight, she could see she'd probably insulted him.

"I know you're more than capable. I mean are you able? Emotionally?"

His face softened, and he stared into the fire for a few moments. When he looked up, the lawyer was gone. "I know what it meant to him, and I know what he wanted—so yeah, I can do that for him and for you."

"Make sure you pay yourself." She felt guilty for dumping her responsibility, but there was no way she could deal with it. Not tonight, that was for damn sure.

"That's worked out in the will, but I'd do it for nothing if I had to."

Thinking it was all settled, Kate leaned back and resumed stargazing.

"Before we end this topic—for now, that is—I want you to know Joey took very good care of you."

"Tommy, please, I really can't think about th—"

"Just listen. File it in the back of your mind if you must, but listen. Financially, you'll be very well off. There are some properties: the loft in Tribeca, of course, and there's a cottage up in Maine . . ."

The delicious numbness she'd felt earlier was evaporating. She squeezed his hand. "I don't want anything, Tommy, but for life to go back to the way it was a month ago. I'll bet there's nothing in your little Prada briefcase that will do that, so for now, please let's drop it. I truly can't listen to one more word."

CHAPTER 33

The patter of rain on the roof made it that much more difficult for Kate to get out of bed. It was soothing, and God knows she needed to be soothed.

How was she supposed to go back to work? She hadn't been able to concentrate long enough to read more than a paragraph in a book these past couple of weeks. How could she be expected to actually write something?

She lay there, head throbbing, heart aching, and recalled what Tom had said about the will. For a split second, she thought about calling him and asking him to define "substantial." Then she threw back the covers. She would never feel right accepting it. Better to just get up and go to work. Be an adult.

Of course, an adult would have made sure she had something to wear for work the night before instead of waiting until morning. She'd been avoiding her closet. The empty rod where Billy's clothes used to hang was too painful to face.

It wasn't any easier this morning.

She grabbed an armload of dresses and jackets and slid them across the bar. It still looked pathetically empty. No matter how hard she tried, there were reminders everywhere that he was gone. Little ones, like his World's Greatest Dad coffee mug, and big ones, like his truck in the driveway, snuggled up to her Saab.

"I know." She took off down the hall, her robe fluttering behind her, to retrieve her winter clothes and evening dresses from the closet in the music room. They would fill the rod, at least, if not the empty space echoing inside her.

The door to Billy's sanctuary had been closed when she'd come home, and she'd left it that way. If she'd thought the empty closet was hard to face, Billy's missing instruments and the photos and other memorabilia there would be even more difficult.

"Here goes nothing."

She took a deep breath and pushed the door open slowly. It wasn't as bad as she expected, mainly because almost everything was still there. The Martin was gone, as was the Strat, but the other instruments still hung in their places. The photos and album covers still lined the shelves.

It looked no different than if he'd been on tour.

"Son of a bitch," she muttered.

If she were being reasonable—which was unfair to expect at this point, wasn't it?—she knew there was no room for his things at Rhiannon's other than the finished basement. As much as she loved her daddy, Rhiannon wasn't about to disrupt her household with an assortment of boxes, instruments, and amps. Billy probably expected to leave everything where it was until he found another place to live. Damn him!

She could even smell him; that warm, spicy scent of lemongrass, and something else, uniquely his own. She inhaled deeply. Probably marijuana. She should open the window, air the room out. It was hard enough not to think about him. The last thing she needed was to keep smelling him. As soon as it stopped raining, she would open that window. In the meantime, she'd stay the hell out of there.

Forgetting the reason she'd gone in there in the first place, she was about to leave, when she spotted an envelope on the shelf leaning against a framed picture of Billy and Jimmy Page. Her name was scrawled across the front. Just seeing his handwriting caused her stomach to tie itself in a knot. How dangerous would it be to actually open it? She stared at it for a few more moments, then reached out cautiously as if it might burn or bite her.

She slipped her finger under the flap, and tore it open.

My dearest Katie,

I'm sorry. There are no words to explain or justify what I've done. I just need you to know that after all these years, you still own my heart. There has never been anyone else. You are still my passion and my madness, and even if I never see your beautiful face again, I'll love you long after I take my last breath and well beyond the end of time.

Always and forever,

Billy

The note slipped from her fingers and floated to the floor as a dam broke loose inside her. How was it possible to still love him after everything he'd done?

~

Kate was an hour late for work. She'd thought about calling in sick, but she had to go back sooner or later. Might as well get it over with. The door to the elevator slid open, and she stepped into the newsroom. It was worse than she expected. She trudged past a dozen desks to her cubicle in the far corner. They all meant well, but hearing a dozen *I'm sorrys* was difficult.

She dropped her purse into her bottom drawer and sat. The first thing she saw was the photo of Billy accepting his Grammy award. She slammed it down so hard the glass cracked.

She mumbled a quiet *sorry* of her own to the heads that had turned in her direction and scraped the photo, frame, and broken glass into the trash while her computer booted up. The phone rang as she waited for the servers to load. The caller ID said JOHN SULLIVAN.

Shit. She put on a businesslike tone. "Newsroom. This is Kate."

"Could you step into my office? Er, please?"

Click.

'Please'? Likely an afterthought, a nod to her grieving, reserved for only when absolutely necessary. She smoothed her palms over the front of her navy Lilly Pulitzer dress—an ironic gift from Joey, who said it was the only Pulitzer she'd ever receive—and headed for the glass-walled office at the back of the newsroom.

Linda kept typing, her head down as Kate passed. "That was quick," she whispered.

Kate's voice was equally low. "I hope he fires me."

"Close the door," Sully said, his sixth sense somehow knowing she was there even though he hadn't turned around. He picked up the phone, motioned for her to sit, then held up his finger as a signal for her to wait. Did he want her to wait before sitting down or just wait?

"Daniel!" he barked into the phone. "Where's the story on the driver ID law? That should have been filed ten minutes ago. If that's not in the system in three minutes, you'll be writing obits for the rest of the year."

He slammed down the phone. "Sit!" he demanded, then reeling it in a bit, added, "Please."

He rose and closed the door she'd left open.

Why couldn't he just fire her? She needed the money, but she couldn't deal with this right now.

"I'm sorry about your friend," he began in a moderated tone that sounded sincere, if not exactly warm. "Joey, right?"

"Yes. Thank you."

"I understand you were very close."

She chewed the inside of her cheek, fighting a nervous desire to laugh in the face of this unexpected response.

"And I understand you're having some issues at home."

Rolling her lips together, she nodded. "Yes, sir."

"Well." Sully cleared his throat as if being nice was a difficult task. He fumbled with some papers on his desk. "I'm glad you're back. It's understandable that it will take you a few days to get caught up, to right your ship, so to speak, so I'm taking you off all assignments for the week. Catch up on your email, get your feet wet, whatever." His continued use of clichés confirmed his discomfort. "If you need to leave early for the next few days, that's fine. Just let me know. Next Monday, however, I expect you back at one hundred percent though. You got it?"

She nodded. Thank heaven for small miracles.

It turned out a low-key week was exactly what Kate needed to try and "right her ship." Sully seemed almost human toward her for the rest of the week. Although she never asked to leave early, he sent her home each day around noon.

She kept herself busy working in the garden. She even had time to put up several batches of tomatoes and raspberry jam, as well as a batch of sour cherry jelly. Her counters and pantry held the fruits of her labors, sparkling with dozens of jars of jewel-toned distraction—more fruit than one person could ever hope to eat.

She wasn't doing well, but she was surviving.

Eileen stopped over early in the week and invited her to dinner. Kate had no interest in round two, but she didn't want to disappoint her friend.

They made small talk over the meal, but clearly there was something on Eileen's mind. She'd unveil it sooner or later. Hopefully later. Much later.

"Have you heard from Billy?" Eileen asked as she cleared away the remnants of a bland, somewhat dense macaroni and cheese. Eileen wasn't much of a cook. Her high blood pressure ruled out the use of salt, so her food was often tasteless, but Kate appreciated the gesture.

"No. To his credit, he's leaving me alone."

"You're not even curious how he's doing?"

Of course she was, but she'd never admit it, especially not to Eileen. "Not really," she lied. "Anyway, Doug stopped by this week to check up on me and said he's fine."

"Fine?" Eileen's eyebrows shot up over the rim of her glasses.

She ticked off Doug's comments like items on a shopping list. "He's trying to get sober. He's not eating or sleeping well. He's also devastated. Other than that, he's fine. Okay?"

"Am I okay?" Eileen gave as good as she got. "I'm fine. Are you okay?"

"Yes. Fine."

Eileen humored her like a spoiled child. "Come sit in the living room."

Kate followed reluctantly. She was about to sit in the wing chair across from Eileen's recliner, but Eileen bypassed it, moved to the couch, and patted the cushion beside her.

"Next to me. I want to show you something."

Several photo albums lined the coffee table. Inwardly, Kate groaned. She didn't want to look at old photos. Even though it was only Eileen, socializing was too draining right now. She just wanted to go home.

Eileen picked up the first album and flipped it open. The pages were yellowed, and most of the photos were black and white. Scraps of paper marked the pages. Eileen flipped to the first one.

"This is Michael when he was two."

Eileen's son had a sweet, pudgy face and bright eyes. His hair was styled into a miniature pompadour.

The corners of Kate's mouth lifted. "He's adorable."

Eileen beamed at the compliment, then picked up another album.

"This is Michael in high school." She flipped to the next marked page.

Tall and handsome, he stood between Marty and Eileen wearing his Belleville Lions basketball uniform. The ball he held proclaimed that he'd scored one thousand points.

Eileen ran a finger over the photo.

"Athletic, too," Kate said. She had a similar picture of herself and Devin, who had also been a standout high school athlete. Billy had been on tour when their son hit his milestone.

Eileen nodded. "And smart. He went to Lehigh for engineering. Did you know that?"

Kate shook her head.

"Here's the last picture I have of him." Eileen pulled out another album. Michael stood next to a Christmas tree, looking nothing like the young man in the earlier photos, especially not the proud teenager. He wore a faded flannel shirt, and his hair was long and stringy. A cigarette dangled from his lips. He squinted as if he'd just woken up. The transformation was startling.

Kate found herself struggling for something to say. "He looks . . . different."

"Believe it or not, it was hard to notice at first. The change was so gradual. He started smoking, which was the biggest shock for me. He'd always been so health-conscious. When he'd come home from college, he'd rarely see any of his old friends. Looking at pictures, the change is dramatic. In real life, it was much more difficult to see."

Eileen snapped the album closed, put it on the coffee table, and turned toward Kate. "My son had a drug problem."

"I'd heard that."

"He needed help, help we couldn't give him. It was easier for us to scold or threaten, to stick our heads in the sand. He promised he'd stop, and we believed him because we wanted to. But he didn't. It had a grip on him stronger than anything we could've imagined."

Why Eileen felt the need to bring this up, Kate had no idea. Michael had died over twenty-five years ago.

"He stole from us when he came home that Christmas. He took my engagement ring and my mother's pearls. He took his father's golf clubs. Even the television from the rec room downstairs. He pawned it all for money to buy drugs."

"That must've been hard for you."

She shook her head. "It was a lot harder burying my son." Eileen's bright blue eyes bore into Kate. "It would have been easier to call the police and have him locked up. Force him to get the help he needed, rather than to put him in the ground."

Kate wanted to look away, but she couldn't.

"Your husband is an alcoholic, Kate, and he has a drug problem. You have your head in the sand like I did. He needs help, and you and your family don't want to see it."

Kate's anger started to rise. This whole invitation had been a setup. "Yes, Billy has an issue with drugs. I'll be the first to admit that, but he's not an addict. He can control what he does. He chooses not to."

"Do you really believe that? Do you really believe that he was of sound mind when he did whatever it was he did to you the night of Joey's funeral? That it was a choice?"

Kate stiffened. "That was different. He said he took something he hadn't used in a long time. He didn't do it on purpose. He would never—"

"So you're defending him?"

"Of course not!"

"Then you're defending his right to use drugs?"

"No, I didn't say that either."

"What *are* you saying?"

"I don't know." Why was Eileen attacking her? She hadn't done anything wrong. She was the victim. "I don't know what I'm saying."

"Let's look at more pictures, shall we?" Eileen gave her a gleaming smile, moving on as if that last flurry of words hadn't happened.

"I have to go." Kate stood. "I'm tired, and I don't want to do this anymore."

"Sit down." Eileen used her best junior high teacher's voice, then continued as if they were having a pleasant afternoon chat. "This is Marty and I on our wedding day."

Kate dropped back onto the couch.

"Beautiful." She was too damn polite, that was her problem. She should get up, and go the hell home.

Eileen showed her more photos: coming home from the hospital with Michael, dancing cheek to cheek at Marty's company Christmas party, standing suntanned and relaxed on the deck of a cruise ship at sunset.

"They're all very nice, Eileen. You and Marty had a wonderful marriage. I'm sure you miss him very much." She meant it, even though her voice wasn't exactly conveying much sincerity.

"I do. And you're right. We had a wonderful marriage, but it was far from perfect."

How much longer did she have to suffer through this trip down Memory Lane? Eileen had always been as sharp as a tack, but maybe she was beginning to suffer from a bit of dementia.

"This cruise here," Eileen tapped the last picture. "We flew to Miami and sailed to the Bahamas to celebrate Marty's retirement. While we were there, he told me about Arlene, his secretary. They'd been having an affair for several years at that point. Since the time Michael died. Arlene had been eager to comfort him, give him an escape. When he tried to end it, she threatened to expose him. Instead of giving in, he decided to retire and come clean with me."

Kate's throat went dry. She'd never seen Eileen and Marty exchange a cross word, let alone argue. He'd always been attentive and loving.

"What did you do?"

Eileen gave her a funny smile. "Well, I told him I thought the whole thing was a little too on the nose, and that I would have expected him to be a little more creative. I mean, seriously, his secretary?"

Kate didn't see the humor.

"I also told him I'd known from the beginning, and then I forgave him."

"You knew?" Her mouth dropped. "You knew and you never said anything? You just let it go on?"

Eileen nodded.

"Why?"

She took a deep breath. "Because we'd made a promise to one another, and just because one of us broke it didn't mean we both had to break it. I knew he felt helpless after Michael died and probably more than a little guilty. Arlene had known him long enough to see the same things. She took advantage of his state of mind. I'm not saying it didn't hurt, because it did. It hurt like a sonofabitch."

"So why didn't you stop it then?"

"Because I knew how much he loved me, and I knew eventually he'd come to his senses. And he did. It took longer than I expected, but I think in part that was my fault."

"Your fault?" Kate sputtered. "You're not serious?"

Eileen laughed. "It was my fault because toward the end, he was being careless. He wanted me to find out. He was feeling guilty, and he wanted me to lash out at him because he believed he deserved it. I wouldn't give him the satisfaction." She looked quite smug when she said this. "I wasn't going to punish him. He would have to do that himself."

"I suppose you're telling me this because you think I should forgive Billy for cheating?"

"Not necessarily."

Exasperated, Kate slumped against the sofa cushions, the less than palatable macaroni and cheese forming a hard knot in her stomach. "You're confusing the hell out of me."

Eileen chuckled. "I'm sorry, kiddo. I just wanted you to know that you're not alone. These things happen every day, and you can come out on the other side in one piece."

She took Kate's hands in her dry, papery ones and held them tightly.

"You're a survivor. You've been through a lot and you're still standing. You're a strong woman, sweetheart. Billy? He's big and sometimes maybe even a little scary, but he's weak. He's at the bottom right now, and I don't know if he's strong enough to climb back out on his own. I just want you to think about that. I know you've had an awful lot thrown at you all at once, and none of it's fair, God knows. But you can grab hold of the things you can control and fix what you can, if you choose to."

Kate tried to keep her voice steady. "I don't think it's that easy. He not only hurt me physically, which I never thought possible. I thought he loved me much more than that. But even with time, if it was drugs and he got help, maybe at some point I could forgive him, but this . . ." She shook her head. "I don't think so. I try not to think about it. I keep myself busy during the day, but when I go to bed, no matter how exhausted I am, I close my eyes and there they are. I see them together, and it makes me sick to my stomach."

"You know who this woman is?"

Kate nodded, wiping angrily at the tears that had begun to fall.

"I know of one. But I'm sure if there was one, there were more."

"Did you ask?"

Ask? Eileen couldn't be serious. Billy was always surrounded by women before and after gigs. He was a good-looking man, and a talented one at that. Of course there were women throwing themselves at him every night. But she'd trusted him. God, she'd been so stupid! Just knowing that he and Christa had been intimate was more than she could handle. To know for certain there had been other women over the years as well? Safer for her to just assume he'd been consistently unfaithful and try and move on. She didn't need or want confirmation.

"No, and I'm not going to. Don't you think I've been hurt enough?" With that, Kate stood. "I'm really beat. Thank you for dinner and for sharing some difficult stories with me. I'll think about what you said. I promise."

She wrapped her arms around her friend and kissed her cool, dry cheek.

"Do you want some macaroni and cheese to take home?"

"I have plenty of food in the house that will go bad if I don't eat it. It was delicious, though."

"Oh Kate, sweetheart," Eileen said with a laugh. "You're such a terrible liar."

CHAPTER 34

Between getting up to speed at work, helping Devin finish packing, and driving him to school Wednesday night, Kate had plenty to keep her mind occupied. It had been good having him home, even if just for a couple of days, but now she had to face her new life. Her new normal. Just her and Charlie. She'd heard nothing from Billy, and even though she'd threatened to report him to the police if he contacted her, she hadn't expected him to listen.

It's not that she wanted to talk to him or see him. She didn't. She couldn't, not after what he'd done to her, what he'd told her. And it wasn't like she'd never been alone before. He was often gone for long periods of time. It's just that this time, she was really alone. And it hurt. A lot.

She'd driven Devin back to school after work the night before. The ride was long and surprisingly quiet. She'd expected him to use the time to try and convince her to work things out with his father, but he'd apologized for being tired, slipped in his earbuds, and napped the entire way. Normally she would have scolded him for being rude, but this time she welcomed it. She tuned in to NPR and listened to Terri Gross interview an author on his new novel about a man mistakenly committed to a mental hospital. The topic was disturbing, but at least it kept her mind occupied and off her own worries.

The two-hour trip to Williamsport passed quickly; the ride home, not so much. It was after midnight before she climbed into bed, and it seemed like mere minutes later when the alarm clock went off at five. By the time she got home that afternoon, she was dragging. If not for the meeting to cover that night, she would have gone straight to bed. She set the alarm for six and fell across her bed, hoping for at least an hour's nap.

When the phone rang just before seven, Kate grabbed her alarm clock, disoriented and thinking it was morning and that she'd overslept. Which was exactly what she'd done, only it wasn't morning. When she'd set the clock, she had failed to change it to evening, rather than morning, and might have slept through the entire meeting if a telemarketer hadn't called to try and sell her on a vacation share in the Poconos. She barely had time to comb her hair and brush her teeth before rushing out the door.

At least nothing ever happened in Washington Township. She'd be lucky if she got anything more to write about than Sedge Stevens's usual outburst. Even that seemed unlikely. According to Sully, although Stevens had called the newspaper after her story ran and had written a profanity-laced letter to the editor, he hadn't shown up at the last meeting. Eight months of causing a ruckus at every meeting, and the first one she hadn't covered, he'd been a no-show. Maybe he'd finally wised up and agreed to clean up his property.

About a dozen cars filled the lot at the municipal building. Kate's usual spot near the door was taken, so she eased her Saab into a spot alongside the building, grabbed her purse and her backpack, and headed inside.

She slipped into a seat at the back of the room next to Eileen. "What're you doing here? You didn't tell me you were coming."

"I was beginning to wonder if *you* were," Eileen answered, offering her cheek for Kate to kiss. "My nephew said they're supposed to discuss that new subdivision ordinance, and if that goes through, I'm thinking of putting that piece of land up for sale in the spring."

Eileen's husband's family had once owned hundreds of acres in Washington Township. Most of the parcels had been sold off over the years, and her nephew Stan and his wife Lora were the only family members still living in the township, but Eileen had been holding out.

"You should've called me. I could've told you what happened, or you could've just read tomorrow's paper."

"Eh, I don't get out enough anyway. I had dinner at Stan's, so I was nearby. Oh, hey!" She dipped into her oversized purse and pulled out a pint jar of bread and butter pickles. "Lora sent these for you."

Kate loved Lora's pickles, and she'd been after Eileen for years to get her the recipe. "Oh, thank you! I made a batch over the weekend, but mine never come out as good as hers. Any luck getting me that recipe?"

"I'm working on it." She gave Kate a critical once-over. "By the way, you look like crap. Are you sleeping?"

Trust Eileen not to mince words.

"I'm hanging in there."

"Tell you what. If these numbnuts don't drag this thing out too late, I'll buy you a cup of coffee."

"Thanks, but—"

"Okay, I'll buy you a cocktail." Eileen winked. "You drive a hard bargain."

Kate gave her a weak smile. "A cocktail might be just what the doctor ordered." She pulled out her notebook and fished around the bottom of her backpack for a pen.

"Have you heard from Billy?" Eileen asked.

Just hearing his name hurt. "Eileen, please."

"I'm just asking. Have you thought about what I said?"

Kate set her backpack on the floor, with the jar of pickles on top of it. "I'm trying not to think about anything. And before you ask, he hasn't contacted me, either, so he's in no hurry to fix anything—not that what he did is fixable."

"Maybe he's just doing what you asked, respecting your wishes."

"Respect? After what he's done, respect is the last thing he's given me." This conversation might actually make her head explode. She stood. "I'll be right back. Could you watch my stuff?"

Eileen called her name as she left the room, but Kate kept walking. If she didn't take a minute to calm down, she'd say something she knew she would regret. Thinking about Billy upset her, and Eileen knew it. Why did she keep pushing?

Kate paced the long hall leading to the secretary's office and a conference room, then darted into the ladies room, where she wet a paper towel and pressed it to the back of her neck and forehead. After a few cleansing breaths, she felt her pulse tick down toward its normal level.

Maybe she should start doing yoga. Rhiannon swore by it.

She tossed the paper towel into the trash and glanced at her reflection. Eileen was right. She looked like crap. Her lack of sleep was glaring under the harsh fluorescent lights. Dark moons were visible beneath her eyes. She leaned toward the mirror; although some of that might be smeared makeup from her nap.

She was reaching for another paper towel when she heard a sharp crack. There were several more, followed by the sound of breaking glass. Someone screamed.

Kate froze. The exit door at the end of the hall banged open. There were several more loud cracks.

Fireworks? That made no sense. But if it wasn't fireworks, the only other thing it could be was gunshots.

Forcing her legs to move, Kate darted into the farthest stall and locked the door. She climbed onto the toilet, where she gathered her legs beneath her. The gunshots continued on the other side of the wall that separated her from the meeting room. There were loud, heavy thuds, shouts, and more screams. What the hell was happening?

The motion-sensitive light in the bathroom turned off. If she stayed still, it would stay off. But her body was shaking so hard. She tucked into herself, squeezing her arms around her legs to keep them still.

A man shouted. More gunfire. Muffled cries seeped through the wall. The emergency exit was located just outside the bathroom, and if the shooter was in the meeting room, she might be able to slip out—

The door to the bathroom was kicked open, and light flooded the room. A scream filled her throat. To silence herself, Kate bit down on her forearm.

The taste of blood filled her mouth. Bullets ricocheted off the floor and into the metal divider. Shards of tile and pieces of mirror and porcelain skittered across the floor. She bit down harder. To move, to cry out would get her shot.

The footsteps moved away, but before the door closed with a soft thud, Kate heard the wail of a lone siren. A few moments later, the light went out. She allowed herself one deep breath.

There was another rapid burst of gunfire from the hall.

Clinging to her perch and afraid to move, Kate mentally made the sign of the cross and began whispering the Lord's Prayer as more bursts of gunfire erupted outside the room. A random barrage of memories played in her head. She closed her eyes against the darkness of the room and let them embrace her: The wonder on Rhiannon's face when she found Easter eggs tucked into her bunny's hutch when she was five; how excited Devin was when he hit his first homerun; the Christmas mornings when the two of them would run for the tree, padding softly in their footed pajamas; Rhiannon being crowned homecoming queen; Devin's high school graduation. And of course, Billy.

They had been together for more than half her life. He'd been her life. This wasn't how it was supposed to end. She'd meant it when she told him she never wanted to see him again.

Yet at this moment, he was all she wanted.

The muffled sound of sirens pierced the walls. There was more gunfire. More footsteps. She wanted to cry. She wanted out. She wanted it to be over.

The door to the bathroom banged open.

"Police! Is anyone in here?"

Don't scream. Don't move. Her mouth was filled with blood; she'd bitten through her lip.

The door to the first stall banged open.

What if it isn't the police?

"Identify yourself!"

Heavy-soled black boots were visible beneath the door. She couldn't breathe.

"Answer me! Who's in there?"

Her voice was frozen in her throat. She made no sound. She couldn't. She made the sign of the cross and covered her face as the door crashed open.

CHAPTER 35

Chances were pretty good he was going to lose his mind. All Billy could think about was how much he missed Kate and how badly he needed a drink. Instead, he was stuck in fucking suburbia, miles from anything, watching a goddamn Phillies game.

If he knew what the twins had done with the remote, he'd change the damn channel. It had been well over thirty-five years and baseball still made the hair on his arms stand up and his need for a drink even stronger. And either there was no alcohol in the house, or Rhiannon had done a damn fine job hiding it.

Until he was ten years old, Billy had eaten, slept, and breathed baseball. He had been a pitching phenom and a Little League starter wherever his father was stationed, right up until the day his father had beaten him nearly to death for fucking with his prized Babe Ruth autographed baseball.

Billy had been raised by his grandparents after that, and while he'd never seen his father again, his mother made an appearance every now and then. He hadn't seen her in twenty years, not since the night she showed up after a gig and convinced him that if he didn't go along with her wishes—to send her money each month—his father might show up on his family's doorstep the next time Billy was out of town.

He didn't trust his mother, not for a second, but he knew there was one thing about her he could count on: greed. As long as he kept paying, she and his father would stay away. Being on the road away from Katie and the kids as much as he was, that monthly check bought him peace of mind. It was worth every cent, but it wasn't cheap. He kept careful track of those payments. Over the past two decades, he had paid his mother close to a quarter of a million dollars. But his wife and children had remained safe, and as far as he knew, neither of his parents had been anywhere near his family in all that time.

Occasionally, his mother would remind him of her existence: the odd postcard, an email wishing him a happy anniversary, a short voicemail message "just to say hi." But last night? Last night, she had taken a step unprecedented even for her. In the midst of all the other shit he was going through, she had chosen last night to text him.

"Nice going, genius. Seems u let ur fists do ur talking just like ur father. Not too smart. Just make sure u figure out a way to honor our understanding before they haul ur ass off to jail or you'll be sorry. Love JJ"

If he hadn't held out hope that Kate might eventually have a change of heart and reach out to him, he would've smashed the phone against the wall or crushed it under the heel of his boot.

JJ. Jessie Jones. What a joke. The alias was supposedly her stage name. What she did on a stage, he could only imagine. It was probably her way to keep from being traced to the checks he mailed her each month.

He was living in the Third Circle of Hell. Fuck Dante. Fuck everybody.

Just one drink. He could live without coke. And smack? That was just stupid. He could probably even pass on weed.

He just needed a little something to take the edge off.

Maybe he'd take a walk. It had to be cocktail time somewhere. He could drop in on a neighbor, introduce himself. Someone might offer him a beer, maybe something stronger. Saliva pooled at the back of his throat.

He fingered a guitar riff along the top of his thigh. He thought about heading to the basement, taking out one of his guitars, but his hands were shaking so badly he was afraid he wouldn't be able to play. If that were true, it would send him over the edge for sure.

He had to get out of there and walk. If he came across some friendly neighbors, all the better.

He made it as far as the patio door.

"Daddy?"

Damn it.

Rhiannon came down the front hall flashing him a smile, his smile—the one she used to charm her way out of things, or into things, just like he did. "The boys want you to kiss them good night."

Billy dragged his fingers through his hair and forced a smile. "Sure thing, honey."

He was screwed. Once the boys were asleep, Rhiannon would focus all her attention on him, at least until Doug came home for his turn to watch Druggie Daddy.

Billy opened the door to the nursery. The twins were all but done in. They blinked at him sleepily from their matching cribs, smelling of baby shampoo and dreams. The smiles peeking out from behind their pacifiers tugged on his heart. He planted a kiss on each head and sat on the rocker to sing an old Scottish lullaby, one his grandmother had taught him. Before he'd finished the second verse, they were both sound asleep.

He pulled the door closed and quietly slipped down the hall. If he could get downstairs and to the front door without Rhiannon seeing him, he might still be able to sneak out.

She called out to him just as his foot hit the last step.

He swallowed a groan and rounded the corner toward the family room. Rhiannon stood facing the sixty-five-inch TV. At least the game was no longer on.

He painted on their trademark smile. "Amazing how they look so peaceful when they're asleep, yet they're such little hellions when they're awake."

She turned to him, her eyes wide and fearful.

"What is it?" he demanded. "What happened?"

The screen behind her showed an aerial view of amassing emergency vehicles and a kaleidoscope of red and blue lights.

"A shooting." She motioned to the television. "In Washington Township."

"Wow. That's hitting a little close to home."

"Daddy! It happened at a meeting."

What was he missing?

"Mom covers those meetings."

He felt the color drain from his face.

She held up her cell phone. "I called her phone, but it went right to voicemail."

Frozen, Billy watched the footage from a news helicopter hovering over the scene. Uniformed officers and the state police SWAT team swarmed about. Police cars and ambulances filled the parking lot. More fire trucks and cars with flashing lights lined the long driveway leading from the road.

The crawl across the bottom of the screen said multiple people had been shot and several were believed dead. It wasn't known how many people were in the building, and there was no information yet on the shooter or shooters.

He stepped closer, as if by sheer will he could spot Kate in the chaos.

"Give me your keys."

"No. Doug will be home soon. He'll take you, or I can. Just wait."

"Give me the goddamn keys! Now!"

He spotted her purse on the counter and lunged, knocking it over. Lipsticks and pens rolled onto the floor. He fished the keys from the pile of makeup, pacifiers, and credit cards and bolted for the front door.

It usually took forty minutes to get to Belleville. With any luck, he could cut that time in half. He raced along the back roads, his mind moving even faster. Every lousy thing he'd ever said or done replayed in his head. This couldn't be happening, yet the images from the screen were seared into his brain, the line of ambulances and fire trucks, the flashing red and blue lights of all those police cars.

Just like the ones gaining on him in the rearview mirror.

"You have got to be fucking kidding me!" Billy pounded his fist against the steering wheel. He glanced at the speedometer. He was doing close to seventy. The Volvo could easily handle a hundred, and he was only minutes away from the municipal building. He stepped down harder on the accelerator.

He crested a hill to two cruisers straddling the road before him, lights blazing. Shit! He pumped the brakes and the car slowed, but not nearly enough. He pressed the pedal to the floor. The car fishtailed to the right and skidded partway off the road in front of the cruisers.

The officers from the blockade stood behind their squad cars, guns trained on him. An officer in the vehicle behind stepped out, his gun drawn.

Billy raised his hands to shoulder level. This wasn't his first rodeo; he knew the drill.

The officers in front took a few cautious steps.

"Exit the vehicle," demanded the officer who had been tailing him. "Slowly. Keep your hands where I can see them."

Billy opened the door, then raised his hand again. "Look, officer—"

"Out!"

He did as he was told and turned to face the car. Within seconds, he was thrown up against the Volvo while the first officer patted him down. He couldn't see the others, but with at least two high-powered rifles trained on him, all he had to do was hiccup and it could all be over.

CHAPTER 36

Kate's body went boneless, and she crumpled. The officer lowered his rifle and was able to catch her before she hit the floor.

"You're safe," he said, propping her up. When she was certain her knees wouldn't buckle, he led her out of the stall, then lowered her to the floor, kicking shards of glass and tile out of the way with his foot.

"I'm Officer Hayden," he said, squatting down beside her. "This is Officer Kotter." He pointed to the officer standing in the doorway. "We're with the Washington Township Police Department."

Kate began to shake so violently her teeth chattered and pain shot up her spine.

"Are you okay?" the officer asked. "Are you hurt?"

She shook her head. "D-did you get them?"

He pinched his lips together. "Them? You saw more than one shooter?"

"N-no. I didn't see anyone. B-but there had to be more. There were so m-many shots. And I heard them. In t-the hallway."

"We're certain there was just the one shooter, ma'am." He held out his hand. "Do you think you can stand? We'd like to get you outside. Maybe have one of the EMTs look you over."

Kate hesitated. She didn't want to stay in there, but she also didn't want to get shot. "Maybe we should stay here. Until you're sure."

Officer Hayden leaned closer, bringing his eyes level with hers, close enough for her to see he'd missed a spot on his chin while shaving. "We're sure. I wouldn't take you out of here unless I knew for certain you'd be safe. Will you trust me?"

Trust? No, she didn't trust him, but she didn't have much choice.

When she nodded, he draped his weapon over his shoulder and helped her to her feet. Her legs continued to shake, making it difficult to stand.

"Just lean on me. Think you can walk?"

"I-I think so."

When they reached the door, Officer Hayden looked down at her. "Kate, I want you to close your eyes and keep them closed. I'm going to guide you."

"Why do I—"

"Ma'am, please. Just let me guide you. You don't want to see this."

She nodded and squeezed her eyes shut, even though her mind had already began to paint a picture of what was out there. They moved slowly, Officer Hayden leading her down the hall, his warm hands gripping her upper arm and waist. It was uncomfortable, and although she assumed she was surrounded by police officers, she felt exposed and vulnerable.

There were others nearby. A foot scraped across the carpet as someone moved out of their way. Static crackled through police radios. Emergency workers called orders to one another. Sirens heralded the arrival of more help, and a steady, staccato rhythm overhead announced a helicopter was about to land.

Kate held so tightly onto the officer's arm, she must be hurting him. They inched forward and the sounds coming from outside grew louder. A warm breeze brushed her face as they neared the door.

"Stop," Officer Hayden instructed. "We're going to move a couple of steps to the right now."

Rattled and disoriented, Kate moved to the left instead, stepping on something soft and pliable. As she lost her footing, her eyes flew open. She'd stepped on a hand. A hand that belonged to a man lying in the hallway, surrounded by a pool of blood. He should've yelled, pulled it away. But he didn't. He just lay there, not moving.

"Don't look," the officer demanded.

But it was too late.

The walls opposite her were riddled with bullet holes and splattered with blood. Beyond that was the entrance to the meeting room. Bodies were strewn about, chairs were overturned. There was blood. Everywhere.

She could see the corner of the metal chair where she'd been sitting. The tan cloth Coach bag Rhiannon had given her for her birthday last year was darkly stained, its contents dumped onto the floor. A bloodied arm was draped across the chair; its familiar fingers gnarled with arthritis. Kate's cell phone lay on the floor, crushed, as if dropped from that hand. Shards of broken glass winked at her, swimming in a pool of blood and pale green onions, mustard seeds, and cucumber pickle slices.

She sucked in her breath and turned. The entrance was just a few steps away, but it was still too far. She doubled over and vomited.

CHAPTER 37

Sharp pain separated Billy's shoulder blades as the butt of a rifle jammed into his back. A second officer patted him down. As soon as he recovered his breath, Billy spoke.

"Please. I need to get to my wife. She was at that meeting in Washington Township."

"Shut up!" The officer commanded. "Put your hands behind your back."

"You don't understand. My wife—" He wasn't sure if he was going to cry or spin around and choke the sonofabitch who'd jammed the gun into his back.

The officer yanked his left arm down and started to cuff him.

"Wait!" The officer who had remained by the blockade called out. "Damn it—Billy? Is that you?"

Billy squinted into the headlights of the two squad cars. It was hard to see with the spotlight trained on him.

"Yeah?"

"What the hell are you doing?" Digger demanded, stepping toward him.

This could either go very badly or work in his favor. "Kate was covering that meeting. She's not answering her phone."

"Which meeting?" Digger's response was measured.

They all knew exactly which meeting, but sarcasm wasn't going to help Billy now. "Washington Township. You've got to let me go."

"Uncuff him," Digger yelled. "This is Billy McDonald."

"No shit? From Stonestreet?" the third officer asked.

Digger grumbled under his breath.

Billy shook his wrist after the handcuffs had been removed. He reached to open the door to Rhiannon's Volvo, but Digger held it closed.

"What do you think you're doing?" he asked. "First of all, you're under suspension. Second, you're driving like a fucking maniac, and you're gonna kill yourself or someone else." He held out his hand. "Gimme the keys. I'll take you."

Billy had no choice but to trust him. It was either that, or risk getting shot if he tried to continue on his own. He tossed the keys to Digger, who handed them off to another officer. He gave the officer Rhiannon's contact information and climbed into the passenger seat of Digger's squad car.

"Buckle up," Digger said, slamming his foot down on the accelerator.

The cruiser raced along the two-lane highway, picking up speed on the straightaways. As they crested the next hill, Billy could see lights on the horizon. A helicopter circled overhead, and the road before them was clogged with thrill seekers.

They reached the first checkpoint, and a state trooper waved Digger through. Squad cars and emergency vehicles lined the road. A state police SWAT team truck sat at the entrance to the driveway, and officers decked in protective gear milled about. Fire trucks lined the perimeter of the parking lot, their bright lights trained on the building, which sat in the middle of a cornfield, giving the scene an eerie sense of day. A row of ambulances were parked closest to the building. Billy had been on several video shoots, and if he hadn't been desperate to find Kate, he would almost have believed this was just another production. It was that surreal.

Digger eased the squad car along the roadway and parked not far from an area designated for the media and guarded by two state troopers.

Looking for an opening, Billy launched himself out of the cruiser and into the crowd. But before he could work his way in, Digger grabbed him by the arm and whirled him around. Billy might have had several inches on him, but the sonofabitch was strong.

"You trying to get yourself shot? You go running up on a crime scene like that, that SWAT team will shoot now and not bother asking questions." Digger let go of his arm slowly, as if he didn't trust Billy not to bolt. "Stick with me and let me handle this, or you're going to find yourself in either an ambulance or the back of a squad car."

Digger was probably right, but he'd better get answers—and soon.

Digger shouldered his way through the crowd, and Billy followed close behind. They reached the yellow tape cordoning off the entrance to the driveway, and Digger addressed a trooper holding a clipboard.

"This man thinks his wife was at the meeting. Kate Donaldson?"

The trooper glanced at Billy and shook his head. "Nobody gets through."

"I understand, but could you just check on Mrs. Donaldson?"

The trooper leaned forward, shaking his head and speaking low enough that only Digger could hear.

Bullshit. He wasn't waiting. Billy backed into the crowd of reporters and photographers, then ducked behind a fire truck. When he was away from the bright glare of the spotlights and certain no one was looking, he ducked under the yellow police tape and headed toward the bank of ambulances, careful to stay away from the action.

The first ambulance was empty. So was the second.

No one paid him any attention. The police and paramedics went about their grisly tasks.

The third ambulance was also empty. His heartbeat drowned out all the other sounds around him. What if they were all empty?

He jerked a hand through his hair, his fingers tangling in the elastic that caught it into a sloppy bun. Angrily, he tore it out and jammed the band into his pocket. He kept moving. Past the powerful lights that had been set up to illuminate the scene. Police officers combed the grass and shrubs. A heavily armed SWAT team stood nearby.

Determined not to be caught, he ducked between two ambulance rigs.

Windows along the front of the building had been shot out and holes blown into the shiplap siding. The doors had been propped open. From where he stood, Billy could see a body in the vestibule. A man's body. An arc of blood splattered the walls behind him.

Billy's chest ached. His heart felt as if it might explode.

What if Kate was still inside? He pressed his open palms against his temples.

"Katie!"

Fear and desperation filled his voice. It was foolish to call out, and running would also bring attention to himself, but he had to find her. Struggling to slow his feet, he approached the next ambulance.

"Katie!"

When he opened his mouth to call out again, he heard her, over the static of walkie-talkies, the drone of helicopters, and the pounding of his own heart.

Wrapped in a white blanket, surrounded by a halo of artificial light, Kate stood outside the last ambulance, calling his name.

CHAPTER 38

If he held her any tighter, Billy was afraid he might snap her in half.

"Are you okay? Are you hurt?" He leaned back far enough to see for himself, then crushed her against his chest before she could answer. Other than a swollen bottom lip, she looked distraught, but whole.

"Oh God, Katie. I don't know what I'd do if I lost you." The words stuck in his throat like bits of broken glass.

"Take me home," she mumbled into his chest. "I don't want to be here."

"Are you sure you're all right?"

Wrapped in a blanket and held tightly in his arms, she was unable to move. She angled her head toward the building. "They're dead."

He relaxed his grip, but only a little. She squirmed until a hand slipped free.

"Eileen's dead. There was a lot of blood." She choked on a sob. "And the pickles. Lora's pickles were all over the floor."

It was hard to understand her, but there was no mistaking the anguish on her face.

"Mrs. Donaldson?" A small woman with a soft voice, a paramedic, approached Kate. "Can I check you out? We want to make sure you're okay."

Kate grabbed a handful of Billy's T-shirt.

"I'm right here. I'm not going anywhere."

Billy guided Kate into the back of the rig, then climbed in and sat in the captain's chair behind the litter after she lay down. She immediately reached up and laced her fingers with his.

"My name's Joni," the paramedic said as she slipped a blood pressure cuff over Kate's upper arm. She checked her pulse, her oxygen level, and when she seemed satisfied that Kate was physically unharmed, she instructed her to rest. "I want to make sure you aren't going to pass out again, okay?"

"You passed out?" Billy asked.

Kate rolled her head back so she could see him and shrugged. "I guess."

"You don't remember?" He looked at the paramedic.

"She fainted a little while ago while Detective Butler was speaking to her. He caught her before she hit the ground."

Fainted. She only fainted. It could have been worse. He cupped his hand under her chin and bent to kiss her forehead.

"Kate? Can I speak with your husband outside for a second?" Joni asked.

Kate's grip on his hand tightened.

"I'm not leaving you. I'm just going to move to the end of the gurney, okay?"

It wasn't easy navigating inside the back of the rig at six foot four, but he did his best, never breaking physical contact. When he reached the end of the litter, he sat and tucked his hand around Kate's knee. An EMT climbed into the seat he'd just vacated and did her best to distract her.

"Your wife's been through a horrible shock. Physically she's fine, but there's no telling how this will affect her psychologically. She might want to see a counselor to help her process what she's been through. I don't think we need to take her to the hospital unless she wants to go."

"She wants to go home."

"That might be best. But if she becomes hysterical or does anything out of the ordinary, you may either want to take her in or call 911. She might need a sedative if she starts to get worked up."

"I'm pretty sure we have something at the house." He glanced at Kate. The EMT was telling her a story about going to school with Devin. "Her best friend was killed a few weeks ago. The doctor gave her something then."

"Oh, man." Joni shook her head and sighed. "She may have a rough time ahead of her. Be prepared." She slipped the stethoscope from around her neck and stood. "I think Detective Butler still wants to speak with her. I'll let him know I gave her the all clear. Oh, and you may want to put some ice on her lip to bring down the swelling."

Billy ran his hand up and down Kate's calf while she listened to the EMT. Usually, when someone spoke to her about one of their kids she would practically gush with pride. Now, she stared up at the girl as if she didn't recognize the language she was speaking.

"Mr. Donaldson?"

Billy assumed the man standing outside the rig was Detective Butler.

"We're going to let your wife go, but we'll need to talk with her again tomorrow. We'll have someone call you in the morning to arrange a time for the investigators to come to your house. She's been through enough tonight."

"Ya think?" Billy didn't know who to be angry with, but he wanted to hurt somebody. This cop was as good as anyone.

"We believe she's safe," he continued, ignoring Billy's comment. "Township police neutralized the shooter, and we're almost one hundred percent certain he acted alone."

"Neutralized? What the fuck does that mean?"

The detective gave him a sharp look. "It means he's no longer a threat—to anyone."

"Who? Who did this?"

"The suspect's name is Sedge Stevens. Apparently he's been in some kind of confrontation with township officials." He lowered his voice. "We also think it's possible he was looking for Mrs. Donaldson, in addition to the committee members he shot."

Billy gripped the gurney so hard his knuckles turned white. "Whoa, whoa, whoa, back up. Why the hell would this guy be after Katie?"

"She claims she didn't know him. Said she only wrote about him. He must've known her, though, because he shot the hell out of her car."

The sautéed squash and tomato salad he'd had for dinner was threatening a comeback.

"We don't have many answers yet," the detective continued. "Unfortunately, we won't have a lot of help here. We'll do what we can. We'll be talking with the editors at the *Examiner* as well, see if Stevens made any threats toward Mrs. Donaldson or the newspaper."

Billy gripped the edge of the gurney. That fucking job.

"Try to keep quiet around her. She may or may not want to talk about it. I think it would be a good idea if she didn't make any statements to her colleagues right now."

"She won't be talking to any members of the press. That's for damn sure."

"I'll have the ambulance bring you to your vehicle. It's best if she doesn't walk through this."

Billy raised a hand to his forehead. "Shit, I don't have a car. The Belleville chief brought me. Digger—hell, I don't even know his real name."

"Dave." Kate had obviously been listening. "Dave Johnson."

The detective nodded. "I'll see if Chief Johnson is still here. If not, one of my officers will take you."

He took a step closer to Billy and motioned for him to do the same.

"And Mr. Donaldson?" He lowered his voice. "You ever walk onto a crime scene of mine again, I will personally see to it that you find yourself behind bars right quick. You understand?"

He stared down at the detective. "Yes, sir. And as long as my wife isn't on the other side of your yellow tape, you'll have nothing to worry about."

~

The ambulance pulled up to the end of the secured area, but they would still have to walk a short distance past a horde of photographers, cameramen, and reporters in order to get to Digger's squad car.

Billy settled his sunglasses on the bridge of Kate's nose. "Keep these on.

No matter what."

She nodded, her face somber.

The doors of the rig swung open. Lights blinded them, and cameras and microphones swiveled in their direction. In some sick way, it reminded him of climbing out of a limo at an awards show.

Billy jumped from the rig and reached for Kate. Her fingers dug into his shoulders, but she didn't move. He plucked her out, then held his arm up to shield her from the cameras.

"Keep your head down and hide your face," he said, covering her as best he could. Digger protected her on the other side.

Someone called her name from the pool of reporters. They already knew who she was? Billy looked up to see a man waving frantically.

"Ignore him," Billy said, feeling her hesitate. "Just keep moving."

When they reached the squad car, he helped her into the back and climbed in beside her.

"C'mere." He held up his arm and she slipped beneath it. Where she belonged. He brought his other arm around, encircling her.

"You're safe now," he whispered into her hair. Closing his eyes, he pressed his lips to the top of her head and breathed in her citrusy scent.

In the back of a cop car, on a night of such mayhem, and with Katie in his arms, it felt like he was finally going home.

CHAPTER 39

The house was dark except for the porch light over the back door. Digger climbed out, scanned the back yard, then motioned for them to get out.

"Do you want me to check the house?" he asked Billy.

"I don't think it's necessary, do you?"

"Nah. They're pretty certain Sedge acted alone. He wasn't smart enough or friendly enough to have a conspirator. He was just a crazy old bastard who'd been pushed into a corner. Sad thing is, I don't think anyone believed he was this crazy."

Billy helped Kate from the car. He was unlocking the back door when he heard the crunch of gravel. Someone was coming up the driveway, and they were clearly in a hurry.

"Get inside, and stay there," Billy said as he opened the door.

Digger activated the lights in his squad car and stood beside it. The driver pulled his compact car behind Digger's cruiser and opened the door.

"Stay in the car," Digger ordered.

The driver rolled down his window. "It's okay. I'm a friend of Kate's. I just need a quick statement. Tell her it's Danny."

Billy recognized the guy who'd been calling to Kate at the scene.

"Get him the fuck out of here." he told Digger.

"Move along, buddy. Kate's not talking to anyone tonight," Digger said.

"Just tell her it's me. She'll talk to me."

"Not tonight," Digger said.

"I have a deadline. I need to talk to her now. She should know that." One foot hit the driveway.

"Unless you want to be arrested for trespassing, I suggest you close that door and back yourself right down this driveway."

The dude didn't budge. "Look. You tell Kate she needs to give me some kind of statement. I was ordered by our editor—her boss—to get something for tomorrow's edition. She can give the rest of her story to them tomorrow, but I'm not leaving without a comment."

Fists curled, Billy started toward the car. He was going to bust this clown's head open. Kate called to him, but he was too far gone.

"I'm gonna give you two seconds to get the hell off my property!"

"I got this, Billy," Digger said firmly. "Go take care of Kate."

The little shit grabbed a camera off the front seat and snapped a photo of Billy coming toward him. "You let me talk to her for one minute, or I'll run this photo and the story we buried about you and your latest arrest, pal."

The guy looked smug right up until Billy grabbed one of the bricks that edged Kate's herb garden and threw it at his back window, shattering the glass.

"You sonofabitch!" Danny cried.

"Get in the house!" Digger ordered.

The only voice that registered was Kate's, calling from the doorway. "Billy, please."

He wanted to yank this chubby, snot-nosed kid right through his broken window, to take out all the anger and frustration of the past few hours and beat him to a bloody pulp.

Instead, he took a few deep breaths to let his heart rate return to normal, and crossed the patio toward the house. Digger radioed for backup, pulled out his ticket book, and wrote out a citation for trespassing. Billy stood in the doorway while Danny argued with Digger about pressing charges for damages until the punk finally got into his car and drove away.

"I'm going to post an officer at the end of the driveway so no one else tries to bother Kate," Digger said.

"Thank you."

"You okay?"

Billy pressed his hand against his neck and rubbed his fingers against the knotted muscles. "I'm fine, but you can just arrest me when the next maggot shows up, because I'm likely to kill him."

"Calm down. You'll be no help to anyone in prison. Lock the doors and take the phone off the hook. You got it?"

There were two ways Billy knew to calm down, and he'd been trying hard not to do either of them. Actually, three—although he was pretty sure sex was off the table now as well.

"I'll check back in the morning. Anybody shows up, just call 911. There'll be an officer nearby."

⌒

Billy stood in the kitchen after Digger left. He'd walked the dog and made sure the doors and windows were locked.

"How about some tea?" he asked. "Sleepytime, right?"

Kate nodded.

"Go sit. I'll bring it to you."

She took a step toward the dining room but then chose a kitchen stool not far from where he was filling the kettle.

"I'll have some, too," he said, although what he really wanted was a big glass of Jack Daniels. Maybe a whole bottle. "Sleepytime all around."

He forced a smile. Kate just stared.

He pulled two cups from the cupboard and dropped a tea bag into each one. Then he plucked a lemon from a bowl on the counter and held it up. She shook her head, and he put it back.

"Sugar or honey?"

"Yes, please."

"Honey, it is."

When the kettle began to whistle, he poured boiling water into the cups and placed Kate's in front of her. She looked at it as if she wasn't quite sure what to do with it.

"I need to call Rhiannon," he said. "I'm sure she's worried sick."

"Yes, please," Kate said, strangely polite. "And Devin."

He couldn't say much to Rhiannon or Devin with Kate sitting there. And while they both wanted to talk to her, he promised them tomorrow would be better. She wasn't herself. Clearly. There was no reason to worry them any more than they already were.

He hung up and noticed Kate hadn't touched her tea.

"Is there anything else I can get you?"

She shook her head.

"Let me bring it upstairs. You can drink it in bed." He didn't wait for a response, since he really didn't expect one. He picked up the mug and guided her to the stairs, then followed her to their bedroom.

Kate turned on the overhead light, the table lamps, and the light in the bathroom. Then she stood in the middle of the room as if not sure what to do next. Her face was blank, but every now and then she winced.

He could only imagine what was going on inside her head.

"Do you want me to help you get ready for bed?"

Her brows furrowed, and she nodded. He set the mug on the nightstand and led her into the bathroom.

The first thing he did was find the tranquilizers the doctor had prescribed when Joey died, and was immediately filled with guilt. There were only three pills left. He'd taken more than half of them himself, and now Kate needed them. He filled a glass with water and handed her the pill. She didn't even ask what he was giving her.

He closed the lid on the toilet and guided her down. Then he took a cotton ball from the jar on the counter and soaked it with makeup remover.

"Close your eyes." He lifted her chin and gently removed what was left of her eyeliner and mascara, first one eye and then the other. He ran a washcloth under warm water, pumped some of her face cleanser onto it. He lifted her chin. At least a dozen freckles were scattered across the tops of her cheeks and the bridge of her nose. She hated them, but he loved every single one.

He stared at her for so long, she opened her eyes. He smiled down at her. "I was just thinking how beautiful you are."

She watched him, unblinking, until he lifted the washcloth and washed her face.

When he finished, he pulled her blouse over her head and placed it on the edge of the tub. He removed each of her shoes and placed them by the door. Then he helped her stand and unbuttoned her pants, holding onto her as she raised each leg so he could remove them.

She was like a little girl, and it frightened him. He unbuckled her bra and gently slipped it off. He trailed his fingers over her shoulders. She shivered. He had taken her clothes off hundreds of times, but never like this. There was passion, but it wasn't the white-hot, sexually charged kind he was used to. An angry, murderous rage filled him now, tempered with fear.

He reached behind the door where Kate usually kept a nightgown, but all he could find was one of his old chambray shirts. He held it over her shoulders, and she slipped her arms into the sleeves.

As he buttoned the shirt, their eyes met again. The bright gray-green had dulled, as if someone had slammed and bolted the doors to her soul. He circled his arms around her and held her close. Her arms dangled by her side.

"C'mon. Let me brush your hair."

He guided her to the side of the bed and reached for the brush she kept on the nightstand. With each stroke, a tear rolled down his cheeks. He'd long passed one hundred, but he kept brushing until her shoulders curled forward and her body tilted. The tranquilizer was working. He lifted the covers, and she obediently climbed into bed.

"Do you want more tea?"

"No. Thank you."

"Okay. I'm going to get ready for bed."

He hurried through his bathroom routine and was glad to see his toothbrush still in the holder next to hers. The face staring back at him in the mirror had aged ten years since morning, and that was after fighting to stay sober for two weeks.

Kate was still awake when he came out. He turned off the bathroom light and sat beside her.

"Do you want me to stay with you?"

"No. I'll be fine." She was struggling to keep her eyes open.

It hurt, but he hadn't expected her to say anything different.

"I'll be down the hall if you need me." He kissed her forehead. Her eyes fluttered, but she was already more asleep than awake.

It was the first time he was ever thankful for a drug that didn't have anything to do with him.

~

Pulling the futon out required more energy than Billy could spare. Instead, he threw a sheet over the cover and grabbed a blanket and pillow from the closet. When he turned out the light, there were so many images going through his head about a story he knew so little of, he couldn't sleep. He reached for the remote and turned on the TV.

CNN was rerunning coverage, but he didn't learn much more than he already knew. The worst of it was the footage of him and Kate trying to get into Digger's cruiser. There was a tight shot of her face. She looked terrified. The report referred to her as "the estranged wife of bad-boy rocker Billy McDonald, who resurfaced to come to his ex-wife's rescue." Somebody was taking liberties, and it pissed him off. Kate was not his ex-wife, and he would hardly call a few weeks out of the public eye "resurfacing."

He pushed aside the stupidity and tried to focus on what mattered: Six people were dead. Three were in critical condition. Several others, wounded. Jesus Christ.

He turned off the TV. Unable to sleep, he got up and checked on Kate. After he was certain she was asleep, he slipped downstairs and pulled out the bottle of whiskey he'd hidden in the back of the cabinet the last time he was home. The weight of the bottle was heavy in his hands, cumbersome. If he were smart, he'd pour it down the drain. He'd gone two weeks without it, without anything.

Because he hadn't been able to get his hands on anything, that's why.

He pulled a glass from the cabinet and filled it halfway. He swirled the amber liquid, then set it down. Again he considered dumping it down the drain, but his hand was faster than his brain. It was gone in one long swallow. He wanted to take the bottle with him, but he knew if he did, it would be gone by morning. So instead, he stashed it back in its hiding place behind the tall boxes of cereal that only Devin ate, and headed upstairs.

He listened outside their bedroom. It was quiet, so he went back to the music room and tried to settle in for the night.

The mattress had to be stuffed with rocks. He shifted and turned, far too big for such a small bed. Lifting his head to flip his pillow, he saw Kate silhouetted in the doorway.

"What's wrong?"

She didn't answer. She just stepped inside the room and began unbuttoning the shirt. He watched as it dropped to the floor. Then she slipped out of her panties.

He lifted the blanket for her to climb in beside him.

"What are you doing, babe?"

Her hands curled around him, but stopped when they reached the waistband of his briefs.

"Take them off."

He wanted nothing more than to take them off, but this wasn't the time. "Katie, I don't think—"

"Please do this for me." For the first time that night, she sounded as if she might cry. "I need to feel your skin on mine."

"Okay."

He did as she asked and when he lay back down, Kate unfolded into him like a flower. Petals soft as velvet pressed against his flesh; her arms and legs fragile tendrils, she twined herself around him like a vine. Her body returned to him just as it always had, fitting perfectly into the grooves and hollows of his own.

"Thank you."

"For what?" he asked, breathing her in.

"For saving me."

CHAPTER 40

The lorazepam did the trick. Other than getting up to climb into bed with him, Kate slept through the night.

Billy, on the other hand, hadn't sleep at all.

His body ached from the cramped futon, and his arms were numb from the weight of her body. It had occurred to him at some point during the night to carry her back to their king-sized bed, but he was afraid if she woke, she would change her mind about needing him. So he suffered through it, if you could call being exactly where he wanted suffering.

Now Charlie was tap dancing outside the door, so he needed to get up and let him out. Gently, he rolled Kate onto her side and climbed over her. She struggled to open her eyes. Groggy from the drug, she wasn't awake enough for memories.

"Go back to sleep," he whispered, stepping into his jeans. "I'm just gonna let Charlie out."

She made a small noise as her eyes fluttered closed. He lingered a moment, wanting to lie back down beside her, but the frantic clicking of nails on the floor below warned him that he could either let the dog out now or clean up after him later. Besides, he needed coffee desperately.

Especially after he turned on the TV in the living room.

Seven dead, including the shooter. Footage from the scene replayed on all the morning news shows, including the video of him and Kate leaving the ambulance. A picture of Kate filled the screen and he almost put his fist through it when the anchor reported witnesses were saying Kate may have been Stevens's target.

"Oh my God. It was my fault."

Shit. He hadn't heard her come in behind him. He hit the off button on the remote, but she snatched it from his hand and turned it back on. He stepped between her and the television, trying to block her view.

"That's not true. Those idiots don't know what they're saying. The guy's dead. No one knows what the hell he was thinking."

Panic filled her eyes. "He was looking for me. He wanted to kill me!"

"You don't know that."

Her hand flew to her scalp and she wrapped her fingers in her hair and tugged. "Did you see what he did to my car? He knew my car. He killed all those people. Eileen."

"He didn't kill you!" He grabbed her shoulders, trying to settle her. "That's all that matters. You're safe."

"That's not all that matters! It should've been me. All those people, and it should have been me!"

"Don't say that!"

He was yelling. He didn't want to, but he couldn't stop. How the fuck could he calm her down when he was losing his shit right along with her?

"Listen to me. He was a crazy motherfucker who didn't care about anyone. He was angry with all those people there. You're not the one who threatened him or tried to take anything from him."

"I stole his privacy, didn't I? I stole his privacy with that stupid story. I even felt sorry for him." She strained against him, trying to see the television.

Billy unwound her hand from her hair, then wrapped his arms around her. The more she struggled, the tighter he held on. When she finally stopped fighting him, he loosened his grip, not quite ready to let go. He rocked back and forth, swaying gently and making soft shushing noises.

The phone jangled. From over her shoulder, he could read the caller ID that popped up at the bottom of the TV screen: EVENING EXAMINER.

"No fucking way."

Kate twisted in his arms. "I don't want to talk to them."

"You don't have to."

"I'm going to get fired."

"Good."

Billy wrested the remote from her hand, turned off the set, and stormed into the kitchen. He practically tore the phone from its base.

"What?" he barked into the receiver. The person on the other end, probably the douchebag reporter from last night, asked for Kate. "No. She can't come to the phone, and don't fucking call here again."

He slammed the phone down so hard he cracked the base.

Kate had followed him into the kitchen where she stood, looking lost, her arms tucked tightly around her waist as if she needed the help to remain upright. "What am I going to do?"

"Right now, you're going to drink some coffee." Why the hell hadn't he made decaf? "Then you can take a shower and get dressed. The detective said the police will need to talk to you today. Are you okay with that?"

Her shoulders slumped. "I don't have a choice, do I?"

"I can tell them not today."

"It won't be any easier tomorrow. Besides, I'm the lucky one, right?"

"You are. I know it doesn't feel that way, but you are. We're all lucky. You always tell me that God has a plan. Well, he must have a plan for you."

"Yeah, right. He must have one hell of a plan for me." She barked out a short laugh, so cold and hard, he almost shivered.

This wasn't his Katie. She had been through a lifetime of hurt in such a short time. Joey's death had damaged her, but she could have survived that.

Then there was what he'd done to her. And now this.

The light in her eyes flickered out. He reached out, tried to give her something to hold on to, but it was too late.

All he could see was darkness.

CHAPTER 41

Billy had never felt as helpless as he did at that moment. He'd rescued her—
or so she believed—the night before, but right now, as Kate sat next to him
on the sofa, he could no longer reach her.

He listened as she recounted her story to the two state police detectives
sitting across from them. He'd tried to hold her hand, but she pulled away,
twisting the linen napkin in her lap until it looked like an old paper bag.

After he'd gotten her calmed down earlier, she'd convinced him to go
to the store—a twenty-minute walk each way—to buy cookies because she
"didn't have time to bake." A police interview wasn't a damn social call, but
he sure as hell wasn't about to point that out.

By the time he returned, Kate had showered, dried her hair, and put on makeup. He blanched at the floral print dress, coordinating cardigan, and short strand of pearls. She'd even pulled out her grandmother's china.

"Will you be joining us?" Her voice was strained and formal.

"Of course. I don't want you dealing with this on your own."

"Too late." She reached for another cup and saucer from the cupboard.

"What?"

The corners of her mouth rose, but it was hardly a smile. "I said too late. It's too late for you to keep me from dealing with this on my own. I already did. You can't be there with me. Besides"—she shrugged—"if you'd been there, you'd be dead now." She dipped her hand into a bowl on the counter. "Should I cut up a lemon?"

She held it up and waited for his response.

Stunned by her lack of emotion, he couldn't answer. She had turned into one of those fucking Stepford Wives.

With a shrug, she tossed the lemon back in the bowl. She moved about the kitchen efficiently, setting the items onto a tray and arranging the cookies on a large glass plate.

When the detectives arrived and had settled in the living room, Kate proceeded to chat about the weather. She poured the tea and told them what was growing in her garden and how many batches of tomato sauce and dilly beans she'd canned.

It was a slow-motion, six-car pileup. You could prepare yourself for impact, but there wasn't a damn thing you could do to stop it.

"I would have baked, but I didn't have time. My husband was kind enough to go to the market. Cookie?" She served up a wooden smile along with the store-bought cookies.

Lt. Cimochowski looked at the plate as if he'd never seen a cookie before, then up at Kate. "Er, no thanks."

Lt. Jones just shook her head and flipped open her notepad.

Kate lowered the plate to the coffee table. Smoothing the back of her dress, she sat beside Billy. She folded her hands together and studied them.

Billy glared at the officers. *Take a fucking cookie.*

"Mrs. Donaldson, could you begin by telling us—"

Kate jumped to her feet. "What was I thinking? Of course it's too early for cookies." She turned to Billy and frowned. "I should've told you to get muffins." She faced the officers. "He can run to the store. It won't take but a half hour or so if he hurries. Better yet, I'll just run to SuperFresh real quick." She wiped her palms over the front of her dress. "I'll be right back."

Billy was up before she could get far. He slipped an arm around her waist and lowered his face until he could force her to look at him. "Babe? It's fine. I'm sure they don't want any muffins."

Kate gritted her teeth and hissed out the words. "Do you have to give me a hard time about everything?" She yanked away from him and dropped onto the couch where she went back to staring at her hands.

Lt. Cimochowski's cleared his throat. "I love cookies. I've been watching my weight, but I have to tell you, these look pretty tempting." He picked up a cookie and took a bite. "Delicious," he said, his mouth full of Pepperidge Farm.

Lt. Jones followed his lead. "Me, too." She transferred two cookies to the edge of her saucer. "I guess I can stand a few more minutes on the treadmill."

"Wonderful." Kate clapped her hands together, whirling from catatonic to bubbly so fast it made Billy dizzy.

When she finally settled down enough to allow the investigators to ask their questions, it was as if she had stepped outside herself. She showed no emotion. She could have been giving directions from the house to the town square.

The same wasn't true for Billy. Listening to Kate's version of what had happened was difficult, and it was hard not to react. He lifted his teacup. It was so small and fragile, he feared he might break it. He swirled the amber liquid and thought about the half bottle of Jack Daniels hidden in the kitchen, then remembered there was pot tucked away in the basement freezer, beneath the chuck steaks.

Feeling guilty, he set the cup down with a clatter and mumbled an apology. Kate was reliving a tragedy, and he was wishing they'd all leave so he could take the edge off. How long was this supposed to take, anyway?

"Mr. Donaldson?"

"I'm sorry. What?"

Lt. Jones addressed him. "Were you aware of any threats to Mrs. Donaldson from Mr. Stevens?"

They were kidding, right? "If I'd known he'd threatened her, he'd have never made it to that meeting last night."

Kate settled her hand on his knee.

"Understandable," said Lt. Cimochowski.

"Mrs. Donaldson, can you fill us in on your history with Mr. Stevens?"

Kate glanced at Billy. "I don't really have one. Not really." She told them about Stevens coming to township meetings and his rants against the committee, and that her editor had insisted she try to get an interview.

"Did anyone at the newspaper think he might be unstable or even dangerous?" Lt. Jones asked.

Kate fidgeted and tugged at the hem of her dress. "My editor called him a ticking time bomb, but I felt sorry for him. They were threatening to take his land and all. He didn't seem quite right, but my editor wanted a story, and if I didn't do what I was told, I could've lost my job."

"Jesus Christ!" Billy jumped from his seat. "I said you didn't need that fucking job, but you wouldn't listen."

He wanted to hit something. Better yet, someone.

Kate grew stiff.

Lt. Cimochowski stood as well. "Mr. Donaldson, I know this is difficult, but we need to ask your wife these questions. If it would be easier for you to wait in the other room . . ."

He scrubbed a hand over his face, then took a deep breath before turning back to Kate. "I'm sorry, babe."

Her head down, she continued to stare at her hands.

"Can you go on, Mrs. Donaldson?" Lt. Jones coaxed.

She didn't answer.

"Would you like to talk without your husband present?"

Billy shook his head. "Not happening."

Kate sat up straighter. She raised her eyes slowly and nodded.

She couldn't be serious! "I won't open my mouth again. I promise."

"I'm sorry." Lt. Cimochowski looked as if he might escort Billy out of his own damn living room. "It might be easier for her. We're almost done. We won't make it any more difficult than it already is. I promise."

"Katie."

She met his eyes for a second, then looked away. *Damn it.*

"Fine. I'll be in the kitchen. Call me if you need me." He gave each of the detectives a warning look.

Good job, Donaldson. Threaten the police. That should work in your favor.

Billy paced between the kitchen and the dining room, catching snippets of conversation coming from the living room, but Kate's voice was low. It was almost impossible to hear what she was saying without hovering in the doorway. He might as well find something to keep him busy, because while he was trying to focus on Kate, he was also trying—and failing—to ignore the bottle taunting him from behind the corn flakes.

He emptied the dishwasher and then busied himself trying to figure out what to make for dinner. He stared into the open refrigerator, but he wasn't thinking about the jar of spaghetti sauce or the leftover chicken. All he could think about was the bottle of JD calling to him, just inches from his face. And if he didn't answer, he just might lose his shit.

Two minutes ago he'd been banging around in the cabinets putting dishes away, but now he moved quietly, opening the cabinet door and slipping out the bottle of whiskey. A bottle of vodka he'd somehow missed the night before was off to the side, next to the waffle maker. He took that, too.

He climbed the narrow stairs, avoiding the creaky second one, and ducked into the music room. He tucked the whiskey into the bottom cabinet where he kept his sheet music, then opened the vodka and took a long, hard pull.

Warmth spread through him, soothing him from the inside. He took another swallow. Feelings of comfort mixed with feelings of guilt. He wasn't drunk. He wouldn't get drunk. He just needed to cope, and this was the only way he knew how. A little hit now and then, just so he could remain calm. For Katie.

The detectives were getting ready to leave when he came back downstairs. "Everything okay?"

"Yes, thank you." Lt. Jones smiled at Kate. "Mrs. Donaldson, we'll be in touch."

"At least you won't have to testify," Lt. Cimochowski said.

With Stevens dead, there would be no trial.

The moment the police left, Kate slumped as if a rod inserted in her spine for the interview had been whisked away, no longer necessary. She opened the refrigerator and stared inside.

"You hungry?" Billy asked. "I can make you some lunch."

"No thanks." She pulled a half-empty bottle of chardonnay off the door, grabbed a wine glass from the cabinet, and filled it near the brim.

His eyes followed the glass to her lips. How had he missed that? "I thought you didn't like chardonnay."

"I don't." She swallowed and slid the bottle across the counter.

If she was testing him, he'd already failed miserably.

She raised the glass to her lips again and shrugged. "Doesn't really matter anymore, does it?"

CHAPTER 42

Billy pulled his Gibson Les Paul from its spot on the wall and tried to work off some stress. He hadn't slept in days. Even before the shooting, his mind was too full of what ifs to let him rest.

Kate had taken another tranquilizer. Between that and the glass of wine she'd had for lunch, she was sleeping soundly. At least he hoped she was. If it helped her relax or sleep, she could stay drunk as long as she wanted. He sure as hell wouldn't judge.

Afraid he wouldn't hear her if she needed him, he opted to forego the headphones he usually wore to practice. It didn't matter anyway because he was too wired to focus. He set the guitar on a stand and wandered down the hall to lean against the frame of the door, listening to the soft, even snoring coming from beneath the quilt.

Every time he thought about what happened—what could've happened—he was torn between wanting to grab her and never let go and wanting to put his fist through a wall.

He was in a constant state of anxiety, and he needed to calm the fuck down.

The weed would help. He slipped down to the basement and retrieved his stash from the freezer. The cops had confiscated his pipe, so he dug through his sheet music cabinet and pulled out rolling papers. He opened the window, lit up, and took a hit, holding it in until he thought his lungs would explode. A light breeze stirred the corn in the field behind the house, and he pictured the tension that gripped his neck and shoulders flowing out of him as he exhaled. The sun was making its descent on the other side of the house, its last rays lighting the tips of the stalks and turning the green to gold.

Already feeling better, he took another hit and rested his head against the window frame. His stomach rumbled. He'd grabbed a sandwich earlier, but Katie hadn't wanted anything. Should he wake her? Hell. They weren't on any schedule. If she wanted to sleep until midnight, so be it. They could eat whenever she was hungry.

"You going to bogart that joint?"

He whacked his head against the window frame. "Jesus. You scared the crap out of me."

"Welcome to my world."

Kate flung herself onto the futon. She was wearing his chambray shirt again and her long, tan legs were bare. Dark smudges were visible below her eyes, and her hair was mussed. And damn if his cock didn't twitch. She was still the sexiest woman he'd ever laid eyes on.

He held out the joint. "Seriously?"

It had been years since she'd smoked pot. With a shrug, she took it and put it to her lips. She took a deep drag and held it.

"Like riding a bicycle," she said, her voice as wispy as the smoke.

She passed the joint back. Billy took another hit.

"Shotgun!" Taking him completely by surprise, Kate pressed her mouth against his, her hand curling around the back of his neck, holding him in place. As if he would pull away. He exhaled slowly into her mouth, not wanting the moment to end.

After sharing a few more hits, he dropped the last of it into a near empty bottle of water. He leaned back, the rapid beating of his heart in direct contrast to the sluggish parts of his brain.

Kate straddled him, grabbed the collar of his shirt, and brought his mouth back to hers.

His mind reeled and his body ached. This was his wife, yet he wasn't sure how to respond. He wanted to wrap his arms around her, but he didn't dare. Whatever happened had to be on her terms.

Grinding herself against him, she kissed him until he was practically breathless and groaning.

"How're you feeling?" he asked, toying with a strand of her hair.

She ran the tip of her nose along his jaw. "At this moment? I'm okay."

"Are you hungry?" He was trying to be a dutiful husband, but she was making it hard for him to think straight.

"Not for food."

She captured his lower lip between her teeth, and he growled. "God, I've missed you." His hand moved beneath her shirt, cupping her breast.

"Wait."

Damn it.

Kate slid from his lap and stood, then took him by the hand.

"Bring that with you." She motioned to the baggie of pot before leading him down the hall, and into their bedroom. She pulled the drapes and lit several candles.

"Give me a few minutes," she said, closing the door to the bathroom.

What he wouldn't give to be able to read her mind about now. He paced the bedroom floor. Kate was sending some pretty clear signals. But still. He didn't want to assume anything.

"Babe?" He tapped on the door. "You want some wine?"

"Sure."

Good, because he needed it.

He went to the fridge to search for the bottle of chardonnay. Instead, he found a pint of fresh strawberries. And, bingo! There was a bottle of champagne in the vegetable crisper.

251

"I couldn't have planned this better myself."

A half-second later he was awash in guilt, recalling the real reason he was there. Idiot. Although the reminder did little to diminish the uncomfortable tightness in his jeans.

He snagged a pair of champagne flutes from the hutch in the dining room, dumped the strawberries into a crystal bowl, and headed back upstairs, taking the steps two at a time. He was uncorking the champagne when the bathroom door opened.

"Nice timing." Kate leaned against the door frame, looking as if she'd just stepped off the cover of *Maxim*.

She wore a sheer black teddy and strappy, high-heeled stilettos. Her thong was cut high enough on her hip to expose the musical heart tattoo she'd gotten to surprise him for their tenth anniversary. Her hair hung in loose waves halfway down her back, and she had fixed her makeup. Her eyes were rimmed in black, and her lips were a glossy peach. A long strand of pearls looped tightly around her neck and trailed between her breasts.

"You like?" She turned, giving him a view from the rear.

"I do." So much, in fact, he could barely breathe, especially when he began to wonder when she'd bought this little number. He'd never seen it before. Their sex life had been nonexistent for months, between being on tour and the shit show their lives had been since he got home.

He shoved those thoughts aside and poured the champagne.

"You look beautiful, Katie. And in spite of the mess I've made of our lives, I'm a lucky man."

She raised her glass, her eyes never leaving his. He felt it at the base of his spine. She was stoned, but there was something else. Her eyes no longer flat, she looked mischievous. Playful. It made no sense. She drained half her glass in one mouthful, set it on the nightstand, and began working the buttons on his shirt.

His brain went to war with his heart. She was fragile, vulnerable. This was not a good idea. Yet he couldn't stop himself, couldn't stop himself from wanting her.

Once he was naked, she pulled him down onto the bed beside her and handed him the baggie.

"You sure?"

She ran her tongue along the inside of his ear. "Like the old days, remember?"

With his dick practically poking him in the chin, Billy rolled another joint. A few hits later, even he was stoned. Kate had to be zoned out of her mind.

She pushed her fingers against his chest until he was flat on his back. Then she reached into her nightstand and pulled out several long silk scarves. She dragged her knee over his belly and straddled him. Her fingers fumbled with the scarves. She knotted the first around his wrist and dragged his hand over his head, looping the other end of the scarf around the bedpost.

"I don't know about this." They'd done some kinky shit before, but he was usually the one in control.

"Shh!" Kate grasped his other hand and attached it to the other bedpost. She ran her hands over the ridges of his stomach and down one thigh, teasing him with her mouth, her fingers. She looped a scarf around each ankle and finished tying him to the bed.

Then she took another gulp of champagne, filled her glass again, and climbed onto the bed, standing between his splayed legs, wobbling on those killer heels.

Not a good idea. She could really hurt him, even if that wasn't her intention. And at this point, he had no idea what was going through her head.

She took another sip, then while trying to maintain her balance, poured a slow stream of icy-cold liquid over his chest and stomach.

"Hey!" He lurched, pulling against his restraints. "That's cold!"

Laughing, she bounced to her knees between his legs, and he cringed. She bent forward to kiss his mouth, her tongue exploring his. Then she moved on to his jaw, planting tiny kisses along his neck, slowly making her way down his chest, her tongue lapping at the spilled champagne.

"Do you want me to stop?" She hovered below his navel, her eyes glittering in the candlelight.

This could be fun if he could just relax.

"What's wrong?" She bit the tender skin around his waist.

"Nothing," he moaned. "I'm just not used to being in this position."

"You've done it to me. You had to learn it somewhere."

Shit. His stomach dropped and the pleasant buzz he'd been feeling faded.

"That was a long time ago, Katie. Long before I met you."

"Come on." That tongue of hers could make him lose his mind. "A beautiful man like you, on the road all the time, with a dull wife at home who grows her own vegetables and sews her own curtains? Don't tell me there haven't been hundreds of women over the years."

The cold words belied the steamy tone in which they were spoken.

"Untie me." The harder he pulled on the scarves, the tighter they grew. It seemed all her years as a Boy Scout den mother had paid off.

She laughed. "Oh, I don't think so."

Getting angry wouldn't help, but he didn't like feeling vulnerable.

"Katie?"

"Hmmm?" Her teeth grazed the inside of his thigh. She nipped him—a little too hard—then kissed the spot.

"I'm sorry. I never meant to hurt you. It was just the one time . . ."

"Oh, c'mon. You're forgetting Tiffany? Isn't this what she did for you?"

Who the fuck was Tiffany?

He began to argue, but her lips wrapped around him and his eyes rolled back into his head. He was suffering through the oddest mix of physical pleasure and mental pain. He wanted her to stop, and he wanted her to keep doing exactly what she was doing.

"I don't know anyone named Tiffany." He strained against the scarves, fighting the urge to throw his head back and go wherever she was leading. Her head bobbed, and he let go a low growl, losing himself in the moment.

"Tiffany," she said finally, as if she hadn't been interrupted by her little detour up and down the length of his cock. She alternated between open-mouth kisses and soft, gentle bites. "Remember? From Bailey Swift's music video? Have there been so many women over the years you've forgotten?"

"Oh for fuck's sake. That was over twenty years ago! Nothing happened. Did Joey tell you?" He lifted his head to look at her. "Okay. I almost did it. I was drunk and upset. You had just dropped a bomb on me, remember? And the other time . . ."

He stopped. This was a bad position to be in for discussing his infidelity.

The look in Kate's eyes sent such a chill through him he went limp.

"You know . . ." She nibbled her way down the insides of his thighs. "It would be easier to believe it was only the one time if you were never drunk or stoned again. But come on, Billy, we know that's not true."

"That's not fair." He yanked on his fist hard enough to shake the bed, even though he was not in a position to argue. "You know how much I love you."

"Life's not fair, babe." She lifted herself up until she was kneeling between his legs. Rocking slightly, she reached out and steadied herself against his thighs. "Put yourself in my position."

"I'd like to," he grumbled.

"Oh, I don't think so." She ran her hands over her waist and then cupped her breasts. She chewed her lower lip, gazing down at him coyly.

"Imagine another man with his hands tangled in my hair." She lifted the heavy mass of hair off her shoulders. "His lips pressed against my neck." Her head dropped back, exposing her throat. She ran her hand along her neck, her eyes half closed. "Pushing me down, his hands parting my thighs, his mouth—"

Billy's blood ran cold. "Stop it, Kate."

Her mouth dropped open, as if surprised by his outburst. "I thought you wanted to trade places with me. If those images are in my head, shouldn't they be in yours?"

Breathing became difficult, and there was the distinct possibility his heart might actually leap from his chest. He couldn't bear the thought of another man touching her. If she didn't shut up, he would lose his fucking mind.

"Stop," he begged. "It wasn't like that."

He squeezed his eyes shut tight, trying to erase the images she'd planted in his brain. Obviously she wanted to hurt him. She was succeeding, too.

When he'd calmed down enough to speak, he tried apologizing. Again. "Katie, I'm sorry for anything I've done to hurt you." He thought about the night of Joey's funeral. "Everything."

It was as if he hadn't said a word. She refilled her glass and held it up. "Thirsty?"

He shook his head, but she held the glass to his lips anyway. He would drink it or wear it. Then she popped a strawberry in his mouth. When he gagged, she lifted his head.

"Smaller bites next time, babe."

This was not his wife. She was teetering on the edge between sanity and madness. And it was dangerous. Billy was sobering up quickly.

Kate picked up another strawberry and took a bite. "Umm, sweet." With the remaining half, she drew lines down his chest and across his stomach. She traced the lines with her tongue, nipping him every now and then. She grabbed another berry and ran it across the curve of her neck and along her collarbone, then positioned herself over him.

He turned his face away. This had become a game to her, teasing and taunting him, making him want her more than he could have imagined possible under the circumstances. And fuck if his dick wasn't playing along, again standing up in full salute.

When he thought he might lose his fucking mind if he couldn't have her, she peeled off the teddy and her panties. Wearing nothing but the pearls and her shoes, she crushed the rest of the strawberries in her hands and rubbed them over her breasts and onto her stomach.

"Do you like strawberries?"

Jesus Christ. The ripe, sweet scent was intoxicating. So was her laughter.

"I do."

"Do you love them?"

"God, yes."

She rubbed her stained hands over his chest, then slipped her thumb into his mouth. He sucked on it until she almost purred.

"Katie, you have to untie me. Now." He was practically growling.

With a knee on either side of his hips, she dipped just low enough to drag her hair across his chest.

"And what will you do if I untie you?" She rubbed the rest of the berries up his arms and across her own. Red streaks dotted with pieces of the pulpy mess covered her body. Her eyebrows arched, and their eyes locked as she waited for his answer.

"Love you. I'm just going to love you."

The hard mask slipped, and her mouth fell open. It wasn't the answer she'd expected—and if he were being honest, it wasn't the first one that had popped into his head. But it was the right one. It was what mattered most and, deep down, what he truly meant. He just wanted to love her.

He'd reached for her without arms, and somehow he'd caught her.

Her eyes burning into his, she untied his legs and then his arms. When he was free, he gently placed her on her back and did what he had promised: he loved her the best way he could, frightened that at any moment she might slip beneath the surface and he would lose her forever.

CHAPTER 43

The bed was empty when Billy woke, sticky and smelling of sex, strawberries, and sweat. Would he ever see a strawberry again without getting a hard-on? Doubtful.

They'd made love twice during the night. And he probably wasn't kidding himself when he believed things seemed almost normal, natural. If Kate had still been in bed, he'd have made it a three-peat.

Her lingerie and heels lay on the floor next to an empty champagne bottle. Billy climbed out of bed and stretched until his fingertips grazed the ceiling. Outside, a breeze stirred the row of arborvitae that edged the yard and rippled across the corn.

In spite of the reasons why, it was good to be home. He'd slept in his own bed, made love to his wife. It was all he wanted. So many things needed to be fixed, but he was hopeful. They would get there. Whatever it took.

He splashed some cool water on his face, brushed his teeth, and pulled his hair into a ponytail.

The aroma of fresh coffee greeted him as he descended the stairs, along with a side of guilt. He should have been up first. Then again, maybe getting back into a regular routine was exactly what Kate needed.

He found Kate sitting at the dining room table, a cup of coffee in front of her. Charlie lay curled at her feet.

"Morning." He dropped a kiss on top of her head and ambled into the kitchen, where he poured himself a cup of coffee. He plucked two slices of toast from the top of the toaster and was surprised to find they were cold. The frying pan on the stove held a greasy smear of congealed butter. An open carton of eggs sat on the counter next to a pair of poultry shears.

The television on the kitchen counter had been unplugged, the cord cut in half and left lying on the floor. He stooped to pick it up, his stomach dropping even lower. He carried it into the dining room.

"Katie?"

The cream in her coffee floated like pond scum. She didn't move.

"Babe." He dragged one of the dining room chairs closer and sat beside her. He rubbed her fingers between his own. "What's wrong?"

"She wasn't even seventeen," Kate said finally.

"Who? Who wasn't seventeen?"

"Morgan."

"Sweetheart, who's Morgan?"

The look she gave him suggested he was deliberately being thick-headed. "Morgan Wilson. She died last night."

"I'm sorry." He had no idea who Morgan Wilson was, but didn't dare ask.

She went from withdrawn to frantic so quickly it should have given her whiplash. "Her birthday was next week. She was trying to get a jump on things. Mr. Scott makes the seniors in his civics class get a firsthand look at local government." The chair scraped across the floor as she stood, her voice rising with her. "She was just trying to get it out of the way! Now she's dead."

He tried to piece together what she was saying. Morgan must have been at the meeting. Of course he didn't know her. Kate probably didn't either—not that it mattered.

She sank back into the chair and dropped her head into her hands. "It's my fault."

Oh shit. "Katie, it's not your fault. You can't keep thinking that."

"You can say that all you want," she sobbed, "but it won't change one damn thing."

He wrapped his arms around her, drawing his hand up and down her back, murmuring softly until her sobs slowed to quiet hiccups. With each passing moment, his anxiety grew. This wasn't his Kate. She was sensitive but smart, logical. None of her behavior made sense now. One minute she was hovering on the brink, and the next she was tumbling over the edge.

Billy remained at home, but other than that one night, Kate didn't welcome him back to their bed. Instead, she slept behind a locked door with Charlie to protect her. When he got up during the night, there was always a sliver of light spilling out from beneath her door.

While she claimed she was fine, she was anything but. She'd stare out the window for hours, a book unopened in her lap. She jumped at the smallest sound and wouldn't leave the house unless absolutely necessary. She had even refused to attend Eileen's funeral, insisting the whole family hated her.

Sleeping on the futon was taking its toll, so with Devin away at school, Billy moved into his room, and for the first night in more than a week, he slept. So well, in fact, he hadn't heard Kate get up, but he could hear her now. And he could hear the man she was speaking with.

He hurried downstairs to find Tom in his kitchen, unloading groceries.

"What're you doing here?" he demanded.

Tom looked up from the cloth sack he was emptying.

"Billy!" Kate sounded mortified. "What's wrong with you?"

"Nothing." His eyes never left Tom's face.

Tom finished unloading the sack.

"I should go," he said quietly. "I have to get to the office anyway."

Kate lifted her cheek for him to kiss, leveling an evil look at Billy as she did. Tom gave her a quick peck, then made a hasty exit.

"I'll call you later," Tom said.

"Yeah," Billy answered, "you do that."

Kate turned on him before the screen door banged shut. "What's your problem?"

"Nothing. What's his problem? He's got his own wife and kid. He should stay the fuck away from mine."

Her look was pure disappointment, but other than a frown and a shake of her head, she didn't comment.

But her words taunted him. Words she'd said before. They slid into the crevices of his brain, mocked him: *his lips pressed against my throat . . .*

Damn it. He scrubbed his hands over his face, trying to erase the memory, and then snatched a cup from the cabinet and filled it with coffee.

"I would have gone to the store with you," he said when he could speak calmly. "You should have woken me up." He surveyed the counter filled with groceries. "I'm glad to see you've got your appetite back at least."

She shook her head. "Not really. But when I was talking to Tom last night, I mentioned that I was out of just about everything, and he offered to take me." She shrugged as if it were just that simple.

The edges of his vision turned black.

"What's the deal with this guy, huh? Is there something you need to tell me?"

"Tom?" She chuckled softly. "You're ridiculous."

It wasn't an answer, but it was all he was getting.

He tried putting the groceries away, but when he had to keep asking where things went, he gave up, poured himself a bowl of cereal, and got out of her way. When she pulled out a quart of fresh strawberries, her face turned pink as she stashed them in the refrigerator. He smiled.

"Come here," he said. "I want to talk to you."

"Not now. I have all of this food to put away."

"We need to talk. That can wait a few minutes." He led her to a chair in the dining room, then pulled a chair across from her and sat so that their knees were almost touching.

"We haven't talked about what happened the night of the funeral."

She tried to stand. "No!"

"Katie, please. We need to talk about it."

"I don't want to." She tried to pull away, but he held tighter.

"We can't just forget about it and make believe it never happened."

Her body went rigid and her voice turned cold. "Is that what you think I'm doing?" "Forgetting about it? Because trust me, Billy, I haven't forgotten. I'll never forget."

This time when she tried to stand, he let her go.

~

They were living in some kind of holding pattern, waiting for something to happen. What that something might be, Billy had no idea. He felt like a caged animal. He hadn't gone this long between gigs since high school, and it was making him more than a little crazy.

Problem was, there was already plenty of crazy in the house.

Kate rarely went anywhere. Seeing Eileen's empty house at the end of their driveway with the FOR SALE sign out front was too difficult. She agreed to see a counselor—not a legitimate psychiatrist, but a religious counselor who kept hours at the Methodist church on Tuesdays. Billy didn't know what they talked about or if the woman was even qualified to handle traumatic stress, but Kate swore she was feeling better. He was certain the only reason she agreed to that counselor was because she could cut through the neighbor's yard and walk to the church, and thereby avoid passing Eileen's house.

He wanted to believe her, even more so when he got a call from his agent about a two-week stint with Dax Fleetwood, whose lead guitarist's appendix had just ruptured. He had minutes to make a decision and call C.J. back.

"Will you be okay if I go?" he asked Kate. "It's only two weeks."

She sat at the dining room table with a cup of tea, rolling and unrolling the string from the bag around her spoon. "Isn't Dax Fleetwood a country artist?"

"Yeah, but I need to play. I wouldn't care right now if someone wanted me to back up Wayne Newton in Branson."

For a second, he thought she might smile.

"Okay, maybe I wouldn't go that far, but we could use the money."

She dropped the spoon into the cup and stood.

"Of course you should go." She patted his arm politely on her way to the kitchen. "You didn't need to stay this long."

"Jesus Christ, Kate." He pushed his chair back from the table and stormed after her. "Don't start."

He yanked the refrigerator door open and stared inside. It made him nuts when she acted like she was some kind of burden he needn't concern himself with.

She stood at the kitchen sink, her back stiff. "When are you leaving?"

"If I can go, C.J. will send a car to take me to the airport in about an hour." He closed the refrigerator and rested his hands on his hips.

"If you can go? What am I, your mother?" She loaded her mug into the dishwasher. "I guess you better get moving then."

He needed to go. He needed a break. But he also wanted her to beg him to stay or even offer to go with him.

"What about your trial? Can you leave the state?"

"Tom worked that out at my preliminary. I'm not a flight risk." Just saying Tom's name made him scowl.

Kate, on the other hand, laughed.

"What's so funny?"

"You. You're not a flight risk, yet you're headed to the airport." She shrugged. "Never mind."

He packed in record time. He'd done it so many times, he could do it in his sleep. The guilt settled in just as he pulled his toothbrush from the holder next to hers. He headed back downstairs.

"Come with me."

Kate was curled up in the bay window. The book in her lap was the same one he'd seen her with for the past two weeks. She used to finish a novel in two days. Three tops. "C'mon. I'll help you pack. You'll be ready in no time."

She shook her head. "No. This is for the best. I need to man up, so to speak."

"Katie—"

"You need to get back to work and on with your life, and so do I. It'll be fine."

Gravel crunched in the driveway. There was no time to argue. If he could split himself down the middle, he would.

"If you change your mind, just let me know. I'll fly you out, okay?"

She tucked the bookmark between the pages of her book. "Where are you going, anyway?"

Shit. Had he been in such a hurry to leave that he hadn't asked? "I don't even know."

A queer look passed over her face, and he hoped she wasn't thinking the same thing.

He put his arms around her. "I'll call you as soon as I land, wherever the hell that is."

For a moment, she seemed about to panic, but it passed.

"You sure you're okay?"

"Fine. Go."

"Not yet." He tilted her chin and touched his lips to hers. Her fingers gripped his shirt. "I love you, Katie."

"I love you, too." She turned away, but not before he'd seen the glimmer of a fresh tear in the corner of her eye.

Crazy as it seemed, he considered it a gift; a sign he might finally be getting through to her.

CHAPTER 44

Twenty-nine pills. That's how many were left in the bottle of sleeping pills the doctor had prescribed over a month ago. Kate had taken one. There was no need to renew the prescription, but she'd done so anyway.

The pill worked. That wasn't the problem. Sleep frightened her. It was like walking into a haunted house knowing what horrors awaited her. Each night, and sometimes during the day even, she would pass out from exhaustion, sleep for an hour or two, then wake in a cold sweat, her voice trapped in her throat, unable to scream.

It was her new normal.

She slipped the two bottles into her nightstand and covered them with a small pillow filled with dried lavender buds Rhiannon had made for her in

Girl Scouts. On top of that, she placed a book of inspirational quotes that had belonged to Eileen. Stan's wife had dropped it off along with her recipe for bread and butter pickles. As if it mattered anymore. Kate had refused to open the door when Lora knocked, and she'd eventually left, leaving the book and the recipe on the porch along with a note and the keys to Eileen's car in case she needed it.

Why were they acting so nice? They should hate her. All of the families should. They should trample her flower beds and throw rocks through her windows. The guilt was unbearable. And their kindness made it even worse.

Kate slammed the drawer closed and went downstairs. She made a sandwich she wouldn't eat and pulled out her laptop. She checked her email. It was full, but she didn't respond to any of the messages from friends or former coworkers. She found a recipe for pecan pie on Pinterest and saved it, although when she'd ever feel like making a pie again, she had no idea.

She wasn't interested in Facebook, Instagram, or Twitter. She didn't want to read the latest news. There was only one thing she was curious about.

She pulled up Google.

"Dosage, side effects, warnings: An overdose may cause excessive sedation, pinpoint pupils, or depressed respiratory function, which may progress to coma and possibly death."

Adding alcohol or other opiates would make it more likely to be a fatal overdose, but she would still need hundreds of pills, which would take months. And even then, it was more than likely she'd be found semiconscious in a pool of her own vomit.

Not a very dignified way to die. Not that she was planning anything. Not really. She was just . . . curious.

Kate pressed her fingers against her temples. She couldn't think anymore today.

She deleted the history on her laptop and closed it.

⌐◠◡

Billy called later that afternoon. Kate debated letting the call go to voicemail, but if she did, he'd just keep calling, as if he knew she was trying to ignore him.

"I'll be home sometime tomorrow afternoon," he said after they'd exchanged the usual greetings.

266

"So you ended up in Branson after all?"

"Yeah, go figure," he chuckled. He sounded good—happy, relaxed.

It made what she was about to do easier.

"About tomorrow. I think it best if you have the driver take you to Rhiannon's."

There was silence at the other end.

"Billy?"

"I'm here."

"Did you hear me?"

"Yeah, I heard you." He spoke in clipped, even tones. "Is that what you want?"

She exhaled heavily. "I think so. I still love you, please believe me, but there's a big elephant in the room that we've been ignoring. I can't keep doing that."

"Katie—"

"Please. I'm not saying it's over—I'm not—but we haven't fixed anything. And so much is broken, especially me—"

"You're not broken, baby." His voice was a soft hug. "You've been through a lot. How can we fix anything if I'm not there to work on it? And when I am, you won't talk about it."

"I don't know, but I think it's for the best."

She pictured him on the other end gripping the phone, his jaw tight, trying not to lose his temper.

"You sure this is what you want?"

"I am." She wasn't. What she really wanted was to melt into him, seep through his pores, and live inside him where she could feel safe again. But that wasn't possible.

"Okay, then," he said, the hurt apparent in his voice.

She didn't want to be the cause of any more pain, but he'd hurt her badly. She still hadn't figured out how to deal with it or even if she could deal with it.

"I'll call you when I land."

"Tell Wayne I said hi."

"Wayne?"

"Newton."

"Oh, yeah. Funny."

CHAPTER 45

It was almost three o'clock when Rhiannon heard the garage door rumble open. Doug and her father had been gone most of the day. The formal arraignment and pretrial conference had been set for nine thirty in the district attorney's office. She had asked Doug to call when it was over, but he hadn't.

To keep her mind off the possibility that her father could be heading to jail, she'd tried to stick to her normal routine. She dropped the boys off at the sitter's, popped into Starbucks, and then spent a couple of hours at the gym. But by lunchtime, she'd been such a nervous wreck she ended up canceling lunch with her two best friends.

That Doug hadn't called had been gnawing at her for the past two hours. She was about to let him know just how annoyed she was when he walked in, but after the look he gave her, she almost wished they'd stayed away a little longer. Her father followed, looking tired and tense. He'd worn the same look that morning.

"Well?" She glanced from one to the other.

Doug glared at his father-in-law. "The DA wants to know to what charges he'll plead guilty. She's willing to give him a deal on a reduced charge, but he's got to decide quickly because she's not going to hold it open forever."

"And?"

"He wants to plead not guilty." Doug yanked his tie loose and unbuttoned his top button. He grabbed a tumbler from the cabinet near the sink and filled it with ice. Then he stalked into the pantry and returned with a nearly full bottle of Scotch.

They had hidden their alcohol for a reason. Now she'd have to find another spot.

"Doug." Her voice carried a smile, but she was shooting him daggers. "Don't drink in front of Daddy."

"It's fine." Her father opened the Sub-Zero refrigerator and helped himself to a bottle of water. His tie was already off, the tail hanging from the side pocket of his suit jacket. He opened the water and straddled the wood-and-leather stool near the island, waiting for Doug to finish telling her what had transpired.

Doug turned to him instead. "You're going to jail, Billy. Like it or not, you're going to jail."

Doug took a mouthful of Scotch. His eyes watered. He swirled the glass so hard several drops of the golden liquid dribbled over his hand.

She wanted to choke him. "You don't know that!"

She knew the charges against her father, coupled with the fact that it wasn't his first drug offense, meant he wouldn't be getting off with a slap on the wrist. But isn't that why people paid good money for attorneys? So they wouldn't go to jail?

"He doesn't want to make a deal, so he has to go to trial." Doug crunched down on an ice cube. "You were drunk. You had drugs on you. And you put a guy through a plate glass window and nearly killed him. Tell me how you're not guilty."

Her father didn't answer. He just let his gaze settle on Doug as he lifted the bottle of water to his mouth.

"Excuse me, but isn't that *your* job?" Rhiannon said.

"I'm a lawyer, Rhiannon," Doug responded flatly, "not a magician."

Men. So frustrating. Maybe if she tried reasoning. It worked with the twins—sometimes.

"Daddy, if Doug thinks you'd be better off making a deal with the DA, why won't you do that?" Doug uttered a low grumble, which earned him a dirty look before she continued. "Do you really think you can win?"

He set down the water on the granite counter. "No, I don't, but that's the only chance I have of not going to jail. If I plead now, then I get sentenced and very likely locked up. And who knows for how long? What about your mother?" He pressed his hand against the back of his neck. "I can't go to jail now. It's hard enough that I'm not with her every day. What if I get sentenced for a few months or longer?"

"I'm sure you won't have to go to jail for that long, if at all." She turned to Doug, ready to pounce. "He didn't even start the fight. Did you forget that? He was defending his friend."

Doug watched her over the rim of his glass. "I know, and I'm sure we can get her to agree to assault instead of aggravated assault. You'll likely have to pay the guy's medical expenses, but we might be able to get the judge to split that, since you didn't start the fight. But it's too risky to go to trial."

The stool scraped along the travertine-tiled floor as her father stood. "Put it off as long as you can. Hopefully by then, Katie will be doing better. Then I'll think about a deal, but not now."

The determined set of his jaw and the look in his eyes warned her that his mind was made up.

"Did you talk to your mother?" he asked, changing the subject.

"Yes," she said with a sigh. "She doesn't want to come for dinner. She says it'll be too late."

"Then we'll go over there. She'll want to see the boys in their Halloween costumes."

Doug rolled his eyes, but Rhiannon's look mirrored her father's.

"That's fine," she answered. "We'll take a ride after dinner."

"I'm gonna pack a bag in case she'll let me stay for a couple days." He stopped in the doorway and turned to Doug. "I appreciate what you're trying to do. I just can't do it your way right now."

CHAPTER 46

It was the part of *Pride and Prejudice* Kate loved most: the drawing room scene. As silly as it might be, it was an utterly romantic moment for her. She'd watched the BBC version of the movie so many times she could recite the lines by heart.

Dressed in a pair of yoga pants and one of Billy's long-sleeved T-shirts, she was curled up on the futon in the music room with a mug of chicken noodle soup and a quilt around her shoulders. There was even a bowl of popcorn in case she was hungry later.

A loud bang on the front door made her jump. No one ever ventured up their long driveway on Halloween, not when they could stay in town and hit ten houses in the time it took to get to hers. Of course, with the house lit up like a Christmas tree, it was hard to miss even from so far away.

The clock on the VCR read seven thirty. Trick-or-treating went on until eight. She had no candy or anything to give. She should just ignore them.

Another knock. Someone seemed determined.

Unable to bear the thought of a disappointed child, Kate paused the movie and pulled the quilt tightly around her. The thought of opening the door to strangers made her more than a little uncomfortable, but when she heard a woman's laughter and recognized the top of Doug's head through the window, she relaxed.

"Tee-tee, Nonna!" Dayton yelled when she opened the door. Dalton mimicked his brother.

She felt a little tug around her heart. "Oh my! Who have we here?"

"Me!" Thing One and Thing Two cried in unison.

Their hair was tinted bright blue and stood up with a bad case of static. They wore red footie pajamas, and each had his particular name emblazoned within a white circle on the chest.

Kate grinned at their beaming little faces, then up at her daughter. "They're adorable. Nonna doesn't have any candy, but I do have some yogurt."

"Much better." Rhiannon gave her mother a peck on the cheek, deposited her Louis Vuitton bag on the dining room table, and shrugged off her cashmere wrap.

Kate was reaching up to hug Doug when she noticed Billy standing at the bottom of the porch steps. Damn if her heart didn't skip a beat.

"And who are you supposed to be?"

"That's Poppy!" Dalton answered.

"That's right." She scooped him up and covered him with kisses. His laughter reminded her how she had once believed that such an irresistible sound could cure the worst case of the blues. Too bad it wasn't true.

She gave Dayton an equal number of kisses, then darted into the kitchen to get the yogurt and two oatmeal raisin cookies.

Rhiannon crinkled her nose. "Store-bought?"

"Sorry. It's my emergency stash. There's no point in baking—or cooking, for that matter—if there's no one here to eat it."

She ignored Billy's frown.

"Do you want coffee or tea, maybe?" she asked. "There's some beer in the fridge." She glanced at Billy. Was he still fighting to stay on the wagon, or had he fallen off again?

"We don't want to put you out, Mom," Rhiannon said. "We just wanted you to see the boys, and . . ." She glanced up at her father.

"I miss you," Billy admitted. "I thought I'd stay for a day or two if it's okay."

The look on his face was just short of pleading, and she felt that if she told him no, he might just drop to his knees and beg her. She didn't like being put on the spot, but she was too exhausted to argue. Besides, having Billy in the house might mean more than just a couple hours of sleep.

"Sure," she said, wishing things were different. "That'll be fine."

⌒

Doug glanced in the rearview mirror. The boys were sound asleep.

"I'm worried about your mother."

"Why?" Rhiannon didn't look up from her phone. "She seemed okay."

"She was okay when she saw the boys, and for a little bit she almost seemed like herself. But it's like the light's gone out of her eyes."

"She's fine. She and Daddy just need to work their shit out. They'll both be fine."

"I know you'd like to believe that, and so would I, but I don't think it's that simple."

This was not a conversation she wanted to have, and Doug knew it. Rhiannon believed that time, and maybe a trip to the spa or a weekend in Cabo, could cure anything.

"Daddy loves her," she pointed out. "If she'd stop being so pigheaded and let him come home, she'd see that."

"It's not that simple. And what your mother is going through is way more than just dealing with your dad, although that hasn't helped."

She looked up from her phone long enough to glare at him.

He lifted his hand in defense. "You know I care about both your parents, but your father has put her through a lot. That on its own would be enough to push someone over the edge. But given everything else she's had to deal with

273

in the course of just a few months? I'm worried. That's all I'm saying. I think maybe we should try to get her to stay with us. And if she won't stay with your father there, then he should go back to the house, and she should stay."

The temperature in the car dropped about ten degrees. "I'm not throwing my father out, Doug."

"I'm not asking you to. But all of this isn't over yet, remember? I can push off his trial for a bit, but it's very likely he's going to have to do some jail time. What then?"

Annoyed, she tossed her phone back in her bag. "Maybe we should hire a lawyer with more confidence in his ability to defend his client."

"I'm very confident in my abilities, sweetheart, and that of the entire firm, but we're not miracle workers. Plus my dad is looking to run for office next year. We can't pull any strings or look for any favors. You know that."

"You just do your best to get him off," she said, "and let me worry about my mother."

⁓

Billy turned off the outside lights and checked the locks on all the doors. Kate checked them several times a day, but he made a show of it for her sake.

"I know it's silly to have all the lights on," she started to say. "All I'm really doing is telling the neighbors I'm alone."

A smile crept across his face. "What do you think they're thinking when they see all the lights out? I bet they think you're getting lucky."

She chuckled. "Yeah, I'm sure that's what they're thinking."

It was good to see her smile, but the rest was disturbing. She was disappearing before his eyes. She'd lost so much weight she was all sharp angles and lines. Lost in one of his old shirts, she seemed fragile and birdlike.

As if reading his mind, she pushed the too-long sleeves up over her elbows. "Are you hungry?"

"Depends what you're offering. If it's kale and tofu something-or-other, I had that for dinner."

She grimaced, then went to the freezer and pulled out a small package of chicken cutlets. "You're in luck. I just went to the store. These aren't even frozen yet."

She unwrapped the meat and pounded it paper thin. She seasoned it, dredged it in flour, and set it to fry in a pan with butter and olive oil. In the meantime, she sliced some mushrooms and tossed them into the pan with some beef broth and wine.

Billy sat at the island watching, his mouth watering. In less than twenty minutes, he was devouring Chicken Marsala.

He made an exaggerated show of rolling his eyes heavenward. "Oh my God," he said, his mouth full, "please let me come home, even if it's just for dinner."

Kate smiled, but it was sad.

"Don't you miss cooking for me?" He held out a piece of chicken on his fork. She hesitated and then opened her mouth.

"I miss a lot of things."

There wasn't a whole lot he could say to that.

Happy that he was able to get her to eat several bites, he felt even better later when she offered to share her popcorn with him as well.

"I was watching a movie," she explained.

He climbed off the stool and stretched. It felt good to be home, even just for a night or two.

"What do you want to drink?" She took a bottle from the wine rack in the dining room. "I'm going to have some wine. Maybe it'll help me sleep."

"Aren't the sleeping pills helping?"

"Not so much. Not really." She pulled a glass from the cabinet.

When he opened the refrigerator, he found some unusual brand of India Pale Ale and water. He held up a beer, eyebrows raised.

Kate shrugged. "I don't know what it tastes like. Tom brought it when he came for dinner last week. I made curry."

Yes, what you made Tom for dinner was the question I most wanted to ask.

He put the beer back and pulled out a bottle of water, unscrewed the top, and took a sip. Noticing her raised eyebrows, he shrugged.

"I'm trying."

She picked up her glass and the bottle and headed toward the stairs. "Well, I'm not."

"Speaking of Tom, he called me this afternoon," she tossed over her shoulder.

Was it too late to snatch a bottle of that designer beer? He didn't. He just slogged up the stairs behind her.

"He's been following up with the NYPD." She settled onto the far corner of the futon.

Billy dropped down beside her, rolling his eyes at the frozen screen. *Pride and Prejudice. Again?*

"They had a couple of leads on Joey's shooting, but nothing's panned out. They're pretty much saying it was random, and the chance of finding out whoever did it is very unlikely."

He captured her hand. "I'm sorry, babe."

She dragged a pillow onto her lap and picked at the threads. "They think it was probably somebody looking to score money for drugs." She shot him a disapproving look. Yeah, he got it.

"Are they just giving up?"

"They're not saying that, but Tom thinks that's exactly what they're doing." She handed him the remote. "To be honest, I never expected them to make an arrest. It was a random robbery. He was just in the wrong place at the wrong time. It's not like someone wanted to kill him."

She didn't say it, but he knew she was thinking it: *Like Sedge wanted to kill me.*

She settled the bowl of popcorn between them while he flipped through the channels.

"Put on whatever you like as long as it's not scary."

When he came to *The Rocky Horror Picture Show*, he waggled his eyebrows.

"Fine." She huffed. "Although I'll never understand what anyone sees in this movie." When he opened his mouth to explain, she pressed her fingers to his lips. "Save your breath."

Partway through the movie, her head began to droop. Billy lifted the glass from her hand and settled her against his shoulder. Her breathing slowed, and he could tell she was sound asleep. He turned off the TV and lifted her off the futon. As he carried her toward their bedroom, she opened her eyes.

"What're you doing?"

"Putting you to bed."

"Okay." She nestled her head against his shoulder.

The state of their bedroom shocked him. The bed was unmade. The closet door stood open, and several pairs of shoes were strewn about the floor. In one corner was a pile of dirty clothes. Clean clothes were stacked on a chair near the closet. Books and magazines covered the table on Kate's side of the bed. Several more were on his nightstand.

He pulled the covers over her just as Charlie jumped onto the bed and began his nightly ritual of looking for a comfortable spot.

"Lucky dog," he muttered, scratching Charlie behind the ear before turning out the light. He left the bathroom and hall lights on in case Kate woke.

Settling back onto the futon, he watched Leno while the half-empty bottle of wine taunted him. He drained his bottle of water, but it was no use. He poured the wine into Kate's empty glass and drank until he'd finished the bottle.

But if he thought the wine had beckoned, it was no match for the pull of Kate asleep down the hall. He stood outside the door, watching her, which only made it more difficult.

"Beat it," he said, shooing Charlie off the bed.

Then he stepped out of his clothes and climbed into his bed next to his wife.

The moon was still nearly full, and the light shining through the windows illuminated her face. Long, dark lashes curled against her pale skin. Her sweet, full lips were parted slightly.

He wanted to kiss her. Kate had always believed in happily ever after, yet she was living a nightmare. What he wouldn't give to be a real prince, able to free her with a kiss. He wanted to reach inside and pull out all the pain and heartache. He didn't know how to help her. She was slipping away, turning into herself. He didn't know where she was going or how to reach her if she traveled too far.

As he drew her up against his chest, her body remembered its place. Her head nestled into the hollow beneath his neck. Her breath warmed his chest. She was asleep and comfortable for now. Hopefully she would sleep through the night. But if not, at least he would be there when she woke.

CHAPTER 47

The bullets fired from Sedge Stevens's gun and the ones that ended Joey's life never touched Kate, yet they tore a hole in her so wide she couldn't fill it no matter how hard she tried. As the holidays approached, she couldn't stop thinking of the empty chairs too many families would face because of her. Yet here she was, still breathing.

It didn't seem fair.

Each day was a struggle. Each sleepless night, endless. And when she did fall asleep, she woke sweating and panting, the screams caught in her throat. The nightmares had become so real that she fought sleep rather than fall prey to its terrifying secrets.

Moving with zombie-like enthusiasm, Kate threw herself into

Thanksgiving preparations with as much zeal as she could muster, further wearing out her already frayed edges. But it needed to be perfect. Her family deserved that. And if Thanksgiving was going to be perfect, that meant a fresh turkey right from the farm.

She drove all the way to Flanders to pick up the bird. On the way, she stopped at a farm stand and bought a giant Cinderella pumpkin for the centerpiece and a dozen tiny white ones to use as place cards. She'd first counted out eight. When she realized she had included Joey, she couldn't bear to put the extra pumpkin back, so she threw in a few more for no reason at all.

It was almost dark by the time she got home and found Devin waiting for her.

He came bounding into the kitchen to greet her. "Hey!"

Worry clouded his face as soon as he saw her, but to his credit, he shook it off quickly. Anyone who hadn't seen her in a while wore that same expression. She was getting used to it.

"Hey, yourself!" She reached up to give him a hug. "Did you just get here?"

"Actually, I got in this afternoon, but I have a date. Can I borrow Dad's truck?"

She tried to hide her disappointment as she handed him the keys. "Oh? With who?"

"Her name's Danielle. I know her from Lyco. Were you expecting me for dinner?"

"No." She could always freeze the pan of lasagna with homemade noodles she'd made that morning. "I know you're too popular to spend the evening with me."

He gave her a quick peck on the cheek and grabbed his jacket. "Don't wait up!"

"Nice try," she called after him.

After he'd gone, she turned on all the outside lights. Then she boiled an egg for supper, took out a couple of blocks of cream cheese to soften, and began measuring flour for a pie crust.

By the time Devin returned several hours later, she was trying to make room in the refrigerator for the pumpkin cheesecake. Recalling the nights they'd sit at the dining room table when he first started dating, she asked if he'd like some cocoa.

"I'd prefer a beer."

She gave him a sharp look.

"But cocoa would be great."

"You're barely old enough to drink," she reminded him.

"You were only eighteen when you met Dad, but if some of his stories are true—"

"Your father talks too much," she snapped. "Besides, things were different then."

"C'mon, Mom. Even you wouldn't buy that excuse."

"Still. You don't need to be in a hurry to drink. Alcohol and drug addiction is rampant on your father's side, which means you could be predisposed to it as well."

This was a lecture she'd given a million times, and the look he gave her said as much.

"It doesn't hurt to be reminded." She turned away to pour the milk into a saucepan.

"Don't worry about me. I'm well acquainted with my father's predilection for substance abuse. I grew up with him, remember?"

Kate had always believed that she'd shielded her kids from Billy's worst behavior. Now it seemed that all she'd really done was make excuses for it. She added *enabling wife* and *ineffective parent* to her growing list of failures.

When the cocoa was ready, she set the two mugs on the kitchen island.

"Whipped cream or marshmallows?"

Devin frowned. "What do you think?"

"Sorry." She dropped a handful of mini-marshmallows into his cup, then topped it with a healthy squirt of whipped cream.

"Damn straight."

She gave her own cup a quick squeeze from the can, then sat down to face him.

"How was your date?"

He smiled broadly. "Good."

"That all? Just 'good'?"

"For now, yeah. That's all you get."

"Nice girl?"

"She is."

"You deserve a nice girl. Is she pretty?"

"Yes, Mom, and that's all. Seriously."

She frowned.

"I don't want to talk about her, okay?"

Devin was no longer the little boy who shared all his secrets. It shouldn't hurt as much as it did, but she was so damn raw she couldn't help it. To cover her disappointment, she took a too-large sip of cocoa and burned her tongue.

"Fine. How's school?"

"I aced midterms, and I should do just as well for finals."

She beamed at him over the rim of her mug. "What's your favorite class this semester?"

"British Lit."

She groaned. "You're your father's son. I hated British Lit. He loved it."

Devin twirled the spoon around his mug. "Funny. I don't think of myself as my father's son at all."

The intensity of his gaze made her uncomfortable. "Devin." She drew his name out slowly, but he blundered ahead.

"He still staying with Rhiannon and Doug?"

She nodded.

"You guys going to marriage counseling or anything?"

"Not right now. There's too much going on, and he's back on the road filling in with other bands when he can."

This was not a conversation she wanted to have. Not with Billy, and certainly not with Devin. She tried to sidestep the issue by assuring him they would all be fine.

"It's not all of us I'm worried about. Are you sleeping?"

"Of course." Not a wink.

"Doesn't look it. You have dark circles under your eyes, and your hands shake like you've had too much caffeine. You're also really thin."

Did she look that bad? How would she even know? She couldn't remember the last time she'd actually looked at herself in a mirror. She slid off her stool and turned her back to him as she rinsed her cup out in the sink.

"I'm fine. Just tired. Knowing you're home safe and sound, I'll sleep like a baby."

As if he needed proof, she yawned.

He came up beside her. "Then go to bed. I'll make sure everything's locked up."

It was a wonderful feeling to have someone look after her, even if it was her twenty-one-year-old son.

"Good night, sweetheart." She reached up to kiss his cheek. "Sweet dreams."

"You too, Mom."

Sweet dreams? Oh, what she wouldn't give for just one.

CHAPTER 48

Kate looked about to hyperventilate, a gloved hand dripping with pumpkin guts pressed to her chest. The way Billy's heart was pounding, he should have been clutching his own.

"Jesus Christ, Katie!" He didn't want to yell, but she'd scared the shit out of him. "You can see it's me. Why the hell did you scream like that?"

"What are you doing here?" she demanded once she'd caught her breath. She snapped off a yellow rubber glove and tossed it onto the table next to the blue-gray pumpkin she'd been disemboweling. Mud stains covered the knees and seat of her pants, and her hair was wound into a messy knot on top of her head.

She eyed the duffle bag he'd just dropped at his feet.

"Devin picked me up. I came to help you."

"He didn't say anything to me."

"Because I told him not to. And don't worry, I'll sleep on the futon."

For a moment, he thought she was going to turn him around and send him right back out the way he'd come in. It sucked that he had to practically plead with her to stay in his own home.

She yanked off the other glove. "Fine. I guess I could use the help."

To prove he was a man of his word, he did everything from cleaning bathrooms to polishing silver.

By six, the entire downstairs had been cleaned, dusted, vacuumed, and polished. The pumpkin centerpiece was finished and set out on a hand-quilted table runner. The table was set, and each place setting included a white pumpkin bearing the name of the family member who would be sitting there. Serving dishes were laid out on the sideboard, each with a scrap of paper that detailed what it would hold the next day, and next to each dish was the proper serving utensil.

The carrots had been peeled and steamed, and so had the Brussels sprouts. The yams had been cooked, peeled, sliced, and caramelized. Even the golden Yukon potatoes had been cooked, mashed, and seasoned, ready to be reheated in a crock pot the next day.

It could have been any other Thanksgiving.

Kate was finishing a batch of homemade cranberry sauce while he sat on a stool and watched. His stomach complained loudly. "I don't suppose there's anything for dinner tonight?"

She shook her head. "I wasn't expecting you, and I didn't think Devin would be home until late."

He chuckled. "Yeah, I think that's getting serious."

"He's too young."

"You were younger than he is."

"Fortunately, he's a lot smarter."

He leaned back, hurt. "Ouch."

Kate's shoulders drooped. "I'm sorry. That wasn't right. I didn't mean it like that." Her cheeks pinked and she struggled to smile. "No matter what happens with us, I'll always love you."

Not exactly what he'd been hoping to hear. "That's small reassurance."

She struggled with something to say, then changed the subject. "You're hungry?"

He nodded. "Yeah, but—"

She gave the cranberry sauce a final stir and turned off the heat. "I have a lasagna in the freezer downstairs. Let me run down and get it."

He stood and tugged the dishrag from her hands. "You've done enough. Let's go out and eat." He forced a smile, even though her remark still stung. "How about a date?"

"A date?"

"Yeah, a date. Dinner and a movie."

Kate snorted. "You hardly took me on dates when we were dating."

He flashed her a smile and leaned against the counter. "We were in a hurry to do other things back then. Now we have time to date."

She picked flecks of dried pumpkin flesh from her shirt. "I don't know . . ."

"C'mon. Go get changed. We'll grab something to eat and catch a movie. *Life of Pi* opens today. I know you want to see that."

To see her face, you would have thought he'd ask her to walk a tightrope thirty stories up. He put his arms around her.

"It'll be fine. I promise."

She winced. "Maybe I'll wait until it comes out on DVD."

"Please? I want to go out with my wife. I want you to relax, and I want you to see that you're safe. I'd never let anything happen to you."

She chewed on her bottom lip. "I do want to see it."

"Good." He almost slapped her ass as she turned but caught himself in time. "Go get ready. I'll find out when the movie starts. It'll be good. We need this."

They needed a lot more than dinner and a movie, but it was a start.

~~~

The evening was a disaster. Billy promised Kate they would get there early enough so she could have her choice of seats, which meant grabbing dinner at a drive-through and eating in the car. Once at the theater, she struggled to find a seat. There were plenty, just none that suited her.

"There." She'd finally pointed to a back corner. "It's close enough to the door, and with our backs to the wall, no one can come up behind us."

She spoke so matter-of-factly, it killed him. He nodded, got her situated, and went to get drinks and popcorn. The burger and fries had only whet his appetite.

By the time he returned, Kate had moved to the seat closest to the wall. He had hoped to sit on the aisle, where it would be easier for him to stretch his legs, but like most things these days, he wasn't about to argue with her.

The previews began and the volume in the theater accelerated to just below ear-splitting. By the time the preview for *Les Misérables* began, Kate was white-knuckled and gripping the armrest.

"I can't," she whispered, her voice tight with panic. "Get me out of here."

He held her hand as they squeezed past the others in their row and led her into the lobby. Her face was ashen, and she was trembling. There was nowhere for her to sit, so he slid her down onto the floor and had her lean forward. By the time her breathing returned to normal, a small group of theater employees and patrons had gathered to gawk at the drama. Her pallor was replaced with the flush of embarrassment.

"Are you okay?" He knelt beside her, brushing a damp strand of hair off her face.

"Can we go? Please? I just wanna go home."

Billy's stomach churned on the drive home. It might have been from the fast-food dinner he'd gobbled down, but he didn't think so. More than likely it was because Kate wasn't getting any better. In fact, she was actually getting much worse.

CHAPTER 49

Kate's exhaustion was bone deep. She had hoped—prayed—that with Billy just down the hall and Devin asleep in his own bed, she might be able to have one night of peaceful sleep. Instead, she woke in a cold sweat, a scream stuck in her throat. The nightmare was so bad she couldn't bring herself to close her eyes again.

The temptation to sneak down the hall and climb into bed with Billy was strong, but she was afraid if she fell asleep again, she'd fall right back into the dark abyss waiting to swallow her.

She was nursing her third cup of coffee when Billy came downstairs. He took one look at her and shook his head.

"You didn't sleep?" he asked, his own eyes barely open. He didn't look exactly ready to start the day himself.

She shrugged.

"Katie, you can't go on like this. If the sleeping pills aren't working, you need different ones, and you need to start seeing the therapist. If you don't care about what happens to you, I do. We all do."

A therapist. That was his answer for everything these days. Why didn't any of them understand that there wasn't a damn thing a therapist could do for her? A therapist couldn't bring Joey back or Eileen, or any of those poor people who died because of her. And a therapist couldn't erase what Billy had done either. What was the point? Nothing could be fixed. Didn't he see that? There was no fixing it.

She rubbed her face with her hands and asked him what he wanted for breakfast.

"I'll take care of that. What do you want?"

What do I want? Such a loaded question. *I want my life back.* "I'm not hungry. I'll just have a piece of toast."

He made her two pieces of toast, then buttered them and sprinkled each with cinnamon and sugar, just like she used to do when Rhiannon and Devin were little.

When she finished eating, he turned on the stereo.

"Dance with me," he said, taking her hand and wrapping his arms around her. Rocking her, he sang softly as he rested his chin on the top of her head.

"Billy." Every time he touched her he threw her into a tailspin, weakened her resolve. He probably knew it, too. She tried to pull away. "I have things to do."

"This is more important."

She let out a long sigh. "Two minutes, that's it." It was easier to give in, so she let him dance her around the dining room. The song ended, but he didn't let go. She reminded him how much work she had to do, but he silenced her with his mouth on hers, holding her so close she couldn't move.

Sometimes he made it seem so easy, as if they could just take a step backward and pick up where they'd left off. He kissed her until her legs turned to rubber. And she let him.

"Come back to me, Katie." He whispered so low she wasn't sure if he'd meant for her to hear.

"How do you do that?" she whispered back.

He arched an eyebrow.

"After all we've been through, and all that has happened, how do you still make me weak in the knees?"

He tucked a strand of hair behind her ear. "Because. You love me. And I love you. Can't you see that?"

She did. But was it enough?

CHAPTER 50

The conversation around the dinner table was loud, jovial, and as far as Kate was concerned, forced. They were each trying to be their most charming, most engaging. She appreciated the effort, but her head throbbed and it was becoming difficult to pretend she was enjoying herself just to make everyone else feel better.

The wine should help numb the pain. She'd already polished off several cups of hot apple cider punch. Hopefully, the Riesling would finish the job.

She stood, and as she did, her chair banged into the wall behind her. "I want to make a toast." She raised her glass. "I know we're all trying to ignore the elephant in the room." Her eyes swept the ceiling. "Yes, Joey, I mean you. I'm sure you're looking down at us right now, wishing you were here."

It was difficult talking around the lump lodged in her throat. She gripped the linen napkin she held in her other hand and swayed, sloshing wine onto the table.

Billy's chair scraped along the floor, but Devin was up faster. "Mom? May I?"

"Please." Kate collapsed into her chair, relieved. Something monumental should be said, but she didn't have it in her to figure out what that something should be.

Devin raised his glass. "To Uncle Joey. There was never a kinder, sweeter, funnier, more generous man alive. You live on in our hearts and in our minds every day."

There were a couple of murmured amens and other unintelligible syllables, followed by an uncomfortable silence. They'd said their goodbyes in July. Moved on. She was the only one stuck.

The chatter started again. Which was worse, the silence or the noise?

She mumbled an excuse and slipped into the kitchen, where she turned on the faucet. Leaving it running, she walked out the back door.

Despite a light breeze that carried the hint of a chill, it was warm for late November. Long strands of hair drifted across her face. Kate tucked them behind her ears before pushing her hands into the pockets of her plaid woolen skirt.

The field bordering their land had been cut weeks earlier. Acres of short, jagged stalks remained, sharp teeth ready to chew up anyone foolish enough to stumble forward. At the far edge of the cornfield, three large boxwood hedges caught the last rays of the setting sun—chartreuse gumdrops against the deepening twilight.

She leaned against the ancient outhouse, which had been reincarnated into a rabbit hutch, and more recently, a garden shed. Shielded from prying eyes, she could finally give in to the tears she'd been struggling to hide all day.

Thanksgiving, and she could think of nothing to be thankful for. Not one thing. Further proof she didn't deserve to be here.

Her knees gave way, and her body began to slide against the worn shiplap siding. Strong hands stopped her descent, catching her before she landed in the damp earth.

Billy pulled her up and held her in place.

She studied his face. His hair brushed his shoulders, multiple shades of gold and not a single strand of silver. His face was clean-shaven and smooth. Tiny lines had taken up residence at the corners of his eyes, but other than looking more tired than usual, he looked like the same heartbreakingly beautiful man she'd fallen in love with. Just a little older, if not any wiser.

He lifted her face in both his hands. Blue-gray eyes searched hers, dipping into her very soul, sparking something—if only for a second—deep inside.

His thumb traced over her bottom lip. "I'm staying the rest of the weekend. I don't care what you say."

Devin was there, she wanted to remind him, but she'd hardly seen Devin since he got home. She settled her hands on Billy's waist and leaned her forehead against his chest.

"Okay."

The sun had dropped below the tree line behind them. The glowing shrubs faded into the darkness, and the cornfield grew more sinister.

"You ready to go back inside?"

No. "Yeah, sure."

Her hand dwarfed in his, he led her toward the house. Rhiannon and Doug, who had been peering out the kitchen window, ducked out of sight.

Billy looked down at her and smirked. "Smooth."

Despite the despair she'd been feeling all day, she couldn't help but smile. "Seriously."

Once inside, Kate slipped into the bathroom. Other than the dark moons beneath her eyes and the pink rimming her lashes, her skin was colorless. She could go upstairs and reapply her makeup, but for what? A fresh coat of mascara wouldn't change anything.

In her absence, the dishes had been cleared and piled on the counter along with the half-empty bowls and platters. Coffee was brewing, and dessert waited on the table, along with bowls of fruit, nuts, and a tray of assorted chocolates.

She refilled her wine glass, which might make it easier to endure the rest of the holiday.

When the twins began to fuss, Billy brought out his acoustic and pulled a chair in front of the fireplace. He started with one of his own songs, but seeing that he was losing his target audience, he began to make up silly songs using the boys' names. Rhiannon pulled two boxes of pasta from the pantry and handed one to each boy so that they too could make music, or so she said.

To see her family happy and enjoying each other would normally fill her with joy. Instead, it made her sad that she couldn't join them. Even worse. She envied them.

A yawn caught her off guard. She tried to stifle it, but Billy must have noticed. He finished his version of the *Blues Clues* song and set down his guitar.

"All done," he said as the boys rushed him yelling for more. "Nonna's tired. Poppy has to put her to bed."

They turned on Kate.

"No, Nonna," Dalton cried. "No bed!"

"Bad Nonna!" Dayton stomped his little foot.

"I beg your pardon?" She snatched him up and planted several raspberries on his belly as he dissolved into hysterical laughter.

Doug shoveled the last of his pumpkin pie into his mouth, then began collecting the dessert dishes.

Rhiannon stood. "You need to help me get the boys ready. It's past their bedtime anyway."

He grabbed a handful of silverware. "We need to help your mother with the dishes."

Help was exactly what Kate wanted, but she wanted something else more. "It's okay. The boys are tired." She ignored the smug look her daughter shot at her husband. "But while we're all here, I was hoping we could talk about Christmas."

"Christmas? Geez, Mom," Rhiannon said. "I haven't even digested Thanksgiving."

"I know, but this is a good time to talk about it."

Now that she had their attention, she wasn't sure how to proceed.

"What is it, Kate?" Doug asked.

She mashed the untouched sliver of cheesecake on her plate into an untouched shred of pumpkin pie. "I was hoping we could do Christmas at your house this year." She studied her daughter as she spoke. "I just think it's going to be too—"

"Our house? I can't manage an entire holiday by myself."

Doug reached for her hand. "Honey, I'm sure we could—"

Rhiannon swatted him away. "Absolutely not. Besides, it's tradition. We always have holidays here. It wouldn't be the same."

"What would we eat?" Devin's question earned him a nasty look from his sister. Undaunted, he continued. "Rhiannon can't cook, so who would do the cooking? I'm not eating kale for Christmas. I don't care if it is green."

Rhiannon glowered. "Ha-ha."

Kate felt nauseous. "I would help you. It's just that this was so hard on me, and you have that big, beautiful house—"

"You don't think it's been hard on all of us?" Rhiannon pressed an open palm to her chest. "You forget, not only do I have a husband and two children to take care of, I'm also taking care of Daddy."

Kate had expected some pushback, but this? This was ridiculous. "Really, Rhiannon. Your father's hardly there, and it's not like he's a doddering fool who needs to be coddled."

"That's beside the point. It's out of the question. I have all I can manage taking care of two small boys. You have no idea how difficult that is."

She did *not* just go there. "True," Kate answered, channeling her late best friend. "You and Devin were born as very short, wholly functioning adults."

"Very funny, Mother. You forget we weren't twins, though."

"Rhiannon." Billy's voice carried a note of warning, but Kate was on a roll.

"No. There was an entire fifteen months between the two of you. I had all I could do to find enough to fill my days, with your father on the road three hundred days a year and me home alone with two small children. And you know what? In all those years, I still decorated, cooked, cleaned, and shopped for every single holiday. I was the Tooth Fairy, the Easter Bunny, and Santa Fucking Claus. And I must've done such a good job no one wants to take my place."

Kate rose so quickly her chair toppled over. "I'm just asking for a break. For just one fucking holiday off!"

Dayton and Dalton had begun to cry, but Kate could barely hear them over the clanging in her ears.

"Good going, Mom!" Rhiannon cried.

"That's enough!" Billy pounded his fist on the table, rattling dessert plates and wine glasses.

"We're done." Rhiannon threw her hands up and stalked out of the room.

Kate slumped against the wall. What the hell had come over her? She'd never spoken like that to either of her children. Ever.

Devin stared at the table, his napkin twisted in his fist. Kate wouldn't look up, but she could feel Billy's eyes on her. She could only imagine what he was thinking. Probably the same thing she was thinking: that she'd completely lost her mind.

Rhiannon returned wearing her coat and carrying her purse and the diaper bag. She thrust the boys' jackets at Doug, then without a word to anyone, walked out the front door, taking the long way back to her car, presumably to avoid having to pass Kate.

Doug spoke softly to Dayton, calming him, before helping him into his jacket.

"I'll talk to her," Doug promised, zipping the boy's jacket. He reached for Dalton. "I'm sure we can have Christmas at our house. We'll hire some help if need be. Please don't worry about it."

Kate waved him off. "It was a silly idea. It's better if I stay busy anyway." She pointed to her glass. "I think I had a little too much vino. I got all maudlin on you."

"We'll talk anyway," Doug promised.

Billy hoisted Dayton into his arms and carried him to Kate to kiss goodbye. His eyes sad, he looked like he wanted to say something, but in the end, he pressed his lips against the top of her head and followed Doug out to the car.

Other than the sound of Devin clearing the table, the house was strangely silent. Kate picked up the cheesecake and what was left of the pumpkin pie and followed him into the kitchen.

"I'm sorry," she said. "I don't know what came over me."

He finished scraping the plate he was holding and placed it next to the sink. He picked up another, scraped it, and carefully set it on the pile. Then he turned to face her.

"I get it, Mom. I do. And I'll be the first to call Rhiannon a brat. But try looking at it through her eyes. In some ways, she's just like you. Married young, two kids right off the bat. Thing is, I'm not sure that was in her master plan. Marrying Doug? That was all her, but I think there were things she wanted to do first that didn't involve changing diapers and scrubbing toilets, at least not right away."

"Your sister doesn't scrub toilets."

"Maybe not, but it's still her job to make sure all the toilets in her McMansion are clean."

It had to be the wine, because none of this was making much sense. No one had said anything about cleaning toilets.

"I think she's kinda lost. To ask her to do something you've done effortlessly is setting her up for failure, and you and I both know she wouldn't like that very much."

"Effortlessly?"

Devin reached for another plate. "You make it seem that way. Our holidays have always been perfect. The best. Even when Dad couldn't be here, you made them special. She wouldn't even know where to begin."

"I said I would help. And besides, you're the one who made that crack about her cooking."

"Yeah. My bad." He scrubbed a hand across his face. "I was trying to break the tension. I'll call her tomorrow and apologize."

Kate felt as if she weighed a thousand pounds. The thought of letting down one more person was just too much. Being angry would've been easier.

She reached up and kissed Devin on the cheek.

"Tell your father I went to bed, will you? And ask him to help you with this." She motioned to the mountain of dirty dishes. "If not, just leave it for me. I'll do it when I get up."

She passed through the dining room and snatched the half-empty bottle of wine off the table. Her foot hadn't even hit the steps before she yanked out the cork and lifted the bottle to her mouth.

CHAPTER 51

Billy cringed at the fear in his son's eyes. He'd bet anything Rhiannon was frightened as well; she just had a hell of a way of showing it. He rested a hand on Devin's shoulder.

"She'll be fine," he said, praying he was right. "I'm going to insist she start seeing a psychiatrist immediately, even if I have to carry her there."

Devin nodded and tore off a strip of plastic wrap.

"Where is she?" Billy peeked into the dining room, surveying the damage. It was hard to believe so few people could make such a huge mess.

"She went up to bed," Devin said, his voice flat.

"I know you have a date. If you could just put the food away, I'll deal with the rest of it later." He headed for the steps. "Lock up behind you."

The bedroom was empty, but the bathroom door was closed. Billy tapped gently. When Kate didn't answer, he turned the knob, relieved it wasn't locked.

Steam filled the room, coating the mirror and the windows. Kate sat upright, the claw-foot tub filled to capacity, her hair floating around her shoulders like a dark nimbus. The slightest movement would send water cascading over the edge.

He knocked on the open door.

"Yes?" She didn't open her eyes.

"You okay?"

"Fine." She reached for a bottle of wine sitting on the floor beside the tub and raised it to her lips. Water cascaded over the edge of the tub as she stretched to set it down.

Billy rescued the bottle and took a mouthful before placing it on the counter. He leaned on the edge of the sink.

"We'll work it out. Don't worry."

"Whatever." Her arm snaked out, searching. He handed her the bottle. Another wave flowed over the side and splashed onto the floor.

Billy unfastened his watch and set it near the sink. He pulled his shirt over his head and snagged an elastic from a sea shell on the counter and slipped it into his hair. Kneeling beside the tub, he plucked the sponge from the mass of bubbles and swept Kate's hair to the side, running the sponge along her neck and shoulders. She rocked under his touch.

He lifted her arm and slid the sponge from her wrist to her ribs. Despite the sauna-like atmosphere of the room, she shivered. He dipped the sponge again and squeezed, allowing the water to flow over her. Eyes still closed, she bent her legs and rested her cheek on her knee as he drew the sponge across her shoulders and over her neck.

When he'd finished, he took her hand. "Can you stand?"

Kate squinted as if he'd just woken her. Water sloshed over the sides, pooling onto the floor as he helped her up.

He gripped her waist with one hand, the other he slid upward along her ribs, up to her breasts, where he lingered, his thumb sweeping over her taut nipple. He repeated the movement, increasing the pressure.

Her chest rose and fell with short breaths. Her eyes, dark and hooded, remained fixed on his.

He grasped the soap and lathered his hands, running them over her body. The sweet, citrusy scent filling his nostrils as he explored her skin, moving over her hips and around the curve of her ass, where he lingered, gently kneading the tender flesh and hoping she wouldn't push him away.

She didn't. Instead, her lip caught in her bottom teeth and her fingertips dug into his shoulders.

He slipped his soapy hand between her legs, running his thumb into the softness of her.

Thoughts of rejection clouded his mind. His need for her was powerful, but more than that, he wanted to free her; give her a release. Even if it would be no more than a few stolen minutes.

He steadied her with an arm around her waist as his thumb probed deeper, moving quickly, strumming the small, round bead. He dropped his head and captured a nipple in his mouth, grazing it with his teeth. Her body vibrated against his.

Holding tight, he plunged two fingers deep inside her. Her head rolled back and she pressed her hips against his hand, her muscles tightening around his fingers. Her arms grasped his shoulders; her fingers tangled in his hair. This woman was the sweetest instrument he'd ever played, and the sound of her coming undone was music to his ears.

"Let go, baby. I got you."

It started from deep within her, a soft, low moan that rose until her cries echoed off the tiled walls. With a deep, low growl, she nearly collapsed in his arms. Billy softened his touch, massaging her gently as her orgasm faded. He buried his face in her neck, kissing the spot below her ear, and gently biting the curve of her shoulder.

"I want you." Her words were barely a whisper, but he heard them.

"You're drunk, Katie."

"I am." She sighed. "But I still want you."

His brain went to war with the rest of him. He had little self-control when it came to his addictions, and his greatest weakness was standing before him, wet, naked, and *wanting* him.

"Are you sure?" The question was almost painful.

Her head bobbed slightly. "Yeah."

He lifted her from the tub and draped a towel over her shoulders.

Between the makeup smudges below her eyes, the wet hair trailing over her shoulders, and the pink flush of her skin, she had a just-fucked look that on its own threatened to derail him. He grabbed the edges of the towel and pulled her closer.

"God, you are so beautiful."

She shrugged off the towel and linked her hands around his neck. She pulled the elastic from his hair and rubbed her fingers against his scalp and through the long, thick strands.

He let her set the pace, waited to see where she would take them. What he wanted was obvious, but it had to be what she wanted. He needed her, but it was so much more than sex. She had been his salvation, his safe harbor, no matter what.

Now it was his turn. She was drifting away, and he would be her anchor.

She gazed into his eyes as if she could read what was written on his heart. Her hands cradled his face.

"I need you, Billy," she whispered. "Save me."

He stepped out of his jeans, then he lifted her up and laid her on the quilt.

The desperation evaporated. The lines in her face faded. There was a softness there now, and a contentment he hadn't seen in months. His lips touched her eyelids, her nose, trailing along the edge of her jaw. He kneaded her earlobe gently between his teeth. Her skin pebbled when his tongue tickled the hollow behind her ear.

She wrapped her legs around his waist and he rolled, flipping her on top, letting her take the lead.

Her skin was velvet against his, and they rediscovered each other, slowly, deliberately. Touching her, holding her. He had missed this more than anything.

Later, Kate slept with her head in the curve of his arm, her hair spread across his chest like a soft, warm blanket. He lovingly stroked each strand, fighting to stay awake. In the morning, she'd be sober, and the safety net he'd managed to wrap around her might snap, leaving her exposed and vulnerable, and tumbling away from him yet again.

CHAPTER 52

Sunlight played across Kate's face. She blinked lazily and tried to remember how long it had been since she had woken to the sun and not the moon? The deadweight of Billy's arm rested across her chest, his leg flung carelessly over her own, pinning her in place. His head rested on her pillow and his hair, golden threads of amber, honey, and wheat mingled with her own chestnut strands. Her head throbbed, but having more than a couple of hours of sleep made the pain tolerable.

She had escaped last night from the jagged edges of her life. For a brief, blissful time, she had not only regained her passion, she had found softness and warmth in Billy's arms. She had remembered what happiness felt like.

But darkness had returned with the dawn, dragging her deeper into its never-ending pit. In spite of the sunlit morning, she was as empty and hollow as ever.

She watched Billy sleep, her heart turning inside out. When she couldn't bear it anymore, she slipped out from under him and headed downstairs.

The mess from yesterday remained spread across the dining room table and kitchen counters, triggering memories of the angry conversation of the night before. More heartache. It would take hours to clean up, but at least it was something to occupy her mind.

Charlie was dancing by the back door, so as soon as she'd set the coffee pot to brew—first things first—she opened the door to let him out.

Billy's truck wasn't in the driveway. The clock on the stove said it was just after seven. Too early for Devin to have gone out, which meant he'd never come home.

Hands shaking, she clawed through her bag for her cell phone. The goddamn battery was dead. She snatched the charger off the counter and plugged it in, then reached for the house phone.

Devin's cell rang several times before he picked up.

"Where the hell are you?" Fear amplified her voice.

"Mom?" he asked, sleepily.

"Yes. Mom! Where are you?"

"I sent you a text." He yawned in her ear. "We went to a party and since we were drinking, we spent the night. I sent you a message."

She sank onto a stool behind her. "I didn't get any message."

"Well, I'm sorry about that, but I sent it." Sounding more awake, he lowered his voice. "Jesus, Mom. Get a grip, will you?"

His anger and frustration surprised her. Her cell phone beeped. The message, sent before midnight, flashed across the screen: "Had a couple drinks. Staying overnight. Better safe than sorry. Leave the dishes, I'll do them when I get home."

Oh God.

"I'm sorry," she stammered. "I see it now. I just got scared when I didn't see the truck—"

"Whatever. I'll see you later." He hung up before she could say anything else.

Kate was standing at the sink, scrubbing dried food from pots and pans that would have done well with an overnight soak, when Billy came up behind her. He slipped his arms around her shoulders and kissed the top of her head. She stiffened.

"How are you feeling this morning?"

Steam curled around her, and she scrubbed harder, her entire body vibrating from the effort. "Good."

She'd tried to hold it in, tried to lose herself in greasy roasting pans and dishes caked with crusty mashed potatoes and pumpkin pie, but on that single word her voice broke.

"Oh, Katie. What's wrong?" He turned off the water and pressed a dish towel into her hands, then guided her to a chair in the dining room. Through tears, she told him about her conversation with Devin. Then she rehashed the fight with Rhiannon. Any other time, either event would have done little more than annoy her. Given everything else, they overwhelmed her.

"That's enough." He tipped her chin and made her look at him. "I want you to see a doctor. You can't keep suffering like this."

Not this again! "How many times do I have to tell you no? I don't want to. It's not gonna help. Why can't you see that?" She dropped her head into her hands, but jumped when his fist came crashing into the table. The stack of clean plates shivered dangerously.

"Bull shit! You're going to see a goddamn shrink."

She started to protest, but he cut her off.

"That's it. No more wallowing. No more excuses. You're getting help."

Spit flew from his mouth, and he jabbed his finger in her face. "I mean it!"

He took a step back and folded his arms over his chest. Billy was stubborn and demanding, and he was used to getting his own way, but not this time. He had no right to tell her what to do, and there was no way in hell she was going to sit on some stranger's couch and relive the worst year of her life. No. Fucking. Way.

When it seemed he'd finally calmed down, he reached for her and ran his hands along her arms until he captured her wrists. Then he lowered his face until she had no choice but to look at him. This time when he spoke, his words were softer, almost desperate.

"I can't bear the thought of losing you, Katie, especially when you're standing right here in front of me."

It wasn't funny, but she almost laughed.

He just didn't get it. It was too late. She was already gone.

CHAPTER 53

Kate sat at the dining room table while Billy called Dr. Mueller, the psychiatrist their family doctor had recommended back in September. The office was closed, but he left a message with the service saying it was an emergency.

"It's not an emergency," she said after he hung up.

"Yes, it is."

She poked at the scrambled eggs he'd insisted on making her. He was treating her like a child, and she didn't like it. She didn't want to see a doctor, and she didn't want to take medicine that clouded her mind. It would just push her feelings below the surface where they would churn and bubble, then spring back when she least expected it.

She swirled her fork through a puddle of ketchup.

"Eat."

"I'm not hungry. I'm having a hard time swallowing."

"Because you never eat!" he shouted. He held up his palms. "I'm sorry. I don't mean to yell, but you've got me so fucking frustrated I don't know what else to do. I'm not going to stand by and watch you shrivel up and blow away."

"I'm fine."

"Jesus, Katie! You're not fine!"

She set her fork down and folded her arms. Would he make her sit at the table until she finished? Wouldn't surprise her. He was treating her like a child.

"I'm sorry." He spoke more softly, although still through clenched teeth. "I'm just worried."

She didn't answer. And while she didn't look up, she could feel his eyes on her. She shifted just enough to turn her back to him and focused on a pine tree outside the window.

He sighed loudly. "I'm gonna take a shower. If the phone rings, answer it, and if it's the doctor's office, take the earliest appointment. I'll go with you."

Yeah, right.

She waited until she heard the bedroom door close, then she scraped her uneaten eggs into the trash. She wasn't going to sit around and wait for the phone to ring. Especially since she had no intention of seeing any doctor.

What she needed was to keep busy, that's all. Devin should be home soon. She would send him and Billy to the tree farm to pick up wreaths for the front windows. Thanksgiving had been such a huge fucking success, she couldn't wait to see what Christmas would bring.

⌒

Climbing into the attic terrified Kate, yet there she was, balanced at the top of the pull-down ladder, trying to hoist herself up through the opening. The muscles in her arms shivered under the strain, and the little bit of breakfast she'd choked down earlier threatened to come back up.

She never went into the attic. Ever. Heights frightened her, and the steep ladder was unnerving. And she was convinced there were bats up there. She could have waited for Billy to finish his shower, but what if the phone rang? He'd expect her to answer it, and that wasn't happening. If she was up in the attic and missed the call, so be it. At least this way she would have a legitimate excuse as to why she couldn't answer. Then hopefully, he'd forget about her seeing any doctor.

With a loud *oomph,* she pulled herself up. There was enough room to stand, but she stayed low, crawling on her hands and knees. Any resident bats would probably be hibernating, but with her luck, one would fly into her hair and she'd end up falling through the opening in the ceiling. With frequent glances into the rafters above her, she searched for the box that held the red tartan ribbons for the Christmas wreaths.

The attic was small. Boxes were wedged tightly against each other. It seemed Billy had organized it into some kind of system. There were several large red and green plastic containers in the far corner. Crawling as quickly and quietly as she could, she skittered across the attic, only to catch her sweater on a shoebox, dumping it over.

"Damn it."

Dozens of identical slips of paper littered the floor. It was difficult to see exactly what they were in the low light, but they looked like checks.

Billy had always been so infuriatingly secretive when it came to their finances. Any other time, she would have been wildly curious, but for now, all she wanted was to get the damn ribbons and get out of the attic. She began scooping up the checks. At first she dumped them into the box, but knowing Billy, there had probably been some kind of order to them. She pulled out a handful. Maybe by date. She could probably gather them by month, at least.

She picked up one and held it to the sliver of light coming from the hallway below. *March 15, 2009.* She picked up another. *December 15, 1997. February 15, 2002. June 15, 2006.*

None were from the same month. She reached for a few more: *July 15, 1998. April 15, 2004. May 15, 2004.*

"What the hell?"

Some amounts were the same. Five hundred. Eight hundred. A thousand.

She dropped onto her bottom. There were at least two hundred canceled checks, some going as far back as 1991, all made out on the fifteenth of the month and all to the same woman: Jessie Jones.

A slow, sick feeling worked its way into her belly. She pawed through more of the checks: *October 15, 2011. May 15, 2006. January 15, 2012.* This year. Fifteen hundred dollars.

The contents of her stomach rose, and bile burned her throat. She swallowed it down.

Jessie Jones. The name wasn't familiar, but why would it be? If Billy had gone through the trouble of hiding these checks in the one place he knew Kate would never find them, it was because he'd never wanted her to see them.

She thought of how many times he'd swore to her that what had happened with Christa was a one-time thing. Maybe it was. But here was proof that whatever had happened with Jessie Jones had lasted more than one night.

Kate shoved the rest of the cancelled checks back into the box and shut the lid. Then she took a deep breath.

If someone had asked her this morning if it were possible for her heart to be any more broken than it already was, she would have said no, definitely not.

And she would have been wrong.

~

Eileen's car started on the first try. Too bad the gas gauge was empty. Worse, she was a couple of miles out of town before she noticed. Billy had still been in the shower when she'd grabbed her jacket and rushed out the back door. She hadn't thought to grab her purse. With no money and no driver's license, she wouldn't get far.

Not that she had a clue where she was going anyway.

She pulled over at the first place she could—a small parking area for an Appalachian Trail access point. A Subaru with Maine plates was the only other car in the lot. Ironic. She and Joey had hiked this trail as teenagers. They had also both loved Maine. If she believed in such things, which she didn't, she might be tempted to think he was trying to send her a message.

For someone who suffered tremors at the thought of walking into the grocery store these days, hiking up the side of a mountain alone was irrational. Had she been in her right mind, she would have returned home as soon as she realized her limits.

Clearly, she wasn't in her right mind.

The ascent up the trail, normally a twenty-minute hike, took twice as long. She'd done nothing physical for months and it showed. Her main occupation had become sitting. Sitting and thinking. It was a terrible occupation.

When she reached the top, she saw that the view was as beautiful as she remembered, but it did little to lighten the heaviness in her heart. From atop the rocky outcropping, she could see the river snaking its way around a bend not far from the Delaware Water Gap. It was quiet. The sun shone brightly. With hardly a cloud in the sky, she could see for miles.

She dropped to the cold, hard ground and leaned against a boulder, trying to catch her breath.

She couldn't do it anymore. None of it.

Losing Joey and then finding out Billy had been unfaithful with Christa should have been enough to destroy her, but she'd survived, only to bring devastation to all those other families.

And now this? He'd sworn the incident with Christa was the only time he'd ever been unfaithful. Granted, she hadn't been willing to discuss it with him; she couldn't. But he had sworn. And now? Having to face the possibility that Billy was supporting another woman somewhere, or a child? Clearly he was lying.

She'd known so many of Billy's friends and bandmates who'd used sex as a power trip or a stress reliever or just because it was so readily available. Why had she ever thought they were above that? That they were somehow better? That they loved each other more?

"You're such a fool, Kate."

She pressed the heels of her hands into her eyes and tried to erase the unwelcome images springing up like weeds. If she could reach inside her head to tear out her brain, she would.

"Stop! Stop, stop, stop!" She twisted her hands in her hair and pulled, screaming at the top of her lungs. As if that would make it go away. All it did was startle a red-tailed hawk from its perch beyond the clearing. It let out a high-pitched screech and soared out over the ridge before dropping out of sight.

She wanted to kick the ground and tear handfuls of her hair from her head, but even heartache required more energy than she could manage. She toppled over and curled up against the wide boulder, her face in the dirt, and cried.

When there were no tears left, and she echoed with the hollowness of her life, she rolled onto her back and blinked up at the sky.

She wasn't supposed to be here. Sedge Stevens had been looking for her. Instead, he'd killed all those other people. Annoyed with Eileen, she'd taken refuge in the bathroom, and that had saved her life. It wasn't fair. Of course she felt empty. Her entire life had been a mistake. Her parents hadn't wanted her. She simply wasn't supposed to be here.

She rolled onto her knees and stared into the horizon. She was so empty. If she stepped off the edge, she would be picked up by an air current, a dried leaf, tumbling and drifting until she crumbled, scattering in a million directions as she fell to the ground where she would spend eternity among the soft pine needles, moss, and detritus lining the forest floor.

It would be a more peaceful existence than the one she tried to endure each day.

She stood and brushed the dried leaves and twigs from her legs. She took several careful steps toward the edge and peered down the steep, rocky embankment. That's what she would do. One final step and it would be over. It was perfect.

She just had to decide when.

And when she did, she would bring the pills, in case she chickened out. And the bottle of French wine she'd hidden away for a special occasion.

Because really, what was more special than dying?

CHAPTER 54

The car door swung open as Kate pulled the keys from the ignition. Billy grabbed her arm and practically yanked her out of her seat.

"Where were you?" he yelled. "You scared the shit out of me."

"I went for a ride." She pushed against his chest. "Let go. You're hurting me."

He shook her before releasing her. "Hurting you? I'd put you over my knee if I thought it would do any good."

She averted her eyes, and as she did, she noticed he wasn't wearing any shoes or socks.

"You're going to get sick," she said as she walked past him toward the house.

He followed close behind.

"Where were you?" he asked again, only slightly calmer.

"I told you." Unable to look at him, she gave Charlie a scratch behind the ears. "I went for a ride."

He pulled something from her hair and held it up. "You don't get covered with leaves from riding in a car."

She ran a hand through her uncombed hair, picking out the remaining stragglers.

"I drove for a little while, and when I realized Eileen's car was almost out of gas, I pulled over and took a walk." She was tired of arguing, but she couldn't help feeling defensive at getting the third degree. "I'm not a prisoner, you know."

Billy took a deep breath and forced it out through clenched teeth. "The doctor's office called. He'll see you Monday morning."

"He?" She shook her head. "No way. I'd rather a woman doctor." Not that it mattered. She wasn't going.

He wanted to strangle her, she could tell, but he was doing an admirable job keeping his temper in check. More or less.

"This is the psychiatrist Dr. Patterson recommended. This is who can see you Monday. This is who you're going to see. Understand?"

"You're not the boss of me!" Gah! That sounded childish even to her.

He threw his hands up in disgust. "What are you? Five? You're acting like a child, so I guess I'm not surprised."

"Maybe it's just how you treat me." She waved her hand. "No worries. I won't be your problem much longer."

"What the hell is that supposed to mean?" The meter of his voice changed, and worry clouded his features.

"Nothing." She shook her head and pushed past him. "I don't know what I'm saying. I'm just not myself these days."

⌇

Billy cursed under his breath.

"What's wrong?" his agent, C.J., asked. "I thought this is what you wanted."

"It is," he whispered into the phone. "It's just . . . the timing isn't good. Katie's—"

"Look, Billy, it's only three weeks, but it's a big three weeks. The new songs are great, but we gotta road test them. You keep this up and I can guarantee you a record deal, but I have to get you out there. People need to hear you. There was a lot of buzz after that performance in Miami this summer, and to tell the truth, the arrest and all the rest of it didn't hurt that angry rock star image, either. There's no bad publicity, not for someone like you, but fans have short memories."

"I know," he agreed, "and God knows I need the money—"

"Look, it's just three weeks. She can't be without you for three freaking weeks?"

Could she? She was getting worse, there was no doubt about it. But if she started seeing the doctor, and if he could talk her into staying with Rhiannon . . .

"I don't know. I guess. I'll figure something out."

C.J. was all business. "Okay, then. I'll have a car pick you up first thing Monday to bring you straight to the airport. I'll meet you there, and we'll sign the contracts. Just leave everything to me."

"Fine."

"And Billy? I had to pull a lot of strings to get you on this leg of the tour. This is the perfect audience for you. Don't screw this up. You're not a cat. You don't have nine lives, and even if you did, you've about run out."

"Yeah, I get it. I'll see you Monday."

"That's what I want to hear."

Now for the fun part: convincing Kate to stay with Rhiannon, and convincing Rhiannon to get her mother to the doctor.

The timing sucked. People only got so many chances, and this was probably his last one. For the past several months, while trying to keep himself sane at Rhiannon's, he'd been writing new songs. He'd even done some preliminary recordings. They were good. It was some of the best work he'd ever done. Not only that, but after his last altercation with Christa, it seems she'd finally stopped fucking with his career. Maybe he should've threatened to kill her years ago.

He dragged his hand through his hair and slipped his phone into the front pocket of his jeans.

"I don't suppose that was the doctor." Kate had showered and dried her hair. She'd even put on makeup. And judging by the look on her face, she knew it wasn't the doctor. Shit.

"Look, Katie. A really important job's come up. I have to leave Sunday afternoon. I'm flying out of New York first thing Monday. I'll be on the road for a few weeks."

He followed her into the kitchen.

"I need to work. I'm sure you understand that, more than anyone. I know I said I'd go to the doctor with you, but I'm not going to be able to now. I wish I could."

The look on her face said she didn't believe him.

"It's going to be a quick tour, pretty much crisscrossing the country, but I'll have my phone on me all the time in case you need me."

"I'll be fine. I told you, you don't need to worry about me." Her voice was flat and unemotional.

She picked up the coffeepot and began to fill it with water. Just what they all needed. More caffeine. His blood pressure was on the rise without it.

"Well, I do worry about you. I want you to stay with Rhiannon while I'm gone."

"Ha! Did you mention that to her?"

"No. I'll call her later. When you take me back Sunday, you can just stay."

"We don't have to wait." She slipped the carafe into the coffeemaker and hit the button. "I can take you now."

"I don't want to go now," he said evenly. "I'll go Sunday, like I said."

"Why do you think you get to call the shots?" she asked defiantly, almost challenging him to a fight.

"That's enough, okay? I'm not leaving till Sunday, and I'm not discussing it." He wanted to put his fist through a wall. Probably not a good idea. "I'm gonna get the Christmas stuff down from the attic, and I'll help you do the decorating. This way you don't have to worry about it."

She turned her back to him. "Trust me. I'm not worried about it."

He ran his fingers through his hair and wondered why he had any left or why it hadn't all turned gray. He reached for her, but when his hand touched her shoulder, she pulled away.

"What happened this morning? Last night was . . . It hasn't been like that in so long. What the fuck happened this morning that all of a sudden you're mad at me again?"

Her casual shrug hurt, as if answering him wasn't worth the trouble. When she turned to walk away, his frustration got the better of him. He caught her by the arm and tugged, causing her to stumble.

"Don't shut me out, Katie. It's not fair."

"Let. Go." She snarled, pulling her arm back. "You made your choice. Obviously it's not me."

"Oh, for fuck's sake. Not that again." He let go. He needed to get it together, or he was going to erupt. "You need to listen. I love you. I've always loved you. Why the hell won't you believe that? I don't want anyone else. I never have." He took hold of her upper arms. His voice was barely a whisper. "I love you more than anything? Can't you see that?"

He searched her eyes for some connection, a spark, but he saw nothing but dull, blank orbs.

"Let me go." As angry as she'd been a few moments ago, now there was nothing.

He wanted to kiss her or take her by the shoulders and shake some sense into her. Instead, he did as she asked. He let her go.

She turned and stomped up the steps.

Fuck coffee. He spun toward the kitchen and the bottle of Jack over the refrigerator, and found Devin and his girlfriend standing in the doorway. Devin's eyes narrowed into cold, dark slits when they met his.

"Here we are again," Devin announced, glaring at him. "Home, crap home."

~

Since coming to her decision, Kate felt strangely detached. As if she was just going through the motions. It was like preparing for a big party or a holiday, only she was the only one invited.

She was sorting through her clothing, trying to decide what she might want to be buried in when Billy knocked. He waited for her to invite him in before entering. Then he took a few tentative steps into the room and waited, his hands shoved into his pockets.

"Do you really want me to leave today?"

She held up a long white dress. Without a tan, it made her look washed out, so she put it back in the closet.

About to say yes, she wanted him to leave, she changed her mind when she saw the look on his face. He looked stressed and anxious. She assumed that was her fault. Had she always made him crazy? That could explain the drinking. She certainly made herself want to drink.

There was another reason she didn't say yes. Despite what he'd done to her, she didn't want his last memory of her to be of them fighting. Besides, she wasn't about to give him to Christa or Jessie or whoever else he was fooling around with any sooner than she had to.

She choked back the lump in her throat and shook her head. "I'm sorry. You can stay."

He didn't smile. He just nodded and looked defeated.

"We got the Christmas decorations down," he said. "Devin went up to White's for the wreaths. When he gets back, we'll hang them."

"So you weren't planning on going back to Rhiannon's today, were you?"

"I would've finished the wreaths and then asked Devin to take me. Like I said, if you want me to go, I'll go. I'm sorry for upsetting you, although I'll be damned if I know what I did."

He looked sincere. And if she didn't know what was stashed away up in the attic, it would have been easy to believe that he was. He would've made a damn fine actor.

"Forget it. I'll be down in a few minutes to make the bows."

This time he did smile. "Devin's girlfriend is working on them."

"Danielle? She's here?"

"Yeah, and apparently she knows how to make bows. Devin says she's hooked on Pinterest or something. They look terrific."

"That's great." Kate swallowed. "You don't even need me."

The smile faded. "Don't ever say that. I'll always need you."

She turned back to the closet, hoping he wouldn't notice the tear that made its way from the corner of her eye.

316

"What're you doing?"

She tugged another dress from the closet and tossed it on the bed. "Just thinking about giving some clothes to the Salvation Army. You know, stuff I don't wear."

"You want me to go through my stuff?"

She shook her head. "There'll be plenty of time for that later."

He was almost out the door before he popped his head back inside. "How about we go to dinner tonight with Devin and his girl? How's Mexican sound?"

"Sounds good," she said, glad for the time she'd get to spend with Devin. "As long as it's not turkey, I'm in."

He closed the bedroom door behind him.

She rested her head against the wall. This would be good. She'd get to spend some time with Devin, meet his girlfriend. After that, she just needed to make her peace with Rhiannon, and then it would be time.

CHAPTER 55

Devin left early Sunday to return to Williamsport in Eileen's car. Kate had called Eileen's nephew and arranged to buy it. At least she had one child no longer angry with her.

After sending him off, she got ready for church. She hadn't been in months. All things considered, it was the right thing to do.

"Do you want me to go with you?" Billy asked as she slipped into her coat.

She stared up at him in surprise. "Since when do you want to go to church?"

"I'll go if you want me to," he said with a shrug.

"Thanks, but no. I'd rather spend my time praying than wondering what you're up to. I'll make breakfast when I get back."

It was too early for nine-thirty Mass. The church was empty. She chose a seat on the far side of the last pew, knelt, and made the sign of the cross.

"Bless me, Father, for I have sinned." She stopped. That was the prayer for confession. Everything in her head was muddled; she couldn't even remember her prayers. At least God knew what was in her heart and why. She didn't need to tell him anything. Would he consider what she planned to do a sin if she was only righting a wrong?

She began again. The words of the Our Father and the Hail Mary, then the Act of Contrition, came back to her by rote. She tried to pay attention to the words, but she couldn't focus. She said a prayer for Joey and one for Eileen and another for the other victims, just like she did every day.

When she finished, she sat on the hard wooden pew. Early worshippers had begun making their way into the church. A few glanced in her direction, some whispered. This was one of the reasons she hated going anywhere. She wished she could just be a fly on the wall and not the subject of Sunday's dinner table conversation. Maybe this was a bad idea.

She stood and was about to sneak out the side door when Father Patrick cut her off.

"Hello, my child," he said in his warm brogue. "It's good to see you." He guided her back into the pew. "How're you doing? I've not seen you in a while."

Kate nodded. "I'm sorry. It's been . . . difficult."

"I know, but remember we're here for you, Kate." He motioned to the mostly empty pews. "We're your family, too, you know."

"I do." She smiled weakly. "Thank you."

"So truly, how are you?"

"Honestly, Father? Not good." Her throat felt tight.

"Aw, darlin'." He patted her hand. "I'll be needin' to get ready for Mass now, but why don't you come see me afterward? You know I'm a fine listener."

"I do. Thank you. Maybe I will."

"That's a good lass." He patted her hand again. "I'll see you in a little while then."

Once he disappeared into the sacristy, Kate slipped out the side door.

She felt guilty, but she couldn't sit down face to face with him or anyone else to talk about what was bothering her. No one could help her, and she didn't want anyone to feel guilty later, wondering what they could have done differently. There was already way too much guilt.

Kate pulled into her driveway and climbed out of the truck to the sound of Billy whaling on his guitar. The amplifier was turned up high enough to fill MetLife Stadium. It was a wonder no one had called the police. She let herself in, then covered her ears as she climbed the stairs to ask him to turn it down.

When she got to the music room, his back was to her. On the amp was an almost full bottle of Jack Daniels—a recent purchase, she assumed—and a half-empty glass. He must have sensed her presence, because he turned.

Without a word, she stormed down the hall. She had no right to be angry, but she was. It was just further proof of his lies and that he would never change.

He called after her, but she didn't stop. She slammed the bedroom door behind her.

He followed—this time, without knocking.

"Don't start with me, Katie. I've got a lot on my mind, and these next few weeks are important. I'm just stressed out."

"I didn't say anything."

"You don't have to. Your face says it all."

"Hey, if drinking helps you make it through the day, knock yourself out. I wish it worked for me." She kicked her shoes into the closet and took off her belt. "Maybe that's it. I'm jealous."

She pulled the sweater dress over her head, leaving her hair in a halo of static. She hurled the dress onto the bed and marched down the hall.

"In fact," she called over her shoulder, snatching the bottle off the amp, "I don't think I've ever tried whiskey. Wine just isn't doing it for me, but I never really gave this stuff a chance."

She tilted her head and took a big swallow of the dark amber liquid. It burned, and her eyes watered. She shivered from her chin down to her knees and began to cough. Oh dear God, this was nasty.

Billy watched with a resigned expression. When she stopped sputtering, she took another swallow. Tears sprang from her eyes and she took several quick breaths, afraid it would come right back up the way it had gone down.

When she tipped the bottle a third time, he yanked it from her hands.

"That's enough," he said quietly. "You still have to drive me to Pittstown, remember?"

She glared at him defiantly, breathing through her mouth and still hoping to keep the whiskey from coming back up. Billy's eyes raked over her, and she recalled how ridiculous she must look standing there in just a bra and a pair of black tights.

She tried to leave the room, but he blocked the door.

His lips curled into a smile. "You know, I'll be away for three weeks. We have a few hours before I need to go."

Caging her against the wall, he gave her a whiskey-flavored kiss. She shivered again in spite of the warmth from the alcohol coursing through her veins.

A part of her longed to return that kiss, to step back in time and sweep all the ugliness from her mind, but it was too late. Instead, she raised her hands and pushed against his chest, causing him to stumble backwards.

"What the fuck?" His hands dropped to his side.

"Don't," she said, searching for words that wouldn't tip her hand or make her sound as if she'd completely lost her mind, but she found none. "Just don't."

She darted down the hall and into the bedroom, continuing on into the bathroom, locking both doors behind her.

This time, he didn't come after her. The walls began to vibrate as a rapid stream of staccato notes played at ear-splitting levels filled the air. He had to have turned the gain up to eight and been pushing the amp into overdrive. The mirror trembled on the adjoining wall.

She slipped back into the bedroom, closing the bathroom door behind her to deaden the sound. The music pumped angrily as she crouched to sort through the jumble of clothing on the bedroom floor, looking for something to wear.

It was so loud, she couldn't even hear the voices in her own head.

By the time she was ready to burn the house down, Billy must have worked out most of his anger. After shredding his guitar for a good half hour, he plugged in his acoustic. Pounding riffs were replaced with the fluid tones of Bach's *Lute Suites*. She stopped packing leftovers to send with him to Rhiannon's and leaned against the kitchen counter, letting the sound wash over her.

The house eventually grew quiet. She put the kettle on for tea and finished packing up the leftovers. She was loading them into a box when Billy came downstairs, carrying his guitars and duffle bag. His eyes were red and she detected a faint whiff of pot.

"You're never going to change, are you?"

He stared at her coldly. "And all you've done is change."

"Forget it." She finished filling the box.

"I called Rhiannon to come get me, but she can't."

Kate rolled her eyes. Did he seriously expect their daughter to drop what she was doing and come running? "Why not?"

"They went to the fucking zoo, and they'll be back too late to drive all the way out here, so you're going to have to take me."

The fucking zoo. That was a new one.

CHAPTER 56

The drive to Pittstown was mostly silent. Billy attempted to start a conversation, even trotting out clichéd comments on the weather and something about how much he was going to miss eating her leftover stuffing. When she failed to respond with anything more than a nod or a clearing of her throat, he gave up.

Since she rarely wanted to listen to music anymore, he tuned in NPR and picked up the Thanksgiving broadcast of *A Prairie Home Companion.* He hoped Garrison Keillor was on his A game tonight. A few times, Kate emitted a one-note laugh. As short as it was, it was a nice sound to hear.

When they arrived in Pittstown, she pulled into the driveway and stared straight ahead, unmoving.

"I feel like this is the end of a very uncomfortable date, and you're not sure if you can kiss me good night or not," he said.

Her fingers gripped the steering wheel.

"You can, you know." He leaned closer.

"Can what?"

"Kiss me good night."

She nodded and gave him a tenuous, almost painful smile.

He leaned across the console, lifted her chin, and gave her a soft, tentative kiss.

"I love you, Katie."

She blinked a few times and nodded. It hurt, but he wasn't going to push her.

He climbed out and grabbed his bag and guitars from the back seat. He stood in the driveway with the door open, waiting, praying she would say something, something he wanted to hear, but she didn't say a word. He reminded her that Rhiannon would be there in the morning to take her to the doctor, then he promised to call every day while he was on the road.

She nodded, her mouth working, but instead of saying anything, she just chewed on her lower lip.

"Okay, then." He closed the door. A sick feeling was brewing in his gut, and his heart was telling him not to walk away. He took a few steps, fumbling in his jacket pocket for the keys. Nothing about this felt right.

He looked over his shoulder. She raised her hand in a sad, little wave, but made no move to leave.

He set his load down and pulled the passenger door open.

"I'm not going. I can't leave you now. I can't do this."

Her mouth dropped in surprise, but she shook her head. "I told you I'm fine. I mean it. Really."

She opened her door and climbed out. He rushed around the front of the truck and met her before she had taken more than a few steps.

The woman who stood before him was haunted, broken. It was killing him that he didn't know how to fix her—more so because he was responsible for some of the deepest cracks.

She put her hands around his neck and rose onto her toes. Then she kissed him—and this time, as if she meant it.

"I love you," she said, pressing her hand against his chest before turning back toward the truck. She said it once more, as if he might not have believed her the first time. Then she climbed in the truck and backed down the steep driveway.

The red taillights were visible for some distance as she made her way along the winding road. He stood there long after they disappeared, debating whether to go after her. At least she'd taken his heart with her. It was always with her.

He just wished she believed that.

CHAPTER 57

According to The Weather Channel, Monday would be clear and in the high fifties. Tuesday would be a good day as well, which meant Monday at sunset would be perfect.

Kate flipped off the television, tossed the remote onto the coffee table, and snatched up her wine glass. There were some details yet to work out, but having a plan made her feel calm, in control. It was like finally figuring out the answer to a complicated math problem that had puzzled her for months. She tossed back the contents of her glass. God, she hated math.

There was a lot to do and less than twenty-four hours to do it in. She needed a list. Devin had always teased her about her list-making. What would he say if he knew about this list? The thought weighed heavy on her, but she pushed it away.

"I can't think about the kids right now," she told Charlie.

Damn. Charlie! If they didn't find her right away, he would starve, and if she left enough food, he'd eat until he got sick. She scribbled his name on her list:

Charlie.

She would have to leave him tied up outside. Someone would hear him barking before too long.

She ruffled the furry head at her feet. "It will be for your own good."

He lifted his tail, then dropped it with a heavy thud, as if he understood what she was planning.

The next items on the list: call the doctor to reschedule. She would cancel, but knowing Billy, he might have anticipated that, and told them to contact him if she tried. Next, she would have to call Rhiannon so she wouldn't come over. She also needed to apologize for her outburst. And she'd call Devin. He had a class at four, but she should be able to reach him before then. She would leave them all notes, but not now. That she would save until last.

Write notes.

She drained her glass and refilled it.

Her will. *Damn it.* She couldn't exactly ask Tom for an emergency update. She tapped the pen against her chin. Maybe if she just wrote out her wishes, they would follow them.

Will and other stuff.

Tom would have to take care of whatever Joey had left her. She couldn't worry about it now.

Despite the comfortable numbness taking over, she felt an annoying wave of guilt. She'd promised Joey she would help Tom. She had tried, but after the shooting, she had nothing left to give. She'd leave him a note, too.

Apologize to Tom.

All of them, they would all have to do the right thing, because she couldn't. She was done. It felt eerie and a little foreign to relinquish control, but she was ready. Relieved, for the most part.

She grabbed the pinot grigio off the counter and headed upstairs but realized once she'd gotten there she'd forgotten the glass.

"Fuck it." She raised the bottle to her lips. She checked her list.

Pills.

She emptied the top drawer of her nightstand onto the bed and rooted around in the jumble until she found the stash of pills she'd been hoarding. Fifty-nine pills wouldn't kill her, but they would make her groggy enough to take that final step, just in case she chickened out at the last minute. She tossed them on the bed next to her list.

Her head swam. She wanted to lie down, but there was too much to do. She still hadn't decided what to be buried in. The white dress was too lightweight and summery. She wouldn't want to be cold for the rest of eternity.

"Of course it could be hot where I'm going." She laughed.

She tried to hook the hanger back on the rod but missed, and the dress puddled to the floor at the bottom of the closet.

Nothing appealed to her.

Grabbing the bottle of wine, she headed toward the music room. Standing in the doorway she stopped. The space was so pervasively Billy she expected him to look up at her from the futon, his Stratocaster in his lap. It was warmer in here than in the bedroom. She touched the amp, thinking it might still be on. Maybe it was the dark red walls, or maybe it was the memories associated with the room.

She closed her eyes and wrapped her arms around herself. If she could stay there, warm and safe, never have to leave, maybe she could survive. She dropped onto the futon. Heaven would be like this. Warm and safe. And she'd never be afraid. Oh yeah, she wanted to go to heaven.

The bottle of whiskey sat open on the table in front of her. She swirled it under her nose, and her eyes watered.

"Must be an acquired taste." She dumped the melted ice from Billy's glass into a half-dead potted fern, then measured three fingers' worth. Just like in the movies.

She took a cautious sip. It burned, but it wasn't as much of a surprise as it had been earlier. She swished it around in her mouth like mouthwash and swallowed. Warmth bloomed as it spread to her arms and legs. It was like getting hugged on the inside.

She carried the bottle back into the bedroom. First things first: she needed to find something to wear up the mountain.

Maybe her black leather pants. She would pair them with an oversized black turtleneck sweater. Black would be good, especially if there might be a lot of blood. Much less obvious. She tossed the clothes on the bed and crawled around the bottom of the closet, looking for her black Uggs. Might as well be warm and comfortable.

Her glass was empty, so she poured another three fingers of whiskey. Holding it in a shaky hand, she wandered back to the music room and thumbed through the dresses hanging in that closet. Maybe the dress she wore for Rhiannon's wedding? She ran her fingers over the heavily beaded jacket and the soft sage crepe de chine skirt. No, it was too matronly. She'd felt old when she wore it, even though she'd only been thirty-nine. Who wanted to feel old for eternity?

How could she have nothing wear? She couldn't go shopping. The mall had closed at seven. Besides, she was drunk—even she knew that.

"Now what?" she asked Charlie, who wandered in and curled up on the Oriental carpet in the center of the room. She raised the glass to her lips, but it was empty again. No longer able to line her fingers up with the glass, she just poured. Half went into the glass and half onto the table.

She settled back against the cushions of the futon, her insides nice and warm. Comfortably numb.

"I know!" She sprang to her feet, only to stagger and fall back down again. "My wedding dress."

She got up, slower this time, and swung into the hall, narrowly missing the door frame. It took several tries to catch the cord to lower the attic stairs, and when she did, she yanked so hard they came crashing down and nearly knocked her off her feet. She surged forward and climbed the steep steps on shaky legs.

Still afraid to stand, she surveyed the small space from her knees. In twenty years, she'd never once come up here—and now twice in just a couple of days. It was still just as creepy. At least she knew the box she was looking for wasn't with the holiday decorations, unless Billy had moved it.

Her eye fell on the box of canceled checks.

"Damn it."

She should bring it down with her and toss them all over the bedroom so Billy would know she was on to him. She crawled toward the box. But if she did that, she would sentence him to feel guilty the rest of his life. And even as fucked up as she was, she couldn't do that to him. Too many people had suffered already.

She pulled out one check, why she had no idea, and slipped it into her pocket. Then she pushed the shoebox aside, and after sorting through containers of Rhiannon's and Devin's report cards and artwork, she found her dress packed and preserved in pale blue tissue paper from Bayonne Cleaners.

She crawled back to the opening.

"Now what?" How the hell was she supposed to get down? If climbing up had been difficult, getting down while holding a large box would be impossible.

There was only one way. She dropped the box through the hole into the hallway below. It landed on its side and split, spilling its contents onto the floor.

After several attempts to step out onto the ladder, Kate eventually lay on her belly and wiggled until she was partially out of the attic. Her feet flailed, scissor-kicking the air, until she was able to hook her right foot onto one of the rungs. She eased herself down slowly, but her foot missed the last three rungs.

Her chin smashed against the ladder. She flew backwards, biting her tongue and landing on her back, hard enough to knock the wind out of her. She lay on the floor, gaping at the ceiling and gasping like a fish, while cold air pooled around her.

When she could breathe, she rolled onto her side and laughed until tears ran from her eyes. What if she'd broken her neck? It would have been the best joke ever, yet no one would have understood the irony. The floor was uncomfortable, but she didn't feel like moving. Only when it got too cold to stay there, did she finally ease herself up, bracing herself against the wall until the hall stopped spinning. When she was certain she wouldn't fall right back down again, she struggled with the attic stairs.

"Fuck it," she slurred, walking away when they wouldn't close.

She gathered up her dress and kicked the empty box out of her way, scattering blue tissue paper half the length of the hall.

She placed the dress on the bed and untucked the rest of the tissue paper. It had been more than twenty years, but it was still the most beautiful dress she'd ever seen. Joey's friend from F.I.T. had designed it for her with his input, and it was perfect. She held it in front of her and looked at her reflection in the full-length mirror.

"Thanks, Joey."

A fat tear rolled down her cheek onto the front of the dress and disappeared into the lace. Through her watery gaze, she saw him, standing on the other side of the glass, watching her, waiting for her. She spread her fingers, reaching for him, but instead of Joey, all she felt was the cold, hard surface of the mirror.

"It's okay," she told him. "I'll see you soon."

Not satisfied just to look at her wedding gown, she wanted to try it on, so she could see herself in it one more time. She slipped out of her clothes and stepped into the dress. It was big on her. Of course, she'd been four months pregnant with Rhiannon when she'd worn it. Now it gaped in the bodice, and she could gather bunches of fabric on either side of her waist.

Even still, she loved it.

She carried the bottle of whiskey into the bathroom, where she stared into the mirror. Her skin was pasty. Dark smudges had taken up permanent residence beneath her dull green eyes. Several silver threads stood out in her hair, which was tangled and knotted. She watched her reflection tip the bottle. Whiskey rolled down her throat and over her chin, stinging the bloody scrape from the ladder and burning her tongue where she'd bitten it.

She stumbled back, then grabbed hold of the sink and brought her face close to the mirror. "You're a mess. What the hell happened to you? You're fuckin' hideous. No wonder he found someone else."

The words were her own, but they hurt as much as if Billy had said them to her himself.

She snatched the hairbrush off the counter and yanked it through her hair. One hundred strokes. She tried to count but lost track so many times she gave up. Her hair snapped with electricity, floating around her head. She smoothed it with the flat part of her palm, but it sprang back up again.

Without taking her eyes from her reflection, she reached into a drawer in the cabinet. She dragged the other hand through her hair, then pulled up a thick, long handful and held it over her head. She began to cut, sawing back and forth, the scissors chewing through the thick strands, until they lay puddled around her on the floor. All of it. Gone. Long strands clung to her dress. Shorter pieces were trapped in the décolleté of her gown, where they poked and tickled.

The room spun, and she held on to the sink to keep from falling.

The person staring back at her was now as ugly on the outside as she was on the inside.

"Fuck you!" she screamed at the monster in her mirror. "Fuck! You!"

An antique glass Mason jar filled with cotton balls was the first thing she could reach. She hurled it at the mirror with such force that shards of glass ricocheted back and struck her face and arms. Flowers of red bloomed on the surface of her skin. She staggered into the bedroom with the whiskey, walking through the glass, too numb to feel it cutting her feet. Her nose dripped and she wiped it on her arm, smearing blood across her face.

She angled for the corner of the bed but missed, hitting the floor and dropping the nearly empty bottle of whiskey. She rescued it before it spilled, and raising it over her head triumphantly, she silently toasted the man watching from inside her mirror.

CHAPTER 58

Before she knew it, Kate was standing in the clearing at the top of the mountain. The sun was warm, and the deepening blue sky was stained with neon threads of pink and orange. The setting sun glowed so bright it set the horizon on fire. Her hand dipped into the pocket of her slacks, fingering the slip of paper. It was still there. Her name and address. For them to find later.

She stepped toward the edge. She had forgotten the pills and the bottle of French wine, but she was no longer afraid. It was the right thing to do.

She took another step. The sky glowed. Music played—angelic voices singing the "Hallelujah Chorus" from Handel's *Messiah*, to be precise.

Goose bumps prickled her flesh. "I had no idea it would be this beautiful."

"It is, isn't it? God is quite the handy man." The voice came from behind her. She spun around and almost fell.

"Is it over?"

"Oh, honey," he said with a laugh. "It hasn't even begun."

He was dressed all in white.

"You look like Mr. Roarke from *Fantasy Island*."

He ran a hand over his jacket. "This old thing?" He shook his head, and his beautiful curls danced. "He wore a white linen suit and a black tie. I'm wearing a white tie. Plus"—he slid his thumbs behind the lapels of his jacket—"this is made of angels' wings."

"Really?"

"No, not really. Don't be ridiculous."

She stood unmoving as he walked toward her. "How are you?"

"I'm dead. How are you?"

She motioned toward the outcropping from which she had been about to step.

He frowned. "I've been meaning to talk to you about that."

"Really?"

"Yeah." His eyebrows rose in a high arch. "Whaddya think you're doing?"

"I can't take it anymore."

"You can't take it anymore? I wish I had the opportunity to decide whether or not I could take it anymore." He called over his shoulder. "What do you think?"

A titter of discordant mumbles rustled above her head. Talking leaves?

"Don't worry about that." He waved dismissively.

She narrowed her eyes. "Don't worry about what?"

"The leaves." He pointed behind him.

"You can read my mind?"

"Oh, sweetie." He smiled. "I could always read your mind. No hocus-pocus there. So, you were saying? You can't take it anymore, right?"

"Yes, but—"

"But nothing. What else?"

"What do you mean, 'what else'? Isn't that enough?"

He shrugged and shook his head. "Not really. That all you've got? You can't take it anymore?"

Her mouth opened and closed, but nothing came out.

"You look like a fish, Kate. What else? Hurry up. The sun's going down. You don't have much time."

She turned toward the horizon. They had been talking for several minutes, yet the sun hadn't moved. In fact, neither did anything else. White wisps of clouds sat motionless. Birds hung suspended in midair, their wings frozen in flight.

She turned back. "You can stop time?"

"Who me? No, but He can." In case she didn't know who *He* was, he pointed in the general direction of heaven.

"Where is He?"

"Everywhere."

"Can I see Him?"

He gave her a sad smile. "No, sweetie. It isn't time for you to see Him. That's why I'm here."

"It is, Joey. It *is* my time. It's past my time."

He sat on a boulder and tapped the spot beside him. "Why do you think that?"

"I was supposed to die in September. This man—"

"I know all about that, but you're wrong. You weren't supposed to die."

"He was looking for me. He wanted to shoot me. Instead, he killed Eileen and all those other people. If he'd found me, all those people would still be alive."

He shook his head. "No, honey, they wouldn't. He would've killed eight people instead of seven."

"It's my fault."

"It's not your fault. Blame the people who sold him the guns or the people who sold him that stockpile of ammunition. Or blame the people who threatened to take his land, or the neighbors who made the complaints. While you're at it, blame his parents for doing such a crummy job of raising him in the first place. You could blame all those people just as much if not more than you can blame yourself—and you know what? You'd still be wrong."

"Why?"

"Free will, Kate. God gave us free will, and Mr. Stevens used his free will to pick up a weapon and kill those innocent people."

"When did you become such an expert on God and free will?"

"We have lectures every Friday night. There's not a very active social season up here. It's like New York in the summer."

"Really?"

"No! My God!" He grimaced. "Oops—sorry," he yelled over his shoulder.

She peeked behind him, but no one was there.

"Old habits die hard," he mumbled under his breath.

He put his arm around her shoulder. "Look, Kate. We know you've been through a lot. An awful lot. I mean, losing me? That had to suck."

She nodded, and he nodded in agreement.

"And then the shooting."

She nodded again, and her lip began to quiver.

"It's enough to make anyone crazy."

"I'm not crazy," she said.

"Yeah, honey, you are. Certifiably. If anyone knew what you were doing right now, it would buy you a room at Bellevue. But that's okay. You're entitled. And although you feel like you can't take it, you can. You just need help. You can't do it alone. You can't do it with Billy, and you can't do it with a bottle. And trust me, you've been hitting that bottle a little too hard lately. Honestly, when I saw what you did to that dress, I was ready to send you to your maker."

"You could do that?"

"Of course not." He smiled, then added in a stage whisper, "But I know people."

She nodded solemnly.

"Listen to me. I gave you the means to take care of yourself, didn't I?"

She shrugged. "I don't know."

"Of course you don't, because you won't sit down and listen to Tommy. And I might remind you, you're supposed to be helping him. I know you have a lot going on, but he's having a rough time too. You don't see him planning his own funeral, do you?"

She shook her head.

"And by the way, wasn't that something?" He smiled. "And of course you can't tell the kids I said this, but bravo!" He clapped his hands, giving them a round of applause. "Devin's eulogy? I couldn't have written it better myself, and don't think I didn't try. And Rhiannon, with the other arrangements? I have a lot of hope for that girl still. Even the rock star did a good job. The music was perfect."

She rolled her eyes. "Bagpipes? Really?"

He shrugged. "Hey, if you're gonna die, you might as well go out with a bang, or at least a churl." He leveled his gaze with hers and leaned close enough that their noses almost touched. "And speaking of death, it's not your turn. You still have a lot to do, trust me. There are people who need you, but you're no good to anyone right now. Talk to Tommy. There's money, Kate, and a place for you to go. I want you to do that, and I want you to see a doctor—a psychiatrist. I want you to get better."

She chewed her lip. "What about Billy?"

"Let him get his own psychiatrist."

It was like nothing had changed. "I mean, is he cheating on me?"

Joey took her hand and squeezed it between his own. "Listen to your heart, Kate. It'll tell you the truth."

She wasn't so sure about that.

"I want you to go home now, but take this with you."

He pressed something cool, hard, and flat into her palm, then closed her fingers around it. She opened her hand to find a piece of pink sea glass nearly two inches wide, roughly tumbled into the shape of a heart.

"It's beautiful. Where did you get this?"

"In Maine. I found it at Nuns' Beach in Saco." He smiled and cupped his hand under hers. "It is beautiful, isn't it? It's really just a piece of garbage, but it's been battered by the waves and the sand. It's withstood a lot and come back better than before. It's all in the way you look at it."

The heart felt solid in her palm.

"Consider it a little miracle from me to you."

Tears stung the backs of her eyes, but before they could fall, Joey shushed her.

"No more crying, Kate. It's enough already." He patted her back.

She touched the side of his face and ran her fingers through the soft tumble of dark curls. "I can feel you."

"You can now, but not usually."

"Usually?"

He nodded and smiled. "All the other times. You can't see me or feel me, but I'm there. I promised you I'd always be there for you."

"I don't feel you. I'm so alone."

"That's because you aren't trying to help yourself. But you aren't alone."

She heard someone call her name.

"You have to go now." Joey folded her fingers over the glass and squeezed tightly. She felt the point bite into her palm.

"Remember, Kate." He stood and pulled her to her feet. "You also have free will. I can't stop you, but I promise, it isn't your time."

The voice drew nearer. "Mom?"

Kate looked toward the trail. When she turned back, Joey was gone. The sun resumed its descent, and the birds called to one another as they soared high above the river.

"Rhiannon?" Kate hurried toward the sound of her daughter's voice. In her haste, her foot caught on a rock, and down she went.

CHAPTER 59

Rhiannon pounded on the door, grumbling and hoping she wouldn't have to dig around in her purse for the key to her parents' house. If she even had the stupid key.

"Mom!" she yelled. "It's me. Open up!"

Charlie jumped and pawed at the back door, barking like a maniac. Actually, like more of a maniac than usual.

"Calm down!" she shouted at him through the window. As soon as she opened that door, he would jump up and snag her new Moncler down jacket. She just knew it.

Trying not to spill her caramel macchiato, she dug some more and finally came up with the key her father had given her.

"Get back," she scolded, pushing the door open.

She needn't have bothered. Charlie bolted up the steps and through the kitchen.

"Mom?"

The coffee carafe was empty. Odd for this early in the morning. Her mother lived on caffeine these days.

Charlie continued barking, ran back to her, spun around, and raced back into the dining room.

"Shut up!" she snarled. "Mom!"

The dog bolted up the stairs, then turned back again. Charlie had always been way too rambunctious, but this was a little much even for him.

"Mom?"

She tossed her bag on the counter and headed for the stairs. Charlie waited at the top, still barking. She should have just let him out. She'd have a goddamn headache by the time she got back in the car.

A cold rush of air hit her. What the hell? The attic stairs were down.

She called up the stairs. "What are you doing? I've been pounding on the door for five minutes." More or less. "You're going to be late for the doctor."

Silence.

She squeezed past the ladder and continued down the hall to her parents' room.

Her mother lay crumpled in a heap at the foot of the bed. Her hair was gone. Bloody streaks covered her arms. The dress she was wearing—her wedding dress?—was splattered with rust-colored spots that grew larger near the hem. Dried blood covered her bare feet. Alongside her was an empty bottle of whiskey.

On the bed, an empty bottle of wine lay next to two bottles of pills. A trail of blood led from the bathroom to the spot where her mother lay.

"Oh, dear God."

Rhiannon searched for a pulse. It was there and relatively strong. She grabbed the bottles—sleeping pills. They seemed to be full.

Rhiannon gently rolled her over. There was blood on her hands and cuts on her face. Her chin and cheek were bruised, as if someone had struck her. Her eyes were closed, but she began to groan.

Grabbing her mother under the arms, Rhiannon tried to lift her onto the bed but couldn't. Instead, she stretched her out on her back, then headed into the bathroom for a washcloth.

In the doorway, she froze. The large mirror over the sink had been shattered. Broken glass covered the floor amidst clumps of her mother's hair.

"Oh, Mom. What the hell have you done?"

Dr. Mueller was much younger than Rhiannon would have expected, with wavy brown hair that brushed the tops of his shoulders and wire-rimmed glasses. His tie had been loosened as if he was at the end of the workday rather than the beginning.

"Sit, please," he said. Taking the third chair in the room, he spun it around and straddled it.

Rhiannon glanced at Doug, who was frowning. She knew her husband well enough to read his mind. He was already planning to find a different doctor.

"The good news is it doesn't appear your mother took any of the sleeping pills. There's only one missing from the one bottle. We checked with the pharmacy. She only refilled the prescription twice. The bad news is, she may have been planning to take them."

Rhiannon chewed on her lower lip. Doug covered her hand with his.

"Also, she's been drinking—a lot. Her blood sugar is dangerously low, and we're giving her IV fluids and oxygen therapy to help flush the alcohol from her system."

He picked up an iPad from the desk and scanned it.

"I understand from the conversation your father had with my nurse that your mother lost a close friend this summer and that she was a survivor of a mass shooting a couple of months ago." He pushed his glasses up on top of his head. "That's a lot for anyone to go through. Has she seen any type of counselor, therapist?"

Rhiannon shook her head. "I don't think so. She said she was seeing someone at the church in town, but my dad thinks she was lying. She just keeps getting worse."

"There's something else, too," Doug offered. "My wife's parents have been separated since July."

What the hell? She yanked her hand away. "Doug!"

"They have, Rhiannon. That could be part of the problem as well." He focused on the doctor. "Billy stays there now and then, but Kate won't let him move back home. No one knows what happened. They sure as hell weren't Ward and June Cleaver, but they love each other. But something big happened, and neither of them are talking about it."

Doug turned back to her. "Full disclosure. You want your mother to get better? She can't keep bottling this stuff up, obviously." He waved his hand at their surroundings. "In the past three months, this is the second time I've had to rush to the ER because of one of your parents."

"Douglas!" He was going to be the next patient in the ER if he didn't shut his mouth.

"Has she done this before?" Dr. Mueller asked.

She answered quickly before Doug could say anything else damaging. "No. My father had a little accident back in August."

"He OD'd on heroin," Doug said.

Rhiannon swiveled in her chair. "Are you gonna throw us all under the bus? Who's next? Dalton whacked Dayton in the face last night when he took his Thomas the Train book. Maybe you should tell him that."

Doug stared at the wall behind the doctor's head. "You just did."

"Folks, we're all stressed here. Let's take a deep breath. C'mon, you'll feel better. Breathe in . . ." He closed his eyes and lifted his face up as he expanded his lungs. His arms made a wide, sweeping motion.

Rhiannon gave Doug a sidelong glance and caught the flicker of a smile. She lowered her head and rolled her lips together. After they took a collective breath, she reached for his hand, and when he took it, she squeezed. He squeezed back—his equivalent of *Can you believe this guy?*

"Better?" Dr. Mueller asked.

"Much," Rhiannon said, unable to look at Doug.

Although she found the process amusing in spite of the seriousness of the situation, she took another deep breath before pulling out her cell phone and scrolling through the pictures. When she found the one she was looking for, she held it up for the doctor to see.

"This is my mother." The picture had been taken in Cape May. Kate was sitting at a picnic table, the sun reflecting off the ocean behind her, a contented smile on her face. She could pass for someone half her age.

Dr. Mueller nodded. "How long ago was this taken?"

"Mother's Day weekend."

"Wow. She's changed a lot since then."

"She's changed a lot since Thursday," Rhiannon said.

He nodded. "I assume that's her wedding dress she's wearing?"

Doug squeezed her hand harder.

She nodded. "That's how I found her: passed out on the floor, an empty whiskey bottle next to her, and an empty wine bottle on the bed next to the sleeping pills. Her hair was laying in piles all over the bathroom, and the mirror was shattered into a million pieces. It doesn't make sense. My mother doesn't even drink whiskey. That's my dad's drink."

"Where's your father?"

"On his way to California. I tried to call him after the ambulance left, but it was too late. His plane had already left. My mother dropped him off at our house yesterday. He didn't say anything when I spoke with him last night, but he's pretty close-mouthed." She shot Doug a look. Unlike some people. "I don't know if anything happened to set her off. Honestly, if he knew she was this bad, I don't think he would've gone."

Dr. Mueller tapped furiously on his iPad, taking notes as Rhiannon spoke.

"So your parents are separated."

She frowned. "Sort of. My mother's just being ridiculous."

His eyebrows rose. "How so?"

"My parents have an unusual relationship," she said, unable to think of any other way to describe it. "My dad's a musician. Billy McDonald?" When he failed to show any signs of recognition, she continued. "He's on the road a lot, and my mother isn't always the most patient person when it comes to what he needs to do. She just seems to be getting kind of resentful the last few years . . ."

Dr. Mueller tapped as Rhiannon spoke. Every now and then, his dark eyes narrowed in on her. She began to feel as if she was the one who'd done something wrong.

"They had some kind of fight back in July, around her birthday. That's when it got really weird. She threw him out for no real reason, and he's been staying with us off and on since then."

The doctor nodded. "And when he's not with you?"

"He's either on the road, or he stays with my mother if she'll let him. He was supposed to stay with her after Uncle Joey died, but the next night, she wouldn't even talk to him. To be honest, my dad was being kind of a jerk that day—but he was under a lot of stress too. Anyway, a couple of days after he came home, he overdosed. He was in the hospital for a couple days, but Devin—my brother—wouldn't let us call her, so she doesn't even know."

He continued tapping. "Does your mother use hard drugs as well?"

She shook her head vehemently. "I doubt she uses any drugs."

Then again, there were the two bottles of sleeping pills.

"Go on."

"After the shooting, my dad took care of her. He stayed for a couple of weeks, but then she started pushing him away again."

The doctor continued making notes.

"She just keeps getting worse. She doesn't want to go anywhere. She hardly leaves the house unless she has to. She's afraid of everything. It seems like sometimes she's not even there, you know? Like she's already checked out."

He gave her an odd look.

"Blank, you know, like her mind is far away." She frowned. "It's hard to explain."

"I'm surprised you've waited so long to get help."

"My dad's been after her for months, but she refused. I guess he put his foot down the other day. She was bad over Thanksgiving, which is understandable. We all tried to pitch in, but she had a total meltdown. My dad got a last-minute gig, and he was afraid she'd try to get out of coming to see you, so he made me promise to bring her." She chewed on her lip until she was certain she could speak. "Thank God, or I wouldn't have found her."

Dr. Mueller set down his iPad. "I want to commit your mother to the psychiatric ward. Obviously she's in a lot of pain, and right now, this is the safest place for her."

Rhiannon shook her head. All she was supposed to do was take her mother to the doctor, not have her locked away.

"I don't think that's what my father wants. He wants me to take care of her."

"Unfortunately, you can't. If she's truly suicidal, she'll find a way. Let us do our job and protect her. We'll get her started on medication to help ease the depression, and we'll start intensive therapy immediately. Trust me, Mrs. Bradford, this is the best thing for your mother."

Doug ran his hand across the back of his neck. "You have to, Rhiannon. Even if we got her to agree to stay with us—and that's a big if—you could turn your back for one second, and she could take off. I don't want that responsibility."

"Can't you just treat her as an outpatient?" She hated the way her voice was rising. "I can't believe she'd really try to kill herself. Doesn't she care about us? What kind of mother would do something like that?"

"Babe," Doug shook his head. "She's in so much pain, she doesn't see that she's doing anything to you."

Rhiannon swiveled in her chair and leaned toward Doug. This was nonsense. Totally unacceptable. How could her mother not realize what she was doing to them?

"No decent mother would put her children through something like this. Killing herself? Jesus, Doug. Then she is fucking nuts, and I'm not sorry she's here."

CHAPTER 60

It was the smell she noticed first. Sharp. Not awful, but in no way pleasant. At the sound of a woman's voice, Kate's eyes flew open. It was dark, but there was enough light for her to recognize that she was not at home. This was not her bed, and this was not her pillow. She faced a large window. The image reflected a glass wall behind her and beyond that, a dimly lit corridor. She drew her legs up slowly, folding in on herself.

A sharp tug on her left hand helped her gain a bit of clarity. An IV needle was taped to her hand, connecting her to a bag of clear fluids hanging above her bed.

She had taken Billy to Rhiannon's. Had they crashed? Her fingers floated to her lips. No. They'd kissed goodbye. On the way home maybe. But other than her cheek and swollen lip, and strangely, the bottom of her feet, nothing hurt. Certainly nothing that would put her in the hospital.

Fragments of memory assaulted her. Nothing tangible. Nothing she was able to reach out and hold on to. She was in a hospital bed, wearing a hospital gown, connected to an IV. She just didn't know why.

From where she lay, she could see a bathroom with no door. A small video camera hung from the corner near the ceiling, pointed directly at her. It was like waking up in a horror movie.

She tried to sit. Cold air hit her neck, and the room started to spin. She raised shaking hands to her neck, then her scalp. Her hair! It was gone, yet she felt it like a phantom limb: long, soft strands sliding down her arms, floating to her feet, catching between her toes. The sound of steel teeth, gnawing and chewing.

Her fingers crawled across her scalp. Some spots were almost bare; others bristled like a porcupine. She slid beneath the covers and began to rock.

The glass wall behind her rattled open.

"Mrs. Donaldson?" a soft voice called.

"Please go away."

"I need to check your vitals. Then Dr. Mueller said you should have something to eat. I can heat some soup as soon as you're ready."

"I don't want any soup. I just wanna go home."

"I know, but I need to disconnect this bag, give a quick listen to your lungs and check your pulse. Besides, I can tell you're hungry. I can hear your stomach growling from here."

Kate didn't want to sit up; didn't want this person to see her. Didn't want anyone to see her.

"Mrs. Donaldson. I'm sure you're confused and frightened, but you're safe here. I promise."

Safe? As if that were even possible. She pulled the sheet around her tighter.

"Could you close the curtains, please?"

"Absolutely."

When Kate heard the fabric being drawn around the bed, she lowered the sheet. The woman standing beside the bed had a mass of curly brown hair gathered into a ponytail atop her head and a kind smile.

"That's better." She tucked her hands into the pockets of her scrub jacket. "My name's Lori. How're you feeling? Any headache or nausea?"

Kate nodded. "Both."

"I'll bring you some ginger ale. That should help. I think once you eat something, you'll feel a little better."

She took Kate's pulse and timed it on her watch. "Sounds good." She brought the stethoscope up to her ears and listened to her heart and lungs.

"Why am I here?"

"What do you remember?"

Kate shrugged. "Not much."

What she remembered was being with Joey. Probably best to keep that to herself.

"I guess you gave your family quite a scare. Dr. Mueller thinks being here is the best thing for you right now."

"What if I don't want to stay?"

"You can discuss that with him later this morning. He came by to check on you around dinnertime, but you were still sleeping."

"What time is it now?"

Lori glanced at her watch. "Two fifteen. How about I get you that soup?"

She was a prisoner. Might as well accept her bread and water and be done with it. She nodded.

Lori turned to leave the room and began to push the curtain back.

Kate's hands flew to her head. "No! Please leave it closed. I don't want anyone to see me."

"Let me see what I can do." Lori left the curtain partially closed. The video camera was likely broadcasting her image to the nurses station, but at least she wasn't on display to anyone passing in the hall.

Lori returned a short time later. She set a food tray down in front of Kate, then pulled something out from under her arm.

"See if this will help." She handed Kate a dark pink cable-knit cap lined with fleece.

"I can't take this."

"Don't be silly." Lori shook her head. "It gives me hat hair. I hardly ever wear it. You can keep it until you leave."

"Are you sure?"

"Absolutely. Here—let me." She slipped the hat onto Kate's head, tucking in one or two strands that had escaped her madness.

"I guess hat hair is the least of my problems."

Lori chuckled. "It looks better on you, anyway." She turned and pushed the curtain back. "I know you're uncomfortable and it seems like a terrible invasion of your privacy, but we have to be able to watch you for the first twenty-four hours. It's for your own safety."

"I'm in the psych ward, aren't I?" The words caught in her throat.

"Look at it this way." Lori pushed the tray table closer. "You're safe here. Nothing and no one can hurt you. It's a chance to catch your breath, get a little perspective." She smiled. "In the meantime, here's some chicken noodle soup, which isn't bad for hospital food, and if you want more, I can get it for you. There are some crackers, too, but try and eat some soup first. Dr. Mueller wasn't sure how long it's been since you've eaten, so he doesn't want you to overdo it, okay?"

Kate wasn't sure how long it had been either.

After Lori showed her how to page the nurses station and work the remote for the television, Kate asked why there was no door on the bathroom.

Lori just smiled. "Not for the first twenty-four hours."

It was beyond uncomfortable; it was humiliating.

"Your daughter dropped off a bag for you. When you're done eating, we'll go through it together."

"Go through it?"

"We need to see what's in it before you can have it."

Of course. In case she stripped the shoelaces from her Doc Martens and tried to string herself up in the shower.

"Lori?"

"Yes?"

"There's no phone."

"Not tonight."

It turned out the soup was as good as it smelled, and Kate even ate the Jell-O, although the thought of eating the crackers made her gag.

Not long after she'd finished, Lori returned with her suitcase. She unzipped it and lifted out each item. The only thing questionable, it seemed, was the hooded sweatshirt. The drawstring had already been removed. Had Rhiannon taken it or had the hospital staff already pawed through her bras and panties?

In addition to her other toiletries, she spotted her makeup kit, which Lori put to the side. Of course Rhiannon would think it barbaric to leave the house without wearing eyeliner. At this point, Kate was pretty sure it would do nothing for her appearance. Rhiannon had also packed the book that had been on Kate's nightstand for weeks. She'd barely read more than a few pages. Focusing on her own life was difficult enough. Following the plot of a novel? Impossible.

When the contents of her suitcase had been inspected, Kate pointed out that she had neither her phone nor her wallet.

"You can't have your phone, and you don't need your wallet. Tomorrow, if there's anyone you want to call, there's a phone you can use, but you still won't be able to have your own. That's for your own protection."

"My husband's going to be really upset if he can't reach me." The irony that she'd said her final goodbyes to Billy hadn't escaped her. She was just stating a fact.

"Your daughter said she'd speak to your family to let them know where you are, and Dr. Mueller will be in to see you around eight. You can talk with him more then."

For a moment, she worried about Billy, but this was probably exactly what he wanted—to have her out of the way. Now that he was running around the country playing rock star again, he would no longer need to worry about who was taking care of her.

Despite sleeping for what—hours, days?—she suddenly felt very tired.

"You can keep the gown on if you wish, or you can slip into your own pajamas. Then you can read or watch TV if you can't sleep." Lori pointed to the book. "What are you reading?"

Kate shrugged. "I honestly don't remember."

She picked up the sleepwear Rhiannon had packed. Two pairs of Ralph

Lauren cotton pajamas, both plaid, and a long-sleeved night shirt, also plaid. All new. All three sets bearing a Lord & Taylor hang tag. That was her daughter. In the middle of a family crisis, she found time to zip to the mall. Kate rarely slept in pajamas, preferring Billy's concert T-shirts or his worn and faded chambray shirt.

Had Rhiannon bought new pajamas because she knew Kate wouldn't have been able to bear the thought of wearing something of Billy's, or had she been embarrassed by her mother's lack of stylish sleepwear? Probably the latter. Regardless, she was grateful.

Grimacing when she put pressure on her feet to stand, she grabbed the top pair and yanked at the tag. With careful steps, she headed for the bathroom where at least she'd find a sliver of privacy.

She looked at Lori. "Thanks for the hat." She would have smiled, but the effort was more than she could manage.

Lori's smile lit her entire face. "No problem."

Kate changed quickly. She tried to avoid the mirror, but when it was time to brush her teeth, her eyes betrayed her. She stared at her reflection. The woman staring back at her was a stranger. Purple smudges stained the tender skin below her red-rimmed eyes. Her lip was cut and swollen. A bruise blossomed on her cheek.

With a shaky hand she reached for the knit cap and slid it off.

She looked like a drug addict or a cancer patient. Someone about to take their last breath. And really, wasn't that exactly who she'd become?

She had officially hit rock bottom.

"Do you have any fight left in you, Kate?" she whispered to her reflection, "or have you already checked out?"

CHAPTER 61

By the time the day nurse came to take Kate to see Dr. Mueller, she had changed into a pair of jeans and a hunter green sweater. The sweater clashed with the knitted cap Lori had given her, but she wasn't about to leave her room without it.

The man waiting for her in a comfortable office seemed to be about her age, which bothered her for some reason. She had expected someone more like Sigmund Freud and less like Eddie Vedder. Just what she needed, another musician. He rose from one of the leather wing chairs and reached for her hand, then clasped his own over it in a gesture she assumed was meant to reassure her.

"Hi, Kate. I'm Eric Mueller."

Eric, huh? Sigmund's patients had probably called him Dr. Freud.

He motioned to the chair opposite his. "Sit, please."

Kate did as she was told, then folded her arms and crossed her legs. If he could read body language, then she was speaking volumes.

"When can I go home?"

He gave her a benevolent smile but refrained from the *now, now* she expected to follow.

"Legally, after you've been here for seventy-two hours. However, if I believe you're a danger to yourself or others, I'll petition to keep you here longer. That being said, I hope you'll consider staying voluntarily."

Her snort should have conveyed how unlikely that would be.

"You have a long road ahead of you, Kate."

"Look, this is a huge misunderstanding. I had too much to drink, and I passed out. Trust me, my husband did it for years, and I never had him carted away in an ambulance. My daughter overreacted. I'm fine."

He crossed one leg over the other and linked his fingers around his knee. Billy never sat like that. It irked her. "What about the sleeping pills?"

"I didn't take any sleeping pills. I took one about two months ago. Reacting to that is even worse than calling an ambulance for someone to sleep off a drunk."

He nodded and waited for her to continue. Instead, she kicked her leg back and forth. Of course, if he thought she was agitated, he might call for a straightjacket. She smoothed her hand down her thigh, stilling her leg.

"Kate," he said at last. "You've been through several devastating losses. Anyone in your position would have a difficult time dealing with them, including myself. The only difference between me and you in that regard is that I'm fully aware of the benefits of seeking professional care to help me process the tragedy. You are not 'crazy.'"

She assumed his use of air quotes provided him some cushion against appearing politically incorrect, instead of employing the more acceptable "mentally ill."

"Some of your behaviors may appear to be bizarre, perhaps, but you are not. You're hurting, and whether you believe it or not, you're crying out for help."

Kate hooked her fingers together around her knee to slow the maniacal back-and-forth movement of her foot. She was agitated, but she was listening.

"The thing about the seventy-two-hour involuntary commitment—I can let you go home the day after tomorrow, and nothing will have changed. Correct?"

"I guess."

The way he was grinning, you'd have thought she'd had some sort of breakthrough. "The thing is, *you* need to change, and you can't do that in just seventy-two hours."

It felt as if he was trying to upsell her before she knew exactly what she had purchased. It reminded her of the time she'd dragged Billy to Atlantic City, thinking she was a finalist in a drawing for a Jaguar XJ6. It turned out she was one of hundreds, if not thousands, of finalists, and the deal was they had to sit through a two-hour presentation on timeshares. After fifteen minutes, Billy had excused himself to use the restroom. She found him in the hotel bar three hours later. She was pretty sure Dr. Mueller wouldn't fall for that.

"In here, we can protect you. I don't just mean in the physical sense, but more importantly, in the emotional sense. You don't have to see or speak to anyone you don't want to. That's why you don't have a phone. If you don't want to talk to someone, if that person's interaction with you will in any way hinder your recovery while you're here, then we don't want them talking to you. If it's a family member, we can schedule a session and monitor the interaction, and if they're hurting you in some way, even if it's unintentional, we can help them learn what they're doing that's stunting your recovery."

Interesting. She loosened her arms but left her hands folded in her lap.

"So if I don't want my daughter to visit, she can't?"

"If that's what you want."

"What if my husband calls?"

Dr. Mueller's head bobbed as if he was giving her question a great deal of consideration. "Same thing. We'll make a list of who you will and won't speak to, and since the calls go through the nurses station, they'll make sure it's followed."

"Okay. Let's do that."

There was a notepad and a pen on a nearby table. He handed it to her.

She hesitated. "Has my husband called?"

He scrolled through his iPad, then shook his head.

"No. Just Rhiannon. She called last night and again this morning. I understand, though, that she notified your husband and your son, so they know you're here."

"Do they, now?" So Billy knew and hadn't even bothered to contact her. Tears stung her eyes, but she blinked them back. She scribbled a name on the pad and handed it to Dr. Mueller.

"Tom Reilly? I'll make sure the nurses station gets this. If he calls, you don't want to speak with him. Is he a relative, employer . . .?"

"No, he's the only one I will speak with. In fact—" She took the pad back and jotted down Tom's cell phone number. "I'd like someone to call and ask him to come see me as soon as he can. Today, if possible."

He looked concerned. "You don't want to speak to anyone in your family?"

"No. I don't. You said I'm safe here, right?"

"Yes, but—"

"No buts. My husband raped me while he was strung out on crystal meth the same night I buried my best friend. And that's not even the worst thing that's happened to me this year. Do you want to know where he is? He said he was going on tour. That may be true, although it came up awfully sudden. But I've also discovered that he might have another child or even a whole family somewhere. So no, I don't want to talk to him, and I don't want to talk to my daughter, who'll take his side regardless, or my son, who thinks I've lost my mind. My family may not have caused all the big hurts that put me here, but they keep piling on the little ones, and I think those are the ones that finally pushed me over the edge."

Even as she said it, she wasn't quite sure she believed it. What she did know is that she was angry, and as ugly as the anger was, it was better than the pain that had been her constant companion for months now.

"Did you report the rape?"

She shook her head angrily. "No. And I'm not going to. He didn't mean it." She pressed her fingers against her eyes. That sounded ridiculous. Maybe she was mentally ill.

"Okay. We can talk about that later. Who's Tom Reilly?"

"He's a dear friend, the only real friend I have left. The others were murdered." She said it plainly, and it was clear by the expression that passed over his face how harsh it sounded. It was the truth, after all.

She wouldn't tell him that Tom was also her attorney. He would just discourage her from attempting to conduct any type of business while she was hospitalized.

And business was exactly what she needed to speak to Tom about.

CHAPTER 62

Late that afternoon, Kate was moved to a private room. There was no closed-circuit camera following her every move, and the bathroom had a door. It was a small victory.

She was sitting in the recliner in her room trying to focus on *Northanger Abbey*, her least favorite of Jane Austen's books, when Lori knocked on the door.

"You're looking rested."

Kate returned her smile. "Sleeping more than two hours a night will do that for you."

"I'll bet. You have a visitor. Tom? He's waiting for you in the dayroom."

Kate followed, giving a quick tug on the knit cap to make sure it was secure before stepping inside. It was a large, bright room with windows on two sides. An older gentleman shuffled between the two windows, mumbling softly, a string of curse words exploding from his lips every few sentences.

Tom sat on a small sofa on the far side of the room, looking uncomfortable. Another sofa was anchored perpendicular to it, with a table and lamp between the two sofas. The table was bolted to the floor and the lamp to the table.

The look of horror on his face when he recognized her was disconcerting. "Kate!" He jumped to his feet.

She snugged the cap down over her ears again, forced a smile, and tried not to burst into tears as his arms wrapped around her.

"Oh, Tommy," she sighed into his shirtfront. "It's so good to see you."

"Kate." He pulled back to look at her, as if he still wasn't sure it was her. "What the hell happened?"

She took his hand and led him back to the sofa. Before speaking, she peered down into the top of the lamp, then ran her hand under the lip of the end table.

"I'm checking for microphones," she whispered. Once she was convinced there were none, she sat. Trying not to fidget, she gripped the front of her jeans, which were now at least a size too big.

"Rhiannon put me here."

"Why?"

"Because she thought I was going kill myself."

His eyes widened.

"I was, but I changed my mind. I saw Joey."

Tom's natural pallor grew even lighter.

"I'm sorry. I know that sounds crazy. He came to me in a dream—but it was so real, Tommy. I touched him." She held out her fingers as if the evidence would be easy to see. "It was that real."

He nodded and gave her a tight smile. Of course he didn't believe her. He probably thought she was crazy, like everybody else. Chances were she wasn't saying anything to change his mind.

She leaned closer. "As you know, I have to stay for seventy-two hours, and then I can leave."

He cleared his throat. "Right."

"I want to go away. Joey told me to go."

"And where did he tell you to go?"

"Maine. He left me a house, right?"

"Yes."

She slid forward so that their knees were almost touching. "I need to go. He made me promise I'd go, and I promised I'd get better."

He thrummed his fingers on his knees as if playing an imaginary piano. "That's a long way to go. Is Billy going with you?"

She shook her head. "Absolutely not. No one. I don't even want them to know where I am."

"Kate—"

"Listen to me." She narrowed her eyes. "If you won't help me as my friend, then you'll help me as my attorney. I'm invoking the attorney–client privilege, and you won't say anything to anyone."

"Now, you listen—"

She held up her hand. "No, you listen. You said the property is mine. I'm taking ownership, and you're forbidden to breathe a word of this to anyone."

"You're putting me in a difficult position."

"I understand that." She struggled to remain calm. "But listen to my side of this."

It was difficult, but Kate told him some of what had happened over the past few months, including an abbreviated version of what took place the night of Joey's funeral.

"There are too many memories here for me right now. That in itself is enough to make me want to get as far away as possible. I can't even come up my driveway without feeling guilty about Eileen." Her voice started to break, but she took a deep breath and recovered. "And there are the other things. My family. I can't deal with them right now. I can't make myself go through Christmas and act like everything is okay. Even Devin snapped at me the other day. My presence is destroying them, little by little. They're fighting with each other. I can't take it anymore."

"Billy is never going to let you go."

She pushed her shoulders back. It was difficult, but she steeled herself against the painful words she was about to say. "That's the thing, Tommy. He already has. There's someone else."

"Oh, Kate. I don't believe that."

"It's true. It's been going on for years. I've been so stupid." The sting of humiliation propelled her forward. "I'm trying to deal with it, all of it, but I can't if I'm here, and it's still going on right under my nose."

"I just don't think that moving four hundred miles away is the best thing for you right now. Yeah, the cottage is yours. That was always the plan, but not under these circumstances."

There was an awkward silence.

"And if you're trying to convince me that you've spoken to Joey and he told you to go to Maine, then maybe here is where you need to be, Kate. I'm not trying to be cruel. I care about you, and Joey loved you—"

"He looked good." This wasn't helping her case, but it was the truth. "And he was as sassy as ever. I can't remember everything he said, but he gave me something, a gift to remember our meeting by. I just don't know what happened to it."

If he walked out that door before she convinced him to help her, she would be screwed.

"What was it?" Clearly, he was humoring her.

"You'll think it's silly, but it meant a lot to me and to Joey."

"Tell me."

"It was a heart. A sea glass heart." If she closed her hand, she could still imagine it there. "Just a piece of broken glass someone tossed in the ocean. I've never seen a piece that color before. It was pink."

Tom blinked and cleared his throat. He was probably trying to think of a way to get out of there gracefully. "How big was it?"

She traced the size against the palm of her hand.

He ran his hand over his mouth and stared out the window.

"Are you okay?"

He gave her a shaky smile and nodded. "Yeah. I'm fine." He took a deep breath.

"So, he looked good?"

"He did. It was wonderful to see him. And Tommy?" She wrapped her hand around his wrist. "He reminded me that I'd promised to be there for you, and I haven't done a very good job. I'm sorry."

He pressed his hand against the back of her neck and pulled her forward, close enough that their foreheads touched. They were so close, in fact, it was impossible to tell he had begun to cry until he let out a short sob. She wrapped her arms around him and held him until an orderly came over and asked if they were okay. Kate nodded and wiped her eyes on the cuff of her sweater.

When the man was out of earshot, Tom took her hands in his.

"I'll help you, but it will take a few days for me to make arrangements and to schedule some time off. And I'll only do it under a few conditions."

She frowned. "No conditions."

"You do as I ask, or no deal."

She didn't have much choice. "Fine."

"First, I want you to stay until Thursday or Friday."

She started to protest, but he held up his hand.

"That's a condition, Kate. Let them help you. Get a jump start on my next condition."

"I'm afraid to ask."

"You immediately go into counseling when you get to Maine. I'll set it all up before we leave."

"Tom, seriously—"

"No deal, Kate. You promised Joey you'd take care of yourself, right? Well, I don't need him coming to me in a dream to tell me what kind of help you need. I love you too, you know. I want you to get better, and you aren't going to do it staring out to sea by yourself day after day."

She chewed on her lower lip, then nodded.

"You promise?"

"Cross my heart and hope to die." She made a face. "Sorry."

"I'll start things on my end as soon as I can. You think about any loose ends you'll need to tie up before you go. If I can get the ball rolling, we may be able to leave by Saturday. We still need to have an official reading of the will."

Oh, crap. "Who has to be there?"

"Just me and you. He left you everything."

She took a deep breath. She had no idea what that entailed, but it was more than she could think about right now.

When it was time for Tom to leave, she walked him to the entrance of the ward. As they waited for him to be buzzed out, she slipped her hand into the crook of his elbow.

"Why did you agree to help me?"

He leaned closer. "Now this may sound crazy," he whispered, "but I was with Joey when he found that sea glass heart."

CHAPTER 63

Rhiannon had just dropped the twins off at the sitters and was heading into Starbucks when her phone vibrated.

"Shit." She'd been saying that a lot lately, especially when her father's number popped up. She sent the call straight to voicemail. She was attempting to listen to the message he'd left when the barista asked for her order.

She glared at the young woman. Couldn't she see she was on her phone? Some people. "Tall, skinny, upside-down caramel macchiato, two Splendas, extra hot."

She hit Play again, then listened while she waited.

"I've been calling your mother for two days and I can't get her on the phone. Is she with you? I'm worried. Call me."

Damn it. She was afraid of that. She pressed Play for the second message.

"I know you're sending my calls to voicemail, so knock it off. If you don't get back to me soon, I'm taking the next plane home."

Yeah, he was pissed. She couldn't put it off any longer.

"Rhianna!"

She huffed as she snatched the cup away from the barista. She was dealing with idiots. Everywhere.

Caffeine would help clear her head, and then she would deal with her father. She tossed her wallet back into her purse, climbed into her Volvo, and took a much-needed sip of coffee.

"Fuck!" She'd asked for extra hot, not blistering. Idiots.

She steadied herself, lifted the phone, and hit redial, but canceled just before it rang.

"I know!" She was practically giddy. If she sent him a text, he couldn't drill her with questions.

Thumbs flying, she typed out a message: "Hey Dad! Can't talk. Heading 2 gym. Mom's fine, just mad u made her go 2 shrink. I'll check on her later & keep u posted. No worries. TTYL! XXXOOO"

She added a kissy face emoji before hitting Send, then turned off her phone. If he called, it would go to voicemail automatically. At least then he couldn't claim she was ignoring him.

⌒⌒

"What's wrong with your phone?" Doug asked later that evening.

The twins were asleep, and Rhiannon was putting the finishing touches on a special dinner for just the two of them.

"Nothing." She pulled a large baked potato and a small sweet potato from the oven, then gave a pot on the stove a quick stir.

He peered over her shoulder. "Creamed spinach? What gives?"

"You love creamed spinach." She bustled around him.

He strode over to the table, where she'd place a wooden bowl with crisp romaine lettuce, the ingredients for a fresh Caesar dressing—her mother's recipe—and a bottle of A-1 Steak Sauce.

"Caesar salad and steak?"

Averting her gaze, she darted around him. "You love Caesar salad and steak."

"I know. And you never let me eat it. What's wrong?"

She faced him, eye to eye. "Nothing. I just wanted to do something nice. I figured you're sick of tofu and kale."

"I've been sick of tofu and kale since the first time I ate it. That never bothered you before."

Jerk. She gave him a dirty look.

"Sorry." He captured her by the waist as she passed, spun her into his arms, and gave her a long, deep kiss, the kind that could end in dinner being eaten for breakfast. "I'm sorry." He dragged his nose along her jaw. "Thank you. This is very sweet."

Much better. She smiled up at him, satisfied.

"Now tell me what's really going on."

Her smile faded. Did he have to be so damn perceptive? No wonder he was one of the youngest attorneys to be a finalist for the state bar's Attorney of the Year.

She huffed at him and wiggled in his arms. "Let me go so I can get your steak off the grill."

By the time she came back inside, carrying a perfectly grilled porterhouse, Doug had opened the bottle of syrah and poured two glasses. The candles on the dining room table flickered.

"How's your mother?" he asked as she sprinkled fresh Parmesan over the salad.

Not a conversation she wanted to have. "Fine. That's all they'll tell me. That, and I can't see her."

"She'll get over it. She's mad that she's there, but it's what she needs. You'll see. Any day now she'll call, and you can go see her."

Rhiannon wasn't so sure. "I hope so, although I'm almost afraid. You didn't see her, Doug. It was awful." She dropped into the chair beside him. "I'm afraid she may never be the same again."

He slipped a large hand over her much smaller one. She loved those hands. Doug wasn't as tall as her father, but he was brawny and big enough that she always felt safe, secure. He was so damn dependable, too, which made him very much not like her father.

"If she's not getting the right help there, we'll find a place where she will. I love your mother. I want her to be well just as much as you do."

Rhiannon's facade crumbled. "Thank you." She was leaning across the table to kiss him when her cell phone rang.

Shit!

"Did you turn my phone on?" Of course he must have, since it was ringing.

He wiped his mouth on a linen napkin. "Yes. I thought you'd turned it off by mistake. What's wrong?"

She darted into the kitchen and snatched it off the counter.

"Damn it! What time is it?"

"A little after eight. Why?"

She held out the phone, waving it wildly. "Then why is he calling me now?"

"Who? Jesus. Just answer it."

Moments after the ringing stopped, the house phone began to ring.

"Sonofabitch!" She stomped her foot.

"What the hell's going on?" Doug pushed back his chair and stalked into the kitchen. Rhiannon rushed him as he reached for the phone, but it was too late.

"Yes, of course. She's right here." He handed her the phone. "It's your father."

"No shit," she grumbled, scowling as she yanked the handset from him.

"Hi, Daddy," she cooed into the phone. "How come you're not on the stage yet?"

"Maybe because it's only five o'clock on the west coast," Doug muttered.

~

Her ears still ringing, Rhiannon hung up. "Why'd you turn my phone on?"

Granted, her father had a temper, but it had rarely ever been directed at her. Not this time. He was beyond pissed. She'd wheedled, cajoled, and finally sworn to God that her mother was fine, just annoyed that they were making her see a psychiatrist. She hated lying to him, but it was for his own good. By the time he learned the truth, her mother would be well on her way to recovery and this nightmare would be over. He'd probably even thank her.

Right now, her most pressing problem was the man in her kitchen giving her the stink eye.

"Why are you lying to your father?"

She sighed. "Because if I tell him she's been committed, he'll come home."

"And?"

"He needs to do this, Doug. His agent said this could be his last shot at a recording contract. This is his life, remember?"

He could be so obtuse sometimes. She stalked across the kitchen and dropped the phone into her bag, but not before turning it off again.

"And what's your mother?"

"What?"

"You think a recording contract is more important to him than your mother?"

She grabbed her glass of syrah and drank. "No, but . . . I don't know. I'm handling this, okay?"

"You're lying. You need to tell him the truth. Let him make his own decision about whether or not he wants to come home."

Rhiannon was a practiced negotiator who'd worked her way out of things for years, from cleaning her room to missing a final exam. None of those skills worked on Doug, however. There was only one weapon left in her arsenal.

She angled her head, exposing the curve of her neck, and reached up and tugged off the tie he'd loosened when he walked in the door earlier. Her fingers drifted over the buttons of his Hugo Boss shirt.

"You don't understand. Being a musician is everything to my father. It's who he is. Without it, he wouldn't know what to do with himself." She slipped a finger between the buttons, running it over the soft skin of his chest. "It's like being a lawyer is who you are."

He shook his head. "No, Rhiannon. Being a lawyer is my occupation. It's not who I am. I'd walk away from all of this right now if you needed me to."

"That's ridiculous. That's not the same thing at all."

He grasped her wrists. "It is. I love you so much, I'd give all this up and live in a one-room shack if that's what I needed to do."

He let her go, picked up his glass, and drained it with one long swallow.

"Your father loves your mother that much, enough to walk away from it all because she needs him. Too bad you can't see that."

He plucked his wallet from the bowl near the mudroom, tucked it into his back pocket, and grabbed his keys. "Thanks for dinner."

Typical Doug. He didn't even slam the door on his way out.

CHAPTER 64

Rhiannon had been convinced she knew what she was doing, that she could handle her mother and her father.

Turned out she was wrong.

Her father was relentless—left her no choice, really. Sending him text messages from her mother's phone probably wasn't the smartest thing she'd ever done, especially when he begged her mother to call him back or answer when he called her. He texted several times a day, swearing how much he loved her, telling her how much he needed to hear her voice.

Texting as her mother, Rhiannon had answered in the simplest terms, keeping her distance but assuring him she loved him as well and that she just needed some space. Thank God he'd bought it. It bordered on creepy. These were her parents, for crying out loud! The things she had to do. Someday they'd thank her, and it better be with something big.

Despite having several days to cool off, her mother wouldn't budge. Rhiannon had driven to the hospital one afternoon, not only hoping her mother would see her, but that she'd also be able to get her to call her father. No dice. So she'd just left her mother's phone there. She was tired of being in the middle.

Other than that, Rhiannon called the hospital every day—well, almost every day. She'd been told her mother had agreed to stay a full week, so she drove to St. Stephen's on Saturday afternoon, thinking if she just showed up instead of calling, her mother might feel guilty enough to see her. But when she arrived, she learned her mother had signed herself out two days earlier. Which was surprising, since the house was dark when she and Doug pulled up Saturday evening. When her mother was home, the place was usually lit up like an overnight highway construction site. The only light now came from the candles in each window, the kind that turned on automatically at dusk.

It was quiet, too, as they approached the back door. Too dark. Too quiet. Charlie would have announced their arrival by now, unless he was still at the kennel. Also very odd.

Icy fingers skittered up her spine. What if it was like last time? Or worse?

Doug took the keys from her shaking hands and unlocked the door. The house was not only dark, it was cold. Really cold.

"Mom?" she called, her voice barely loud enough to carry into the next room.

"Kate?" Doug's voice boomed.

The echo of their voices was hollow.

"Are you sure she was released?"

She gave him a sour look. "I'm not an idiot, Doug. Of course I'm sure."

They ascended the steps into the kitchen. Rhiannon called again, louder.

"Wait here." Doug turned the lights on as he moved through the kitchen and dining room. Taking the steps two at a time, he disappeared upstairs.

Between fear and the chilly room, Rhiannon shivered. She tossed her purse on the counter and flicked on the light over the island, then wrapped her arms around herself to stay warm.

Leaning against the large glass canister where her mother kept the flour was a note addressed to her and Devin. She ran her fingers over the wide, loopy script.

"She's not upstairs." Doug barreled down the narrow stairs and headed for the living room. She called to him, but her voice was little more than a squeak. He didn't hear her.

Her hand shaking, she slid her finger along the edge of the envelope. Slipping out the single page, she unfolded it and began to read.

Dear Rhiannon and Devin,

I'm not really sure what I should say, so forgive me if this doesn't make much sense. I think it's safe to say I've not been myself lately.

I've decided the best thing for all of us—and me especially—is to go away, so that's what I've done. I need to be alone. I need time to heal, if that's even possible, and to figure out what comes next.

Please don't try to find me. Tommy can reach me in an emergency, but please also understand that I won't come home. You're all adults. You don't need me.

I know you're angry. I don't blame you. I have to wonder what kind of a mother goes off and leaves her family. Certainly not the mother I wanted to be, but there you go.

I want you all to be happy and go about your lives. It should be easier without having to worry about me. Always remember how much I love you, and try not to be too angry and disappointed. I'm already so disappointed in myself.

I hope you still say your prayers each night like I taught you. If so, please pray for me. Ask God to forgive me and guide me. I will pray for you all as always.

Love,

Mom

P.S. I tried to write to your father, but I just couldn't find the words. Tell him he's free to move on. He'll know what that means.

She handed the letter to Doug. He read it silently, then folded it and put it back in the envelope.

"I told you to tell your father, didn't I?"

Not this again. She tucked a strand of hair behind her ears. "What good would that have done?"

He dragged his hand across the back of his neck before looking down at her. The disappointment on his face crushed her. "I don't know, but if he were here, he would have stopped her."

His open palm slammed against the countertop, and she jumped.

"Jesus Christ, Rhiannon, as far as she knows, he didn't even try to contact her while she was in the hospital. She probably thinks he doesn't care."

"Don't make this my fault." She yanked a paper towel from the spool sitting near the sink and dabbed at her eyes. "I did what I thought was best. She hates me for putting her in the hospital, and she probably thinks I hate her and that's why I did it. Obviously she's not thinking clearly. I can't believe she talked Tom into this. He must be as crazy as she is."

She paced back and forth before collapsing onto a kitchen stool.

"What the hell are we gonna do? What am I gonna tell my dad?" She wanted to vomit. "How am I gonna tell him? He has two more weeks yet. If I tell him now, he'll come home, and then what?"

Doug closed his eyes and rubbed his temples. He pulled out his cell phone and dialed Tom's number, only to be told by his wife that he was out of town on business and wasn't expected back until Tuesday or Wednesday. He tried Tom's cell, but it went straight to voicemail.

"Tom. It's Doug Bradford. You need to call me. Now." He sounded threatening, or maybe desperate.

He tucked his phone back into his pocket and gave Rhiannon a long, hard look.

"You already know what I think. Other than that, I don't know what to tell you. You need to decide what you're going to do. I'll be in the car."

The door clicked quietly closed behind him.

Rhiannon stared at her phone. Her boys—Dalton, Dayton, and Doug—smiled back at her. The clock in the dining room ticked loudly. It was almost seven thirty. Her father was still out west somewhere. He was probably already at the venue. He might not even have his phone with him.

She'd give just about anything to put this off a little longer.

Doug was right. She'd fucked up. Big time. Chewing on her lip, she scrolled until she came to her father's number. He answered on the second ring.

"Hi, Daddy. It's me."

CHAPTER 65

Billy stood in the doorway to Tom's law library. The bastard had his back to him as he scanned a row of books. Part of him didn't even want to give the sonofabitch the chance to answer. But if he acted on his first impulse, Tom would be unable to speak when he was finished with him.

"Where is she?"

Tom startled, nearly dropping the book he had just plucked from a shelf. "How did you get back here?"

"You don't ask the questions." Billy filled the doorway, his hands jammed in the pockets of his jeans. "I'm gonna ask you once more. Where's my wife?"

"Kate's fine." Tom's voice squeaked like a cartoon mouse. He cleared his throat and pushed his glasses up his nose.

Billy stepped into the room, closed the door, and locked it behind him. "Don't make me ask you again."

Tom licked his lips and pressed the tome close to his chest. Billy could see he was shaking. He gestured toward the row of chairs on Billy's side of the table.

"Sit down, please."

"I'm not here to socialize, but I'll give you a word of advice. I suggest you answer my question while you still can." Billy moved closer. His hands were out of his pockets now, and he pumped his fists open and closed. He'd wanted to tear into this fucker for months now and little was going to hold him back.

"Don't threaten me," Tom said, foolishly trying to stand up to him. "Just sit down, and I'll tell you what I can, but I won't tell you where she is. I gave her my word."

"You sonofabitch."

It took seconds for him to scale the table and wrap his hands around the collar of Tom's suit jacket. He lifted him up and slammed him into the tall bookshelf. Tom let out a sharp whoosh of air and the shelf wobbled dangerously.

"Where the fuck is my wife?"

Tom looked as if he were going to either faint or vomit. Or worse. Maybe even piss his pants.

A key turned in the lock. Billy let go and stepped back just as the door swung open.

"Do you want me to call the police, Mr. Reilly?" the ancient receptionist asked.

Billy shot Tom a warning look, then turned and smiled at the woman.

Tom straightened his collar and smoothed his jacket into place. He glanced at Billy, maybe hoping for some sign that his homicidal urge had passed.

Nice try, fucker.

Tom cleared his throat. "No, Maisie. I think we're okay. Just a minor misunderstanding."

Billy grinned. He clapped his hand on Tom's shoulder, burying his thumb in his clavicle. "Absolutely. Just a misunderstanding." He flashed Maisie the same grin.

Unlike most women he came across, she didn't seem to be buying it. Tom nodded when she turned to him for confirmation. With a warning look at Billy, she stepped back and left.

When the door had closed all the way, Billy dug his fingers in deeper. He gave Tom a shake, then let go.

Tom reached for the chair nearest him and sat. When he motioned for Billy to do the same, Billy kicked one of the chairs out from under the table and lowered himself into it.

Tom cleared his throat again. That was one fucking annoying habit.

"I can't tell you much for two reasons. First, Kate is my friend, and I'm abiding by her wishes. And second, she's my client, which prohibits me from sharing confidential information."

"And you don't think the fact that I'm her husband counts for anything? Or that she's sick?"

"I know this is difficult—" He leaned back in his chair, arms open, chest exposed. He was either very brave or very stupid.

Billy leaned forward, his voice rising. "You don't know shit!"

Tom closed up like a starfish.

"You have no fucking idea what I'm going through. Your wife didn't run off with someone you thought you could trust."

"Wait, what?"

"You heard me. You must think I'm pretty fucking stupid. I know something's been going on between you and Katie for a while now."

"You think Kate—and me?" he sputtered. "Me?"

Maybe he wouldn't wait for Tom to reveal Kate's whereabouts. Maybe he would just snap his neck and get it over with. He stood and leaned forward menacingly. "Yeah, you. And after Joey died, I tried to be there for her. I wanted to comfort her, console her. Instead, she turned to you. She's *my* wife, for fuck's sake."

Tom gaped up at him, not moving. When he opened his mouth to speak, Billy cut him off.

"I heard all the whispered phone calls between you two. And then I find out, after she throws me out, you're over at my house having dinner, doing God knows what."

For a split second, he thought Tom was going to laugh. Good thing he didn't, because Billy was prepared to beat him to a bloody pulp.

Tom shook his head, slowly at first and then faster and faster. "You have it all wrong. You don't know how wrong. There's nothing going on between me and Kate. Yeah, I love her—of course I do, but as a friend. A wonderful, caring friend." He pressed a hand to his chest. "You know how much you love her? That's how much I loved—still love—somebody else."

This clown must think he was a fool. "I've heard you and your wife don't get along that well, so don't even—"

"I'm not talking about my wife." Tom stared up at the ceiling for a moment, then down at Billy. "Joey."

He said it so low Billy wasn't sure he'd heard him correctly.

"Joey," Tom repeated.

Billy dropped back into his seat. "What?"

"I said Joey. I've been in love with Joey. For years. It was a secret. Even Kate didn't know until the night he died."

It was Billy's turn to look incredulous. "You and Joey?"

He nodded.

"I can't—" He ran his hands through his hair. "Joey Buccacino?"

Tom had been close to tears, but now he chuckled. "Yeah. Joey Buccacino."

"How long?"

"Not long enough."

Fat snowflakes fell outside the tall windows of Tom's library, clinging to the wreaths decorating the windows. Billy turned away. He couldn't even think about Christmas.

He watched Tom trace his finger slowly over the titanium band on his right hand.

"It started in high school, really, but I was always too afraid. No one knows I'm gay. No one except Kate, and now you. Even Stephanie doesn't know, although I think she suspects. We have a marriage of convenience, and now, because of our daughter, I can't leave. She's already threatened to keep Lian from me if I do anything to embarrass her."

Billy felt deflated. "I'm sorry, man. About Joey and—and everything." His anger was quickly deflating as well. "I won't say anything. You have my word." He cracked the smallest of smiles. "I'm glad you're not fooling around with my wife, and I'm also glad Joey had somebody."

Tom nodded. "It wasn't the perfect situation, but when we were together, we were happy."

Billy gave a brusque swipe to his eyes, then rapped his knuckles on the table. "You still owe me some answers."

"I can't, Billy. All I can tell you is she's fine. Well, maybe not fine. She's dealing with a lot of heartache and pain, but she's safe. She needed to get away from here. Do you know how close you came to losing her?"

Billy slumped lower into his chair, no longer feeling so tough. "I didn't until Saturday night. Let's just say my daughter is lucky she doesn't live at home anymore."

Tom scrubbed a hand across his face. "Rhiannon probably thought she was doing what was best. Kate was safe in the hospital, but she was angry—and honestly, she wouldn't have seen you. I think she understands committing her was the right thing to do at the time. For now, she's on medication, and she'll begin seeing a qualified psychiatrist this week. She has a lot of work to do, Billy. If she's going to pull through, she can't do it here. There are too many things to set her off. She's in a safe place, and I will speak with her every day. And I truly believe she wants to get better. If I didn't, I would've never gone along with this. If at any time I think she's getting worse, I'll step in before anything can happen. Trust me."

Billy rubbed his hand over the stubble on his face and stared out the tall casement window. Hurt filled his chest, the wound so deep he was surprised he could breathe.

"What about me?" he asked. "I won't survive without her. I can't."

"You have to. You have a lot of work to do yourself. You want Kate back? You need to fix Billy. She'll come through this, and when she does, she's going to be stronger. To be honest, if you haven't moved forward as well and can fight all those demons on your own, then it might be over for real. In her state of mind, she thinks the best thing she could've done is go away and let you all go on with your lives. She values herself so little, she thinks you're better off without her."

Tom shifted in his chair. "She's also convinced you're seeing someone else."

"God damn it!" Billy slammed his hand against the table. "I made one stupid mistake twenty years ago. I was fucked up and—" He stood so quickly the chair slammed into the bookshelves. He stalked to the window and stared out at the street. Normal people moved about, living their lives, going about their business. And he was living in a nightmare of his own making. He faced Tom again. "There's no excuse that will ever make it okay, but I've spent the last twenty years feeling guilty. I can't change the past, but I have no intention of repeating it."

"Then isn't this the perfect excuse to get sober?" Tom asked. "You're looking at jail time. I'm sure Doug's already suggested that you go into rehab voluntarily, which is exactly what I would've told you if I were still your attorney."

Billy nodded.

"Then do it. You want Kate back? Do what you need to do so you're ready to fight for her when the time comes."

There was a sharp rap on the door and Maisie walked in, followed by Digger.

"Chief Johnson is here to see you, Mr. Reilly." She cast an evil eye in Billy's direction.

Nasty old bat.

"Thank you, Maisie. Digger, good to see you."

The officer stood in the doorway, looking confused. "Everything okay here?"

"Yes," Tom said. "I think we're done, aren't we?"

Billy moved slowly. It felt as if an extra hundred pounds had been piled on him since he'd walked through the door earlier.

"You need a ride?" Digger offered.

Billy ran his hands through his hair, then crammed them into his pockets. He'd never felt so alone and defeated. "Yeah, thanks. I'd appreciate that."

Maisie continued to glare as he moved toward the door. He turned back to Tom.

"Will you . . . will you tell her I love her and that I'll be waiting?"

Tom nodded. "I will. If she'll let me."

CHAPTER 66

Billy stood in the kitchen. The light over the stove cast dim shadows over his guitar cases and his duffle bag, right where he'd dumped them before he'd gone to find Tom. Kate was safe, and she was getting help. It was what Billy had wanted all along, but he also wanted her here. Home. With him.

The house was cold and still. The silence screamed at him, filling his brain, flowing through his veins like ice water, leaking out from all his broken places.

How in hell could he act like everything was okay? Go back out on the road and play like nothing happened, then come home and deal with Christmas?

He swept his arm across the kitchen island. Glass canisters shattered at his feet, sugar and flour falling like snow.

How could she do this? How could she leave him like this?

He ran his hands through his hair and over the scruff on his unshaved face.

Fix himself? How the fuck was he supposed to do that when there was nothing left to fix? What he needed was a drink.

The cabinet above the refrigerator was empty. Wine. There was always wine.

He opened the refrigerator door and gagged at the stench. Food leftover from Thanksgiving and God knows when filled the shelves. He grabbed containers and began throwing them into the sink. When he pulled opened the vegetable bin, he thought he would vomit for sure; decaying lettuce leaves lined the bottom of the drawer, mixed with moldy cucumbers and rubbery celery.

Cursing, he scooped up the slippery mess. Cold, wet sludge slipped between his fingers. He tugged open the cabinet under the sink and plunged his hand into the trash. Pushing the contents down to make room for the rest of the slop, his fingers caught on something soft, unexpected. Familiar.

He yanked out his hands. Strands of long, dark hair clung to his fingers, held in place by the dark green slime. His knees gave way.

"Oh, Katie."

Horrified, he tore the trash can out from under the sink. Buried beneath blood-smeared paper towels and shards of glass were great mounds of hair. Hair that he'd touched, played with, buried his face in. Hair that he'd wrapped around his hands in some of the most tender, most passionate moments of his life.

He wiped his hands on his pants. Then he reached into the trash and gently lifted out as much of Kate's hair as he could separate from the mess.

Doubled over, he clutched it in his fists and began to wail. His mind replayed everything he'd ever done wrong, every hurt he'd heaped on her, even the hurts he'd had nothing to do with that had also destroyed her. He pressed his hands to his face, breathing in the hint of citrus hidden within the foul stink of garbage, and held on tight.

He remained there long after his body began to ache. Then he gathered her hair in one hand and reached into his pocket for his cell phone.

"I'm ready," he said when Doug answered. "Make it happen."

If Kate was going to save herself, it was time he did the same.

CHAPTER 67

MARCH 5, 2013

Billy stood stiffly, his hands clasped before him, staring at the words inked along the side of his right hand: *You are my madness and my love.*

Doug jabbed an elbow into his arm. He lifted his eyes to meet the judge's.

"Mr. Donaldson, you are in agreement to enter a plea to the lesser charge of simple assault? It that correct?"

"Yes sir."

"On that charge, how do you plead?"

"Guilty, Your Honor."

The judge rattled through the rest of the charges. Billy answered guilty to all of them.

"I also understand you've taken it upon yourself to undergo inpatient rehab for your drug and alcohol problems."

"Yes sir."

"How long were you there?"

"Just over sixty days."

"And did you successfully complete the program?"

"Yes sir. I was released this morning."

"And you're prepared to begin your sentence immediately?"

"Yes sir."

"Very well, then. Mr. Donaldson, I sentence you to ninety days incarceration, but I will give you credit for those sixty days. You will, however, serve the remaining thirty days in the county jail forthwith. Following that, you will serve twenty-one months of probation. I also sentence you to one hundred hours of community service. You are to reimburse Mr. Jaworski for one-half of his medical bills, and you are to pay one-third of the costs associated with the damages that occurred on the evening of July 19, 2012, at the Hilltop Tavern in Andrewsville. You will also pay all fines and court costs associated with this case. I order you to undergo a drug and alcohol evaluation and impose zero tolerance for any drugs or alcohol during the duration of your sentence."

The judge lowered his head and regarded Billy over the bifocals perched at the end of his nose. "Given your history, I strongly suggest you consider making that a permanent life choice."

The judge banged his gavel, rose, and left the courtroom. A sheriff's deputy appeared at Billy's side.

"Can I say goodbye?"

"Make it quick."

Rhiannon threw her arms around him. "I'll be out to see you Wednesday."

He distanced himself enough to look down into her tearstained face and shook his head. "No. No visits."

"Daddy!"

"Rhiannon, please. I don't want any visitors. It's only a month. You've gone much longer than that without seeing me. I need time alone to get into my head and figure some things out. And I also don't want my little girl coming to see me in jail."

She continued to argue.

He turned to his son-in-law. "I mean it. No one."

Doug slipped his arm around his wife. "Don't worry."

Devin watched, his face grim, his mouth a thin, straight line. Their eyes met, and Devin held out his hand.

"Nice try." Billy pulled him in for a hug. He squeezed a little tighter when Devin's arms circled around him.

He was raw. His grief over Katie was as fresh as if she'd disappeared that morning. Saying goodbye to his children—again—was just as painful.

The deputy moved in. "Time to go."

Cold steel snapped over his wrists. He took one last look at what was left of his family.

"We're gonna be okay. I promise."

It was what he'd told himself every day for the last one hundred and four days, ever since his heart had been ripped from his chest.

And once that iron door clanged shut and the key turned in the lock, it would be the only thing he would focus on—making good on that promise.

NOTE TO READERS

Reviews are important to independent authors. If you decide to leave a review after you've read this book, please email me a link to your review at klcmaterialgirl@gmail.com, and I'll send you a *We All Fall Down* bookmark as a thank you.

ABOUT THE AUTHOR

Karen Cimms is a writer, editor, and music lover. She was born and raised in New Jersey and still thinks of the Garden State as home. She began her career at an early age rewriting the endings to her favorite books. It was a mostly unsuccessful endeavor, but she likes to think she invented fanfiction. Karen is a lifelong Jersey corn enthusiast, and is obsessed with (in no particular order) books, shoes, dishes, and Brad Pitt. In her spare time she likes to quilt, decorate, and entertain. Just kidding—she has no spare time. Although she loves pigeons, she is terrified of pet birds, scary movies and Mr. Peanut.

Karen is married to her favorite lead guitar player. Her children enjoy tormenting her with countless mean-spirited pranks because they love her. She currently lives in Northeast Pennsylvania, although her heart is usually in Maine.

ACKNOWLEDGEMENTS

This wasn't an easy book to write, and I found myself in tears many times. There are a lot of difficult scenes in this part of Billy and Kate's story, and I agonized over each of them. I pulled back on some, softened them a bit, but on others, I had to go with my gut. Please don't hate me too much.

I did a lot of research for this book, and I spoke with a lot of people, all of them experts in their fields. In most cases, I took everything they told me as gospel, but here and there, I may have tweaked the truth a bit for the sake of the story. I hope I haven't deviated too much, and if so, I hope the experts will forgive me.

One of the first people I'd like to thank is Dr. Cara Guilfoyle. Shortly after publishing *At This Moment*, I learned I had breast cancer. Cara was my surgeon and guided me through one of the scariest times of my life. And as a fan of *At This Moment*, I was able to turn to her for help in guiding me through difficult medical scenes for this book. She read and re-read those scenes to make sure they were accurate. So thank you, Cara, for saving my life and my story. Thanks also to her husband, Dr. Gregg Guilfoyle, who suggested an entirely new scenario when I learned the first one I'd written didn't really work. Thanks also to Beth DeJoseph Hamburger, PA, and Dr. Shari Brandli. And a big gold star to my friend Joni Gestl, a paramedic, who not only advised me on several different scenes, she listened to me blather—on more than one occasion—about this series, and still invited me to spend the day with her on the ambulance for a closer look at what she and her colleagues do every day.

I'd like to thank the following law enforcement officials for spending time with me, answering my numerous questions, and sharing their vast knowledge: President Judge Roger N. Nanovic, Chief of Police Joseph Schatz, NYPD Sgt. Matt Soblick, and District Attorney Jeanne Engler.

Thank you to my beta readers: Patty Morgan, Diane Lane Stone, Ace Leccese, Beth Yaroszeufski, Amber McKenney, Allison Hart, Dena Williams, JudiRae Kessner, Amy Levasseur, Sally McGarry, Shasta Anderson, Rhonda Donaldson, Deidre Popp, Valarie Savage Kinney, Marge Ayers, Nicole Redden, Tyra Hattersly, Sarah Shanley, and Stacy Hagemann.

Lydia Fasteland and Ann Travis, you guys are the best. And Lori Ryser, thank you for tons of feedback and again, for being the last pair of eyes to scour these pages before publication.

My friend, Liz Vigue, you were my earliest cheerleader, and you encouraged me to start at the very beginning. For that I am so grateful. You are always in my heart.

For my editor, Lisa Poisso, thank you again for guiding me, firmly but gently, and for polishing my words and making them shine.

Thank you to my cover models, Garrett Cimms and Annmarie Mazur. And thank you, Garrett, for another awesome cover design. Jade Eby, thank you for the beautiful interior design.

Nancy Blaha, thank you for your encouragement and for helping me learn to believe in myself.

To my author friends, Lisa Clark O'Neil, Valarie Savage Kinney, Whitney Barbetti, and Fiona Cole, you are all so talented, generous, and kind. Thank you for everything.

Thank you Karla Sorensen, Kerry Palumbo and Laura Broullire for helping me tighten my back cover copy.

To my children: Karen, Margaux, Garrett, and Amanda, thank you for being you. I love you guys. I hope I make you proud.

And of course, all my love and gratitude to my husband, Jim. Thanks for doing it all so that I can write. Thanks for keeping me in nachos. I couldn't do any of this without you. I've said it before, and I'll say it again, thank you for making me a musician's wife. What a ride! You will always be my favorite lead guitarist.

SNEAK PEEK

Turn the page for an exclusive sneak peek from *All I Ever Wanted,* the final book in the *Of Love and Madness* series. Due for release this spring.

EXCERPT

The first couple of days were damp and dreary. Not cold enough for snow, but cold enough for a chill to settle deep in her very core. Kate woke early the morning after Tom left. Gray light filtered through the barren branches outside her window. Strands of pale pink stained the horizon.

She dressed quickly and rousted Charlie. Together, they descended the steep hill down to the water. She shoved her bare hands into the pockets of her lined jacket and stood at the edge of the steps that led to the dock. Her breath floated in tiny clouds about her face, mimicking the mist atop the water. A cormorant skittered across the glassy surface, then lifted out of the water with a great disturbance of air and headed toward the open sea. The expanse of ocean that lay before her was deserted. A smattering of empty docks lined the cove, but the boats that harbored there had long been pulled out and stored for the winter.

A forest of dense pine ringed the inlet, which at high tide seemed more like a lake than a finger of the Atlantic. The rising sun illuminated a thin band of white clouds hovering above the tree line, which remained black against the fading darkness. Fifty shades of orange, from palest apricot to deepest tangerine, streaked the horizon until Kate was finally forced to shield her eyes as the sun burst above the trees in a neon ball of butterscotch, blinding in its brilliance.

The imprint of the fireball seared itself upon her closed lids, and in spite of the cold, she felt the memory of its warmth on her upturned face. Her senses awakened. She breathed in the tang of the salty ocean and marshy shoreline and listened to the haunting cry of sea birds springing to life as darkness surrendered to day.

It took her by surprise, but there it was—a fleeting hint of promise, no more than a flutter, really. Her heart was heavy, and it was nearly impossible to see beyond the sadness, but somewhere deep inside, an errant ray of light had squeezed its way through a tiny crack and called her name. It was gone in a blink, like a memory, but she recognized it all the same: hope.

It was time to move forward. She pulled her cell phone from her pocket and turned it on. Forty missed calls and messages. She hadn't listened to or read any of them. She shouldn't look at the pictures, either, but she couldn't stop herself. Determined to ignore pictures of Billy, she doted over pictures of her children and her grandchildren, but she couldn't stay away from his face.

The last picture on her phone was from last spring. She was smiling at the camera, and Billy was smiling at her. She'd loved that picture and had meant to have it printed for her desk at work, but life had fallen apart not long after it was taken and she'd forgotten about it.

She ran her finger over the image, touching his face. If it were even possible, her heart broke a little more. She shoved the phone back into her pocket. Careful of her footing on the slick, frost-covered boards, she picked her way to the end of the dock. It bobbed under her weight, sending gentle ripples into the cove.

When she reached the end, she retrieved the phone from her pocket, took a deep breath, and then hurled it as hard as she could. It traveled less than twenty feet before dropping into the frigid water with a soft plop. A lifeline to her past, it bobbed to the surface, spun once, and then disappeared into the murky stillness.